# Let There Be Dragons

Kim Cormack

Mythomedia Press 2754 10th Ave

V9Y2N9 Port Alberni BC

# ACKNOWLEDGMENTS

To my wonderful children, you are everything to me. Thank you for putting up with mom's endless hours of writing. XO

To my incredibly supportive friends and family. I thank god for you each day.

To Haley McGee thank you for the hours spent reading through scenes that turned both of our faces fifty shades of red. Our little beta reading and editing routine is always way more fun than it should be. I have my pink flamingo glass and a bottle of wine, all ready to go. Perhaps, next time we should add Twinkies?

To Leanne Ruissen, my cousin and grammar queen. All hail to the grammar queen. You have an eye for catching those little things that totally would have made it into print. You have an incredibly unique mind. Thank you both for your editing genius. You lovely ladies catch everything and you rock! XO

To Tasha and Jenna for joining on as series beta readers.

Props to Karrine at KM-Creative for the amazing Children Of Ankh series branding.

## WARNING

The information contained within this book is not intended for mere mortals. Reading this may inadvertently trigger your Correction. If you show great bravery during your demise, you may be given a second chance at life by one of the Guardians of the in-between. For your soul's protection, you must join one of three Clans of immortals on earth. You are totally still reading this, aren't you? You've got this. Welcome to the Children Of Ankh Series Universe. *This is not a fairy tale. This is a nightmare. Let's do this.*

*The girl that looked to fields of bees for solace was gone. She couldn't be the girl who saw purple flowers and reminisced about her best friend slipping one into her shoe as a child. He was gone. She wanted to burn this whole field to ash and kick it into the air. She wanted to do that to every memory she had of him. He'd slit her throat during the Testing and left her to bleed out into the sand. When she'd retaliated, she'd become a Dragon. She wanted to destroy everything beautiful and right, for it was all a lie...*

## TO MY CHILDREN OF ANKH SERIES READERS.

I would like to personally thank you for your support. The wonderful reviews and the way you've embraced this series keeps me going strong even when life becomes difficult. Thank you for every retweet and share. I appreciate the pictures of you holding the books and the letters. I will treasure them always. There is a side series with Lexy of Ankh as the main character, "Wild Thing." You know how I feel about Dragons. I hope to keep you swept away in my universe for many years to come.

*Kim Cormack XO*

Fresh out of Immortal Testing, our antiheroes are traumatized after being killed thousands of times in increasingly ghoulish ways to prove themselves capable of being Immortal. Kayn has become a Dragon, capable of shutting her emotions off. Zach has been made her Handler. It's a hard knock afterlife.

# 1
# TWO DRAGONS

She walked with Lexy for what felt like hours into the backdrop of the glorious crimson sunset. Something changed and the warm, soothing sensation of her steps in sand gave way to the rustling of grass underfoot. They were now standing in the centre of an endless field. *Her soul had brought her to see something beautiful. The scenery before her that she'd once adored, now felt like a devastating symbol of her mortality.* The field was overflowing with delicate purple flowers. She closed her eyes and listened to the soothing hum of the bumblebees, hoping it would bring her back to a better time. Visions of her childhood flashed through her mind. *There they were as children, lying in the field together, watching clouds drift by. She couldn't even think of this.* Kayn ran towards the bees, waving her arms and they took flight. She crawled around on her hands and knees, yanking flowers from the soil. Lexy made no attempt to stop her. *The girl that looked to fields of bees for solace was gone. She couldn't be the girl who saw purple flowers and reminisced about her best friend slipping one into her shoe as a child. He was gone. She wanted to burn this whole field to ash and kick it into the air. She wanted to do that to every memory she had of him. He'd slit her throat during the Testing and left her to bleed out into the sand. When she'd retaliated, she'd become a Dragon. She wanted to destroy everything beautiful and right for it was all a lie...*

Lexy broke the silence by saying, "I didn't know about the plot to make you a Dragon. I understand why it had to be done but, I didn't know beforehand."

*Lexy wasn't one to sugar-coat things. She would have told her if she'd known and chosen to keep her mouth shut about it.* Kayn met Lexy's eyes as she disclosed, "I knew we had to kill our enemies during the Testing. He slit my throat. I never believed he'd be able to do it. When I woke up, I felt nothing but all-encompassing rage. I killed everyone who crossed my path until I caught up with him. I'll never be able to forget the expression on his face as I embraced the hollow sensation within myself and slit his throat. I was lost for a while after that and my memory of that time is sketchy, to say the least. All I can recall is the warmth of the blood as it sprayed on my skin and how good it felt. I fought and died over and over until the pain didn't matter anymore. When Kevin coldly tossed me into a room full of demons, I was eaten alive and that was the moment I understood we were both gone."

After a drawn-out silence, Lexy clarified, "You're not gone. Your perception of everything has been altered. All you have to do is embrace the change and accept the new version of yourself."

"How do I do that? I used to imagine myself as a noble creature, a golden stallion or perhaps a lion. I know better now. I'm a hurricane, a plague, I'm an apocalypse. I am a Dragon. I'm a method of destruction." Kayn knew Lexy understood what she was saying. *She was also meant to be a method of destruction.*

Lexy pointed at the lush landscape and exclaimed, "We can burn this field to ash if you want to. My instinct has always been to burn it. Even though you are meant to be a warrior, you will always have a choice. We choose to work with the Clan, instead of against them. We choose right over wrong. We choose when to be a lion and when to be a Dragon. We choose to be warriors instead of methods of destruction. You're still the same person. You just need time to sort through what happened to you during the Testing. Some of the dark things you've done will stay with you always. Those acts are important. You now know you can survive the darkest of times. You led your Clan through a dark place and came out on the other side. You found your way back to the light because you're a survivor. You can choose to be a lion. My attachment to Grey allows my Dragon to sleep. I know having Zach as your Handler might be complicated. It takes time and it's not always easy. You'll both make mistakes manoeuvring through this situation you've found yourself in."

Kayn felt a tickle and noticed a tiny red ladybug walking across her barefoot. She had the urge to step on one foot with the other but didn't. *Baby steps.* She glanced up at Lexy.

Her fellow Dragon teased, "Is that big bad ladybug bothering you?"

*It was bothering her. It was a reminder that she'd changed on the inside. She'd been happy with who she was as a person. She was funny and dorky and a little bit strange and now she was just angry. She was enraged by the beautiful colours in the sky. She was furious that the bumblebees hadn't heeded her warning and settled back down in the flowers around her. Their buzzing had once been a soothing song and now it was as irritating as someone methodically scraping their nails down a chalkboard.* Once again, she fought the urge to stomp on the tiny insect. It remained there, taunting her as it continued its ticklish stroll across her foot. Lexy playfully shoved her and the ladybug spread its tiny wings and flew away. *Now, she wanted to punch Lexy right in the face.*

Lexy winked and teased, "I wouldn't try it. You can't take me, Brighton."

*She wasn't sure about that anymore. She'd never felt stronger.* Lexy had obviously hitched a ride on her train of thought again. She was grinning at her and shaking her head as they continued their stroll into the scenic backdrop of the in-between.

They wandered aimlessly for quite a while in silence before Lexy continued her, it's good to be a Dragon speech, "Being a Dragon isn't a bad thing. The good and the light need Dragons to do what they can't. They don't want to step into the dark. Not even to do what's right. It's not always light outside when it's time to make a stand for what is right. Dragons can be beautiful things when properly attended to. I love my Dragon and occasionally, I let it out to play. My Dragon enjoys the kill. My Dragon's a warrior and that's what warriors do."

*She'd enjoyed the kill.* She heard the rustling of footsteps in the grass. Kayn spun around, it was Grey. She saw the apology in his eyes before he attempted to speak.

Grey shook his head and confessed, "We didn't know about what Kevin had been asked to do, until after the three of you were already in the Testing. They were right not to tell us."

*It wasn't an apology. With his concerned expression, she knew he hadn't known of the Clans plans beforehand.* Kayn didn't want to talk to anyone else right now, nor was she feeling like one of Grey's, 'you just need to take time to smell the roses speeches.' *The talk with Lexy helped, but she needed to be angry. The fury made her feel strong.* Grey cautiously inched closer. Kayn scowled, her furrowed brow a silent suggestion she still required personal space.

He paused, gave her one of his overly charming grins and disclosed, "Kevin was ordered to kill you. It was a means to an end. You know I liked the kid. In destroying you, he more than likely destroyed himself. He was asked to do this to help you evolve into what you needed to become to survive. Your survival outweighs the trauma you went through, in the long run. You don't see it now, but someday you will. The plan was set in motion so the three of you could make it back home. People tend to lose their marbles in the Testing. It could be that Kevin lost his while trying to do what was best for you."

*He was ordered to kill me. Kevin had said the words but she hadn't believed him capable of doing it. She'd been lying to herself about so many things.* Kayn wiggled her toes in the luxurious grassy carpet of brilliant green underfoot, expecting the act to be followed by a feeling of happiness but it wasn't. *This was bullshit. Complete and total bullshit.* They started to walk as a trio, their footsteps rustling in the grass. Kayn noticed a lone bumblebee pollinating a flower. She stopped walking and stood there mesmerized by the movements of the tiny legs caked in pollen as the others continued to walk away. A vision of Kevin and Chloe as children lying in the grass on their stomachs watching bees caused her heart to feel nothing. She stomped on the bee and felt the burn of its stinger on the arch of her barefoot. *Pain felt good. It felt like she'd discovered something intensely personal about this new version of herself.* She glanced up to see how far the others wandered without her. They'd remained close by, watching. Her face felt warm. Confused by her reaction to pain, Kayn placed her hands on her cheeks. Lexy's lips slowly turned up in a knowing smile. *She was aware of how the pain made her feel.* Standing slightly behind Grey, Lexy raised a finger to her lips as a signal to keep it a secret between Dragons. *Pain was a turn on, interesting. She'd always been curious about Lexy's motivation. Now she knew her secret. If she could feel rage and arousal, it did stand to reason that she'd be able to feel joy again.* Kayn glanced at her wounded foot. *There was nothing there. No stinger and no mark.* The in-between was a magical place. A place where you could feel the pain but not suffer any permanent physical repercussions because your body was elsewhere. That made her think. *Were they the first ones out? Had any of the other Clans made it out?* She pressed her lips together so she wouldn't ask the question threatening to spill from her lips. *Had he made it out?*

From behind Grey, Lexy responded to the question she'd only asked in her mind, "Triad made it out."

Kayn couldn't allow her face to register a reaction.

Grey cautiously clarified, "They were the first Clan out of the Testing."

Kayn's heart was quiet. *Maybe she'd be happy he made it out someday but right now, all she could see was what she'd lost during the Testing. Her mind wrapped around the concept. If Triad made it out and Ankh made it out, that meant Trinity was lost. Leanne and the others were trapped within the Testing.* She responded with a question, "That means Trinity didn't make it out?"

Tenderly cupping her chin in his hands, Grey assured, "It's

okay to be happy he survived. The Testing is meant to destroy what's left of your mortal emotions. Don't let them do it. That's why we fight to keep them. Your spirit can only be broken if you choose to allow something to break you. You are truly immortal now, in every way. You fought your demons and survived the Testing. Now fight like hell to get the Kayn we all know and love back. You have to try to find the joy in everything again. If you spend time looking for it each day, you'll find it. If you consider yourself ruined, then you will be. It's simple, cause and effect. They can't destroy you physically once you are claimed by a Clan but they can and will continue to try to destroy you emotionally."

Grey pulled her into a brotherly embrace but her body remained as stiff as a rail. *She couldn't let them in. She couldn't allow herself to feel because she wasn't prepared to feel everything.*

He stroked her hair gently and whispered, "Let it go. That is the secret to a happy life. When somebody hurts you, let it go. Take the pain as a learning experience and move on."

Where tears would normally come, there was nothing. She willed her body to relax against his but she couldn't. *It was going to be a long way back to the girl she'd once been.*

Lexy joined their sappy conversation and this was a peculiar thing for her to do, "I know where you are inside of your head right now. You don't want to feel anything and until you do, you won't. Just take all the time you need." Lexy wrapped her arms around them both and whispered, "I wish I could heal you emotionally but that's the one thing I can't heal."

She felt like the cat from one of those old Pepe Le Pew cartoons, being hugged against her will, but let it happen, knowing Grey needed to try to make her feel better. *He probably felt bad about the lack of Handler attention she was getting from Zach. Where was he? Wasn't he supposed to be her Grey? Oh, yes. He didn't want this job. His reaction probably would have been hurtful if anything mattered right now.* This hug had started out uncomfortable, and now, it was taking all she had to stop herself from squirming away like the cat in that cartoon. When they finally freed her from the unwanted embrace, Kayn released an exasperated breath as she sat in the grass, where it would be more challenging to hug her without it getting weird. She plucked a handful of grass from the ground and allowed it to slip through her fingers and settle on the bare skin of her legs. Kayn brushed it off, laid down and rested her head on the pillow of lush greenery. She inhaled the fresh scent while quietly observing the clouds drifting across the sky. She'd taken note of the exquisite silken texture of the grass cushioning her body but was incapable of feeling joy as she once had. *Her memory flickered and she was a child in the grass with her best friend sprawled next to her. They were guessing what the clouds resembled. The memories that would have broken her before caused not a twitch in her heart. They were just images now. What if the joy of these moments never returned and all they ever were, was a reminder of her lost humanity? She wanted them gone but knew she could never get rid of the clouds in the sky on a whim.* The grass rustled as Lexy and Grey laid next to her. She heard another noise. Without looking, she knew Mel and Zach had joined them. Grey shimmied over leaving a place for Zach, so he could sit beside her. *He was here to apologize. She could see it in his eyes.*

Zach spoke, "I reacted unfavourably regarding my new job."

Kayn nodded and replied, "I'm sorry you have to be my keeper, Handler, whatever it means. I don't think I'm going to need one. It's going to be easy. I wouldn't worry about it." Grey started to chuckle. Lexy socked him in the stomach. Zach squeezed her knee tenderly. *She didn't want to punch him in the face. It was a good start.*

Her new Handler grinned as he said, "I just wanted to say I'm sorry and I'm in."

Kayn couldn't help but crack a smile at the blatant lie he'd just told. *He didn't want to be in. Zach had no lying ability, none whatsoever. She did note that his presence made her feel lighter.*

Zach pointed at the clouds as he observed the sky above and remarked, "I see something in that cluster of clouds to the left."

Mel brushed her auburn hair away from her eyes as she stretched out in the grass and scrutinized the clouds above. After a second or two she answered, "I'll bite. What do you see?"

"Can't you see the moose? It's obvious. The antlers are over there and wait, there's Frost driving the RV in the next cloud."

*He was trying to make her laugh. He wanted her to reminisce with him about happier times. That moose versus RV incident had been a harrowing couple of days, for her. She hadn't been able to heal as quickly back then. It probably wasn't the best example to use.* Giggles erupted within the group of immortals lying in the grass. Kayn felt her heart begin to thaw, just a little. The moose in the clouds joke made her think of something sort of related. Kayn stated, "One of you has to teach me how to drive."

Grey playfully tossed a handful of grass at her as he volunteered his services, "I will. We can start after the banquet."

She smiled again. *With each smile, she felt a little bit lighter inside. Wait a minute, did he just say banquet?* Kayn scowled as she asked, "What banquet?"

Grey plucked a flower from the earth and tried to tuck it behind Lexy's ear. She started swatting him away as he replied, "There's one for the survivors of the Testing and their Clans. They're just giving us time to unwind before we have to go back there."

*She was going to see him. She was going to be sick. There her emotions were.* Attempting to keep her cool, she closed her eyes. *She'd hoped it would be years before she'd be forced to lay eyes on Mr. Smith again. Judging by Lexy's expression, she'd once again deciphered her thoughts.*

Lexy leaned in and whispered, "Don't worry, you'll sit beside me. I'll remind you that you're a badass and strong until you feel that way again. That's what friends are for."

*It was ironic that the other person with the same emotional defect was the one trying to be supportive.* Kayn sensed more people approaching. Haley and Astrid were standing above her grinning.

Astrid smiled and asked, "Mind if we join you?"

Grey nonchalantly tossed a handful of grass up into the air, it came back down and landed on his face. He brushed it away from his mouth with his hand as he replied, "Feel free. We're guessing what the clouds look like."

Haley was beaming as she made herself comfortable in the plush bed of greenery and sighed, "I can't even tell you how much I've missed this place. I never thought we'd see it again."

The new girl's grin was contagious. Kayn smiled then looked away. *What was wrong with her? Those two had been lost in the Testing for twenty years and she was hyper-focusing on the fact that her ex-boyfriend killed her. Her woes seemed ridiculous when she put them in context.* There were now seven Ankh lounging in the heavenly meadow, peacefully staring at clouds. *This felt right. It felt like this was exactly where she was supposed to be.*

Lexy pointed to the sky above and proclaimed, "I see a Dragon."

Grey met her eyes as he whispered, "Isn't it magnificent."

Kayn knew what they were trying to say. She sighed, "Yes...yes. I guess it is." Zach threw a giant handful of grass right at her face. She almost smiled as she spat it out and wiped it away.

"I must be a strange anomaly," Zach exclaimed as he shifted in the grass and added, I became Enlightened in the Testing and I still don't know what I am."

"Worry about your position as Brighton's Handler. Your abilities will come," Lexy assured.

Grey sat up, averted his gaze to Melody and probed, "How are you doing with the whole Testing thing Mel?"

Melody didn't meet his eyes. She continued to stare at the clouds as she replied, "I'm healed on the outside."

*They all understood what she meant.* Grey plucked another handful of grass out of the ground and tossed it behind him. *He was making her think about someone she didn't want to think about until she had to.*

Astrid looked directly at Kayn and chuckled, "Isn't that the story of our life?" She nudged her. Kayn nodded mechanically, giving her a response. *It took her a second to get it. They were still talking about Melody's healed on the outside statement.*

Zach inched closer to her in the grass. He whispered, "I think Frost is keeping his distance. You know about the getting Kevin to kill you deal, they made with Tiberius. Yes, it's messed-up but it was a means to an end. Even I can see that and I'm not the deepest guy around."

Kayn cracked an enormous grin. *Good one, Zach.* She remarked, "Whatever do you mean? You are super deep." *She was starting to feel peaceful.* Beneath her fingertips, the grass was softer. Above her, the colours in the sky were more vibrant. She felt the warmth of the air and the tickle of a faint breeze. Kayn smiled, relieved to be feeling anything at all, besides anger. She nodded as she assured, "I'll go talk to him. I just need a few more minutes of this."

Sprawled on his back, with his arms behind his head, Zach teased, "Look at how emotionally evolved you've become. I'm personally impressed."

*Oh hell, she might as well just go and get this over with.* Kayn sighed as she got up and brushed the grass off her sparse white attire.

Zach got up and said, "Wait a second." Chuckling, he plucked grass out of her hair and declared, "Go get him tiger."

She rolled her eyes as she wandered away from the group thinking, *we'll see how emotionally evolved I am if I can stop myself from blowing up everybody at the banquet.* She strolled away in the lush emerald grass. *She'd followed Zach's suggestion even though she hadn't really wanted to. That was strange.* There was a blinding flash of white light as the scenery changed and she was standing in waist-high purple heather. *What was this place supposed to signify? She'd never been here before.* The vegetation rose, surrounding her with twisting budding stems until she could no longer see the sky. The purple flowering plants appeared to be living breathing beings, dancing around her as they reached up to the clouds. She worked her way through the sea of greenery, shoving the stems to either side, forcefully creating a path until she heard something rustling in the brush up ahead. She paused. *Something golden was moving through the towering stems. It couldn't be? It was the stallion.* Her heart flickered. *She could choose to be a stallion.* She reached to caress its tender satin nose and the creature morphed into a lion. She yanked her hand away. The magnificent being rubbed up against her as though it were nothing more than an oversized house cat. It knocked her over and she landed on her behind in the shrubbery. The act of falling startled her, Kayn reacted as though she were still in the Testing by crossing her arms above her head to shield herself from its powerful jaws. When nothing happened, she peered up. The King of the wild was gone and she was on her butt in a forest of towering heather stems only inches from what appeared to be a baby Dragon. *She was from Vancouver Island. When you see a baby animal you always assume the mother is nearby. She'd better not touch it. No matter how tempting it was, with those large innocent eyes and shiny scales that glistened in the sunshine. It was sort of adorable. It was going to leave. No, don't go.* Kayn couldn't see the significance of the encounter until the fledgeling Dragon shrieked, spread its wings and flew away. In awe, she parted the overgrown sea of green stems that obscured her view to watch it soar through the pink and orange-hued sunset above her. *The sky had changed again. How long had she been here?* She stood in the overgrowth watching as the magnificent creature vanished in the distance. *She realised what she'd been shown. These were the versions of Kayn Brighton. She wasn't just one thing. She could still be as graceful and unbridled as the stallion or as majestic as the lion but when she needed to be, she was capable of being a Dragon. She was now many things.* The purple brush shrunk and the stems were sucked back into the earth all around her, revealing Frost, standing twenty feet away. *Forgiveness was a tool she'd always used most generously.* It flickered within her even though her emotions were still dull and stagnant. *Yes, his deception had hurt her but she was still undeniably drawn to him.*

Walking towards her, he started to explain, "What we did, helped you survive in there. I'm not going to make excuses. I'm sorry I hurt you but I'm not sorry we did it. I hope you can find it in your heart to forgive me someday."

*That wasn't much of an apology.* Too mentally exhausted to play his games, she shook her head. *It served no purpose to hold a grudge. She needed what little inner peace she'd managed to find to continue, even if it was only for a little while longer.* He cautiously closed the space between them and as he took her in his arms, the icy indifference encasing her heart melted away. The strength of their connection completed the thaw.

He whispered in her ear, "I wanted to hug you the moment I saw you but I knew you'd clock me."

*She might have.* Kayn whispered in his ear, "It's probably a good thing you waited." He chuckled in her ear. She whispered, "Just one question."

He spoke against her hair, "Anything."

She hesitated, already knowing the answer. Kayn placed her hands against his chest to put some space between them, so she could think rationally. She needed to look into his eyes. She probed, "Would you have left me in that place?"

Frost's eyes met hers as he replied, "Why do you think we were willing to do whatever it took to trigger your Enlightening? There's no way to get anyone out." He got down, yanked the long purple flower from the earth and gallantly handed it to her on bended knee. He taunted, "You're not going to make me sing or recite poetry, are you?"

*He was smooth, so damn smooth.* Kayn shook her head and

provoked, "I don't know. Poetry might work." She accepted the flower.

With a playful grin, he chuckled, "There once was a guy from Nantucket."

Laughing on the inside, she spun around and strutted away, leaving him on bended knee in the field of now normal sized flowers. *She'd always enjoyed these naughty flirtations and right now, this was exactly what she needed.*

Frost called after her, "What's wrong beautiful? Do you already know that one?"

*He'd catch up. It would do him good to think she was mad for a few seconds.* She heard him behind her, shuffling his way through the flowers. He smacked her butt. She stopped walking and sighed, "That sweet apologetic behaviour lasted all of five seconds."

He put his arm around her and teased, "Would you really want me any other way?"

Looking into his mischievous eyes, she countered, "Who says I want you now?" Kayn slipped out from under his arm and swung her flower at him. He ducked out of the way and chuckled. They began the trek back to the others, strolling side by side. He laced his fingers through hers and she let it happen.

He paused with a gentle tug on her hand and their eyes met as he suggested, "I don't want to go back yet. There's somewhere I've always wanted to see. Come with me?"

She met his inquisitive eyes, knowing she wanted to go with him but not entirely certain she should. *Before the Testing each step, she tried to take in Frost's direction had been blocked by something or someone. She suspected they'd be an unsavoury combination for obvious reasons. She was a Dragon, and he was, Frost.*

She hadn't yanked her hand away even though she'd had the urge to. Staring at their intertwined fingers, she nodded as her response.

Taken aback, Frost provoked, "Really? I honestly didn't think you'd say yes." He smiled and tempted, "Let's go."

The scenery altered again with an explosion of blinding light and they were standing on the edge of a cliff, barefoot in the snow. They both started jumping around; laughing because standing barefoot in the snow was a ridiculous thing to do. *Why would he even think of this place?* He started to run and it only took her a second to figure out what he was doing as she noticed the steaming pool of water. She chased him to the hotspring. He hopped in and began to curse. She jumped in and her senses exploded. To go from snow to steaming water had them both laughing and swearing up a storm. When her body assimilated to the heat, she relaxed in the liquid heaven and met his eyes, feeling alive. *He'd shocked her senses and made her feel pleasure again. Why couldn't he be like this all of the time? Why did he do ten stupid things for every sweet one?* Frost left his perch on the opposite side of the shallow pool and slowly made his way closer as the steam rose around him. She found her eyes glued to his muscular abdomen and chiselled chest. *Frost's presence had never prompted rational thought on her behalf.* He relaxed beside her. *He was far too close and everything about him was alluring.* She was mesmerized by the beaded droplets of water on his chest. *She'd only spent a short time in his presence and she was already feeling like doing something reckless.* She bit her lip. *She was feeling. This was why he'd taken her to this place. For a second, she'd forgotten everything that ailed her.*

He sighed, "Now this was a great idea, wasn't it?

Kayn grinned as she answered, "An amazing idea but we're going to have to get out of this heavenly pool eventually and stand in the freezing snow barefoot again."

"But it was worth it," he teased.

*She saw what he was getting at. He'd just pulled a Greydon.* She splashed his face. He sputtered and choked but ended up laughing. He splashed her back and for a moment she wondered if this was what it'd be like to be with him. *Would he always make her feel this reckless and wild? The need to throw caution to the wind and do whatever felt good always seemed to snuff rational thought when she was with him. Frost would have been an amazing Handler.*

He got up, grimacing from the cold. Frost questioned, "A penny for your thoughts?"

"I'd be stinking rich if I had a penny for every time you've used that line on me," she taunted. *She didn't want to get out.* "Can't we just stay here," she pleaded, pouting just enough to intrigue him. *If she got out, they'd have to go find the others, then she'd have to deal with this infamous banquet where she'd undoubtedly see Kevin.* Kayn stiffened in the icy air as she rose out of the water. *It was painful but not in a bad way.* Frost cleared his throat. She noticed his agonized expression. He was standing in the snow enduring the pain with his hand gallantly extended in her direction to help her out of the water and into the icy torture that awaited her toes. She took it and stepped out of the warm caress of the pool into the frigidly tortuous snow. They laughed as they dashed away from the pool towards the edge of the cliff. *This time it was different. The pain of the snow beneath her feet felt oddly incredible.* The agony of her icy feet had summoned the Dragon within her and given her an overwhelming urge to do something dangerous. She let go of his hand and winked at him as she leapt off the cliff into the powdery fog of the unknown.

Frost peered over the edge and hollered after her, “Seriously!”

Cackling, Kayn disappeared into the mist. Wind rippled through her hair during her pulse racing downward spiral. *She didn’t know how far she had to fall, but it didn’t matter, she had no intention of stopping. She wanted the pain that came with the end of this ride. It was more than that, she needed it. Was this what she had become? She was now a creature in search of pain.* She felt a tug. Frost grabbed her sarong. *Party pooper.* With another yank, he had a good hold on her arm.

He yelled, “I don’t want to lose you when we hit the bottom! I’m guessing you don’t want to stop before we hit?”

With her hair whipping around, she gave him nothing in response but a smirk. He cursed as they hit the ground with a surge of excruciatingly magical agony.

EVERYTHING WAS HUMMING AS SHE CAME TO. *THAT WAS AWESOME.* Feeling the warm sand beneath her fingertips, she smiled. *The in-between had given her a clean slate.* She raised her head, spit the sand out of her mouth and started to giggle.

Ten feet from her facedown in the sand, Frost groaned, “You suck.”

Scrambling to her feet, she wandered over as he fought to operate death-stunted spaghetti limbs. Kayn held out her hand, teasing, “Come on, princess.” She yanked him to his feet. They strolled away barefoot in silky sand under an ever-changing glorious sky.

"Give Zach time. He'll get used to the Handler thing," Frost urged as he took her hand.

She nodded without responding. *It was all too much to process.* He gave her hand a reassuring squeeze. She looked at him and the scenery exploded with brilliant light as they were transported back to the rest of their Clan. The others noticed their arrival and enthusiastically waved them over. Kayn sat beside her fellow Dragon in the grass.

Lexy gave Frost an ominous look as she warned, "You'd better be nice to her."

He flirtatiously responded, "Whatever do you mean? I'm always nice."

Everyone began throwing fistfuls of grass at Frost. He shielded his face laughing until they gave up and sprawled on the grass as a group to watch the crimson-hued awe-inspiring sunset, swirling a magical path across the horizon.

Haley randomly piped in, "After 20 years in Astrid's happy place, I keep expecting there to be clowns."

Perched on his elbow, Grey enquired, "There were clowns?"

Grinning, Haley replied, "There were always clowns."

"I can vouch for that," Zach chuckled. "Her happy place was getting a little warped."

Frost's eyes lit up as he dared, "I say we all check out this happy place right now."

Grey gave an immediate response, "No thank you. I'm good."

"Oh, come on. Don't be a wuss," Lexy taunted as she tossed grass at Greydon.

Kayn had been quietly watching the exchange. Frost was intentionally pushing Grey's buttons. She came to his defence by saying, “The last time I was in her happy place, the balloons were really chainsaws and the clowns tickled us when they caught us.”

Grey jumped up and stammered, “Like hell!”

Lexy kissed Astrid square on the lips. She leapt up, chased Grey and tackled him into the grass. Against his will, she planted a long kiss on his lips. *He kissed her back. She’d seen his response. Something must have happened between these two while they were attending the Summit. She was dying to ask but knew this wasn’t the time.*

Staggering, with her head in the palms of her hands, Lexy giggled, “This is so messed up.”

The others became curious. When Lexy says something is messed-up, you just know its absolute insanity. Astrid worked her way through the group, kissing them all. It only took moments for her ability to take effect. They were all on the same page as dozens of clowns skipped across the field of floating bubbles towards them to the tinkling music of an ice-cream truck, wearing brightly coloured outfits, towing bouquets of swaying balloons. Kayn stood calmly beside a grinning Lexy. Creeped out by the idea of being tickled by clowns, everyone else scattered. Laughing hysterically, the Dragons joined the twisted game. There was an explosion of light as the rest of their Clan appeared. The freaked-out Ankh sprinted past the others.

Markus hollered, “What in the hell are you guys doing?”

Kayn was having a blast playing clown tag when her chest tightened. The hallucination disappeared and reality sucked. *Her chest was on fire.* She dropped to her knees, finding it difficult to breathe. *What’s happening?*

Immediately at her side, Markus whispered, “It’s going to

be okay, just breathe through it. The Enlightening isn't one moment. Sometimes it's a process that takes days or even weeks. The Testing was only the beginning."

His words rang in her ears. *The Testing was only the beginning. She was at the beginning once again. She'd travelled in a circle and she was standing in the same place.* Grey sprinted past her terrified, narrowly escaping imaginary clowns. Kayn laughed through her agony.

Markus crouched beside her and whispered, "What are they running from?"

The pain passed. Exhausted, Kayn peered up and said, "Clowns. They are running away from clowns."

Markus chuckled as he held out a hand to help her up. Lexy and Melody were already healed. The two girls casually strolled over, laughing as Grey raced by again.

"I guess we can let Grey do a few more laps before we go," Markus laughed.

Out of thin air, Jenna appeared. They stood together watching Grey run laps. He was the only one left under the influence. "What is he running from?" Jenna asked.

Kayn grinned as she replied, "Imaginary clowns."

Jenna chuckled as Grey narrowly escaped his invisible assailants. She commented, "I always miss the good stuff while I'm doing Oracle things." Leaving her, Jenna went over to Markus. She whispered in his ear. Concerned about something, their leader was staring at Kayn.

*Well, that's never a good sign. What now? Maybe, she didn't want to know.* Kayn took a deep breath as she changed the subject, "What is this banquet?"

Lexy gave her a straightforward reply, "They're going to

bathe and dress you up. There will be some form of entertainment, food and dancing."

Kayn knit her brow and replied, "Refresh my memory as to why would I allow a stranger to bathe me? I'm not a toddler."

Grinning, Lexy sparred, "If I had to allow strangers to bathe me, then you do. It's a respect thing. We take any respect we can get from the Third-Tier."

Kayn felt apprehensive as goosebumps rose on her skin. *It was a warning.*

"Is everybody ready to go?" Markus bellowed.

*No, not really.* Kayn didn't like the way she was feeling. *Perhaps it was the lack of choices. She preferred to make her own decisions. This felt forced.* Standing, they joined hands. Kayn was awaiting the stomach-churning sensation of the tomb travel, but instead, they all began to disintegrate into the air. She held her palm in front of her face as it turned to sand and the delicate grains of her essence floated away on a breeze.

# 2

# UNCOMFORTABLE SITUATIONS

They solidified in the air above the deserted coliseum and landed on their feet in unison. An explosion of dust rose. For the first time, Kayn noticed how massive the coliseum was. *She'd been out of it when the stands were full.* Someone cleared their throat. A buffed, gorgeous guy strolled over and began shamelessly flirting with Lexy. Kayn glanced at Grey. *He looked annoyed.* Kayn nudged Grey and whispered, "Who is that?"

He whispered back, "That's Silas. He's Ankh. He won the Summit a long time ago and chose to stay. He appears to have a crush on Lexy. She was the star of the show this Summit. Silas has always been a fame whore."

"Keep it up and somebody might think you're jealous," Kayn teased as they followed the others.

Grey winked and quietly responded, "She's my friend. I'm just looking out for her. Let's just say, she's made a few questionable choices as of late."

Grinning, Kayn hip-checked Grey, teasing, "Right, just friends." He wasn't expecting it and laughed as he came close to toppling over. *Lexy just fought everyone by herself. As always, she was unaffected by the violence she'd survived. Dragons could tuck traumatic emotions away. They appeared undamaged in the aftermath of a storm.* Lexy's scarlet hair flickered in the wind like crimson flames. Kayn's hair ended up in her mouth. She tucked it behind her ears and glanced at her wrist, noticing its lack of always present elastic bands. *She felt someone's eyes.* When she peered up, Silas was grinning at her plight.

Silas spoke, "I've heard impressive things about you. It's a pleasure to meet you, Kayn."

Kayn took the immortal's hand. He gallantly turned it over, kissed her palm and closed it. She felt sick to her stomach. *Kevin used to do this. There's no way he could have known. It was from a children's book.* With an uncomfortable smile, she held the hand he'd kissed protectively. *Kevin... she was going to be forced to see him again. She wasn't prepared for that. What difference did the timing make in the long term? What was done was done. They were done. Her best friend had now taken on a new role as her enemy. He didn't matter anymore. She just had to keep repeating that to herself. He doesn't matter anymore.* The group followed an overly exuberant Silas from the coliseum through an intricately etched archway of gold. *Maybe this bathing thing wouldn't be that bad? She could use some pampering. She hadn't had the opportunity to have a nice hot bath in what felt like forever.* Kayn smiled as she watched Silas strolling along with one arm around Haley and the other around Astrid as he yammered on about how amazing it was that they survived twenty years in the Testing. The group joked and laughed like old friends. Unable to shake the feeling of impending doom, she quietly followed, keeping her distance. *It felt like she was walking slowly to the end of a plank.* She kept trying to meet Frost's gaze. He appeared to be deep in thought. *She felt queasy. It felt like something was off and she knew what that meant. Something was coming. Something was wrong. Did everyone else feel this way? Was she walking into a trap?* They strolled through another spectacular gold intricately engraved archway into a white room of round steaming pools with flower petals floating on the surface. There was an intoxicating scent in the air. On the left side of the enormous room, there was a rich burgundy curtained off area. *Was it a change room?* Silas gestured the five Testing survivors into the curtained area. Behind were six small pools of water full of flower petals. Standing around the pools were dozens of scantily clad men and women. *This was going to be so uncomfortable.* Confused, the newbies stood together. Strangers began removing Zach's sarong. His only coverage dropped to the marble floor in front of a flock of people. He didn't appear to be the least bit concerned as he stepped into the water. Both men and women bathed him. Melody, Haley and Astrid were next. Kayn tried to take off her sarong by herself. Half a dozen people scurried around helping. With an arm concealing her chest and her hand over her privates, she got into the steaming, fragrant pool. *This was mortifying.* She noticed Zach staring at her and glared at him.

He winked and mouthed the words, "Relax, it's nothing I haven't seen before."

She giggled out of sheer nervousness. *Zach walked in on her while she was changing countless times. They'd shared a room like siblings. Why was she stressing out about people she'd never see again?* She was passed a large goblet of red wine. Instead of declining it, she took it. *If there was ever a time to take a glass of wine without a second thought, it was right now.* She downed the entire glass without coming up for air. When she lowered the goblet from her lips, the pool was full of grinning faces. *They were here to wash her. Awkward.* Stranger's hands began soaping her down. She felt like shrinking under the surface where nobody could touch her unless they were willing to dive under to do it. *It was an invasion of privacy. She wasn't accustomed to having anyone's hands on her body.* It went without saying, multiple ones would make her uncomfortable. *Was this supposed to be pleasurable because it wasn't?* Backed into the corner of the pool, Kayn squeezed her eyes closed. *Happy place. Happy place. She felt like a cat being forcibly washed against its will.* She was trying hard to look like she wasn't mortified by the experience. *She didn't want to offend anyone.* When she opened her eyes, the male servants had disappeared. She took a deep breath and tried to relax in the absence of strange male hands. The wine started to work its magic as leaves were placed over her eyes and mud was plastered on her face. *She smelled something minty.* Trying to enjoy the pampering, she laid her head back. She thought she'd been left alone to soak in the tub with a minty concoction on her face when someone began washing her feet without warning. *It tickled so much. She couldn't help it.* She squirmed around, giggling. Her face was washed off. When she opened her eyes, she had an audience. Two fancy attired men were standing above her. She crossed her arms over her chest.

The younger man seemed entertained by her attempt to conceal her body. He spoke with an accent she couldn't place, "You are the Conduit?"

*He was waiting for her to answer his question correctly. It felt like he wasn't clarifying what he wanted on purpose to make her feel uncomfortable. After a goblet of wine, she was in an unfiltered state. She'd have to choose her words wisely.* Smiling pleasantly, even though she was irritated, Kayn answered, "I guess I am."

He smirked and replied, "You guess you are... what?"

She had to stop herself from rolling her eyes. Kayn raised her eyebrows while reining in sarcastic wit, sensing it would be lost in this situation. She responded, "I am."

Looking frustrated, he questioned, "You are what?"

With her best fake Chloe pageant smile, she replied, "I am the Conduit." *This guy was an anal-retentive douche. What a pompous ass.*

Glaring, he enquired, "I understand what pompous ass means but what do you mean by anal-retentive douche?"

Zach began clearing his throat loudly.

*Her thoughts were not private here either. Whoops. She'd have to rein them in.*

Harnessing her inner Chloe, Kayn coolly responded, "It means you are overly concerned with small details."

Intrigued by her candour, he teased, "Yes, I guess I am. It's a pleasure to meet you Conduit."

*He was purposely toying with her.* The man extended his hand to her limply and sideways. *What did he want her to do? Was she supposed to shake it? Was she supposed to kiss his ring?* He was openly grinning at her now. *She knew he could read her mind. He could help her out here.*

The arrogant stranger clarified, "I'm an Oracle. I need to touch your forehead."

She inched closer and knit her brow as he placed his hand on her head and smiled. She noticed the symbol of Trinity on his hand as he pulled it away.

"An unbroken Dragon after the Testing," he indifferently announced. "Thank you. That was all I needed to know."

*Yes, I'm unbroken. Was he checking to see if she was still sane? That would depend on what level of sanity you were looking for and who you spoke to. Am I going to wear you as a skin coat? Well, probably not. She only made skin coats out of people on Tuesday.* Kayn smiled at her off-kilter humour. *She could entertain herself for hours with her own wacky thoughts.* She submerged herself underwater except for her eyes and watched him walk away. *Why hadn't he stopped to talk to anyone else?*

Zach teased from the pool next to her, "You look like you're imitating a rhino at the zoo."

She almost giggled underwater because she was lurking under the surface making messed-up jokes in her mind. *This was why nobody asked what she was thinking anymore.* She sucked in a mouthful of water and spat it at Zach in the next pool. The servants appeared to be mortified at her immature behaviour. *She'd done it without thinking. Lots of people were in this water. Gross.* Kayn sunk under the surface as he shot a mouthful back, opting out of retaliation for obvious reasons. She surfaced and asked, "What do you think that was about?"

Zach ribbed, "Maybe he was trying to decide whether or not he should have you executed for calling him an anal-retentive douche?"

"That guy wasn't royalty or anything. He's Trinity. I saw his symbol," Kayn countered. *Hoping he wasn't right.*

He splashed her and scolded, "You are still supposed to behave yourself, Miss Brighton."

The servants that attended to her bath led her out of the tub and gestured for her to follow while still dripping wet into a small sauna chamber. They motioned for her to go inside. *Against her better judgement, she did.* The door was closed behind her and she was standing in the dark. *Well, she didn't like this, not one bit.* The room began to hum, it became uncomfortably warm as a strong wind blew her entire body. The sound stopped and there was a loud click. A girl opened the door. Kayn was completely dry, including her hair. *That was kind of cool. It would have been far cooler if they'd explained what they were doing first.* She was dressed in an exquisite gold shimmering gown. *It was the most beautiful dress she'd ever seen. It was a bit big on her though.* They led her to another room the size of a shower stall. A lady asked her to step inside. *The last stall had been okay.* She didn't hesitate and just entered. She stood there for a second in the dark with another humming sound. She winced as she was blinded by flashes of light. They opened the door and she stepped out. She looked at the lady who'd guided her to each room and questioned, "What was that room for?"

The tiny built stern-looking woman replied, "See for yourself."

She led Kayn to a full-length mirror. *Some things were obviously the same here.* Kayn was shocked as she stood in front of it. They had old school bathed her and then pimped her out alien style in five minutes. Her dress had been altered and she had makeup on. She was strikingly beautiful. Stunned by the transformation, she'd never felt more gorgeous. Her eye shadow was oranges, teals and yellow. Her green eyes looked amazing. Her naturally curly blonde hair was all free-flowing perfect ringlets. Her skin was golden tanned and flawless. Her lips were glossy and tinted red. *She felt like a woman. She looked like a goddess from ancient Greek mythology*. Staring at her reflection in awe, she said, "Wow, I didn't know I could look like this."

The lady warmed up as she whispered, "You are just as pretty as your mother."

This caught her attention, she turned to look at the woman and whispered, "You knew her?"

The lady's eyes softened as she replied, "I knew her well. She was a good friend of mine. She stayed with us here for almost twelve years. The King was very much in love with her when she disappeared without a trace. She left without saying goodbye to anyone. If you see her, tell her Cassis misses her terribly."

*Her Clan pretended they didn't know where she was. If Freja was hiding from the Third-Tier who oversaw everything, that would explain Ankh's silence on her whereabouts. Was the King her father?*

Hearing her thoughts, Cassis answered, "She came to stay with him in lieu of being entombed for creating you. She was his prize. I'm not certain his feelings were ever returned by Freja. The King is a volatile, unforgiving man. I'm concerned for your safety this evening. Do not leave the safety of your Clan for any reason."

*Her mother had been held here for twelve years. So far, it really didn't seem like a bad place to be. Poor thing was probably dressed up like a princess and paraded around by a King.* She smiled at Cassis and gave her a hug as she explained, "I've never met Freja and the Clan acts like they have no idea where she is. Don't worry about me, I'll be fine. I survived the Testing. I'm tougher than I look."

The lady who'd been close with her mother warmly teased, "I bet you are."

Silas walked through the flowing velvet curtains beside her. He caught his breath. It took him a moment to speak. He whispered, "You look so much like her."

*Once again, she resembled somebody else as she had for her entire life. She just wanted someone to say the words, Kayn, you look beautiful. She didn't want to hear that she looked like Chloe or the woman who'd been her egg donor. She just wanted to be Kayn. Hadn't she earned the right to be an autonomous person?*

Smiling at her, Silas said, "You're beautiful, Kayn. You resemble her but don't look exactly like her. You have the same hair and green eyes, but that feisty personality is all yours. I'm just used to seeing you in a ponytail and shorts. You were always my favourite twin. You've always been beautiful to me."

*Everyone could read her thoughts here. Also, she apparently had a stalker.*

Silas chuckled, "I prefer to think of myself as a friendly observer. I was asked to keep an eye on you." He motioned for her to follow him and stated, "They're waiting for you. We have to stop by the treasury on the way."

Kayn followed him down long dimly lit passageways until they reached a stone wall. He walked right through it. She hesitated for a second before shutting her eyes for impact and following. Her eyes were still closed as she came through on the other side. *She'd gone through one of these walls before. It was one of those things her mind couldn't quite grasp. The instinct to not walk into the wall was far greater than the trust that she would come through unscathed on the other side. Perhaps, she'd walked into too many walls as a child?* She froze as she took in the awe-inspiring room before her. A golden room full of jewels. The security wore gold loincloths and held swords adorned with gems. *If she touched anything, they'd frisk her. That wouldn't necessarily be a bad thing, they were gorgeous. If she was just a little more experienced, she'd be trying to get caught stealing from these two.* Silas was grinning. *She seriously had to start remembering her thoughts were being listened to.*

Silas pointed around the room and announced, "Choose anything you want to borrow for the evening but make it quick. They're waiting for us."

*She'd never really worn jewellery. It rarely left her jewellery box. When you are naturally clumsy, you tend to leave expensive things at home.* She wandered up to a wall of exquisite necklace and earring sets. *She was always overwhelmed when someone gave her a ton of choices.*

Silas started to laugh. When she looked at him, he teased, "Would you like help?"

"Yes, this is way out of my element," she replied. Silas pointed at a few different ones. The guards climbed up, took them down and they were placed in see-through cases in front of her. Getting a good look at one of the guard's bits and pieces as he climbed, her cheeks reddened. Kayn looked away. Silas grinned but didn't tease her.

Taking one out of the see-through case, Silas enquired, "Do you mind?" He put a necklace on her, did up the clasp at the nape of her neck and passed her earrings. She put them on. Medium-sized yellow stones surrounding a large green one and diamonds. *It looked like Emeralds, diamonds, and Topaz, but she didn't really know.*

Taking a good look at her, Silas preened, "Absolutely stunning. Do you want to try on something else? Do you need to take look in the mirror?"

*This all felt so ridiculous. She had just survived the equivalent of her own personal hell and she was standing here picking out jewellery.* Kayn admitted, "That's not necessary. I'm sure it looks great. I'll wear what I have on. This is all way out of my comfort zone. I'm not a girl that is overly impressed with shiny things. I mean, I'm sure they're beautiful but I'd be just as happy with a flower in my hair."

"Where have you been all my life?" He teased as he grabbed her hand and playfully towed her back through the wall.

As they strolled arm in arm down the long corridor, Kayn sparred, "I thought you already knew?"

Silas chuckled, "You have to keep up. There's no time for messing around. You're going to be late. Trust me, you do not want to make your grand entrance alone."

Grateful she was barefoot, she trotted along next to him. *Had someone forgotten to give her shoes?* She glanced down at Silas' feet. *His were bare. Interesting, these people didn't wear shoes. Lexy must be downright traumatized.* She followed him through another fancy archway into a large room where her friends had all congregated waiting for her to arrive.

Zach's jaw dropped open, he mouthed, "Wow."

They all wore stunning gowns. Melody looked like an angel in a delicate white lace dress. Astrid was in a blue strapless satin dress. Haley had her natural blonde hair piled up into a bun but it still had pink tips. She looked like a ballerina with soft tendrils of loose hair framing her face. Zach also looked incredible but none of them had been done up to the degree that she had. *What was going on? Maybe, she'd just downplayed her looks for so long that any effort made a shocking difference.* Kayn stood before her Clan in her form-fitting glistening gold gown with a slit on one side that travelled all the way up to the curve of her hip. *She felt like a lion. She had power over the uncomfortable situation she was about to walk into.* Zach grabbed one of her hands and Melody grabbed the other. Astrid and Haley joined the line on the other side of Zach.

Zach leaned over and whispered in her ear, "Triad is already in there."

Melody whispered in the other one, "Just don't make eye contact. Avoid it completely. If you act like you don't even see him, then you win."

*Had anybody won?*

"Zach looks like the luckiest man alive," Silas stated as he anxiously surveyed the room.

Everything became quiet and the muffled sounds of chatter subsided. Their Clan was announced. The doors opened revealing a dimly lit coliseum style banquet room with dining on each level. *Oh good, because there's nothing I love more than eating in front of people.* They entered the hall to the music of a trumpet. *That was incredibly weird.* She was trying to stop herself from smiling but when the trumpeter began playing a well-known pop song, she was forced to press her lips together to stop herself from laughing. *Her emotions were all over the place.* Both Clans were sitting at the same long table. She scanned the room and saw where the open seating was. She met Frost's eyes from across the room and knew the other end of the table would obviously be Triad's. She made sure to look away before she accidentally made eye contact with him. She stared directly at Frost as she walked towards the open seating at the table without taking her eyes off him.

Melody squeezed her hand and preened, "Good girl, just pretend he's not even there."

*All eyes were on her.* She tried to make sure she didn't even glance at the King. *There was that feeling of foreboding again.*

Curiosity got the best of her. Out of the corner of her eye, she snuck a peek. *People resembling famous actors and musicians from Earth were at the long table where royalty was seated. Weird.* Kayn sat between Frost and Lexy. *It felt like everyone was staring at her. Silas had attempted to make her feel better but she must look enough like Freja to render everyone speechless.* Kayn accepted a goblet of wine as it came around on a tray. What appeared to be silken ropes dropped from the ceiling. At least twenty women dressed in white came in a procession through the door. They wrapped the ribbons around their wrists and began to dance. They wrapped and entwined themselves up higher and tighter until they were suspended in the air performing. *It was incredible. She had seen acts like this but never with this kind of precision and fluidity.* She was entranced by what they were doing. *It was as though they were dancing in the air.*

Frost leaned over and whispered in her ear, "You look absolutely breathtaking. Don't spill wine on your dress love."

Glancing up at him under a veil of eyelashes, Kayn responded, "Thank you, I'll do my best." She smiled, instantly feeling much better. *Leave it to Frost to lighten her mood with well-timed sarcasm.* She felt his eyes on her and noticed he was staring at her exposed hip at the top of her dress. Seductively crossing her legs, Kayn whispered, "Is something wrong?"

"You're not wearing any underwear," Frost teased.

A little concerned, she innocently replied, "I hadn't thought about it. With the no shoes thing, I just assumed everyone wasn't wearing any."

Frost sipped from his goblet, and as he lowered it, he chuckled, "Now, there's a thought."

She whispered, "Am I the only one who isn't wearing underwear?"

Leaning over, Lexy whispered, "None of us are. Ignore him, he's messing with you."

Kayn smacked Frost's knee under the table and he laughed.

He looked at Lexy and complained, "Party pooper."

*There was no cutlery? They had machines you walk into to save time getting ready to alter your clothes but no forks.* She looked around the table and noticed everyone else pulling apart food with their fingers. *They had buns, fruit and meat she didn't recognize.*

Frost put some on her plate, saying, "If you don't eat anything, it's an insult. Just eat it. You don't want to know what it is."

She ripped it apart easily, put a piece in her mouth and chewed. *It had a strange texture. He was right, she probably didn't want to know what it was.*

Grey tossed a flat thing that looked like a thick rough-edged tortilla across the table at her and urged, "Make sure you eat lots of this if you're drinking tonight."

He pointed at her empty wine glass. She took a bite and smiled because it tasted like bread. They brought around bowls of orange soup. Kayn glanced around, watching people pick up the bowl and drink from it. Others were dipping tortillas in it. They began to laugh and joke around as the wine took hold of the room. Kayn caught herself glancing at this King that kept Freja here for twelve years. *He was watching her eat.* She smiled pleasantly at him and looked away. She watched Grey wrap the meat inside the tortilla. He dipped it in the bowl and ate it. She did the same. The soup was spicy but delicious. Enjoying the meal, she ceased to care about what kind of meat was in her tortilla. Cakes and pastries were passed around the table. Selecting a few, Kayn smiled at the boy serving and politely said, "Thank you." He smiled back but appeared confused.

Frost nudged her and explained, "They aren't supposed to speak to us. Let me rephrase that, they aren't allowed to."

Kayn picked up a pastry and stared at it critically as she replied, "That's pretty stupid."

"Yes. It is," Frost responded, watching her.

Sniffing the pastry, she asked, "What's in this one?"

Frost took it from her and placed it on his plate. He found her a different one and whispered, "Open your mouth."

She bit her lip as she met his devious eyes. *She'd played this naughty game with him before.* She parted her lips as he slipped the creamy filled pastry into her mouth. She slowly chewed the dessert. *It was delicious.* Frost seductively licked the cream from the treat he'd fed her off his finger. She watched him, knowing he was doing his best to entice her. He ate the one he'd taken off her plate and grimaced. She grinned and whispered, "What was in that one?"

Frost swallowed it. Smiling back, he stated, "Nothing good." He motioned like she had something on her face. Her eyes widened as she unsuccessfully attempted to lick it off. He chuckled and whispered, "Let me get that for you." Touching her face, he showed her the cream on his finger and asked if she wanted to lick it off.

Lexy piped in from the other side of her, "Lick that cream off your own finger, Romeo."

Before she had the time to see Frost's reaction, music began and from the wall on the far side of the room something that resembled a rock-climbing surface slid up from the inside of the floor. It kept going until it was flush with the ceiling. Then instead of smooth rocks, pointed spikes slid out. The whole set up appeared to be made of sculptured ice. Kayn leaned over and whispered in Frost's ear, "What is that?"

He replied, "Our entertainment."

A nervous young man was on a circular platform, ten feet from the sculpture. It rose into the air. *What was he going to be forced to do?* The platform stopped, hovering forty feet in the air. Six others appeared, walking to the base of the structure. They climbed to different positions. *If they slipped, they'd either fall to their death or become impaled on frozen spikes.* Extending themselves with athletic majesty from the structure, they performed a climbing dance routine. This went on for the remainder of the meal. *It was hard to look away.* The muscle tone it would take to move lengthwise was nothing short of miraculous. *How had they managed to keep it up for this long?* She watched in awe as one of the climbing dancers lost hold of the rigid surface and fell. Kayn's mouth dropped open. He was bleeding to death to raucous applause. A pool of blood formed beneath him on the marble floor. A fancy man in a red gown with intricate gold threading around his neck and waist strolled over. He clicked something resembling a flashlight. The injured man solidified and turned grey. The gowned man kicked the fallen one's form and he turned to dust. A woman in white swept up the dust with a golden broom and walked the pile of what had once been a Second-Tier under the elaborate archways and out large double doors. As the doors swung closed behind her, there was another applause. *This was messed-up. She understood they were immortal. Death was nothing more than entertainment to this crowd.* Kayn whispered, "What in the hell was that? Why are we applauding?"

"They are prisoners," Frost whispered back. "They're all Second-Tier, they can't really die. I'd imagine they were offered a chance at freedom if they were willing to be a part of this evening's festivities. The ones that survive, will be released. We're applauding because we don't have a choice. Play along, Brighton."

Trying to control her reaction to the knowledge that there was a society of immortals who thought of Second-Tier as nothing, Kayn asked, "How many usually survive?"

Frost chuckled and replied, "No one, they have to keep going until the King says dinner is finished. Nobody has the endurance to continue doing that bullshit for hours. One by one, they'll all die."

*Why were they even here?* Kayn clarified, "So, in this realm you have to win the Summit to be treated with respect. The rest of the Second-Tier are being held captive?"

He took another drink from his goblet. Nodding Frost explained, "Some are offered service and performing roles instead of entombment. Always chose entombment, at least when you're set free, you return to your Clan. They can always find a reason to extend your term if you are in a service role. Try to stay under the radar while we're here. The royal family can do whatever they want with you. I'm sure you've noticed Lily sitting at the head table. There's no option to say no and the King is a violent son of a bitch."

Kayn glanced at Lily intently listening to the prince, feigning interest while drinking from her goblet. Feeling the wine, she enquired, "What rights do we have?" *She'd been pacing herself, knowing she had to keep her wits about her this evening.* She reached for another piece of tortilla to lighten the effects.

Seeing what she was doing, Frost commented, "Good idea. Pass me one too."

She grabbed one and handed it to him. Their fingers touched. Her breath caught in her chest with a peculiar mix of emotions.

He continued his explanation of all things Third-Tier, "This realm is under monarchy rule. We're not from here so we have no rights. Earth is nothing but a farm. We are the harvest. We're here as delegates for our planet. You made it through their Immortal Testing, so you've proven yourself in their eyes to some degree. Worthy of breaking bread with and sharing a bed, but in no way equal to that family at the head table. No Third-Tier in this realm is considered close to equal."

Kayn asked the obvious question, "Why would we come here if we might be held captive or mistreated?"

Frost grabbed for another piece of tortilla on the plate in the middle of the table. He disclosed, "The only beings the royals in this realm fear are the three Guardians. We have a treaty. If we don't break any of their rules, we are reasonably safe. By reasonably safe I mean, they aren't allowed to detain us and keep us here unless we murder a member of the royal family or attempt to stage a revolt."

She took another sip from her goblet and laughed a little on the inside before saying, "But they can't be killed, they're immortal."

Frost smirked as he replied, "Oh, they can kill us for shits and giggles but if one of us accidentally bumps into one of them and they so much as stub their toe, we can be entombed.

I never said any of this was fair. Just do what you're told and you'll get to go home tomorrow. Anything that happens to us while we're here, is the price we pay for being immortal."

The room gasped as another acrobat slipped and impaled themselves on the spikes. The man with the strange flashlight gadget strolled over and turned it on the girl. She turned to dust and disintegrated into a pile on the floor. The lady with the broom swept up what was left and walked her out of the large, sculptured archway. She'd just left when three exhausted acrobats plummeted to the marble floor with a splat. The man in red with the light swooped in and turned them into piles of dust. This time more than one lady in white swept up what was left and walked their remains out through the majestic archway. The crowd continued their applause as the final Second-Tier was swept out of the double doors. The blaring of trumpets startled her. She glanced over just as the spiked wall slid into the floor with no evidence it had ever been there. With odd timing music began. Good music, easily comparable to what would be playing on the radio back home. The entire table stood up and she followed suit. *What's going to happen now?* They partnered up and strolled out onto the open dance floor in front of the head table. *She had a feeling dancing was also not a choice.*

Frost took her hand, whispering, "Try to have a good time but don't piss anybody off."

He led her to the dance floor and found somewhere difficult to see from the head table. She suspected he was trying to disguise her in the crowd. Frost pulled her against his chest and they swayed to the music. She was relieved nobody was attempting any kind of organized dance. *She would have stood out for sure in that scenario.*

He whispered in her ear, "You look stunning this evening, Froggy." She not so accidentally stomped on his foot. Frost laughed, "Alright...alright, I'll stop calling you Froggy but there's a condition."

Kayn whispered back, "You realise I could just make up an embarrassing nickname for you like snuggle butt or honey muffin cakes? I don't have to play these games with you." His breath against her hair made her shiver. She'd been doing a great job of ignoring the fact that Kevin was here. She knew Frost was trying to distract her. *He was doing an excellent job.* She'd almost forgotten everything but the sensation of his breath against her hair and the rhythm of his heart against her chest. She allowed herself to become lost in the music as they drifted effortlessly around their hidden area of the dance floor, with her eyes closed and her head resting on his shoulder.

As the next song began, he whispered against her hair, "Admit it. You love playing these games."

She didn't get the opportunity to answer. Grey swooped in as per usual to steal her away.

Frost let her go, quietly suggesting, "Keep her on this side of the room."

Dancing with her for a minute or two, Grey stopped moving. He gave her an enormous brotherly bear hug and whispered, "You have no idea how happy I am that you all found your way out of the Testing."

*All found your way out of the Testing. Those words jogged her memory and reminded her of the one person she was actively trying to forget.* Her heart tightened as she opened her eyes. *Don't look for him. No good can come from looking for him. It didn't matter what she told herself because she could feel him close by.* She peered over Grey's shoulder as he skillfully spun her around.

*Kevin was only a few feet away, dancing with someone from the head table.* Kayn closed her eyes again and willed the boy she used to love to go away. *Why in the hell couldn't he go dance on the other side of the room?* She opened her eyes with perfect timing. Their eyes met and it was like seeing a ghost, the essence of who they were still lingered in the space between them. *This was the moment she'd been desperately trying to avoid.* The look in his eyes was similar to the one he'd given her a second before she'd slit his throat. *Disbelief mixed with a flash of fear.* He mouthed something to her, but Grey spun her before she could decipher what he was trying to say.

Grey whispered in her ear, "Are you alright? Did you see him?"

She quietly replied, "I think he was trying to tell me something, but it doesn't matter anymore. I'm fine, forget about it. I already have." He fluidly spun her around and elegantly dipped her, dangling her precariously. It made her laugh. *He was good at changing someone's mood.*

With her suspended sideways, Grey disclosed, "You don't have to be tough when you're with me. We're friends and breakups always suck." The music changed and he propped her back up on her feet, grasping her arms.

Smiling, Kayn assured, "I'm alright. He chose his road, I chose mine. We're both exactly where we're supposed to be. I'll get over it."

He grinned at her as he affirmed, "You will get over it but that's enough talk of drama for this evening. Let's dance!" Soon their entire Clan joined in. The repetitive song had a club vibe. They began singing along. For the first time in a long time, Kayn felt capable of coordinated dance moves. *Was it because she'd been Enlightened and taken on more of Chloe's characteristics?*

She glanced at Kevin a few more times and it stung less than she'd thought it would. He was talking to a seriously hot familiar guy. *Wait a minute, where was Patrick?* She scanned the writhing pack of dancing fools. *Where was he? She hadn't seen him all night.* She danced her way over to Lexy and asked, "Have you seen that Patrick kid?"

Lexy giggled as Grey grabbed her from behind. He kissed her neck while swaying her back and forth. She laughed, "Stop it Grey! I can't even think!" Lexy struggled out of his grasp and hinted, "Picture him without the extra weight and take another look around."

Kayn tried to inconspicuously dance her way closer to the one hot guy she didn't recognize. *Holy crap, it was him. It was Patrick. How had he changed that much?* Zach took a page out of Grey's handbook as he grabbed her from behind and startled her. She laughed aloud as she turned to face him.

Her Handler took her hand, twirled her around and as they started dancing, he whispered in her ear, "You look incredible tonight, but this isn't my favourite version of you. I think you look best as you normally are. A freckle-faced girl with a ponytail and a streak of mud on your cheek. All of that stuff makes you the beautifully weird, flawed force of nature that you are."

She moved to the music in his arms as she teased, "That might have been the smoothest line I've ever heard. You should have absolutely no problem sealing the deal with Haley."

Zach kissed her cheek and assured, "You're one of my best friends Kayn. That wasn't a line. It was the truth."

"You're one of my best friends too." Kayn gave him a giant bear hug, rivalling Grey's.

Melody appeared behind them and joined in as she baited, “By the looks of things you won’t need that daily kiss I promised you in the Testing.”

Zach grabbed Mel and forcibly planted a kiss square on her lips. “You’re not getting off that easy,” he taunted.

Their whole Clan danced until they were breathless. After a little while, they began the joke dance moves. They did the lawnmower and the sprinkler. They began to make up new ones like the race car and the teacher. Kayn added the tiger lizard and spider rat to her goofy repertoire. Grey included Frost driving. *Frost didn’t find that one funny.* It turned into a giant game of dance charades. They kept making up new ones until they were all doubled over laughing. Kayn snuck a few peeks at the table of Triad. They’d left the dance floor when things started getting weird. She was pretty sure she’d seen a few smiles from some unexpected Triad. One last slow song came on and everyone began to partner up. Kayn scanned the dance floor but she couldn’t find Frost. She was about to sneak away and take her seat at the table when Grey grabbed her and said, “I know you’re looking for Frost, will I do?”

Kayn smiled at the friend she thought of as a brother and hugged him, agreeing to dance without saying a word. This night had done a lot to fill the empty spaces in her heart. *It was funny how a few kind words, hysterical laughter and a giant hug could heal a soul.* The song ended and there was silence. The announcer asked everyone to take their seats. They all wandered back. Grey pulled out her chair before he went to find his own seat. She didn’t want the dancing to end, she’d been having a great time. *Markus kept looking down at their end of the table. Was he looking at her?* Kayn turned around to see if anyone else was looking his way. She scanned the room for

Frost and caught sight of him standing beside Jenna's chair. She was whispering in his ear. He was visibly upset as he left her side. Lexy sat down beside her. Kayn smiled her way as she drank from her refilled glass of wine. Kayn grinned at Lexy and asked, "Do I have purple teeth?" *A logical reason for feeling like everyone was staring at her.*

Lexy assured, "No, you're fine. Fun fact, this makeup stays on for a whole month here. It's like a temporary tattoo. Kind of cool, isn't it?"

"I wish it was a permanent tattoo," Kayn replied. "I'll never be able to copy this masterpiece. I had no idea I could look like this. What's going to happen now?"

Lexy looked away as she answered, "Another sick and twisted show."

*That was a little weird.* Frost sat down beside her and kept staring straight ahead. *He was furious. He was so angry she was afraid to ask why. It wasn't her problem. She didn't need to go looking for drama, not today. She'd far surpassed her drama quota for at least twenty years and that was probably just this month.* She began to watch Haley and Zach. *They seemed quite into each other. It was probably good for him to find a hobby that didn't include taming her. It was more than a little adorable.* Haley's dress had a long frilly tutu. *She looked like a naughty ballerina.* Melody was staring across the table at Frost. *She seemed sad.* Grey was still grinning. *Nothing could rain on his parade.*

Lexy touched Kayn's arm and confessed, "I love seeing him like this."

Kayn grinned at her as she replied, "Me too."

Lexy took a drink of her wine and said, "I'm proud of you guys. You were amazing in there."

Kayn went to take a sip of hers. *There was a yellow flower floating in it. Weird?* She fished it out with her finger as she asked, "Could you see us in the Testing?"

Still smiling at Grey's beaming face, Lexy replied, "No, but Winnie kept Jenna informed. The Guardians were able to witness parts of the Testing."

*She'd been certain she heard Winnie's voice in the Testing. Had Winnie played a part in their arrangement with Kevin to trigger her Enlightenment? She'd had no part in her response. Her vengeance had been her own.* She glanced down the table at Kevin. *He wouldn't look at her. She sucked at this pretending somebody wasn't there game. She'd done so well, but she was curious. She wanted to know what he'd been trying to say to her. Had he been trying to apologize? What was she five years old? They weren't kids anymore. He'd slit her throat, not pulled her pigtail.* She took another sip of wine and shook her head at herself. *Seriously Kayn, would it really make a difference if he said he was sorry? He'd defiled her trust in their friendship by slitting her throat and then solidified it by feeding her to demons. If he was being forced to kill her, there were quite a few less torturous ways in which to accomplish that feat.* She looked at Frost again. He was pensively staring into his goblet of wine, tracing the rim with his finger. *He was acting weird.*

The trumpet played and a man in flamboyant clothing marched to the centre of the room. He cleared his throat and announced, "As decreed by pureblood immortal law. The unbroken Dragons shall surrender themselves to the King."

*What did he say? Did the unbroken mean everyone who survived the Testing? Everyone wasn't a Dragon.* She glanced at Frost. *He was looking at her now. Everyone appeared to be staring at her. He wasn't talking about her, was he? What in the hell was going on?*

Frost whispered, "Stand up and walk over there. You have to go, it's not a choice."

Recalling the random visit with the Oracle while she was having a bath, the word unbroken registered. *Was this about her virginity? You've got to be kidding me.* She glanced at Lexy and whispered, "This isn't seriously happening?"

Lexy squeezed her hand under the table, looked into her eyes and said, "If you don't go willingly, they'll take you by force. Do you trust me?"

Kayn responded, "Of course I do."

Lexy squeezed her hand again and instructed, "Stand up with all of the grace and dignity you can muster and walk to the centre of the room."

Kayn could see the expressions of her panicked Clan. *It wasn't just her own Clan.* She scanned the room as she rose to her feet. *The entire table was furious.* She met Kevin's eyes. *She knew that look. He was afraid for her.* Their eyes met and he looked down at the table. Even Stephanie, who openly despised her appeared personally violated by what was about to happen.

Markus mouthed the words, "You have to go."

Kayn walked around the table with her head held high. She began to recite a poem from her childhood in her mind as she stood in front of the man who'd summoned her, '*with the grace of a woman and not the grief of a child.*' She looked back at the room of upset Clan. *This wasn't really happening. She had already been to hell and back. Could they not give her five minutes peace before forcing her to enter that vile realm of depravity once again? This was insanity. She was not used to feeling like the only sane person in the room. So much for holding onto her first time so it could be special. This was not special. This was humiliating. She wouldn't allow this to change her. She had survived a simulation of the bowels of hell. She knew she could survive anything.* She looked at the head table. *They were already gone.* She glanced back at the table full of friends and sworn enemies as she mouthed the words, "I'll be okay." The frilly man summoned her to follow him. She went with him. He didn't speak to her, not one word as they walked through the archway.

Silas appeared and as he escorted her, he whispered, "Don't fight back. He can be a sadistic son of a bitch when he's been drinking. Just remember, you're stronger than any of this crap. You will be gone from this place tomorrow and this will just be something else on the list of things you need to forget." Silas placed something in her hand and whispered, "So you can find a better place."

She discreetly opened her palm to see what he'd given her. *It was a yellow flower that resembled a buttercup. She'd removed one of these flowers from her wine.* Kayn stared at the flower in the palm of her hand for a second and then looked up to thank him, he was gone. *He'd admitted he'd been watching her. He'd known buttercups meant something to her.*

They stopped walking. The man who hadn't uttered a word to her whispered, "It will be over before you know it. If you fight back, you'll be entombed."

She repeated the last words she'd spoken to her Clan, "I'll be okay."

He smiled as he reassuringly squeezed her shoulder and opened the door, revealing a room that reminded her of a scene from Arabian Nights. The canopy and tapestries on the walls were rich shades of crimson velvet. The man told her to wait inside. Kayn stepped into the room, wandered over to the bed, sat down and started to laugh. *She hadn't seen, 'virgin sacri-*

*fice' coming but, why hadn't she? Her life had been a comical collection of epically messed-up worst-case scenarios for years.* She looked at the bed. *How horrible could it possibly be? She'd just strolled out of her own personal hell and the King was only a man. She'd just close her eyes and pretend she was somewhere else. Tomorrow she would get to go home.* She noticed the wine on a tiny table by the balcony, got up and strolled over to it. Kayn poured a glass from the carafe and accidentally dropped the buttercup into the wine. She watched it float around for a second or two. *Why bother digging it out? She'd just drink around it.* There was a noise outside the door. She quickly downed the wine including the buttercup.

The King staggered in and slurred, "Did you really believe that you could just walk away from me? Did you think you could just leave me as though I meant nothing? Nobody leaves me."

*Oh, wonderful. He was disgustingly hammered. He thought she was Freja. There would be no point in attempting to point out the King's mistake with him in this state.* He was standing there staring at her. He raised his hand. She thought he was just going to touch her face when he swung back and struck her. Her pulse raced as her mind began screaming at her to shut her emotions down. *She couldn't do that. She had to keep the Dragon within her at bay.* Blood trickled from her nose. She wiped it off on the back of her hand. *Take it. Don't run. Predators get more excited when you run.*Scowling, she declared, "You're mistaking me for somebody else. I've never hurt you. I never left you."

Smirking, he slipped a hand around the back of her head. Clutching a handful of hair, he yanked it tilting her head back.

The King spat in her face, hissing, "You will be whoever I want you to be."

*With everything inside of her, she wanted to beat this disgustingly vile piece of shit senseless. Was this what Freja's life had been? Twelve years with an angry abusive drunk.*

He let her hair go and drank wine from the carafe. The King altered his entire demeanour as he politely enquired, "Would you like some?"

*And he's completely insane.* Kayn softly replied, "No, thank you. I'm fine." He swung back and savagely smoked her cheekbone with the heavy carafe. She almost lost her balance but remained standing, coldly indifferent to his show of strength. *Don't fight back. You can't fight back.* Her cheekbone was burning, the room was spinning. Shielding her face with her hands, her ears started ringing. She lost her footing and staggered backwards. The wall stopped her from falling. She heard a few thumps. She removed her hands from her eyes. *The King disappeared.* She pushed away from the wall. *What was going on?* She could barely stand. *She felt funny. He'd hit her hard, but it was her face, not her head.* The floor shifted underfoot. *What was this?* She closed her eyes, feeling dizzy every time she tried to open them. *Had she been drugged?* She opened her eyes to find Tiberius standing in front of her.

Tiberius winked at her and teased, "He tagged me in. The King was far too drunk to keep going."

Barely able to stand, Kayn gasped, "What?" *Tagged him in?*

He laughed, "I'm only joking, don't get your panties in a twist."

She quietly slurred, "Did you drug me?"

Tiberius gently touched her face where she'd been injured,

looked deep into her eyes and countered, "You drugged yourself."

She staggered sideways to the tapestry on the wall and grabbed it to stop herself from falling. She was clutching it as she crumpled to the floor and felt the heavy material land on top of her. All she could see was the colour of the velvet as the lights went out.

Kayn awoke in a strange room. *She wasn't in the King's bedroom anymore. Her head was killing her. What happened? Had Tiberius been there? Had she been dreaming?* She sat up in bed and saw two blurry people standing in the doorway.

They noticed she was awake. One came to her and said, "We're not going to hurt you. You were drugged to subdue the Dragon. You don't recognize me, do you? It's Patrick and this is Prince Amadeus. You'll have to stay hidden in here with us for a little while longer."

Kayn felt her face. *It smarted.* She groggily questioned, "Am I remembering this right? Did Tiberius just help me?"

Patrick grinned as he replied, "It was actually Lexy and Tiberius. Oddly, they were in on it together. Shocking, I know, but none of us were down with the new sacrificing a virgin policy."

Prince Amadeus rationalized his part, "I'm friends with Lexy and I was also close friends with Freja. I helped her escape. He won't know what happened. He usually blacks out when he's been on a bender. He never remembers a damn thing. We'll need to make it look convincing though..." Amadeus walked over carrying a couple of large chamber pots. He placed them on the floor, handed her a knife and said, "We're going to need a lot of your blood. Enough to cause embarrassment to the royal family. That way, none of this will be questioned."

Kayn sliced her arm. Blood slowly dripped into the pot.

Patrick grinned as he exclaimed, "There's no time for that Kayn. We don't even have time for you to use blood from both wrists. You do it or I'll do it for you. We're all involved now."

*She knew what he meant. He wanted her to slit her own throat and drain it into the pot. He didn't know what he was asking of her.* The sensation of Kevin slicing her throat flickered through her mind. *This had to be done and at least this time it was her choice.* Kayn grabbed the knife, leaned over the bowl and ran the blade across her throat. She felt the sticky warmth of her blood as it escaped from her body. Patrick rushed to her side and held her, making sure they didn't lose the precious evidence of the violence she'd been forced to inflict upon herself. Her eyelids grew heavy and closed.

In what felt like seconds, her eyes opened. With the sting of the blade fresh on her delicate skin, she clutched her throat.

"Do you usually heal this quickly?" Tiberius enquired. "You should see what that room looks like. The King's going to wake up and think he went all Hannibal Lector on your ass." He held out his hand and she reluctantly accepted it.

Kayn ignored his question and responded with, "Thank you, I guess. Where's Lexy?"

Tiberius chuckled, "She's riling up the rest of your Clan. Once they see what he's done, they'll allow us to sneak your body out of here to avoid the embarrassment. Playing dead won't be enough if they check you. Do you understand?" He handed her a handful of yellow flowers. She looked into his eyes and understood what he was asking her to do. She ate them, knowing what only one of those flowers had done to her. She felt Tiberius lift her. She was being cradled in his arms and then she felt the sensation of being carried. Her vision started to flicker just as she felt herself being placed on a warm sticky surface. *That metallic scent was her blood. All of this madness to preserve her virginity?* She felt the unforgettable sensation of her throat being sliced by the blade once again, followed by the gooey warmth of her essence flowing from the wound. The noise became hushed and when it was gone, she was...

# 3

# THE HANDLER'S MANUAL

Her mind flickered. From a distance, Kayn was aware of the whispers of horror and anger but couldn't open her eyes. She was being carried but wasn't sure who had her. *All she knew is that she felt safe in their arms.* The movement ceased. She was placed on a hard surface. She heard grinding stone and opened her eyes as soon as it stopped, knowing she was safe. *She was confined in a tomb.* She looked at the tiny handprint on the top. *It was much too small for her hand. It gave her hope. Maybe this tomb was meant for one of the original Children of Ankh?* While waiting for the strobing lights, she noticed the colour of the stone. *It wasn't pink. It wasn't rose quartz. This wasn't an Ankh tomb. What did that mean?* The tomb strobed with blinding turquoise light. She closed her eyes. *I'm going somewhere. Where? How is this working? Wasn't she supposed to turn to dust by touching another Clan's tomb?* She sensed a change in the light around her and tried to open her eyes. The pulsing ceased and she wasn't falling through the sky into the in-between. She opened her eyes. *Pink, the inside of the tomb was pink now. What in the hell?*

The top of the tomb began to open. The grinding of stone on stone usually meant she'd arrived home but this time, she had no idea what was going to happen. *Above her everything was white. Where was she?* She sat up and saw the youthful version of Winnie standing beside Azariah. *Was she in the in-between?* Kayn climbed out of the tomb. As she took a step towards the heavenly duo, a light flashed behind her. She spun around and the tomb had vanished. She met Winnie's welcoming smile with a look of confusion but still walked into her open arms. The embrace seemed to absorb the residual anxiety within her. *Winnie was still the only grandmother Kayn had ever known. Her age had been altered but the love in her eyes remained the same. She didn't want the embrace to end.*

Winnie squeezed her tighter as she praised, "You did well my child. I've missed you."

Kayn realised she was being rude to Azariah.

Azariah smiled sweetly as she read her mind and said, "Don't stop hugging her on my account. I find it most entertaining. I'm off now. You two have a lot of catching up to do." With an explosion of divine light, Azariah was gone.

She spent an hour or two wandering the warm sand of the in-between with Winnie, chatting about the afterlife as memories of the virgin sacrifice returned in scattered confusing images. She remembered Lexy's words, '*Do you trust me?' Lexy was a Dragon and her word was written in stone. It was all coming back. The yellow flower being pressed into her hand and the feeling that it was her duty to do what she was told. The hilarity of the virgin sacrifice situation and the knowledge that there could be nothing worse than what she'd experienced within the endless torture of the Testing.* This woman that strolled by her side had been Kevin's elderly grandmother back in her mortal life, but in the in-between Winnie was a stunning young woman with ginger hair flowing behind her like a ribbon of silk glistening in the sunshine. *Even in her youthful state, Winnie still made her think of Kevin. At first glance, there was no family resemblance but when you followed the line of her smile you could see a hint of Kevin in the curve of her lips. Why was she allowing him to cross her mind? What was the point? He was gone.* She concentrated on the calming sensation of the sand as it slipped between her toes. As she stopped moving, it enveloped her feet in soothing warmth. She stood there staring at the swirling pastel sky above. *Even though Winnie remained by her side, she'd never felt more alone. This was the price of being a Dragon. She noted that the scenery was beautiful but didn't feel it in her soul. It was now just a picture that didn't move her. A beautiful thing that meant nothing at all. She knew it would come back. She'd regained her emotions before the banquet. Would they always come back? What if they didn't? What if she continued to feel this hollow for months or years? Would feeling nothing become normal?* Kayn stopped torturing herself with what ifs and sat down in the sand. She noticed that Winnie had taken a seat, quietly by her side. She stared at the sand for a moment before methodically drawing a squiggly line in the sand with one of her fingers. It felt lovely but her senses were still muted. Kayn picked up a handful and allowed it to slip through her fingers until all the sand had disappeared. One lone grain remained in the palm of her hand. She stared at the solitary grain of sand and noted that this was what she was. A single grain of sand in the vast desert of the unknown. Every grain that had slipped through her fingers represented an emotion or loved one she'd lost and now she was back at the beginning of a new life. One solitary grain of sand. *The possibilities were endless. She could build a new life, all she had to do was to find a way to rejoin the others on the inside.* She licked her fingertip and pressed it against the grain in the centre of her palm and lifted it into the air. She puckered her lips and was just about to blow when Winnie blew on the tip of her finger and the grain of sand disappeared. She glared at Winnie and said, "What in the hell?"

Winnie chuckled, "That was a deep conversation you were having with yourself for someone choked up over lacking the ability to access her emotions. Life is all about change. Stop overthinking everything and just get on with your life."

Kayn couldn't help it, she smiled. *Winnie was right. Her emotions were not gone, they'd been dulled. If she could feel upset about her inability to feel things, that was still an emotion.* Kayn stood up and declared, "I should try to find my Clan. I'm sure they're here somewhere."

Grabbing her arm, Winnie scolded, "You're not going anywhere, my dear. It's not your job to find him. It's his job to find you."

*Him? What was she talking about?* Kayn knit her brow and questioned, "Are you talking about Zach?"

Winnie replied, "Bingo! It's been hours, he should have found you by now. This isn't the original pairing, we were forced to improvise. We're expecting complications. Grey might be able to help Zach understand his duties."

Rolling her eyes, Kayn sighed, "Well, I'm sure Zach will be thrilled about that."

The woman she'd known her whole life scowled and questioned, "Are you being saucy with me? I've known you since you were a child. I've never known you to have a sassy bone in your body. If I didn't know better, I'd think I was talking to Chloe."

Kayn pressed her lips together to shut her mouth but a few giggles snuck out. *She was starting to feel better. A little bit lighter on the inside.*

Winnie shook her head slowly from side to side. She rolled her eyes and sighed, "Alright you comedian, just spit it out."

Kayn grinned as she corrected her, "Theoretically, you are talking to Chloe."

"Touché child. I keep forgetting you're both in there now," Winnie sparred as she scanned the horizon for Zach. With no Handler in sight, she complained, "This is ridiculous. It's been hours. How do you feel about staying here alone with him for a while?"

Kayn's eyes widened as she pled, "No. Please. I want to go back with the others. I'm so tired. I need to get on with my life. I have to move past this whole Dragon thing." *In all fairness, they hadn't even started doing the whole Dragon Handler thing.*

Taking her hands in her own, Winnie sweetly explained, "There's no moving past this Dragon thing and there is no life other than this one. Someday you'll see that the pain you've gone through was nothing but building blocks in the evolution of the women you were always meant to become."

*She felt a presence.* The area exploded with blinding white light. When it became bearable, Kayn opened her eyes.

Zach strolled over and sighed, "There you are."

Embracing her, he gently stroked her hair and kissed her cheek. She made a conscious effort to relax her body against his but remained slightly rigid in his arms.

Zach whispered in her ear, "Are you alright? Did he? Did they get to you in time?"

*He was obviously talking about the virgin sacrifice thing.*

She heard Winnie scold Zach, "You should have found her a long time ago, Handler."

He winced at being addressed as her Handler. *Nice, that wasn't insulting at all.*

"It's not like there's a Handler's manual. I was trying to find her," Zach explained.

Winnie shook her head, scolding, "Find her faster next time."

"Yes, of course," Zach replied, sheepishly.

The sky above altered and caught their attention. The swirling pastel sunset began to shift as though someone was stirring paint as the divine backdrop transformed into various brilliant shades of blue. They were both entranced, watching the sky's magical transformation.

They heard Winnie say, "Zach can find you in the in-between. This is good." Before either one had taken their eyes away from the glorious display, there was another incapacitating explosion of light. They cowered, shielding their eyes from the glare, barefoot in the sand. When they were finally able to open their eyes, the two rose to stand and Winnie was gone.

Zach spun around, asking, "Where did she go?"

"I think she just wanted to see how long it would take you to find me," Kayn answered, scanning the horizon.

Annoyed, he complained, "I didn't realise I was being timed. I guess I'm supposed to be a babysitter and a psychic now."

*She'd been feeling much calmer, almost back to normal, but every word in that sentence had pissed her off. His frustration hadn't been directed at her. He'd said he was fine with being her Handler, but his mannerisms suggested otherwise. She tried to just let it go but it wasn't that easy. Not anymore. That spark of anger ignited, turning the simmering embers within her into a raging inferno. She didn't know how to put it out.* Her pulse raced as adrenaline began coursing through her now clearly visible veins. She looked up at the beautiful sky, trying to think happy thoughts. *It was too late for that. With each passing second, rational thought became more difficult. She needed to fight something or someone.* She glanced at Zach. *He was afraid. She smelled it in the air. It wasn't helpful. Punching him right in the face would make her feel better, but it wouldn't help their floundering Dragon Handler relationship. Instinct told her she needed to feel pain. She needed to heal. She could do anything she wanted in the in-between. She needed an adrenaline rush. There were plenty of dangerous situations she could think up and put herself in, but she'd have to bring her Handler along.* She smiled. *He should start choosing his words more wisely. His insensitivity put her back into a volatile state. So, it was only fair he come along for the ride.*

Zach started to walk away, "Come on, Brighton. We need to find the others. I don't know what I'm supposed to do." He spun around to face her when he realised she wasn't following. In an exasperated tone, he reprimanded, "I've wasted hours looking for you. I'm sure everyone wants to get the hell out of here and back to reality."

*He wasn't helping himself.* He started to walk away again. She allowed him to get a touch ahead as she took some, 'me time,' to plot her revenge for his insensitivity. Kayn stepped on something sharp. She glanced down at the normally silky sand. *It was a seashell.* She lifted a leg to look at her foot. There was a thin trail of blood oozing from a cut. She touched it with her finger, stared at the spot of red and licked it off her fingertip. *Interesting, blood still tasted like blood even if it was in the in-between. If she picked up that shell, bad things would happen. She needed bad things to happen.* She picked up the shell and tossed it into the air, catching it in the palm of her hand. Kayn grinned at the horizon. *There was a wall of blue speeding towards them. Fun. She couldn't fight a forty-foot wave, but it would make her feel better to run from it.* She shouted, "We should start running."

Zach spun around, noticed the shell in her hand and hissed, "Seriously Kayn."

She winked and mouthed the words, "Behind you." He turned and froze, before spinning around and sprinting past her. She caught up and they ran side by side. *She loved this feeling. The rush of adrenaline and the silky sand between her toes that felt heavier when you tried to run on it.* Her hair rippled behind her. *She felt as she was meant to, wild and free.* Their feet rhythmically pounding the sand in unison. *Where was that cliff?* As soon as she thought about it. They were there at the end of the sand as the mountain-sized wall of water surged forth. They both leapt over the edge, knowing this was an excruciatingly painful demise. *Fun fact about Dragons, she didn't care.* The water rushed over the edge of the cliff, creating a waterfall that became a tsunami beneath them, demolishing everything in its path. By sheer force of the water, their bones would snap as they pummelled against submerged trees in the swiftly moving current. She opted out, satisfied with the surge of adrenaline from outrunning the wave. *Think of somewhere else.* While lost in the aftermath of adrenaline's euphoria, she thought of the giant spiders. *It just popped into her head.* In the time it took to exhale, they were bobbing in the water by the island neither one dared swim to. They endeavoured to stay afloat as the waves forced them under. They were doggy paddling as fast as they could in the opposite direction but only managed to stay in one place as the current tried to deliver them to the beach.

Zach sputtered, “Have you lost your frigging mind?”

It was surprisingly difficult to laugh while swimming against the current sucking them towards the beach where three enormous spiders the size of trucks had gathered to ingest the spoils of the sea.

Zach managed to make his way closer. As soon as he was touching her, he sputtered, “Think of somewhere else. Anywhere.”

*She wanted to, but she was laughing inside so hard that her mind wasn’t cooperating.*

“Let me try,” he gasped between waves. He grabbed her hand and they sunk below the surface of the water.

*She knew if this didn’t work, they’d be deposited on the beach by the tide, where they’d be meticulously cocooned in a sticky silken web and carted off to lord knows where.* Before she had an opportunity to get her thoughts straight, she was no longer underwater. They were lying flat on their backs in the warmth of the sand.

Hacking up water, he choked out, “You’re welcome!”

She sighed, “Thanks Zach.”

Lounging in the sand, Zach raked his fingers through it and asked, “Why did you pick up that shell?”

“You were being insensitive,” she countered.

He scowled and dug deeper, “And the spiders?”

She shifted to face him. Perched on one elbow, she sparred, “Well, that was obviously an accident.”

He started laughing, he glanced at her and sort of

attempted to apologize, “I’ll try to be more sensitive if you try not to murder me again for a couple of weeks.”

She heard voices, sat up and scrambled to her feet. “Did you hear that?” In a flash Zach was standing beside her. They both heard Melody’s echoing voice calling out but couldn’t see her. They started walking towards the sound of her voice.

Zach questioned, “How do you think we’re supposed to find our way back to the others? I bet it’s something simple.”

Kayn shrugged. *She had no bloody idea but it felt like they should keep walking towards the echo of Melody’s voice.*

Zach extended his hand to her and teased, “Do you have big plans to murder me within the week? Is there a reason you can’t promise me that?”

She took his hand and taunted, “I can probably give you a week.” She winked at him and he started to laugh again as they strolled together through the endless desert of glistening ivory. *It probably was something simple.* She caught sight of their hands with fingers intertwined. *The Ankh symbols on the palms of their hands. It’s probably something to do with their symbols.* She tugged on his hand and they stopped moving. She let go of him and held up her Ankh branded palm. He grinned, understanding what she was planning without words. He held up his, they pressed their symbols together and thought of the others. There was an incapacitating flash of light. They squeezed their eyes shut and when they opened, they were standing with their Clan. *Why were they staring at her like that? Oh, yeah. The virgin sacrifice that hadn’t happened.*

Rushing over, Frost hugged her, whispering in her ear, “Are you okay?”

His heart was pounding against her chest. Lexy gave her a strange look. *It was a mixture of guilt and something else.* The pieces of the puzzle began to sort themselves out in her brain. *Lexy hadn't given them any details because Tiberius was one of her accomplices. So was Prince Amadeus and Patrick from Triad. Yes, that would be difficult to explain. She'd kept her promise and saved her dignity by making a deal with the devil and a couple of other extremely unlikely coconspirators. It was clear that most of her Clan still thought she'd been defiled by the King. Did Lexy want her to pretend she had been? Zach must have known there was a plan to stop it.* She started to giggle quietly at first, but soon she was doubled over laughing hysterically. *She couldn't catch her breath.* Kayn looked up when she noticed, she was the only one laughing. *Nope, they all thought the King had his way with her. They also now believed she'd lost her marbles. Perhaps she had?* She noticed Lexy whispering in Frost's ear, followed by his expression of relief. *She'd obviously just filled him in.*

Markus wandered over, laid his hand gently on her shoulder and said, "I'm so sorry that had to happen. You know we didn't have a choice."

*She guessed she was supposed to go along with it.* Kayn emotionlessly responded, "I've been through worse."

"Let's go home." Markus announced.

He kept glancing back at her while the group gathered to wait for Orin to summon them back to the land of the living. She felt something in her hand but didn't look at it. *She didn't have to. She knew what it was, it was her stone.* Kayn rolled it around and squeezed it in her palm. As she held it, the smooth rose quartz stone began to heat up. *Weird?* She glanced down to look at it just as it dissolved into her Ankh symbol. She kept looking at the symbol on her palm, *was that normal? Who was she kidding? The word normal should no longer be a part of her vocabulary.* There was no way to fully prepare for this kind of spiritual travel. Her body arched backwards. The scenery flashed with an explosion of light, as the entire group was yanked into oblivion. She travelled upwards at such a speed, there was no room for rational thought. Just when she thought she couldn't take the G-force anymore, her body stopped moving, offering the briefest moment of reprieve. She heard her heart sluggishly thudding, as though time had slowed to a snail's pace. Her stomach twisted, and in the next heartbeat, she sensed the solid rose quartz tomb. The strobing blasts of light made it impossible to open her eyes. She sensed Zach's presence. Her fingers were splayed on the smooth rose quartz her body was encased in. She tried to reach out for Zach in the milliseconds before the tomb lurched and began its spiralling stomach-churning descent into the land of the living. Unable to move, all she could do was listen to the repetitive warbling noise, growing louder with each rotation of the tomb. *They were almost home.* When the strobing ceased and everything became quiet, she knew it was safe to open her eyes, even though she wasn't sure she wanted to. *Everything had changed. She'd changed. She had gone into the Testing as one girl and come out another. What would her life look like now?*

# 4

# TO KEEPING OUR SHIRTS ON

Kayn heard more than one voice as she opened her eyes. Zach, Melody, Haley and Astrid were with her. *They'd been packed into one tomb like partially immortal sardines in a tin. Her fellow Ankh's joy would have normally dragged her out of any slump. It felt like she was merely observing their happiness, not a part of it. She understood there was always going to be a way to snap out of this vacant state she kept falling back into.* The familiar grinding of the tomb's stone as it opened brought her back to reality. *They were alive. They'd survived.* Her brain was still scrambled from the trip home as Orin's grinning face appeared above where she lay. Everyone began to climb out. With tears in his eyes, Orin embraced Melody. The daughter he'd never allowed himself to know. Kayn remained where she was. She lay motionless on the rose quartz and made no attempt to join the others. She inhaled and then allowed the air to slowly escape from between her slightly parted lips. She knew it was only a matter of time before somebody gave her crap and told her to suck it up and get out of the tomb, so she did. *There was nobody left in the room. Nothing but the four seemingly solid stone walls around her. She knew she could walk through one of them but which one? They all appeared to be solid. Always trust your instincts.* She chose a direction and walked through the wall into another room. She could hear the animated sounds of celebration but didn't feel like joining in. As powerful as she'd felt when she'd become a Dragon, she understood that this would always be the cost. She kept slipping into this feeling of empty seclusion. She'd find her way out with a moment of laughter and then fall back into the emotionless abyss. Kayn chose another wall without second guessing her decision. She strolled through the stone into the familiar dark corridor gently lit by the torches flickering on the walls. As she took each step down the long hallway towards the voices of her fellow Ankh, she had this feeling of rebirth. When she stepped out into the open space, she realised everyone had been patiently waiting for her. Her eyes met with Lexy's. *She knew without words that her fellow Dragon was the only one capable of understanding where she was in her mind.* She saw the excitement but couldn't empathize. Haley and Astrid's over exuberant reaction to the act of climbing the stairs and stepping out into the lush green forest they'd left behind twenty years ago, left her wishing she could let it back in. *They were overwhelmed by joy.* Her throat grew tight and dry, so she swallowed. Her heart warmed a touch. *No.* Panicked, she shut off the flicker of emotion by touching her throat and recalling the sensation of Kevin's blade sliding across it.

Jenna's voice praised, "That's good. You're figuring it out. It will become easier to turn it on and off at will. Shutting it off is always easier in the beginning than the act of turning it back on. I've seen you smile. You're farther along than most. I'm sure you've already figured out how to turn it off. Now you just need to figure out what turns your emotions back on and keeps them on."

Kayn didn't respond. *There wasn't really a need to. It had been a statement, not a question.* She continued to observe her fellow Ankh in silence. Grey kept trying to mess up Lexy's hair and she kept swatting him away like a bothersome fly. Frost was standing beside Lily. They looked like obscenely sexy cake ornaments. Markus and Arrianna were strolling ahead of the rest, holding hands. Orin was having an animated conversation with his daughter and Zach was trying to flirt with Haley. Astrid walked up to stand on the other side of Frost and his cheeks cracked into this sweet and genuine smile. *He had his friend back.* She felt a flicker of something. *She'd played a part in that miracle. She'd had a hand in creating that smile on his face. Perhaps she could live vicariously through them for a while, until she found her way.*

Markus announced, "Triad is long gone, and I don't imagine Trinity is going to be in the mood for a fight if they're still around. I say we pack this campsite up, drive into town and get something to eat."

Haley cleared her throat and announced, "I would kill for a burger."

Markus winked at her and teased, "I'm sure murder won't be necessary, just beef."

"A burger and onion rings. That sounds like heaven," Astrid sighed, with a skip in her step.

Kayn saw things clearly. *Why was she complaining after only a short time in the Testing? Haley and Astrid had been stuck in the game for twenty years.* She smiled like everyone else. At first it was a pretend smile but as each one of her Clan members returned her smile, she felt the weight on her heart begin to lift. *She understood now. Happiness was a decision.*

Jenna met her smile with one of her own. She leaned in and whispered, "That's the spirit."

As always, Kayn found herself scanning the group in front of her for a glimpse of Frost. *She didn't need to speak to him, nor did she require one of those sappy sentimental moments where their eyes would meet. She just wanted to know he was close by.* She altered her pace and position in the small crowd to walk directly behind him. She'd been staring at his butt for a while, without really thinking about it as she followed the group. He glanced back at her, without missing a step. The timing of it made her wonder if he'd caught her staring at his behind. *Did she care? Not really.* They strolled peacefully down the trails towards where they'd left the RV. When they arrived, Astrid and Haley appeared disappointed.

Markus chuckled, "Did you honestly believe we'd be driving the same RV twenty years later?"

"Astrid had something hidden. Something important to her," Haley explained, squeezing Astrid's shoulder.

Frost's eyes lit up as he said, "Wait right here." He disappeared inside the RV and reappeared with something clenched in his hand. He opened his palm and inside of it was a locket.

Astrid teared up as she took it from him, held it against her chest and whispered, "Thank you. You kept this for twenty years?"

He nodded as he replied, "Of course I did. You were important to me and I knew this was important to you." He placed an arm over her shoulder. They looked at it together, without opening it.

*She thought they weren't allowed to keep any pictures of their family.* Curious, Kayn wanted to see what was inside. *What else could it be?* Astrid placed it in her pocket. Having it with her made her overall demeanour more peaceful.

Frost interjected, "I know where she used to be. I'm afraid I don't know where she ended up but if you want to know where she is now. It'll probably only take me five minutes on my laptop to find her."

Astrid repeated Frost's statement, "Laptop?"

Frost grinned as he announced, "It's going to be so much fun to show you guys what you've missed over the last twenty years."

Lily piped in, "We watch movies in the back of the motorhome on a big flat screen TV."

Haley and Astrid wandered down the hallway and from the back, Astrid hollered, "This TV is enormous!"

"How long do we have to relax before our first job?" Lily asked, directing her question at her father.

Markus responded with, "Let's just pack up the campsite, drive into town and get some rooms. I say we enjoy the night off. If you need a moment to grab your things, do so now."

Haley interjected, "But we don't have any clothes?"

Mel smiled at her and said, "You look like you're the same size as me. We'll share mine until you have a chance to get some of your own."

*Astrid was a tall girl. Kayn was five foot nine and she was much taller than her.*

Glancing at the girls, Astrid commented, "I'll have to borrow something to wear from one of the guys."

"Take anything you want from my bag," Frost offered.

Kayn knocked on the bathroom. *It was occupied. Of course. She'd been sharing clothes with Lexy.* Reading her mind, Lexy chuckled her a clean tank, underwear and shorts from her bag. She caught them in midair, tossed them on a bunk, then slid under the blankets to discreetly change. *This place was becoming crowded, claustrophobically so.* The buzzing of voices and sounds of people fumbling about was much louder than usual. She had to get out from under the covers on this cubby-hole of a bunk. She tossed the sheets aside. *There, that felt better.* She felt bold enough to slip her dirty top off without covering herself up. As she put on the fresh one, she realised Zach was standing right in front of the bunk she was changing on. *Well, this was awkward. He didn't say anything because he'd seen her in her underwear plenty of times while eternally serving his term in the friendzone. She wasn't about to waste time waiting for the one tiny bathroom to be free.* Kayn shimmied past the group chatting in the narrow hallway. When she got to the kitchen area, she knelt by the fridge, grabbed a peach cider, and twisted off the top. About to take a sip, she stared into the green-tinted bottle and went to the cupboard to get five plastic flamingo wine glasses, recalling the first moments of this life. *Her family was dead. Kevin had been taken by Triad.* She grabbed a few more bottles of cider out of the fridge and began pouring the liquid in equal amounts into the plastic wine glasses. *She had to continue to push for her emotional return. She would do the same welcoming ritual for Haley and Astrid that Grey had done for Melody, Zach and her.* She smiled at the tacky pink flamingo plastic wine glasses. *They meant something to her.* She called over the rest of the five from the Testing and passed them each a glass. They all took one and appeared to be awaiting her toast. Kayn raised her glass and saluted, "To a new life."

They all smiled, clinked flamingos and echoed her toast, "To a new life."

She took another sip of the sweet liquid and took in the jovial faces of her peers. *They looked like normal teens having a few drinks together. You'd never know they'd all just made their way out of the immortal Testing. A place far worse than hell. This mismatched group of five had died thousands of times to prove they were capable of being immortal. She imagined Astrid and Haley had died countless times in twenty years. Yet, they appeared to be fine. She was a cold, isolated, emotionally stunted mess after a short period and those two were just happy to be alive. It occurred to her that those were still emotions and perhaps her emotional recovery would come sooner rather than later.* She heard something smash outside. It startled everyone but her.

Orin hollered, "It's nothing!"

They were packing up the site. Half of the group didn't come back in. She heard the truck's engine start. *They must be travelling in the truck.* The five found a place to sit at the table as the motorhome's engine started humming. Kayn got up to refill their glasses before they started to move. She lost her footing as the RV lurched but recovered. Feeling like she had the agility of a cat, she began emptying the contents of the tinted green bottles into glasses. *Pouring cider into glasses while moving proved to be more difficult than anticipated.* They drove over a bump and she soaked her tank top. Kayn sighed as she passed the unopened bottles to the group at the table. They were all grinning, thoroughly entertained by her clumsy behaviour. *She'd been agile as a cat for five seconds. Some things never change. She'd come to claim her position as the comic relief.*

Kayn road surfed her way to the washroom to change her wet shirt.

"Hey," she heard Lexy's voice. She spun around as her fellow Dragon tossed her another tank top. Kayn smiled at her. Feeling less awkward as she reached the bathroom door, she tried yanking on the handle, but it was locked. *Of course, someone was already inside.* The RV swerved, she braced herself against the bathroom door. *Someone was taking their sweet ass time in there.* Kayn heard the handle move and stepped back. The door opened and it was Frost.

With a flirtatious grin, he teased, "You're supposed to drink cider, not wear it."

*She really didn't have the patience to deal with his flirtatious passive-aggressive crap right now.* "Pardon me." She tried to get past him, he blocked her path. *Not now.* Each time she tried manoeuvring past, he moved in the same direction and grinned. Certain he was doing it on purpose, Kayn sighed, "Come on Frost. I need to change my shirt."

He grinned and whispered, "Don't let me stop you."

Kayn smiled, *she wasn't the girl that was going to allow him to have the upper hand, not anymore.* She baited, "Fine." Without breaking eye contact, she boldly took off her wet top right in front of him. Frost's expression lit up. Intrigued by the new loosened up version of her, it looked like he was about to say something when the RV swerved again. They lost their balance and toppled backwards into the bathroom. She landed on top of Frost, straddling him on the cramped bathroom floor with her lips hovering a breath from his. The door slammed shut. *She should get up and go.* Kayn licked her lips, pressed them together and noticed where his eyes were. *She was still topless. She hadn't had the chance to put her shirt on.* They went over another bump. *This felt dangerous. Danger was what Dragons were created for.* Frost didn't attempt to move his eyes from her cleavage. Not even for the sake of being polite.

His expression softened as he whispered, "I'm glad Lexy found a way to stop..."

Cutting him off mid-sentence by covering his mouth with her hand, Kayn shook her head. *She suspected her friend's interference in her deflowering by the King was something Lexy could be entombed for.* She removed her hand from his lips.

"Why are you still in here?" He whispered as he tilted his head and watched her reaction as he seductively trailed his hands down the length of her arms.

She gasped in response to the shivers of pleasure he'd caused.

Gazing longingly into her eyes, he tucked one of her loose curls behind her ear and whispered, "As tempting as you are, you're in that pesky train wreck stage and I know better."

*He wasn't wrong. Her sentimental, mushy emotions were stifled by an intense, driving need to do something crazy. Being this close to him was intoxicating. She wanted him to kiss her.* Kayn bit her lip and asked, "Why are you still here?"

Frost's eyes flashed as he stated the obvious, "You're sitting on top of me." They went over another bump on the road and his expression altered. His whole demeanour became intensely dark.

She gently touched his cheek and allowed her fingers to slowly trace the curve of his masculine jawline. *He was so beautiful on the outside but innately flawed on the inside. She was flawed on the inside too. The way that he lived his life had never made sense to her before. Frost was infamous in the Clans for his endless chain of meaningless flings. He was all about pleasure while avoiding the pain of emotional attachment. It made complete and total sense to her. She was different now.* She'd been staring at him, without saying a word.

Frost whispered, "Listen Brighton. Put your clothes back on and go or take them off and lock the door."

He seductively cupped her hips with his hands. *He was calling her bluff.* A part of her had always wanted him, and in this moment, it felt like a brilliant idea. She was a Dragon now, the urge to take what she wanted was a driving force within her.

He groaned and looked away, "You're killing me Kayn. You're not thinking straight."

Kayn's lips parted, she leaned in and just before her lips met his, she whispered, "Maybe, I'm tired of behaving myself." Without a hint of hesitation, she placed her hands on his muscular chest. She'd always wanted to touch him like this but never had the nerve. She allowed her fingertips to travel before laying them flat on a certain spot. *What was she doing?* Her hands heated until warmth travelled up the length of her arms into her chest. *She was siphoning his energy.* Remembering what happened last time, she yanked her hands away, grateful she was able to remove her hands from his skin without a struggle. She closed her eyes as the mind-blowing euphoria of her ability coursed through her and lit up her senses. Gasping as she opened her eyes, Kayn raised her hands to look at her palms.

"It's a pretty amazing feeling, isn't it?" Frost whispered.

*She wanted more.* She nodded.

He took her hands, placed them on his chest again and whispered, "Five more seconds, then you really need to go." Her hands warmed as they made contact with his flesh. They became hot as his energy travelled up both of her arms at once. This time she had to force herself to take her hands off his rigid muscular chest. Goosebumps rose on every inch of skin as another euphoric burst of adrenaline released and the unexpected happened, an intoxicating scent secreted from her pores.

Frost's eyes widened as he spoke, "Honey, the game just changed. Get out of here. I won't be able to control myself."

Someone cleared their throat and they snapped out of the seductive game they'd been playing. Kayn spun around to see who was at the door. *It was Zach.*

Zach chuckled and teased, "Isn't this against the rules?"

The sound of Zach's voice felt like someone had just tossed a bucket of ice water on her. She clicked back to reality, scrambled to her feet and noticed her tank top on the floor beside Frost. *Shit.* She attempted to explain, "I fell on top of him."

"With no shirt on?" Zach toyed. Giving her a strange look, he peeked behind the door, questioning, "Lily's not in here too, is she?"

*She'd absorbed some of Frost's ability and used it. This was amazing.* Kayn managed to stop herself from smiling as she replied, "I hadn't had the chance to put my shirt on when I tripped." She finessed her way past her friend. Zach was rather skillfully attempting to block her escape from an awkward situation. She had the urge to smack that Cheshire cat grin off his face but ignored it and chose to just get away from temptation.

She heard Zach ask, "Was that smell coming from her?"

Frost casually replied, "Let's just say, she's learned how to do something new."

She heard creaking of movement. *One of them was coming.* Someone grabbed hold of her arm, halting her escape.

Frost's seductive voice baited, "That's quite the ability you have there." She glanced back as instinct screamed at her to get away from him. *He was right. She wasn't thinking straight. All she wanted to do was to tug him onto one of those bunks with her, witnesses be damned.* She tried to walk away again but he still had ahold of her arm.

He teased, "Don't you need your shirt?"

*She'd forgotten all about her shirt.* Kayn took a breath, spun around and yanked the tank top out his hand. She was staring right at him as she slipped it over her head and expected to still see him standing there watching her when her vision was clear of tank top material, but he was gone. *He couldn't have gone far because they were in an RV travelling down the highway. He'd never be far.*

Lexy's voice came from her bunk, "You might want to let the dust settle from one relationship before you get into another. Just a thought."

Kayn nodded and made her way to the table where the others were sitting, drinking and laughing together like the Testing hadn't happened. She'd just slid onto the bench when Zach appeared. He shimmied onto the seat behind the table beside her. Haley handed her a cider. Opting out of pouring it into a glass, Kayn took a swig from the bottle, savouring the sweet, tasty drink.

Zach leaned over and whispered in her ear like the annoying brother figure that he was, "I see you found your shirt."

She shook her head, opting out of a witty comeback. *She didn't have one. She knew what the rules were. There was no frater-*

*nizing allowed in the RV.* She'd been a second from losing control of both her inhibitions and her ability when Zach interrupted.

Zach leaned over and whispered, "You were in there siphoning some of Frost's ability, weren't you? Do I have to babysit you?"

Kayn whispered back, "I'll be doing whatever I want." *She hadn't meant to be rude. She was so frustrated. She was still too turned on to think straight.*

Astrid was staring at her, she grinned and ribbed, "Nice scent you're wearing, strangely familiar. Are you sure this is the right timing for that?"

*Alright, she got the hint. She knew it wasn't.* Astrid winked at her. Kayn explained, "It wasn't planned."

Holding a drink, Haley saluted, "To unplanned things."

Zach raised his glass, and toasted, "To keeping our shirts on for at least the first day."

Kayn smacked him and the rest snickered. She noticed Melody was missing. "Where's Mel?"

"She's up front with Grey," Astrid answered as the RV slowed and stopped.

# 5

# TRAIN WRECK

Someone rapped on the door. Astrid hopped up to unlock it. Markus came in and announced, "Grab your overnight bags. Make sure you have extra clothes. We're going to eat here and stay the night in a motel."

They all raced down the tight hallway, grabbed their bags and rushed to catch up with the others. Kayn didn't feel the same sense of urgency, wandering to where she'd stowed her backpack at her leisure. When she grabbed her bag and turned around, Frost was standing there.

He provoked, "We really have to stop meeting like this, especially when you still smell like that."

*He'd been hiding out in the backroom to avoid her.* She made an awkward attempt at conversation, "Big plans tonight?"

Frost grinned at her and sparred, "I'm not sure where we are but if you want me to check in with you tonight, I'll text you the pictures."

*There he was, the king of all douches. He was trying to push her buttons.* She edged past him and made her way to the door. *She loved these naughty sparring matches. He'd lit a fire within her earlier. She couldn't help herself.* Walking away, Kayn verbally jousted, "I already know everything I need to know about you. There's no need to send me pictures." He followed her out without speaking, proving her earlier thought. *He was being an ass to put a stop to what they'd started earlier. He'd quite effectively put the brakes on her steamy fantasy. The reality of Frost was that he had her in the catch and release program. He'd lure her in with his seductive ways and then remind her of why she shouldn't bother.* They were waiting for them, outside of the lobby with room cards in hand.

Markus gave Frost his own card and questioned, "Are you coming with us to have dinner or do you have other plans?"

He took the card from Markus. Looked directly at her with a blank expression and said, "I could eat first."

*Was he still trying to make her jealous? He'd been all heartbroken, worried she was mad at him after the Testing, and before the end of the first day, he was already back to his old games. What else had she expected from him?*

Markus addressed the group of Testing survivors, "You five are sharing a room. After tonight, we'll start building the Dragon Handler bond, between Kayn and Zach."

Kayn glanced at Zach. They simultaneously rolled their eyes before following the others to the room they'd be sharing.

Markus hollered after them, "Meet us in the restaurant downstairs. The one next to the pub, in fifteen minutes."

Kayn wandered in following the group. The room was beige. The bed, the walls, even the carpets. There was a comically out of place painting of a colourful parrot on the wall. The room had two queen-sized beds and a fold out couch.

Zach leapt on the couch and sighed, "I guess I have to sleep here?"

Kayn grinned without looking at him as she dug around in her bag. *That bright parrot on the wall was bothering her way more than it should. She wanted to smash it and rip it up into tiny shreds.* She scowled at it.

Astrid sat on the couch, flung her arm over Zach's shoulder, and offered, "I'll sleep on the couch if you want to sleep with Kayn."

Zach dove onto the queen-sized bed, causing Kayn's backpack to bounce off. He managed to grab it before it landed on the floor.

Astrid started to chuckle as she rose to her feet and announced, "Let's go. They're probably sitting there waiting to order."

Kayn reluctantly stopped plotting the hideous painting's demise and followed the group. They were chatting about what they wanted to eat. She was famished but sensed the pangs of hunger she was feeling had little to do with anything she could order in a restaurant. The others were discussing music and dancing. *They sounded like they had one of those go hard or go home nights planned. Except for Melody. She'd been awfully quiet.* Kayn hung behind the group and walked beside her understandably silent friend. *She could empathize with how Melody was feeling. Astrid and Haley were so ecstatic to be out of the Testing that they were in a completely different mindset.* Kayn and Melody were the last ones through the door. Everyone was already sitting at one long table goofing around and laughing as though they hadn't just fought their way out of hell. *She was impressed with Zach. He hadn't missed a beat.* Kayn was gapped out, staring at the forest green tables. *Why did they annoy the hell out of her?*

"Earth to Kayn. Are you planning to sit down or just stand there and stare at Frost all night?" Zach provoked, peeking up from behind his menu.

*Oh, she was going to kill him. For the first time, she hadn't been staring at Frost while being accused of it. Of course, there was only one empty seat left and it was directly across the table from Frost.* She avoided eye contact with Frost as she sat down. *Zach was a horrible Handler. All he'd been doing was poking the Dragon she was trying to put to sleep.* She focused on the plastic flowers on the table but the sight of them made her feel hostile. *Apparently, now all she would get to feel with any ease was angry and turned on.* At that thought, she glanced at Frost. *He was making plans to hang out at the pub with Astrid. She wasn't the least bit jealous. She knew Astrid was into girls.* Kayn grabbed for her glass of water and Lily grabbed for the same glass. Their fingers touched and she got a little shock.

"I was already drinking out of that one," Lily laughed.

Kayn apologized. She was used to being shocked on car doors etc. She didn't give it a second thought as she shrugged and grabbed a full glass from the other side of her. The waitress came and took their orders. *She didn't know what she felt like. Usually she ordered one of three different things, but tonight none of her regular cravings felt right. She wanted something spicy.* Kayn ordered a chicken caesar wrap and politely stopped the waitress before she walked away from the table to ask her to put an absolutely disgusting amount of hot sauce on it. *This was something Chloe would have ordered.* She went to grab another drink of water. *Which glass was hers? Her brain was a pile of mushy goo today.* Her dinner arrived quickly. The waitress grinned at her as she gave her an enormous side of hot sauce. Kayn unwrapped her wrap and dumped the entire container into it. It was overflowing from the sides as she took her first giant bite. Hot sauce dribbled all over her face and down her chin. Frost grinned and passed her a napkin. She wiped her face off. When she looked at the napkin, the hot sauce looked like blood. He continued to stare at her, obviously awaiting her response to the crazy amount of hot sauce but she gave him none. *It was delicious. It was exactly what she wanted. Actually...it could have been hotter.* Another shiver of adrenaline coursed through her.

She heard Grey say, “Next time we come across a hot sauce eating contest, you’re our girl.”

Kayn looked towards his voice. Everyone was staring at her. *She didn’t need to ask them why. She knew she was doing strange things. She had a feeling, this was only the beginning.*

The waitress placed a beer in front of her. *She didn’t recall ordering one.* After feeling another jolt of adrenaline, she excused herself from the table and rose to stand. There were visible goosebumps prickled up on her arms and her balance was off as she made her way to the bathroom. *Okay, she’d just had a half dozen shots of adrenaline in a row for no reason.* Her gross motor skills were a tad sketchy as she grabbed for the handle and missed. Voices had become so loud she could hear every conversation in the restaurant. She opened the bathroom door and closed it behind her. Feeling a touch of relief once the chorus of voices were muffled, she locked the door and stared at it, wondering if she could just forgo eating and stay in here. *These new ability glitches were mentally exhausting. There had to be a way to shut them off.* Someone rapped on the door.

Jenna's voice urged, "I think you should let me in."

Kayn unlocked the door and opened it to Jenna's concerned expression. She manoeuvred around her, closed the door and locked it. *The Clan's Oracle obviously knew she was having a difficult time.*

With a maternal smile, Jenna said, "It's going to take some time to learn how to control when and where you siphon abilities from people. I'm curious, did your twin eat everything with a gross amount of hot sauce?"

Kayn nodded without answering aloud.

Jenna grinned and added, "Your brain's growth can be overwhelming and sometimes this part can take months, even years. Your brain is trying to sort through a crazy amount of information. I can make a bracelet that might calm things down for you. For tonight, you'll have to dull the voices with alcohol."

*That didn't sound like a bad idea.* She followed Jenna back to the table and sat down. Then glanced over at Lexy. Grey was sitting beside her with his arm draped over her shoulder protectively. *No, Zach wasn't Grey. Zach probably hadn't even noticed she'd left the table. He was still having the same intense conversation with Melody.* Jenna whispered something in Zach's ear. He glanced over with a guilty look in his eyes. *He didn't want to do this. He didn't want to be her Handler and she didn't want him to have to be.* She gazed at the full beer in front of her, but she didn't feel like a beer. *Why did she feel like cranberry juice and vodka?* She glanced at Lily. *That's what she was drinking. There was some weird shit going on tonight. Her senses were all over the place.* She picked up the beer and took a giant swig of it. *It wasn't bad.* She took another drink. She watched Frost take a sip from his glass and lick a droplet of beer from his bottom lip. She was staring. *Everything felt like it was happening in slow motion.* Her leg accidentally brushed against someone else's under the table. Frost was staring at her. *It must have been his leg. Why did he have to be this sexy?* She looked down at her glass and traced the rim with her finger. She looked up just as Frost leaned across the table, stole her glass and took a slow seductive sip.

He whispered, "You might want to pace yourself. Pick a drink and stick to it. If you mix beer, cider and those sweet drinks Lily likes, your night will end badly."

She reached across the table, stole one of his fries, dipped it in his ketchup and popped it into her mouth. She replied, "This isn't my first time."

Frost slid her beer back across the table and teased, "I warned you."

She licked the ketchup off her finger, picked up her glass and took a sip. Kayn shivered as the fluorescent lights began to buzz loudly. She winced in response to the overwhelming amount of sound and quickly downed the rest of her beer.

Markus stood up, saying they were calling it a night. She assumed he meant Arrianna and him. After saying their goodbyes, they left the diner with the jingling of bells on the door. The entire group was preparing to leave. Kayn listened as they made plans.

"I'm out of here," Frost announced. "Are you guys still coming with me?"

Grey glanced at Lexy and said, "Are you sure you don't want to come with us?"

Smiling, Lexy answered, "I'm all good. I told Orin I'd watch a movie with him. Have fun. Don't do anything I wouldn't do."

About to walk away, Grey paused and provoked, "After

your shenanigans at the Summit, I guess that leaves me pretty open."

Glaring at him, Lexy ominously teased, "You like to live dangerously, don't you?"

Grey yelped, "Shit!" As Lexy leapt out of her seat and chased him out of the jingling door into the parking lot.

Mel looked at Frost and asked, "Should we help him?" The group strolled towards the door.

Frost snagged a delivery menu from the counter as he passed by and chuckled, "Nah, she won't hurt him, that badly."

Kayn wandered back to their motel room, somewhat detached from the conversation the others were having. Frost, Astrid and Grey separated from the group on the floor below theirs, raring to start their night of debauchery. She climbed that last flight with only Zach as Haley and Mel raced ahead for first dibs on the bathroom. As they entered the girls were wandering around in underwear like normal teenagers trying on clothes before a night out.

Zach paused in the doorway. When nobody bothered to cover up, he shrugged and made himself comfortable on the bed. He turned on the TV, saying, "I'm ready to go." He started clicking through the channels. Most were nothing but black screen with a message asking you to subscribe. He complained, "There's no free channels in this place."

Acknowledging his observation by smiling, Kayn rifled through her disorganized bag of crumpled stuff, inevitably deciding to wear what she was already wearing, running shoes and all. She wandered into the bathroom as Haley was putting on her final touches in the mirror.

Applying lipstick, Haley glanced back at Kayn and declared, "It's hard to believe we were in there for twenty years.

That's two decades hallucinating in a floating crypt. Honestly, I thought the world would have changed more. The TV's in the hotel rooms are different but stuff like this lipstick here." She held up the tube. "The little things are the same."

Kayn smiled, clarifying, "That tube of lipstick may look the same but there's also stay on lipstick along with twelve-hour eyeliner and mascara. Wait until you hear the music and check out what computers are like now. Everyone has one. She picked up Mel's phone and said, "We use cheap disposable cell phones, but most people's phones are just as powerful as their laptops."

Haley stepped away from the mirror and sang, "Your turn."

Mel hollered from the other room, "Zach's panties are in a twist! Hurry up!"

Kayn grinned as she surveyed her rough reflection. Her wild frizzy curls had escaped from her ponytail. She usually checked on the state of her hair during the day. It hadn't even occurred to her. She called out, "Give me a second to freshen up, and it's on!" She heard rustling behind her, Zach was standing in the doorway.

Crinkling his nose, Zach taunted, "It's on? Don't talk like that, Brighton. It freaks me out a little."

He wandered away without waiting for her reply. *Good, she didn't want to give him one. She wanted to have a good time. She needed to forget about the Testing and just enjoy being this fearless version of herself.* Leaning closer to the mirror, Kayn applied dark lipstick and way more makeup than she usually wore. She let her hair out of the ponytail, wet it and messed it up. It fell in a seductive damp lion's mane of curls. She put a dollop of oil in her hair to tame the frizz and strutted out, looking way sexier than usual.

Zach was sitting next to the girls on the bed, he stopped aimlessly clicking through the channels and ribbed, "Who are you and what have you done with Kayn?"

"That's exactly the look I was going for," she teased, grabbing her purse off the bed. They gathered what they needed and headed out. A gentle evening breeze moved through her hair. It felt like someone was running their fingers through it. Noticing something fluffy floating in the air beside her, she allowed it to land in the palm of her hand. The breeze stopped and it didn't float away. *It was a dandelion seed.* Her mind travelled back to her childhood. She recalled spinning in Granny Winnie's yard with a handful in her hands as tiny parachutes took off in flight. An image of Kevin's smiling face as a child flickered through her mind. She squished the delicate seed in the palm of her hand. *She couldn't think of him anymore. Never again.*

Zach's voice broke her out of her thoughts, "What did you just squish in your hand?"

"Nothing," Kayn decreed. "Absolutely nothing." She brushed it on her bare leg as she followed the others down the stairs.

The pub downstairs was playing dance music and there was a lineup of boys outside. *No girls in the lineup. That was strange?* The bouncer called them up to the front of the line and explained, "It's ladies' night tonight. The men won't be allowed in until after ten."

He tried to stop Zach and Kayn explained, "He's just one of the girls."

The bouncer flirtatiously winked at Zach. He waved him past, but stopped him, and whispered in his ear, "Come see me later."

Zach scowled at Kayn and whispered, "One of the girls, seriously?"

She laughed and teased, "He let you in, didn't he?"

Zach shook his head as he trailed her through the crowd. "Funny, you're pretty frigging hilarious," he sparred.

She turned back. Grinning, Kayn taunted, "I try." She scanned the room as they manoeuvred through the crowd. *No Frost, Grey or Astrid. They must have gone somewhere else.* Haley appeared out of nowhere and towed her out onto the dance floor. With the pressure gone, she gyrated to the music with her pack of friends. They did shots of tequila and danced until all thoughts of the Testing had been snuffed out. There was nothing left but the beat of the music and a feeling of freedom. Every so often, she noticed a strange expression on Haley's face and wondered if it had to do with Astrid's absence. *They'd been constant companions for twenty years. If they could endeavour to find blissful moments after twenty years in immortal purgatory, then she had no excuse, Dragon or not.* Zach towed her over to the bar. He ordered a shot covered in whipping cream and told her she had to drink it with no hands. She didn't even give it a second thought. She was having far too much fun to care if her face was covered in whipping cream. A crowd gathered to cheer her on. They did shots of tequila. *They tasted like hell but she felt amazing.* She pranced out onto the dance floor, spinning to the beat of the music, lost in the blissful euphoria of freedom. She was dirty dancing with a random cute guy with no embarrassment or fear. She planted a kiss square on the lips before leaving him on the dance floor to get a drink. She recalled the conversation they'd had in the Testing and mentally ticked, kissing a stranger off her unbucket list. She gyrated and wiggled her way over to the bar to the beat of the music, where a girl she'd never met offered her shots. She did them, hooting with strangers when they were done. *It felt amazing to be a normal girl out with her friends, cutting loose.* The girl towed her back out onto the dance floor and the pack of strangers danced together. *She'd never been this drunk.* The room began to waver. She felt queasy but wasn't about to let that stop her. She danced until perspiration trickled down her brow. Making her way back to the bar, Kayn found a stool. *She had to sit down for a minute.*

"Hey rock star," Zach teased. "Are you alright?"

She gave him a wobbly thumbs-up as he handed her another shot of tequila. They clinked their tiny glasses and downed their shots without even thinking about salt, lime or taste. Kayn had something else to say. She spun around and he was back out on the dance floor. *She didn't want to dance anymore.* A flock of men were lined up for drinks. *It must be after ten.* A hot one sat beside her and placed a bright pink shot in front of her. She swallowed it without thinking. *It was sour.* Something was floating in it. *Yucky, it had a bitter aftertaste.* She crinkled her nose and giggled, "I think I just swallowed a bug."

The guy winked and flirted, "Extra protein."

They chatted for a while about music and life. He was an interesting guy with the darkest eyes she'd ever seen. She couldn't help herself as she stared into them. They were so dark, she couldn't tell the difference between his pupil and iris. *It was creepy but who was she to judge?* He ordered them a few more shots.

When the waitress brought their drinks, she looked directly at Kayn and said, "Are you feeling alright?"

The dark-eyed stranger answered the question for her,

"She's fine." He towed her out onto the dance floor. A slow song began. She went with it. With her arms around his neck and head resting on his shoulder, she moved to the music, without a thought crossing her mind. *This was just what she needed.* Her vision wavered, her knees felt weak. *Oh crap.* Her dance partner pulled away to ask her if she wanted to go for a drive. She could see the colour of his eyes in the strobing lights on the dance floor, they were dark brown. Kayn knew she shouldn't go anywhere but she wanted to.

She pointed at her friends and slurred, "I have to tell them."

He led her through the gyrating crowd to the door as he shouted over the music, "Let's sneak out!"

Helping her walk, he steered her to the door. *She couldn't think.* A wave of nausea washed over her. She mumbled, "I think I'm going to be sick." He changed directions and deposited her back at the same barstool he'd taken her from, saying he'd be right back. Her vision wavered again. *She felt unusually sedated. She could barely keep her eyes open.* The bartender took one look at her and slid her a glass of water. Kayn tried to say thank you and wasn't sure what came out, but it wasn't that. She took a sip of the water and it felt like it was going to come right back up. The cute guy came back and sat next to her. He told her she could use some fresh air. *That sounded great.* Kayn tried to get up and go with him but she couldn't walk. She told him he'd have to carry her as she laid her head on the bar and closed her eyes so the room would stop spinning. The lights went out.

She heard Frost's voice and tried to open her eyes, "Oh, honey. You're going to regret this. Where's Zach?" He sounded choked but she couldn't open her eyes. *It felt like someone was carrying her. Yes, she was moving.* She tried to open her eyes and the room started spinning again. It wouldn't stop and she started to gag. She threw up and heard, "Shit Kayn." *It was Zach's voice.* She blacked out and came too poised over a toilet, staring into the vomit filled porcelain god before her. *How did she get here?* She heard voices in the next room as she began tossing her cookies in a ridiculous way. Someone was holding her hair and rubbing her back while she vomited. She blacked out again and woke up to the sun streaming through sheer curtains. *No, no. It hurts. Everything hurts.* She buried her face in her pillow, groaning dramatically.

She heard Zach's voice, "I'm so sorry."

She lifted her face off the pillow mumbling, "Sorry about what?"

Zach questioned, "What's the last thing you remember?"

She couldn't dredge up a single thought. "I can't think. Please, don't ask me to try." Her head was pounding. "How drunk was I last night?"

Zach's expression changed. He confessed, "You were pretty drunk, but we suspect it was more than that. Frost thinks that guy you were hanging out with drugged your drink. I'm sorry, you looked like you were having a good time. I didn't want to bud in."

Her mouth felt like she'd eaten a container of minty vomit flavoured paste. She didn't remember dancing with anyone. Kayn mumbled, "I don't remember a guy?"

"I'll do better," Zach assured as he held out a hand to help her up. "I promise."

Kayn didn't want to remove her hands from either side of her pulsating head to get up. She said, "It's not your fault. If I wasn't that drunk maybe I would have noticed somebody drugging my drink. Where's everyone else?"

Smiling, Zach replied, "Waiting for us in the restaurant."

*There was no way in hell she could eat.*

He leaned closer, whispering, "Want me to go get you runny eggs and toast?"

*Oh crap*, she leapt from the bed and sprinted on her legs of jelly into the washroom, barely making it to the toilet before, dry heaving. *It felt like she was dying and she'd actually died on many occasions.*

He was standing behind her in the doorway chuckling to himself. She heard the tap running. Zach suggested, "You should drink water. It probably won't stay down but it will make your throat feel better."

She took the glass of water from him and drank it. It stayed down. Kayn stayed there for a while hugging the toilet, groaning. When her stomach settled down, she got up and looked at her reflection in the mirror. She expected to see black mascara streaming down a blotchy swollen face. Her face was swollen but clean. She rewashed it and brushed her teeth, then gargled with mouthwash.

"You had a bath last night," Zach explained. "We even washed your hair."

Kayn paused, afraid to ask. "Who gave me a bath? What do you mean by we?"

He was silent for a second before answering, "Well, I helped hold you up while Grey gave you a bath. Frost and Lexy were here too but they waited out there."

*This was so humiliating.* "Why were two boys giving me a bath while I was unconscious?"

Nervously clearing his throat, Zach explained, "Frost had

to shower first. You threw up all over him and when he got out, you were out cold. I couldn't put you to bed like that. Nobody would've been able to sleep in here. You smelled rancid. Grey showed me how to bathe someone unconscious. I guess he's done it for Lexy a few times. With your dead weight, it was a two-person job. You were covered in vomit. It was gross. The girls slept in Frost's room because we couldn't get rid of the scent of bile."

*Well, that probably killed that. Puking on the guy you have a thing for was the least sexy thing you could do.* She stared at her reflection. *Welcome to the all humiliation Kayn channel. I'll be your host. Today I'm going to get roofied and puke all over the hottest guy I've ever seen. Just for shits and giggles, I'm going to vomit all over myself and smell so rancid everybody has to leave the room while I'm bathed by two boys.*

Zach was still standing behind her in the doorway. He came closer, gave her shoulder a squeeze and apologized, "I'm sorry. I should have been paying attention. I'm really not very good at this Handler thing."

She smiled at him in the mirror and replied, "I'm an adult. This is my fault, not yours."

He smiled back at her, teasing, "Next time I get drunk you can take care of me and give me a bath."

Kayn started to laugh as she gave her response, "Of course." She winked at him.

He placed his arm over her shoulder and whispered, "If you were a mortal, you would have been in the hospital getting your stomach pumped last night." He kissed the side of her head and teased, "Come on, rock star. It's time to face the firing squad."

Grabbing their backpacks, they went to the lobby to return

the key and made their way to the restaurant. All eyes were on her as she walked in, but they carried on eating and, nobody said a word about it. She ordered dry toast and tea, saying a silent prayer it wouldn't come back up with every mouthful. She kept inconspicuously glancing at Frost and was secretly relieved when he didn't look at her. Everyone appeared to agree there was no need to discuss it. Once the group finished eating, they left the table and made their way to the RV, temporarily taking up multiple parking spots.

Markus called her over and whispered, "Don't worry about it. Sometimes you have to learn the hard way."

"I'll definitely never do that again," Kayn mumbled.

Markus messed-up her hair as he teased, "Good, I'm holding you to that. This is your free one. Go find an empty bunk and sleep it off."

She sheepishly made her way past the group already sitting at the table grinning at her. Kayn stowed her bag, climbed up onto a bunk, pulled the covers over her head and closed her eyes. She drifted off to sleep. In her dreams, she went somewhere she hadn't gone in quite a while.

# 6

# DANGEROUS THINGS

She was standing in front of the enormous picture window at Kevin's family's lakeside cabin, staring at the glassy surface of the lake. A long trail of shimmering light created by dawn's first rays made the surface of the water appear to glitter like someone had dropped a trail of floating sparkling diamonds. A fish jumped and she wondered if the fishing rods were still in the closet. Kayn wandered over to the rustic cabin's closet door. She opened it and the rods were still there. Just before she closed the door, she noticed the grooves on the inside of the closet. There was a growth chart for Kevin and Clay carved into the wood. She reached out and traced one of the grooves that read, *Kevin, seven years old.* Kayn smiled as she remembered him at seven. He'd been a goofy kid with messy dark hair and innocent eyes. Then she spotted her own name with the number seven. Kayn ran her fingertip over it and got a sliver. She put her finger in her mouth and nibbled the shard of wood out of the tender flesh of the pad. She took one of the rods out of the closet. *Had Kevin ever come back to this cabin in his dreams?* A part of her hoped he had. Only through remembering his past would he recall the real reason he left with Triad. She understood why he did it. He had to save his mother and brother. He'd destroyed their relationship for a noble cause. That wouldn't prove to be worth anything at all if he never recalled the reason and followed through with saving the surviving members of his family. She wanted him to remember the sensation of his mother's healing kiss on a wounded knee. She wanted him to dream about sitting on the edge of that dock with his brother, with their feet dangling in the still water, while they waited for a tug on their fishing lines. A memory of them as children running barefoot down that dock and leaping into the water filled her heart with the adoration she'd felt for him back then. *Shit, she couldn't think about these things anymore. He was gone.* A knock on the door startled her and her heart tightened. *No, she didn't want to see his face. The sight of his face had confused her into seeing what she wanted to see not who he really was.* It wasn't locked. The doorknob began to turn. Kayn backed away from the door. *She wasn't ready to see him.* It started to open. She grabbed the rod and raised it in the air, ready to fight.

Zach's voice was echoing in the distance, "Wake up. You're dreaming. Wake up Kayn."

Kayn opened her eyes to the sound of humming tires. *She was on her bunk.*

Zach scooted in beside her and began stroking her hair as he whispered, "That was quite the nightmare. Which nightmarish version of death from the Testing were you dreaming about?"

Kayn didn't answer, all she could think about was the panic

she'd felt at the slightest possibility of seeing Kevin again. They were supposed to be enemies in the Testing. It hadn't started out that way but by the time the Testing was over, they were.

He whispered, "You don't have to tell me. I'd imagine we're all going to be haunted by nightmares of that place."

*She was supposed to be a Dragon, damn it!*

Zach kissed her forehead and reassured, "Hey, it's alright. You're here with me. Your heart is pounding a million miles an hour Brighton."

She found herself wishing they'd use something else as her nickname. *Her mortal last name made her think of the Brighton's that hadn't survived. Her brother Matt, her mother and father. Chloe was now as alive as she was. They were one. There was no line between them anymore.* She curled up against Zach and closed her eyes. *She couldn't allow herself to be vulnerable. Dragons never cry.*

She felt the warmth of his breath as he kissed her hair and whispered, "Let it out. It's okay, I won't tell anybody."

Kayn allowed a few shuddering breaths to escape. *This was humiliating. Some Dragon she was turning out to be. Her first acts after the Testing had been to allow herself to be a virgin sacrifice, then she let a drunk King beat the crap out of her because her Clan told her she wasn't allowed to fight back. Oh, the insanity hadn't stopped there. She'd taken energy from Frost, almost made out with him in a bathroom and proceeded to get so drunk she didn't notice someone roofied her. She barfed all over the guy she had unresolved feelings for and was given a bath by two boys. Under train wreck in the dictionary, there was probably a smiling picture of her.* She felt Zach shift, so he could lie down next to her and hold her. She closed her eyes and allowed herself to drift off to sleep, feeling safe in his arms. *She'd worry about the mess she'd made tomorrow.*

When she awoke, she felt no movement. *The RV was parked somewhere.* She swung her legs over the side of the bunk and slid off, landing with the agility of someone that hadn't been wasted the night before. Still embarrassed by her behaviour, Kayn grabbed her backpack along with her toiletries and padded down the hall to the bathroom. *The RV was empty. Where were they?* She brushed her teeth, washed her face and put on fresh clothes. *There was no point in dwelling on what she'd done, it couldn't be changed.* Feeling more like herself, she sauntered down the hall, tossing her backpack on the bunk as she passed. Kayn could hear the others outside and when she opened the door, she was surprised to discover she'd lost an entire day. *It was already dark outside.* She walked down the steps to the gravel. *They'd already set up camp.*

Lily's voice ominously announced, "It lives."

Kayn shook her head, knowing this was only the start of her penance for her night of overindulgence.

Grey, Zach and Lexy were at a firepit roasting hotdogs over the flames. She was starting to feel hungry. *They smelled amazing.*

Grey sweetly offered, "If you'd like a beer, there's a six-pack in the fridge." Her eyes widened and she shook her head slowly from side to side. He chuckled, "Didn't think so."

She looked around for something to cook her wiener with. Lily motioned towards the bushes. "Frost is out there trying to find one for himself."

*Seven of them were missing.* "Where did everybody go?"

Grey chimed in, "They have a job."

Kayn nodded, knowing what that meant. *Already? That was*

*crazy.* She took the hint and ventured off into the overgrown brush in search of a stick to roast a wiener with. The trees weren't tall and there was no breeze at all. *Where were they? She didn't recognize this campsite. She'd never been here before.* She wasn't even able to hazard a guess as to where they were. There was thick long grass, odd looking trees, and as she ventured into the brush, she soaked her shoes when the land underfoot became swamp. *Where was she?* She could hear toads croaking and the dense foliage was lit up by an unusually large amount of firefly's dancing above her. Batting a mosquito off her arm, she stopped moving to appreciate the firefly's exquisite dance. *They were beautiful, like stars whirling in the sky.* She found herself so mesmerized by the firefly's hypnotizing dance that she almost forgot the reason she'd ventured off into the bushes in the first place. *She was there to find a stick but wasn't in a hurry.* Kayn sat on a stump and took a moment to just appreciate the foreign sights and sounds. A twig snapped behind her. Kayn knew she wasn't in danger. *Well, not physical danger.* She spoke softly in almost a whisper so she wouldn't scare the fireflies away, "Did you find a stick?"

Frost answered with his normal tone, "Why are you whispering?" The fireflies scattered.

Her heart sank. She pointed at the empty sky and sighed, "That's why."

He sat on a stump facing her and asked, "Was this the first time you've seen that many fireflies at once?"

She felt like pouting. *They'd been beautiful but they were gone and she was disappointed.* Frost was holding three sticks in his hand. He passed one to her as a silent apology for wrecking her bliss. She took it. *He'd even sharpened the end.* Touching the point with the tip of her finger, she said, "Thank you."

Frost grinned, as he got up and held out his hand. She took it, grateful he wasn't going to make a big deal out of the fact that she'd vomited all over him the night before.

Still holding her hand, he suggested, "Allow me to help you find your way out of this swamp in the dark."

*A swamp? That made sense.* Kayn laughed, "My socks are already soaking wet."

He shook his head as he pulled her towards him and teased, "You knew I was out here. If you'd called me, you could have avoided those uncomfortable wet socks."

*He was acting completely normal. She wasn't sure how to take it. Was this a trick?* She whispered, "Zach told me I threw up on you last night. I was embarrassed." Frost tucked hair escaping from her ponytail behind her ear and her heart flip-flopped beneath the thin material of her tank top.

He whispered, "Don't worry about it. It's much faster if you learn the simple life lessons the hard way. We've all been there. Granted, most of us were much younger than you but it happens to everyone at least once."

She heard the buzzing song of the fireflies and stared up at the dancing lights. *Minus the talk of vomit, this was a memorable moment.* Smiling as she watched the lights dancing across the sky, she whispered, "They're so beautiful." He was beaming at her when she met his eyes.

Frost cupped her chin gently and confessed, "I'm glad you found your way back."

It took her a second to realise what he meant. When it sunk in, she felt it in her soul. *What Grey taught her about looking for beauty in simple moments in the year before Testing brought her back.* She was fully able to embrace the splendour of the repetitious croaking, chirping symphony of swamp creatures. Their musical masterpiece was made even more wondrous by flickering light as they strolled through the brush hand in hand. When they saw the campfire through the foliage, Frost let go of her hand. *She understood why. Once again, he was in the position of being her emotional crutch. If he was still holding her hand in front of the others, they'd probably give him shit for it. She'd been holding his hand for a good five minutes without the slightest urge to take energy from him. Had that moment of beauty tamed the Dragon within her?* He started to make his way out of the bushes and stopped when he realised she wasn't following him.

His silhouette in the moonlight spoke to her, "Aren't you hungry?"

*She was starving.* Kayn answered, "I'm famished." She snapped out of her inner dialogue and followed him towards the glow of the campfire. They stepped out of the bushes to their friends enjoying well-deserved downtime. Frost strolled over and handed a sharpened stick to Lily. She grinned and moved over to give him a place to sit beside her on the log. They sat around the campfire talking about the weeks ahead. She devoured the best hot dog she'd ever eaten by the warmth of the flickering flames. Everything within her was calm. *This was her new life and these people would be her family for countless years to come.* Having lost her mortal family, she found peace in the fact that they would always be together, for they could never die. Kayn tried to lean the stick she'd used to cook her wiener against the log she was sitting on and it fell into the dirt. *Damn it. She wasn't finished eating.* When Kayn reached for it, her stomach cramped. *Crap. Here we go again.* The symbols on their palms lit up and flashed once. She was instantly on her feet.

Frost chuckled, "Hey killer, sit down. In this situation, there's no need for us to move a muscle unless all of them go down. That just means somebody's been wounded. Six, are still standing."

Her heart constricted in her chest. *The sonata of the night that had been glorious only moments before now had ominous lyrics prompting her to kill something.* Their palms flashed again in unison. Kayn's adrenaline surged. *She couldn't ignore this feeling. She wasn't capable of it.* Lexy was grinning at her. She could tell by the look in the other Dragon's eyes, she was feeling the same. Grey signalled to Zach, the Handlers shifted positions to sit within arm's reach of their Dragons. Their palms flashed again.

Zach held onto her arm. In a soothing tone, he assured, "There's still three standing. It's not time yet."

*The urge to kick something's ass was overwhelming.* Surges of adrenaline pulsed through her as her palm flashed a fourth time.

She scowled as Zach tightened his grip on her arm and calmly affirmed, "Not yet. It's not time yet."

Her brain was humming. *The discomfort gradually increased with each thud of her heart. She couldn't ignore this instinct. She had to go.* An explosion of incapacitating pain made her clutch her head and wail in agony. *Her mind was about to explode. It was her duty to protect her Clan. Dragons were the first line of defence. She couldn't take it anymore.* Their palms lit up again. This time, everyone stood up. Zach released his grip on her arm and nodded. Her headache ceased, and in the absence of his touch, she felt a hollow sensation flow through her being, silencing all sense of reason. There was nothing but the overwhelming drive to find the wounded Ankh. Both Dragons sprinted away.

Lily hollered, "Now! Stop her!"

Kayn was aware of the pounding of her heart and the blood racing through her veins. She heard footsteps beside her and knew it was Lexy without looking. Keeping pace with each other, their feet pounded a steady rhythm in the moist earth. Aware of other footsteps, Kayn didn't care who it was. They were inconsequential. She darted through the trails with the agility of a predator in pursuit of its prey. Fury grew inside of her with each thud her feet made in the dirt. Violent images flashed through her mind, fanning the flames of rage within her being. Zach's voice calling her name registered. *She had a job to do. Nothing else mattered. She felt her distressed Ankh. They were close. She was almost there*. Kayn sprinted to where every cell in her body told her they would be and came upon them standing there unharmed. *What? No.* She spun around in search of what hurt them. *There was nothing*. Her heart rapidly palpitated. An explosion of excruciating pain caused her to double over clutching her head. *She couldn't catch her breath. She couldn't think straight.* Adrenaline raced as unreleased fury pulsed through her being. She spun around in search of Lexy. *Grey had her. What was this?* She whirled around again, her mind reeling.

Zach soothed, "Kayn. You need to come back to me now. This was just a test. Nobody's hurt. It was a test."

*She couldn't. She didn't want to. Her chest felt like it was on fire. The headache was excruciating. The unspent energy felt like it was devouring her from the inside out.* She grabbed her temples. Shrieking, she dropped to all fours in the dirt. Zach edged closer to where she was doubled over in agony.

He spoke softly, "I'm sorry I'm such a lousy Handler. I don't even know what I'm supposed to be doing. We'll figure this stuff out together. When my abilities kick in, you can help me. You know how much I care about you, don't you? You have to know that by now."

*His voice was numbing the pain.* She stopped pressing on her temples and looked up at him. He inched closer and held out his hand. *She wanted to take it. It all made sense. His hand was her lifeline. He could save her from the rage consuming her.* As Kayn took Zach's outstretched hand, her pulse stopped racing and she felt peace. *She was tired.* She rested her head on his lap and he began gently stroking her hair. Her heart stopped pounding and the fire within her ceased to be an inferno. Kayn closed her eyes for only a moment.

She woke up on her bunk with Zach caressing her hair. For a second she was confused, but then she remembered.

He whispered, "Don't be angry. We needed to bring you back, set you off and bring you back again, under controlled circumstances. Markus wanted to see if I could bring you back before they sent us on a job alone."

Kayn felt empty, numb inside. Zach stayed with her. Understanding why they did it, didn't fix the hollow feeling submerging her soul in icy nothingness.

Kissing her head, her Handler tried explaining, "They cut themselves to trigger and test your ability. It had to be done before they could send us on a job. I'll be back in two seconds. Frost got you something."

She remained unmoving and emotionless until Zach returned with something covered by a dishtowel.

"Mel, turn off the lights," he requested.

The lights in the RV went out and there was darkness.

Something was glowing under the dishtowel. Zach yanked it off and inside of the jar was fireflies. Her emotions sprung back to life. The moisture from her tears blurred her vision. Kayn took a deep shuddering breath as she whispered, "Let's go outside and set them free." She saw Zach's smile by the light of the fireflies as she followed him to the door and down the steps to where everyone else was sitting with sticks dangling over the fire. Her Handler took off the lid, releasing the fireflies into the night. Kayn wasn't watching the fireflies though, she was staring into Frost's eyes through the flickering flames of the fire. *He'd done this. She knew it was him.* She walked over and kissed his cheek. Shocked she'd done it in front of everyone, Frost smiled. She grabbed a stick. Placing a wiener on the end of it, she sat beside Zach across the fire. The old version of Kayn never wanted to burn her hotdog. The new one dangled her stick directly into the flames and watched it scorch until it was blackened. Zach was sitting beside her, cooking his wiener over the embers. She took hers out, blew on it and tried to remove it with her fingers but it was still far too hot to touch. Lily handed her a napkin to shield her fingertips from the heat.

Orin shouted, "Heads up!" A bun came soaring through the air in her direction.

She caught it in midair, proud of herself. *Cool moves were few and far between in her world. Too bad he hadn't thrown the squeeze bottle of mustard too.* A mustard bottle came flying at her without warning. Kayn caught it a second before it smoked her. She sat there staring at it, amazed it hadn't hit her in the face. She held it up and stated, "How did I catch this? I wasn't even looking."

Their leader disclosed, "Heightened sensory awareness.

You'll find your eyesight and hearing better too, but it's about much more. We can sense danger. You'll have an upset stomach and just know something's coming. We use a larger portion of our brains. Well, some of us." Markus winked at Frost. "You'll find it handy to hear each other's thoughts when you're on a job. It takes both parties being receptive to non-verbal communication. When you're new, your thoughts are unfiltered until you figure it out. For us, only Oracles hear our thoughts when we don't want them to. We'll teach you how to close off your thoughts when you want them to be private. If we can't there's magic to tone it down."

*She'd had many responses to her inner commentary over the years. Sometimes she heard random thoughts, but not often. She'd heard Kevin's thoughts a few times, shortly after they'd first met Triad. She didn't hear Frost's thoughts, but knew he'd heard hers at least a few times.* She heard Frost's voice in her head, *'You have endless inner commentary.'* She drew her eyes up to meet his. *Shit.* He started to laugh. Kayn shook her head and tried answering using only her mind. *Even the naughty thoughts? I've been thinking about that incident in the bathroom for days.*

Frost choked on his hotdog. Lily started smacking his back. She laughed, "Are you alright?"

He nodded as he replied, "Thanks, I must have inhaled that last bite of my hotdog."

Kayn bit her lip. *Now, that she was consciously trying not to think naughty thoughts about him it was all her mind wanted to do. She could still feel his hands on her hips. Stop it. Stop thinking about it.* She felt someone staring at her. *It was Zach.*

"I say just go for it. Live a little," he provoked.

Kayn whispered, "You heard what I was thinking?"

Chuckling, Zach draped his arm over her shoulder and teased, "I didn't need to. Some things are painfully obvious."

*Was it really that obvious?* She glanced at Frost. He was grinning and shaking his head, staring into the flickering flames of the fire.

Markus announced, "Get some sleep. There's a long drive ahead of us." He got up and Jenna, Orin, Arrianna and Lily followed him into the second RV.

*It felt strange to have both groups travelling together. They usually split-up, didn't they? Mel was still hanging out with everyone else. Frost was gone. Was he in the RV? A part of her wanted to go to look at fireflies but a much larger part wanted to find an excuse to be alone with Frost.* Kayn stood up and announced, "Well, I'm going to bed. Goodnight guys." She climbed the steps.

Zach taunted, "Sweet dreams."

She paused as everyone started to laugh. *They totally knew she was following Frost. She didn't have to be stalking him. Maybe, she was tired?* Clutching the handle, Kayn went in, and let it swing shut behind her. *He wasn't sitting at the table.* She wandered to the bunks, grabbed her toothbrush out of her backpack and made her way to the bathroom. She heard noise from the TV in the back but decided to brush her teeth before venturing in. When she was ready for bed, she popped her head in to see what he was watching. *He wasn't alone anymore. They were watching a movie on Netflix. She'd been in the bathroom all of five seconds.* Mel smiled and patted the carpet next to her. Kayn politely declined, "I'm going to bed. Enjoy the movie." She climbed onto her bunk. Resting her head on her pillow, she closed her eyes to the humming of television and muffled laughter. *Maybe she was missing out?* She heard the door open and closed her eyes, knowing who it was. She felt the pressure of someone sitting on the mattress and her stomach flip-flopped.

Frost slipped under the covers, stretched out beside her and whispered, "I know you're awake. You just left the room."

Grinning, Kayn bit her lip as she opened her eyes. *She'd known it was him. She also knew she'd been pushing his buttons and he was here to call her bluff.* She whispered, "I just wanted to thank you for catching those fireflies."

On his back, looking at the bottom of the top bunk, he disclosed, "I thought it might help. I know those little things have always meant a lot to you."

She shifted to face him. *He'd always known that even before they'd had the opportunity to really get to know each other.*

He made himself comfortable under the covers as he probed, "I bet you lost the ring I gave you."

She innocently teased, "The one from the bubblegum machine?"

"I thought it might be too soon for a real one," Frost flirtatiously sparred.

Meeting his eyes, Kayn whispered her reply, "I haven't lost it. It's in the front pocket of my backpack." All she could think about was how badly she wanted him to touch her. Anything, the slightest graze of his fingertip. The covers shifted with each breath he took.

He stared into her eyes as he whispered back, "It's been a long time since someone's randomly kissed me on the cheek."

*He had the thickest eyelashes.* She bit her bottom lip as their gazes locked. *His eyes were magnetic. There was something intensely intimate about unbroken eye contact.* Breathless with anticipation, she felt the covers shift as he slid his hand closer, resting his palm intimately on her hip.

He whispered, "I've been thinking about what Zach walked in on for days too."

*She was still embarrassed about the whole vomiting on him thing even though he acted like it wasn't a big deal.* Kayn grinned and probed, "Even after I puked on you?"

Frost's face cracked into an enormous grin, he taunted, "It definitely wasn't one of your sexiest moments."

The urge to test her boundaries was so enticing, she couldn't help herself as she baited, "What was my sexiest moment?"

Seductively squeezing her hip, he confessed, "I could watch you eat Twinkies for hours."

She felt his hand slip from her hip. *He'd remembered what she did to him right after that. She'd given him the, I'm not over my ex speech.* Kayn grabbed for his arm to stop him from leaving and missed. *Boy, did she miss.* He froze as her eyes widened. She yanked her hand away, stammering, "I didn't mean to do that."

Frost smirked, boldly moving closer. He slid his hand onto her hip and aggressively tugged her against him. She shivered as he nibbled on her earlobe and groaned, "If we were somewhere with a little more privacy, you'd be in big trouble young lady."

She felt him straining against her. *The urge to do dangerous things was now a part of her being. He was a dangerous thing.* Frost sensually hooked one of his fingers around the strap of her tank top and naughtily followed the material until the palm of his hand grazed the thin cotton close to the peak of her breast. She shuddered. His eyes penetrated hers as he observed her blissful reaction to his touch. His lips were slightly parted. *Kiss me, damn it!* His finger moved beneath her top. She arched against him, breathily pleading, "Don't Stop."

Grinning, he whispered, "Now's not the best time for this."

Gazing into his eyes, clutching his hair with a hushed voice, she promised, "I'll be quiet, don't stop."

He knit his brow, groaned her name under his breath, with his hand on the button of her shorts. She willingly tried to help him take them off. *She wanted him and didn't care where they were.*

Grabbing his ears, with his face contorted in pain, he gasped, "Damn it, Kayn. We're not allowed to do this here." He scrambled out from under the covers and left her there, aching for him.

*Oh, Come on!* Every inch of her was vibrating with need. *He couldn't possibly walk back into that backroom in his current state.* She heard the bathroom door slam. She smiled, rolled over, pressed her face in her pillow and screamed into it. She rolled over and started to giggle. *What in the hell? Did they expect her to stay a virgin forever? Seriously. She'd bloody well died a virgin. Wasn't this the time to enjoy the life she'd been granted? She wanted to do this before someone tried to take it from her by force again. Her body was still tingling everywhere he'd touched her.* She fought the urge to lure him into the woods and remained on her bunk dying inside with frustration.

# 7

# NO REST FOR THE WICKED

After spending the night reliving her twin's steamy X-rated experiences with Frost, Kayn was even more frustrated as she awoke. She felt the pressure of someone sitting on the bunk beside her and opened her eyes. *It was Mel.*

Mel leaned over and whispered in her ear, "That was not an inconspicuous dream you were having last night. I bet you moaned Frost's name fifty times. Don't worry, they all crashed in the backroom. Well, everyone except for Frost and me."

*Of course, he'd heard her moaning his name. Why wouldn't her life continue to play the all humiliation Kayn channel on repeat? It had been stuck on the same damn station for years.* Covering her face with her hands, Kayn sighed, "Oh, the joys of merging souls with my dead twin sister."

Mel laid down beside her and chuckled, "Don't give me that crap. You want him bad."

Kayn smiled at her and admitted the truth she'd hidden from absolutely nobody, "I do, but every time something starts to happen between us, they stop it. He had me so turned-on last night, I wanted to scream when he walked away. Hell, I did scream into my pillow."

Laughing, Mel tried to play devil's advocate, "Maybe, it's not the right time or person?"

Kevin popped into her mind and she willed the intrusive thoughts of him away. *She couldn't ever think of him that way again. He was her enemy. That was over. They'd murdered each other. Murder was a deal breaker for any relationship. She understood why he'd killed her the first time but feeding her to those demons was excessively cruel. What was wrong with her? The people that they were before this life didn't exist anymore. They'd died the second they'd been marked. They just hadn't known it at the time.*

"Who are you thinking about? Is it Zach?" Mel asked.

Kayn laughed uncomfortably, "What? No. Never, that's so gross!"

"Are you sure?" Her friend prodded.

Kayn grinned and said, "One hundred percent. Why would you even bring that up?"

Smiling, Mel whispered, "Zach kissed me a few nights ago. I mean really kissed me. He took off to take care of you and never brought it up again."

"You actually like him, don't you? I guess it's true what they say, water can break down a mountain given enough time," Kayn taunted.

"It's not like that," Mel whispered. "It's not like he broke me down. He took me by surprise. He grabbed me and kissed me on the dance floor, until my knees were weak but since then, he's been ignoring me completely. It's messing with my head. Now, it's all I can think about."

*That move sounded familiar. Frost must be giving Zach lessons on how to be a player. As soon as she got Frost alone, she'd ask him about it.* Resting her head on the pillow, Kayn said, "I think that might be a good thing. You and Zach, I mean."

Mel sighed, "I had no idea he was capable of that. He's an incredible kisser."

Kayn grimaced and smacked her with a pillow.

"What was that for?" Mel laughed.

"I don't need a mental picture," Kayn groaned. "I have to be with him all the time." Mel scowled at her. Kayn chuckled, "I mean, good for you. I hope it lasts forever."

"Funny Brighton. I was sent to get you up. We're doing a job on our own for the first time," Mel revealed, smiling.

Assuming it would be their base group, Kayn got ready, went outside and realised what Mel meant. *Everyone else was gone. It was just the five survivors of the Testing. Frost left without saying anything. She'd never done anything without Grey, Frost, Lily and Lexy there. What if they messed up?* The new Ankh were hanging out, drinking coffee and chatting. *They appeared to be fine with the situation. She wasn't. It felt like a recipe for disaster. Didn't they understand she had no idea what she was doing?*

"Here," Mel passed her a coffee.

*Yes, she could use a coffee or ten.* Kayn wandered over, perched her backside on the log beside Zach and took a sip of the steaming brew. They made small talk like normal people whose plans for the day didn't include morally questionable activities. *How long did they have to do this job? What was it? Why wasn't anybody talking about it?*

Zach squirmed on the log and animatedly exclaimed, "I heard your thoughts! I totally heard that!"

*He was staring directly at her.* Kayn knit her brow and sarcastically replied, “Congratulations?”

All excited, Haley exclaimed, “Do me! Do me!”

Zach flirtatiously teased, “Well, if you insist.”

Haley scowled and hissed, “You know that wasn’t what I meant.”

“Okay, think about something,” Zach instructed while grinning. Haley stared into his eyes. He concentrated for a minute and then sighed, “No, sorry. I’ve got nothing.”

Clearly disappointed, Haley shrugged and remarked, “It was worth a try.”

Mel sat down with her coffee and baited, “I know you’re dying to do me.”

Kayn grinned, knowing her friend meant to ply Zach with innuendo.

Casually glancing at Mel, Zach toyed, “I already know what you want.”

Kayn choked on the gulp of coffee she was trying to swallow.

Astrid gave her a few sturdy pats on the back, teasing, “You’re supposed to swallow it, not breathe it in.”

Her eyes were watering from both the near choking experience and the fact that she was trying not to laugh. Kayn said, “Thanks.” *Frost had used a line quite close to that on her.* She glanced at Mel. It was obvious she was intrigued. Their sparring match of innuendos was so entertaining, she’d almost forgotten the pressing issues of the day.

With a devious glint in her eyes, Mel got up. She walked over to Zach and ordered him to stand. He rose to his feet. Mel leaned in like she was going to kiss him. His eyes widened. She blew a tiny gust of air from her parted lips, wiped his cheekbone with her finger and explained, "You had an eyelash." She spun around, strutted back over to where she'd been sitting and took a casual sip of her coffee.

Kayn placed her hand over her mouth to stop the laughter about to escape. *Mel was obviously not the girl to play games with. She had experience and wasn't afraid to use it.*

Astrid shook her head and said, "As entertaining as this little game is, I think we should talk about the job. We need to get going. We're supposed to drive south on the closest highway for roughly six hours. We'll know who the new girl is when we see her. We have to steal her from Trinity and continue driving south on backroads until they contact us."

Kayn's eyes travelled the group. *Those were seriously vague instructions.* She questioned, "Do we have money for a room or are we staying in the RV?"

Astrid smiled, took a card out of her pocket, waved it in the air and said, "You're guess is as good as mine. We have this card for expenses and no idea where we're going but we have to keep driving after we steal the girl from Trinity."

Confused, Kayn knit her brow as she clarified, "They're sending us to steal someone from another Clan. How do we do that? We've never seen them do it."

Haley piped in, "We have. Granted it was twenty years ago, but they just snuck up on them, killed everyone and ran. It's pretty basic."

Kayn was trying to pay attention but a mosquito had begun to feast on her arm. She observed it snacking on her flesh without slapping or squishing it. She pinched her skin on either side, causing it to gorge itself to death on her blood. It dropped off her arm and she smiled.

"Alright then," Zach announced. "Let's get on the road. I'll drive first. Kayn, come with me and keep an eye out for Trinity. Should we just start driving and do the regular three-hour stints before changing off."

"Sounds good," Astrid replied.

Kayn got up and followed Zach into the motorhome while the others took the braces out from under the tires and made sure they had everything packed up. She placed her travel mug in the sink, grabbed a bottle of water out of the fridge and chugged it. *She was unusually thirsty*. Zach was already fumbling around upfront. She hollered, "I'm going to dive into the bathroom!" As she started walking to the back of the RV, her stomach grumbled. *She was hungry.* She backtracked to the kitchen to grab a granola bar from the cupboard. After scarfing it down, she shuffled down the hall and into the tiny bathroom. *It felt extra claustrophobic this morning.* As Kayn was washing her hands, she noticed her veins were unusually pronounced on her chest. *She knew what this was from Testing. It was something to do with her Conduit ability.* She traced the tip of her finger along one of her brilliant green veins. *Hopefully, she'd be able to keep her ability in check.* They'd made sure the Dragon could be controlled, but the Conduit part of her was still up in the air. Aware she'd only touched the surface of what she was capable of, she opted to keep quiet about it. *There was no reason to stress everyone out. Anyone the least bit observant would notice her overly pronounced veins. Oh, well. What could she do about it? Not a damn thing.* She wandered to the front and sat in the passenger seat, ready for the drive ahead. As the engine began to purr, he plugged in his cell and started his playlist. She mentally prepared for three hours of metal from Zach's playlist. A dance track came on. She glanced over.

He laughed and said, "I'm not an asshole. I know you're going to be stuck up here with me all of the time now so I downloaded songs I knew you'd like."

She smiled as she enquired, "When can we stop for breakfast?"

Playing with the rearview mirror, he replied, "I was thinking we'd stop for brunch in a couple of hours? It'll cut our driving time in half. We can get some fresh air and stretch our legs."

"Sounds like a plan," Kayn responded as they slowly pulled out and began cruising down the long winding gravel road towards what she assumed would be a highway. *No such luck. It was miles of bumpy road.* She disliked gravel roads, especially if they were stuck on one for a long time. At least she was upfront with the driver and not in the back trying to play cards or read. Zach cleared his throat and she glanced his way.

He probed, "Have you had a chance to talk to Mel alone since that night you got sick?"

*She knew what he was digging for.* She grinned and baited, "Maybe."

"She told you. I knew it," Zach chuckled, shaking his head. He reached over and switched the song playing.

Kayn looked at him so she could read his expression as she countered, "So, Frost gave you some lessons on how to hook and reel a girl."

Concentrating on the winding gravel road ahead, he grinned, ran one of his hands through his short jet-black hair and far too casually responded, "Why would you think Frost had anything to do with it?"

*Oh, come the hell on. I wasn't born yesterday.* Kayn rolled her eyes at her rather inept Handler and ribbed, "So, that's a yes?"

*This was a seriously hazardous gravel road they were on. She could hear it pinging around underneath the RV.*

Grinning, Zach answered, "Well, I didn't exactly have any reliable male role models to learn from."

*He called Frost a reliable male role model. That was hilarious.* Kayn's stomach complained, even though she'd recently eaten a granola bar. *Man, she was starving this morning. Why was she so hungry?* They went over a large bump and heard a chorus of swears from the girls at the table behind them.

Zach suggested, "You should grab a snack? That grizzly bear under your shirt is distracting."

*Kayn knew what he meant. She could have taken it many ways. If she wasn't starving to death for some strange reason, she would have cracked a joke.* Her stomach complained again, he started to laugh. *She'd just eaten a granola bar. What in the hell?* She nodded and asked, "Do you want anything?"

"Another cup of coffee would be awesome," he sweetly requested.

"If you can handle sitting up here all by yourself for five minutes, I'll grab you one," Kayn sparred as she got up, steadied herself and manoeuvred her way back to the small kitchen area. Kayn always felt like using a knife to cut open a snack wasn't the greatest idea while in a moving vehicle. *Especially if you were one of those accident-prone people.* While they were driving, her munchie choices were rather limited. Someone already made a fresh pot of coffee, so she could check that chore off the list. Kayn glanced over at the table where the girls were stubbornly struggling to play cards while being jostled around. Haley's fanned out cards flew out of her hands onto the floor. She was about to get up to retrieve them when Kayn crouched down and passed them back. She thanked her. Kayn smiled while attempting to pour the coffee into a couple of travel mugs, surfing the bumpy road. *There was an art to backroad surfing.* With two travel mugs of black coffee in her hands and nowhere to place them as she grabbed creamer, she giggled. *She hadn't thought this out.*

Astrid got up, took them from her and teased, "The last time I was on coffee duty I spilled it everywhere."

Kayn smiled, silently thanking her without having to say the words. She countered, "Where was I? I would have helped you."

"You were out cold and epically hungover," her new friend ribbed. "If I'd asked you to help, I would have been cleaning up coffee and vomit."

They managed to get creamer into coffee and put the lids on balancing while being jostled by bumpy terrain. Chuckling, Astrid sat down. Pressing both coffees against her chest, Kayn snagged a box of cookies.

Haley tossed a water bottle cap at her, scolding, "Don't you dare bring him a box of cookies. He'll never stop for breakfast. I'm starving, my stomach won't stop grumbling over here."

They went over an enormous bump. Kayn fell with a thud to the floor, somehow managing to not spill either coffee. *I am Batman.*

They were all still laughing as Zach hollered, "You guys okay back there? What's taking so long, Brighton?"

*I'll tell you what's taking so long, you dumbass. You're driving like you just escaped from a frigging sanitarium.* Kayn sat there on the floor, scowling as she wedged coffees between her thighs. *She was eating these damn cookies. It was happening and he could just bloody well wait until she was done.* She popped one into her mouth and offered the box to the girls at the table. They declined.

Haley rolled her eyes and asserted, "We need real food and soon. It sounds like there's a table full of angry dogs back here. He'll stop if you ask sweetly. Isn't he supposed to take care of your every need? He's your Handler and you're hungry."

Stuck on the floor, Kayn commented, "I wouldn't hold my breath. He said he was going to stop for brunch in two hours. I'm starving too. I was taking the cookies for me."

"Go batt your eyelashes," Haley directed. "Maybe he'll stop sooner, I'm dying over here."

Smiling, Mel explained, "That's not Kayn's style." She placed her cards on the table, deviously chuckling, "Read 'em and weep." They placed their hands down. Mel raised both arms in victory.

"I'd go up and batt my eyes but he'd see me coming. He knows I'm into girls," Astrid pressed.

Rolling her eyes, Kayn sighed, "I'll try." She scrambled to her feet and put the cookies back in the cupboard before making another attempt to bring coffee to the front.

Swatting her as she passed, Mel said, "Kayn."

Kayn paused mid-step to humour her friend. *She was going to fall.*

"Tell him I'll kiss him if he stops," Mel toyed.

Kayn grinned as she teased, "Now, that might work." When she reappeared, she could tell by Zach's expression that he'd heard everything they'd said. She passed him his coffee.

He put his to-go cup into the holder with one semi free hand and baited, "I think Mel forgot about that promise she made in the Testing."

Kayn sipped her coffee, knitting her brow. *What was he talking about?* She responded, "Refresh my memory."

Grinning mischievously, he sparred, "Think about it."

It popped into Kayn's head. She whispered, "Oh, you mean when Mel promised she'd kiss you every day if we got out of the Testing."

*She'd guessed correctly.* Grinning, he purposely drove over a huge pothole way too fast to shake up the gossiping table of girls. Kayn nearly tossed her coffee at the windshield as everyone at the table cursed up a storm. Zach was giggling like a naughty kid. Leaning closer, Kayn whispered, "I'm not sure she meant that in a romantic way."

He shook his head and whispered back, "I know she didn't. A guy can dream, can't he?"

They drove in silence for a few minutes as she dwelled on how starving she was while watching unimpressive scenery flashing by the window. Her stomach let off a hilariously loud complaint.

Zach rolled his eyes and sighed, "Fine. I'll pull over for breakfast at the first place I see." The table cheered. He laughed, "How much can they hear back there?"

Kayn laughed out loud and teased, "How much could you hear of our conversation when I was back there trying to get us coffee while you drove like an asshole?"

"So, everything then," Zach whispered and winked.

It took forty minutes to find a restaurant with space to park an RV. Even then, they had to park across the street. The girls were halfway across the parking lot before they made it out of the door.

He made sure the door was locked and casually asked, "Be honest with me. Does she like me in that way?"

Kayn elbowed her friend as she smiled and countered, "Do you think Frost likes me in that way?"

"Come on, he's always liked you in that way. You knew that." Zach sparred as they darted across the busy street and strolled towards the entrance to the diner. He stopped her before they went in and enquired, "I'm serious. Did she say anything or am I just wasting my time?"

*She might as well just tell him.* Kayn gave his shoulder a squeeze as she replied, "That kiss rocked her world."

He couldn't stop grinning as he shoved the door open. Zach held it open for her. They were already sitting at an orange pleather booth. *Everything was way too bright. Why were the fluorescent lights humming so loudly? Oh shit. She was having an ability related issue. She knew what she needed.*

Sensing her distress, Zach whispered, "Give me your hand."

As she took his hand, an instant sense of calm sedated the Dragon within her. Grateful for the sensory reprieve, Kayn kissed his cheek, messed up his hair and whispered, "Thank you." She let go of his hand as they made their way over to a way less obnoxiously coloured table. There was another humorous chorus of loudly complaining stomachs as she reached for her menu. It occurred to her that none of them should be this hungry. *This was something else. Why had they left them to figure out this supernatural crap on their own?*

The waitress came to take their orders before they'd had a chance to look at the menu. A friendly petite girl with a contagious smile asked where they were headed. Mesmerized by her, Mel kept the conversation going, asking her about the town and if she was from here. *If she hadn't known Mel was straight, she would have thought she was flirting with the waitress.*

Kayn was so busy listening, she forgot to peek at the menu. When the waitress asked her what she wanted, she drew a blank. Pointing at Mel, Kayn said, “I'll have whatever she's having.” A creepy chorus of stomachs sounded off again. *This was getting weird.* Kayn was in the booth with her back to the door as the bells jingled, announcing a patron's entrance. *Why did these diners always seem to have bells?* She caught the shock on Mel's face. She'd become sickly pale.

Astrid mouthed the words, “Holy shit!”

Kayn stealthily turned around. Half a dozen Trinity just strolled in. *Shit! What were they supposed to do now?* Mel made a speedy beeline for the bathroom. *That was smart. They would have recognized her for sure.*

Covering half her face with a napkin like she was wiping her mouth, Astrid coughed into it and whispered, “I don't recognize anyone. Maybe they won't recognize us? We've been in the Testing for twenty years.”

Haley casually took a drink of water and whispered, “Unless your old booty call walks in.”

Kayn and Zach didn't dare look behind them, they'd be recognized for sure. They were trapped at the table.

“I didn't see her,” Astrid whispered.

Kayn turned to look out the window as she enquired, “Is Thorne here?”

“I didn't get a good look,” Astrid answered normally. She took a sip of her coffee and added, “One of them went to the washroom. It looks like they're just picking up an order. They must be staying at the motel next door.”

Their sweet waitress delivered their meals with perfect timing, blocking them from sight as one strolled past the table. As Trinity left with their orders, one was bitching about someone taking forever in the bathroom. The door jingled as they left and the nervous giggles began. *That was close.*

Mel slinked back into her seat and said, "Well, I guess we've found Trinity. They must have the girl up in one of their rooms. Now, we just have to figure out where she is and how to kidnap someone."

Haley snickered and then began boisterously laughing louder. It sounded like she was losing her grip on things as she silenced herself by taking a big gulp of coffee. As she began to eat her breakfast, they watched uncomfortably as she periodically laughed between mouthfuls.

Astrid turned around and hissed, "That's enough! You're starting to freak me out!"

Haley chuckled, "We're sitting in a diner. It's been less than a week since we survived a place worse than hell and we're trying to figure out how we're going to kidnap someone. We don't even know what she looks like. How is that anything other than hilarious?" They all grinned and started to giggle.

Zach announced, "First things first, we need to find out which room they're in and none of us have compulsion as an ability. We don't even know what alias they're registered under."

Mel glanced up and piped in, "I might recognize an alias if I can get a look at the computer at the front desk."

Kayn was silent. *She'd stolen a touch of Frost's ability in the bathroom but had no idea how to access it. She suspected the purpose of this first mission alone wasn't only to find the girl. This was the immortal version of teaching someone how to swim by chucking them off a dock without a lifejacket. They were teaching them how to use their abilities. They'd have to work together to find a solution to this problem. They had given them a puzzle to solve. A puzzle with a shitload of pieces missing. It was rather ingenious.* She ate her breakfast and continued to think. *Frost's and Lily's abilities were triggered sexually. So, she'd probably need to be turned on to access it, if she still could.* She glanced at Zach. *Not a chance!* She surveyed the room. *There was nobody she found remotely attractive.* When she looked up the group was staring at her.

Haley wiped her mouth with a napkin, looked directly at her and casually probed, "So, you can access any ability you've fed off?"

*Haley had heightened intuition. Her instincts were usually dead on. It was confession time.* Kayn smiled at her intuitive friend with the brilliant pink hair and replied, "I might be able to. I took some of Frost's energy a few days ago and I think I accidentally took some of Lily's when I touched her. We all know how they use their abilities. I just have to figure out how to trigger mine and use what I took."

Astrid grinned and teased, "How difficult can that be? You probably just need to be turned on."

Everyone stared at Zach. He grimaced and sighed, "All right. If I have to."

Scowling at her Handler, Kayn repeated his words, "If I have to. Really? It's not like I want you to be the one to do anything." *This wasn't going to work.*

Mel raised her hand. They instantly stopped bickering. They all smiled. A table full of partially immortal teens had been silenced by mortal elementary school programming. Pressing her lips together to stifle her grin, Mel suggested, "We'll get a room. If Zach can't bring it out in you, we'll rent a two-million-dollar dirty movie and leave Kayn alone to watch it."

*This was going to be an absolutely mortifying experience.* Kayn shuffled her behind out of the pleather seat and winced because her thighs were stuck to it. *Short shorts and pleather seats were always a bad idea.*

Noticing her uncomfortable predicament, Haley joked, "I left the back of my thighs behind twenty years ago on a pleather seat in a diner in Arizona. I've grown to embrace jeans for various reasons."

Laughing as Astrid went up to pay, they made their way out of the air-conditioning into sweltering midmorning air. Their RV was parked across the street. *It was going to be a dead giveaway when the parking lot was empty.* Astrid suggested Zach move it now and text for the room number.

He took the keys out of his pocket and jingled them in the air. Zach pointed at Kayn and taunted, "I'll be back to turn you on in a few minutes."

*Gross.* Kayn grimaced and sighed, "Listen, this is never going to work. Why don't we sneak around the motel and try to figure out where they are?"

Grinning, Astrid stated the obvious, "We can't be seen. The rooms have outdoor entrances on three levels. If they open their door, where do we hide? Come on, Brighton. Take one for the team."

*Why did she have to be the one to take one for the team? Oh, yeah. She was a Dragon and a Conduit. It was in her job description.* Astrid went into the office. When she returned with their room key, she declared, "Good news, there's a hot guy working at the desk."

*It would be much easier if she could just stroll in there, snap his neck and look at his computer screen. Oh, how her ideals had changed since Testing. She'd been mortified by Frost's insensitive behaviour before, but it made perfect sense to her now.* They snuck up to the second floor, listening for familiar voices as they passed by each room until they found their mustard-coloured door with slivers of paint missing. *This hotel room might be a nasty one.* Just as they were trying to get in, the doorknob moved next door. Astrid fumbled with the key, desperately trying to open the door so they'd remain unseen until they were ready. She couldn't open it. Her eyes widened as an elderly gentleman stepped out. They all took a breath.

Haley took the key from her, whispering, "Let me try."

The elderly gentleman suggested, "The locks are sticky. Try wiggling the key first, then pull the doorknob up."

Haley wiggled the key, pulled the doorknob up, and sure enough, it worked. They thanked the man, scooted inside, darted across yucky carpet, and flung themselves on the beds. *Nothing was going right. This was not a good sign.* Kayn sat up, saying, "Oh, Crap. We don't have our bags."

Astrid went to see what they had in the bathroom. She stuck her head out of the door and said, "There's soap in here and shampoo. Mel always has makeup in her purse. I saw a bunch of personal items for sale in the lobby. They had toothbrushes and hairbrushes." Astrid stared directly at her, teasing, "Even condoms."

Kayn shook her head, sparring, "How far do you think I'm willing to take this, accessing abilities I've siphoned plan. Not that far. I can promise you that. We should just bust down every door in this place until we find Trinity and kick their asses. We can take the girl and be on our way. No toothbrush necessary."

Rolling her eyes at what she'd suggested, Astrid sighed, "I was joking, Brighton. Also, there's that pesky mortals aren't supposed to know we exist situation. It's just a guess but, Markus might frown upon us beating up everyone in this motel." Someone knocked on the door and everyone jumped. Astrid looked through the peephole. She opened the door without missing a beat.

Scooting inside, Zach handed everyone toothbrushes and toothpaste from the lobby.

"I've already got a toothbrush in my purse," Mel said.

He grinned and ribbed, "Of course you do."

# 8

# THIS IS AWKWARD

Escaping into the bathroom, Kayn locked the door. She moved the curtains, perched on the edge of the tub and stared at the pastel blue sink fixtures. *Everything appeared clean. This was good. She had to get rid of the ball of anxiety building in the pit of her stomach. These stored abilities had to be easier to access. She was supposed to be a Conduit for heaven's sake. She had absolutely no idea what she was doing. Why had she told them she might be able to access Frost's ability? She didn't even know how long she kept one after borrowing it.* Someone knocked on the door. She got up, wandered over and opened it. Zach came in with a bottle clutched in his hand. She sat on the side of the tub and remarked, "If that's a peace offering in your hand, you've got the wrong person."

He removed the plastic from a couple of glasses by the sink and poured some of the amber-hued alcohol into each one. He sat on the edge of the tub as he passed her a glass and urged, "I'm sure this is the last thing you want to do. I know it's only been a few nights since puke fest. Humour me, it may loosen up your inhibitions enough to figure out how to access Frost's ability."

*He was trying to get her drunk. It wasn't the smartest idea but why the hell not. What did she have to lose?* Kayn raised her glass and saluted, "Bottoms up." She downed the entire glass like a shot. It burned as it went down, then felt like it was going to come right back up.

Still holding his almost full plastic glass, he whispered, "You're supposed to sip cherry brandy." He held out his hand for her empty glass. She passed it to him. He filled it with water and gave it back to her. She downed the liquid. Zach laughed, "You'd better have another glass of water. You drink like a teenager that snuck alcohol from their parent's liquor cabinet. You're an adult. Take your time. It's not about getting drunk. It's about enjoying the taste and taking time to relax."

*That made sense. She hadn't had much experience with drinking when she was mortal. She'd snuck wine to drink with Kevin at the lake a few times but hadn't gotten into it. Kevin... She hadn't meant to think about him. He was in most of her mortal memories. She'd never be able to reminisce about that time without thoughts of him and what they used to mean to each other.* Drinking her second glass, emotion numbed as the brandy worked its inhibition loosening magic. Zach was watching her. She met his gaze.

He questioned, "Is it really that impossible to think of me as anything but your friend?"

She stared into her glass of water as she replied, "I'm sorry about my reaction. I wouldn't even be contemplating anything after having my heart stomped on. My feelings for Frost were already there. I want to say it's because of how Chloe felt about him but it wouldn't be the truth. He makes me feel reckless. I don't know, it's hard to explain." Zach poured himself another and offered her one. *She wasn't sure if she should.* She nodded and he passed it to her. This time she took a sip instead of downing the whole thing. *Yes, that's way better.*

He raised his glass and saluted, "To finding someone who makes you feel reckless. That doesn't sound like a bad idea for me either."

She almost slipped off her perch and decided to sit inside. She got into the tub, resting her arms on either side. Zach grinned and got in at the opposite end. It reeked of bleach, and there was no room for their legs, but neither cared. *They were chilling, enjoying the effects of the brandy.* Kayn announced, "Cherry brandy isn't bad." Blissfully relaxed, she felt her Handler's eyes on her. He climbed out and held out his hand. She took it. As he helped her out, he went for a kiss. *Oh, why not give it a try.* She kissed him back. After a few seconds, the awkwardness was unbearable. When he tried to deepen the kiss, she pulled away. They started laughing. It felt like she was trying to make-out with a relative. By the shade of his cheeks, he felt the same way about her.

He shoved her and taunted, "Mystery solved. That'll never happen."

Playfully pushing him back, Kayn declared, "Maybe, I should just go down to the office and flirt with the guy at the desk?"

Zach grinned and teased, "You're drunk and it's just past noon. If you feel like you can do it, go for gold."

They left the bathroom to hopeful eyes. Kayn shook her head, announcing, "Time for Plan B." It was a telling moment because Mel appeared relieved. *She did really like him.* Kayn winked at her and enquired, "Are you coming with me?"

Mel stood up and asked, "Where are we going? You guys can't talk in drunk code and expect us to decipher it. We're sober. You know, like most people at lunchtime."

Kayn gave Mel a curt yet hilarious explanation, "I'm going to seduce the guy working at the front desk while you sneak a peek at the computer."

Astrid's face burst into an enormous shit-eating grin as she asked, "How much did you guys drink?"

Zach placed his arm around her and preened, "I have confidence in our Kayn's ability to seduce someone. Not me, but someone."

Haley leapt up, saying, "You're not going down there like that. Give us five minutes to put makeup on you." She tried to tug Kayn's ponytail out of her hair but it was tangled in her curls. Forced to improvise, she asked, "Does anyone have a knife?"

Kayn grimaced and stated, "There's no need to cut my hair, I'll get it out." She managed to free the elastic band held captive by her unruly mass of curls. Mel put makeup on her. Zach appeared with a glass of water and tossed it on her white tank top.

Kayn scowled and hissed, "What in the hell was that for?"

Astrid grinned, winked at Zach and chuckled, "He's a genius. Now, it doesn't matter how awkward you are. That guy will definitely be staring at you long enough for Mel to catch a glimpse of his computer screen."

*She didn't get it.* They put a bunch of makeup on her and soaked her tank top. She peeked out of the door. *The coast was clear.* Kayn walked outside and complained, "Now, my tops see-through." A lightbulb clicked on above her head. *Oh, she got it. So much for trying to inconspicuously make their way downstairs.* They descended the stairs as quickly as they could and darted into the lobby. A cute guy was intently staring at his cell. Kayn tried speaking to Mel using only her mind, *can you get behind him and peek at the screen? He doesn't even know we're standing here.* Mel nodded. *She'd heard her.* Mel ducked, crawled on the floor, and stood up behind the boy who still hadn't looked up from his phone. *His earbuds were in, he was off in his own little world.* Mel smiled and waved. *She'd found the name she was looking for.* She was crawling back when he noticed Kayn standing there with a soaking wet top. Mel was stuck but concealed from his line of site.

He took his earbuds out. Taking her in, he cleared his throat nervously and said, "Can I help you?"

*It was showtime.* Kayn provocatively bit her lip as she leaned over the desk and flirted, "I'm on a trip with my dad. I'm bored stiff. What's fun around here?"

Inching closer, he replied, "I get off in a few hours. I'd be happy to show you around."

Harnessing her inner Chloe, she seductively responded, "What would we do first?" *This guy had incredible eyes. They were deep chocolate brown with flecks of gold.* Her gaze travelled to the curve of his smile. *He looked like he'd be a great kisser. What was wrong with her? He was a stranger.* He grinned at her, and when he did, she noticed unbelievably sexy dimples and a tiny scar on the left side of his clean-shaven chin.

His eyes appreciatively wandered from her face to the wet tank top as he answered, "I'd take you for dinner at this place downtown. After, we'd grab something from the liquor store and go to this beautiful spot with a view only locals know about."

Tucking loose curls behind her ear, Kayn whispered, "That sounds fun."

When Mel tried to move, the floor creaked. Before he could turn around to look, Kayn slid her hand over his and whispered, "I think I'm going to like this town." She felt an intensity building as her pulse began to race. Kayn shivered as pheromones released from her skin. *Mel already had the information they needed, but she wanted to see if the ability she'd borrowed would work.* She leaned in and kissed his lips. His eyes became blank. Kayn felt free to push her limits as she enquired, "I'm looking for my friends. I need to know what room they're in. Have you seen five or six reasonably good-looking people wearing gloves on one hand?"

He mechanically responded, "They are in rooms 305, 306 and 307."

Mel crawled out as Kayn whispered, "Thank you. Now, I want you to go lay that gorgeous head of yours on your desk and close your eyes for ten minutes. When you open them, you will have forgotten about this conversation. You have a flu. You need to call in sick. You'll feel fine in the morning." He nodded as he closed his eyes. In seconds, he was out cold. The girls managed to keep themselves from laughing until they were sprinting up the stairs to their room. It was only then that it clicked. *They were on the second floor. Trinity's rooms were directly above them. They could have heard them at any time.* Mel quietly rapped on the door as Kayn stared at the balcony above. There was a pause before Zach flung open the door. *He was much more attractive than he'd been only moments before. It must be the ability. Perhaps, it didn't just make her more attractive to other people. It also made everyone else more appealing to her. This was interesting.*

Zach's eyes followed her as she walked past him and sat on the bed. He commented, "I see you've figured out how to use those new abilities."

Mel grinned and replied, "Like a rock star. She had him eating out of the palm of her hand in five seconds flat. By the way, their rooms are directly above us."

Astrid panicked, "You have to turn it off. They'll sense it. To the other Clans, the scent of those pheromones means Frost or Lily are close by."

Zach held his hands out and explained, "If it works to calm other Dragon glitches, why not this one?"

Hesitantly, Kayn took his hands. *She didn't want to let this ability go because it made her feel powerful. Perhaps, it was more than that. This ability should belong to her.* After a minute of contact with Zach, she shivered and felt normal again.

"Do you think they know we're here?" Mel asked while staring at the ceiling.

The five of them sat on the beds, holding their breath, hoping Zach covered up Kayn's ability in time.

He whispered, "If one of the other Clans are close by, shouldn't our stomachs be warning us?"

"Not if we're not in any danger," Astrid explained.

Mel sparred, "Our stomachs were complaining."

"Well, I don't know. Your guess is as good as mine." Astrid replied as she stretched out on the bed.

Haley shoved Astrid as she sprawled next to her and suggested, "They have three rooms. The girl we're looking for must be in one of them. I guess we'll have to do a little recon."

"According to Jenna, you'll know who she is," Kayn

reminded. "We have the room numbers. Why don't we just wait until we're certain everyone's asleep and break in. We just need to get in and out without making a sound."

"We'll need keys to the rooms," Zach pointed out. "Maybe Kayn should go back to the lobby and see if she can get us copies of their keys. Mel should be the one to sneak in and out of their rooms. If someone wakes up, she can just claim she's looking for Thorne." He winked at her.

"That won't work," Mel countered. "We've already talked and let things go. He's not stupid."

He disputed, "True, but it might confuse the situation long enough for us to subdue Trinity and grab the girl."

"Subdue them with what? They didn't leave us any weapons," Astrid responded, staring at the stucco ceiling.

He got off the bed and asserted, "Hold that thought. Come on, Brighton. Let's sneak down to the lobby and see if it's still open. You guys order a pizza. We shouldn't risk going down to that diner again, we're too exposed."

The pair cautiously snuck out of the room. *The coast was clear once again.* They dashed down the stairs, and when they reached the office door, it was locked. There was a sign saying it was closed until 9 am and a number to call in case of emergency. *They had absolutely no idea what they were doing. Why had those dumbasses sent them out on their own to do something this important?* The diner door chimed. *There was nowhere to hide. They didn't know if it was Trinity so they couldn't risk even glancing in that direction.* Kayn panicked as she met Zach's eyes. *He understood what she was about to do. There was no other choice.* She seductively kissed him. They backed into the shadowed cement alcove by the office doors as they took their public make-out session far enough to make it seriously awkward for onlookers. *His hands were travelling to places they shouldn't be.* Playing along, Kayn clicked, *her glove. The one gloved hand was a dead giveaway. She had to hide it.* She slipped her hands under his shirt and they began to heat as she touched his rippling abs. She shivered in response. *They were at the bottom of the stairs. No, no, this was not the time to set off that ability. Zach was turning her on.* Kayn heard a part of the conversation as the group began scaling the stairs. She recognized Thorne's voice. *Now, she was certain it was Trinity. They were planning to have a few drinks and watch a movie. They'd probably all be in one room. It was a struggle to concentrate on what they were talking about with Zach's surprisingly impressive seductive skills.* He added kindling to the fire with his creatively hidden hands. An intoxicating heat grew stronger until it surged within her, the pheromones released from her flesh. *Now, she didn't want to stop. She couldn't.* Zach grew more aggressive as her pheromones worked their carnal magic. He was also incapable of stopping himself as they switched positions with neither one capable of rational thought. She fumbled with the button above his zipper.

"I want you so bad," He whispered against her hair.

*She couldn't think about anything but being with him.*

A voice hissed, "Call the number on the door and get a damn room."

It was like a giant splash of cold water. They shoved away from each other and saw a man strolling away. Kayn covered her kiss-swollen lips with her hand. *What in the hell were they doing? They'd almost done something ridiculously stupid.* Zach leaned back against the wall and slid down it until he was sitting in the corner on the cement with his face in his hands. She did the same against the other wall in the alcove. They were both trying to breathe slowly so they could calm their racing pulses. *The ability she'd siphoned from Frost had almost made them do something they really didn't want to do.* She met his confused expression with an apology in her eyes. *This was going to make things awkward for a while.*

Zach gave her a weak smile. He whispered, "That's one powerful gift you've unwrapped, Brighton. Five more seconds and I would have taken you right here in public. Without any ability for rational thought, I might add. Do you get to keep it, or does it go away?"

"Honestly, I have no idea," she answered. Her pulse was beginning to regulate. A sense of calm washed over her, and this time, it happened without even having to touch Zach's hands. They sat in the shadows, confused over their inability to stop. *You can't be blamed for anything you do while under the influence of magic.*

Zach struggled to stand up and chuckled, "My legs feel like they're made of Jell-O. For future reference, that's how you kiss a guy." He gave her a roguish smile as he held out his hand.

She took it. He gallantly towed her to her feet. Kayn grinned and commented, "You didn't do so bad yourself. That would be what has Mel so hot and bothered." She brushed her shirt down and wiped the lipstick off his face. She attempted to fix his hair. If she looked half as ravaged as he did, it was going to be obvious to the others.

He shook his head as he returned the favour by trying to fix her smeared lipstick. Zach grinned and teased, "If you'd kissed me like that earlier, we'd still be in the bathroom."

*Mel just came to her and told her she liked him. She was a shitty friend if she'd steered him away.* Zach was grinning at her.

He responded to her thoughts, "We were drugged by your

ability. I was kidding about the bathroom. We're friends. We're always going to be friends. Just friends. I know that. In this life, we're going to have to do things we normally wouldn't. This doesn't have to be a big deal if we don't make it one. We kissed and it was hot, but we did it so Trinity wouldn't see us. There was a method to our madness. On a happy note, you calmed yourself down faster this time. If they'd sensed the pheromones, they'd be down here already. We'll just go back upstairs, tell them what happened and figure out another way to get into the room."

She smiled at him and responded with a slow nod. As they climbed up the stairs, Kayn noted it was still absurdly hot outside. *She was starving. She wasn't just hungry, she was ridiculously ravenous.* They made it to the room and quickly glanced at each other before entering.

Zach repeated his earlier words, "It's not a big deal."

Mel's face exploded into an enormous smile as they entered. She announced, "We've just concocted a brilliant plan." She came over holding the bracelet Jenna spelled to stifle Astrid's ability.

*Taking Astrid's bracelet off didn't feel like a good idea.*

Mel began to explain, "We do have a weapon. Astrid's saliva is a hallucinogenic toxin. We just have to figure out how to administer it to three rooms full of Trinity. Were you guys able to get the keys?"

Zach shook his head as he answered, "No, the office is closed until 9 am."

Mel seemed aggravated as she probed, "What took you guys so long?"

*This was awkward.* Kayn replied, "We ran into Trinity. We were forced to improvise."

Her friend's eyes widened as she kept the increasingly awkward line of questioning going, "They didn't see you, did they?"

She felt far too guilty to meet Mel's trusting blue eyes. *These abilities were going to cause serious complications in her life.* Kayn danced around the touchy situation by saying, "Not exactly." She tried to change the subject, "Did somebody order pizza?" She strolled over, grabbed the yellow menu off the table by the landline and began flipping through it.

Haley knit her brow, smiled and repeated Kayn's last words, "Not exactly?"

Zach tried to steer their conversation away from the topic, "I don't think they know we're here, but we heard them say they were planning to have a few drinks and watch a movie. Maybe they'll all be in the same room?"

Mel wandered over, snatched the menu out of Kayn's hand and asserted, "Can you stay focused for a second? We need to figure out a way to get Astrid's toxin into their alcohol. Can you still use Frost's ability?"

*No, she couldn't stay focused. Focus had never been one of her strong suits and yes, she could use Frost's ability, but she shouldn't.* Kayn manoeuvred her way past the group gathered in the middle of the room and flopped down on the bed with her limbs spread out like a starfish. She started to giggle. *How in the hell were they going to pull this job off? They had no idea what they were doing and she was a loose cannon. This gong show was only going to get more comical. What did they have? Haley had instincts. Astrid had poison. Mel was a Healer and Zach had no idea what his ability was yet. She had the ability to use all of those abilities at once.* Kayn rolled over and buried her face in the pillow. *It was quite possible she wasn't thinking straight. So far today, she'd made out with Zach twice and seduced some guy working at the front desk and made him think he was sick. They hadn't accomplished anything but not being caught. Now, the big plan was to roofie Trinity.* She started laughing even harder.

Zach sat next to her and enquired, "Are you alright?"

Kayn raised her face off the pillow, grabbed it out from under herself and smoked him with it as she responded, "Think about it. Our big plan is to break into each room and roofie Trinity. There has to be a faster way to do it?"

Astrid sat on the edge of the bed and said, "Alright, if you have a better idea, let's hear it."

She suggested, "What if I borrowed Astrid's ability and try to use Frost's at the same time? I'll intercept one of the Trinity, kiss him and ask him nicely to spit in everyone's drinks. Once they're out, we'll stroll right in and take the girl. Why make this more complicated than it needs to be?"

Looking at her, Mel questioned, "I know you managed to use it on the clerk at the front desk but can you use it to control one of us?"

Kayn glanced at Zach. He was next to her on the bed. Their impromptu make-out session was still fresh in both of their minds.

He rather bluntly answered, "Trust me, it's not going to be a problem."

A look passed between the two. *He knew she couldn't control that ability, any more than he'd been able to control his reaction to it. It was in both of their best interests to just pretend it hadn't happened.* Kayn's stomach rumbled loudly. *She wished they'd ordered that pizza someone had mentioned earlier. They didn't have time now and once their plan started, they'd have to run as soon as they got their hands on the girl they were searching for. They'd probably be eating cookies, granola bars and gas station subs in the RV for days.*

"Well, let's do this," Astrid declared. "Take some of my ability so we can get this plan underway."

*Astrid's gift wasn't one, she wanted to keep.*

Astrid extended her hands to Kayn nervously, winced and whispered, "Be gentle with me."

Kayn smiled as she took her friend's hands. Almost immediately hers began to heat up. The energy travelled up her arms into her chest, where it caused the embers of her Conduit ability to combust. Every nerve ending in her body lit up. Now, there was no control. Intense waves of euphoria rocked her soul as her body absorbed the new ability. Astrid's eyes widened. She began to struggle.

Zach stepped in and asserted, "Kayn. That's enough. You're hurting her."

*She'd lost herself for a moment there.* Kayn released her grasp on Astrid's hands, catching a glimpse of the clearly visible veins on her arms. *She needed more. Why bother drugging anyone? She could just walk upstairs, pound on the door and ingest their abilities. She was absolutely ravenous. The primal instinct to continue to feed her ability caused her to gap out staring at Mel.*

Mel nervously cleared her throat as she glanced at Zach and hinted, "Duty calls."

*She could just take her healing ability. She wanted it and it was becoming increasingly difficult to talk herself down.*

She heard Zach's voice say, "Are you still with us?"

Kayn snapped out of the trance enough to ominously respond to his voice without removing her eyes from Mel. *Her next logical meal,* "I need more."

Zach knelt before her and whispered, "Come back to me.

Remember where you are and what we're supposed to be doing."

Mel dared to come closer, "Kayn's not going to hurt me. She'd never hurt me. I'll give her some of my ability."

*Yes, by all means, come closer and make this easy.*

Zach stood his ground as he cautioned, "She's not in control. I can feel it."

Kayn glared at her Handler. *He needed to move out of the bloody way and let her do what she needed to do.* She touched her fingertips together and they sparked with energy. She slowly started to pull them apart.

"Brains before brawn!" Haley announced as she tossed a bucket of ice water at her.

*What in the hell?* Instantly brought back to reality, Kayn shook her head as her breathing returned to normal. She regained her ability for rational thought. After a drawn-out silence, she laughed. The tension in the room instantly dissipated. She looked at Haley and exclaimed, "Thank you, I needed that."

Cupping her cheeks in his hands, Zach confessed, "That Conduit ability is getting a wee bit freaky."

*She was a wee bit embarrassed.* She apologized, "I'm sorry, I guess it takes time to learn to feed in moderation. I think I'm alright now. We might as well get this ridiculous plan underway."

# 9

# IT'S A DRAGON THING

She strolled across the dated mustard yellow carpet to the door.

As Zach followed her, he asserted, "I'm coming with you now, for obvious reasons."

She shook her head as she turned the knob, opened the door, and walked right into Thorne. *Oh, crap!*

The immortal's lips curved into a knowing smile. Thorne chuckled, "I figured I'd stop by and make sure you're aware we know you're here before you kids try something epically stupid." He stepped closer to the door and said, "Aren't you going to invite me in so we can speak freely?"

*She was sure she could take him.* Kayn stepped back into the room, allowed him to come in and closed the door.

Thorne locked eyes with Mel as he confessed, "I'm glad you made it out of the Testing."

Mel appeared to be at a loss for words, so Zach pretended

Thorne was speaking to everyone as he replied, "I'm sorry Trinity didn't make it out. They were good people. We really liked them."

Thorne directed his response to Zach, "They were a great group of kids."

The conversation paused for a minute before Thorne continued to speak, "I'd imagine we're all here for the same person. We haven't found her yet, so there's no point in drugging us for someone we don't have. I just thought we could skip all that unnecessary drama and have dinner together at the diner next door. I have a few questions about the Testing and banquet afterwards. We're all dying to know how two members of Ankh made it out after twenty years. It gives us hope that maybe the next group can bring the people we've lost out."

Zach asked the question they were all thinking, "Aren't we supposed to be enemies?"

Thorne grinned as he replied, "There's no need to start fighting until one of us has the girl." He locked eyes with Mel.

*The connection between them was impossible to ignore.*

Zach's gaze darted to his love-struck crush. He rolled his eyes as he replied, "When do you want us there?"

Trinity's leader turned to leave. As he shut the door, he responded to Zach's question, "See you in half an hour."

They all stared at the closed door. Nobody spoke, until Haley confirmed, "They aren't going to hurt us. He wasn't lying."

*Haley was an intuitionist. She had heightened instincts and impressions of people. She knew what they should or shouldn't be doing.* Kayn hadn't known her for long but she trusted her ability. They all got up without discussing the insanity of meeting a rival Clan for dinner. *They were going to dine with the enemy. Were they even allowed to do this? Would they get in trouble? Was Thorne playing them because Trinity couldn't find the person they'd been searching for?*

Zach responded to her inner thoughts, "There's only one way to find out."

Kayn turned and smiled at her Handler. *He was getting good at that.*

Once again, he answered what she hadn't spoken aloud, "I only hear your thoughts."

She responded without speaking aloud, *Prepare yourself for a wacked out experience. My thoughts are all over the place.*

He flung his arm around her while teasing, "That was always obvious, even before I could hear them. Aren't you going to get ready?"

She answered aloud this time, "I'm not feeling the slightest urge to get all dolled up for dinner with Trinity." She left his side, sprawled on the bed and began flicking through the channels. Zach climbed onto the bed beside her and observed her trying to find something to watch. Mel strolled out of the bathroom, looking gorgeous. Kayn slipped a hand over Zach's to inconspicuously console him. *She wasn't feeling guilty about that kiss anymore. Mel was stoked to be spending time with Thorne. Poor Zach. After they'd kissed at the bar that night, he'd assumed things had changed. He thought he'd finally made his way out of the friendzone. He had to be disappointed.* He gave her hand a squeeze before letting go.

There was a faint flash of guilt in Mel's eyes but nothing more as she urged, "We're going to be late."

*That had to sting. She personally had no desire to impress Trinity with prompt arrival. She wasn't even sure they should be going. It felt counterproductive. Why were they wasting time socially entertaining a Clan who was after the same girl?*

Haley and Astrid were laughing as they came out of the bathroom. They strolled past Zach as Mel opened the door and they left.

Kayn wandered over to stand beside Zach. She took his hand, nodded, and prompted, "Let's go."

He turned to her and explained his hesitation, "It's going to be tons of fun watching the girl I like flirting with her ex all night. I just can't wait to get down there."

With an understanding smile, she whispered, "When you've had enough and you want to leave, I'm with you." He smirked and she wasn't sure how to take it. *She recalled Tiberius' words at the banquet before the group left for the Summit. She was a consolation prize.* She bit her lip and decided she wasn't going to let Tiberius' words affect her. *There was no point. They didn't apply here.* She loved Zach as a friend but knew he wanted Mel. She'd even promoted it and Mel was going to submarine the whole thing just as it was starting for a dance through her past with Thorne. Karma came over and gave her a shove as she realised she'd done something like this to Frost. Her situation mirrored a mistake her friend was about to make. She wanted to catch up with Mel, shake her and tell her to quit kicking herself but she knew she wasn't going to listen. *She wouldn't have listened if one of them had said the same thing about Kevin. She'd have to watch her make this mistake and be there for her when it was over.* The group descended the worn wooden stairs in record time. Zach held the door open as they entered the diner. She gave him an empathetic smile as they strolled in. Kayn stopped him and whispered, "She may still want him but she can't have anything real with him, not anymore. This is nothing." *She knew this to be the truth. She'd learned this the hard way.*

Zach nodded as he whispered his reply, "I really wanted something more with her. I always have. Even if I'm just kidding myself."

*He wasn't. He had stirred up feelings in Mel but there was no point in trying to clarify anything now.* Kayn draped her arm over his shoulder and quietly added one last commentary on his situation before they reached the table buzzing with conversation. "I'd suggest trying to make her jealous but I have no idea what I'm talking about. So, there's no point in taking advice on your love life from me."

He winked and teased, "Probably not but feel free to flirt with me."

She shook her head at her friend slash Handler as they slipped into the only free seats at the table. *They weren't sitting in a pleather booth this time. The skin on the back of her thighs would thank her later.* She noticed a familiar man at the other end of the table. It was Frey, her uncle by genetics alone. She'd met him at the banquet before the others left the newest members of each Clan at that campsite for a week while they attended the Summit. *It had been awkward to say the least. What do you say to a relative who never played a role in your life? He was in an opposing Clan which meant he never could.* He looked up from his menu and smiled. She returned the gesture. Neither one attempted to start a conversation. *What would be the point?* Mel glanced over at her and winked before turning her attention to Thorne. *She'd been where Mel was and look at how that turned out for her.* With the desire for something spicy, Kayn scanned the menu, silently cursing at the bland choices. When the waitress came by to ask for her order, she hadn't decided. Following Zach's lead, she ordered a steak. When asked how she wanted it she felt the urge to order it rare and ask for hot sauce.

Glory smiled at her as she remarked, "You know that's a Dragon thing."

Kayn looked up from her drink and felt her stomach curdle. She responded to Glory by saying, "I didn't know that." Mel appeared to be in seventh heaven hanging out with her new Clan and her old one. Her stomach tightened again. *Something was about to happen. Maybe, they were about to poison their food. What were they doing? They knew better than this. Thorne hadn't been lying about the fact that they didn't have the girl. From her vantage point in the conversation, she knew they also had no idea who she was. It was a girl. That's all the information either Clan had to go on.* Thorne was speaking to her. She hadn't been listening at all.

He cleared his throat and repeated, "I heard about the virgin sacrifice thing. I just want you to know that will never happen again. I heard the Guardians were livid."

*The leader of Trinity asked her a loaded question and she had to respond without lying, because he would know. That was his ability.* Kayn gave him a one-word reply, "Good." Her stomach knotted again. She changed the subject. "So, what's the real reason behind this dinner? Are you trying to get into Mel's pants or are you planning to drug us and leave us tied up somewhere?"

Grinning, Thorne shook his head, admitting, "I found it

difficult to believe you turned out to be the Dragon. I see it now. Shall I be blatantly honest? Can you handle it?"

Kayn nodded. She'd always been intrigued by Thorne. He was charming but not in the same way as his brothers. He radiated calm sensibility and had kind eyes. She knew he would tell her the truth.

He stared directly into her eyes as he confessed his true motives, "They've obviously thrown you guys into this job without explaining a damn thing to you to see if you'll sink or swim. I get it. We saw you in the diner. We knew you were here and suspected you were alone. When you took the room below us, you forgot to circle the room with salt so we couldn't detect you. We were sitting upstairs while our friend Jakob over there." Thorne pointed at a guy who waved at everyone. "Was listening to your conversation, relaying your rather inept plots to the group. When your plans started to venture into the ridiculous, we decided to let you know we knew you were here. Normally, we'd just go down there, kill all of you and leave you there, but some of us still have a soft spot for Mel. We're still dealing with the loss of our people in the Testing and Mel used to be one of us, so we decided as a group to help her out. None of us know who the target is, but once we do, we'll take her. If you find her first, we'll take her from you, by any means necessary. We're having dinner together to let you guys know where you went wrong."

Zach spoke first, "We didn't even bring salt."

Thorne grinned as he replied, "Well, for future reference, you're always going to need to have some on hand."

*Glory was staring at her.* Kayn met her unwavering gaze and asked, "Is there something in my teeth?"

Glory smiled as she replied, "Nothing in your teeth. I'd just love to see what you can do. You've got Frost or Lily's ability. There's no hiding from anyone with those potent pheromones. What else can you do?" She met her eyes, eagerly anticipating Kayn's response.

"Anything I want," Kayn boldly decreed.

The gorgeous Trinity smirked and provoked, "Except hide from us."

With a genuine smile, Kayn admitted, "You obviously have me there."

Their meals arrived and as it was placed before her, she stared at the still bloody steak. *It looked good, really good.* She dumped a grotesque amount of hot sauce on the slab of oozing meat and cut off a bite. *Heavenly.*

Zach grimaced, displaying his displeasure to what she was eating. He shuddered as he continued to eat his own steak that didn't look like it was capable of getting up and running away. *It felt like someone was watching her.* When she looked up, it turned out to be everyone. *They were all staring.* They quickly averted their gaze as she noticed. Everyone except for Frey, her absentee uncle.

Frey knit his brow and asked, "Does that actually taste good?"

She took another bite and responded with her mouth full by nodding.

Her uncle intently watched her for a moment before blurting out, "Were you really a virgin?"

Kayn choked on her meat. Zach slapped her back a few times and said, "You alright?" With a partially immortal lie detector sitting across the table from her, she answered his question with a question, "Are you really concerned or just asking out of sheer curiosity?"

With a sombre demeanour, Frey confessed, "Honestly, it's a little of both."

*She would have to change the subject.* Kayn coldly met his eyes and stated, "Haven't you heard? I'm a Dragon. I have no feelings on the subject." *This was true, she didn't.*

Frey took a drink from his mug and sparred, "I don't buy into that Dragons don't have emotions crap. If you can feel rage, you have emotions."

Thorne corrected Frey by saying, "Dragons are just able to compartmentalize them easier than the rest of us can. They can dull their emotional responses down when it's required of them. That's why Dragons are usually the best warriors." Thorne smiled at her and raised his glass to salute her before having a drink of his beer. He looked directly at Kayn and said, "Let's just take that topic off the table." *He was an observant guy.* The waitress came around with a jug of water to refill their glasses. Kayn thanked her and the depressed looking girl gave her a forced smile as she left. Mel was mesmerized by her. *The girl with the puffy eyes, was having a difficult time keeping it together in public.* Kayn always found herself curious about people's stories. *Had she just been dumped? Had she just been chewed out by her boss in the backroom? She'd been crying.* Mel took a drink of her water and excused herself, saying she had to go to the bathroom. She glanced back at Kayn and swiped a saltshaker from a table as she passed by it. *What's going on here?* Intrigued, Kayn had a drink of water and excused herself from the table. She leaned over and whispered in Zach's ear, "My monthly visitor." *She knew Jakob had amped up hearing. The fastest way to shut down a boy's curiosity was to bring up cramps or girly issues.* Kayn pushed open the bathroom door. Mel was standing in front of the mirror. She turned pointed at the circle of salt on the floor and Kayn stepped into the circle.

Mel whispered, "Let there be silence outside of this circle. Let there be silence inside this circle? One of those should work."

She whispered, "Does that door lock?"

Mel quietly replied, "No, it doesn't. We'll have to be fast. That waitress, she's the girl."

"How can you tell?" Kayn whispered back.

"It's her aura. I've been seeing them since we came out of the Testing. Hers is mostly yellow. They said I'd know. I'm not sure how, but I just do."

The door creaked to signal that someone was about to come in. They managed to kick some of the salt under the sink. *They were about to be busted. It was Astrid.* They both exhaled and laughed.

"What's taking you two so long?" Astrid whispered.

Kayn continued to hide the salt on the floor as Mel mouthed the words, "I found her. We need to lose Trinity. I need a pen and something to write on."

"I only caught half of what you said," Astrid admitted.

Mel mouthed the words, "We need to lose Trinity."

They strolled out of the bathroom Mel staggered and collapsed. *What in the hell?* Astrid went down to. *The whole restaurant was asleep. What in the hell?* Kayn's vision wavered. *They'd all been drugged, including Trinity. Now, there's a plot twist nobody anticipated.* The door jingled as her vision clouded. *It was Triad.* She tried to remain standing. Her knees couldn't hold her weight. They buckled as she dropped to the floor.

Tiberius knelt beside her, taunting, "Interesting, you lasted the longest, Candy Kayn. We'll be taking the girl." He kissed her square on the lips and whispered, "Good try though. Better luck next time kid."

In her barely coherent state, she remembered she'd taken Astrid's ability and smiled. *Enjoy the ride, Asshole.* The lights went out.

# 10
# HEALING GAMES

She stirred to the familiar steady hum of tires and opened her eyes. *She was on her bunk in the RV. They'd come out of the bathroom, everyone in the restaurant was out cold. What happened after that?* Kayn heard laughter coming from the backroom. *Was she the last one awake?* She yawned and stretched. *She recalled seeing Tiberius. Triad had drugged both Clans. They were probably heading down the highway in pursuit of the girl.* She swung her legs over the side of her bunk and valiantly attempted to manoeuvre her way to the bathroom even though she still had weak legs. *The TV was on.* Kayn peaked into the room and saw the sleeping bodies of the four Clan members she'd been on the job with. *Who was driving?* She bolted back down the hall and through the tiny kitchen area into the front with adrenaline induced agility. Lexy was driving and Grey was in the passenger seat sound asleep.

Lexy shook her head slowly and probed, "I'm curious. Why

would you guys be in a diner having dinner with Trinity? What in the hell was that about?"

Kayn held onto the back of the seats to steady herself as she replied, "I knew it was a bad idea. Thorne showed up at our room and told us they knew we were there and they'd heard everything we'd been talking about because we hadn't used salt."

Lexy knit her brow and questioned, "Used salt?"

They drove over a bump and Kayn almost lost her footing as she explained, "The salt circle and that chant. Silence inside or outside of the circle. You know what I mean."

Grinning, Lexy stated, "Jakob was there. He's good. He can tune into anyone, anywhere." She scowled in Grey's direction and said, "Smack him for me, he's not supposed to be asleep."

Kayn smacked Grey and his eyes popped open. He looked at Lexy, wondering how she'd slapped him from way over there. Kayn giggled and Grey noticed she was standing behind him.

He smiled at her and ribbed, "Oh, I see. She got you to do her dirty work."

Lexy chuckled, "It's a good thing we were following you guys. Rule of thumb...if two of the Clans are at a job then the third is bound to show up."

*How much had they seen?*

Grey grinned at her and teased, "Yes, I totally saw that. You're a glorious kisser. Anytime you want some more practice, feel free to call on me."

Lexy glared at her obnoxiously flirtatious Handler and sighed, "Oh, just go ahead and smack him again."

Kayn laughed as she smacked him. Chuckling, Grey rubbed his head, pretending to be wounded. She held onto the back of the seats as they went over another bump and apologized, "Sorry we screwed up and lost the girl."

Grey glanced at Lexy and smiled as though they had a secret.

Kayn probed, "What?"

"We didn't lose anybody," Lexy replied. "She's locked in the bathroom. We haven't had time to deal with her yet."

Glancing back, Kayn said, "What if someone gets up and goes in there?"

"She's out cold and there's a sign on the door," Grey explained.

Looking back at the bathroom again, Kayn smiled and shook her head. *They were driving down the highway with a kidnapped waitress in the back of the RV.* She asked, "How did you get her from Triad?"

Grey piped in, "Let's just say, Lexy's Summit shenanigans came in handy. Hey, did Astrid kiss Tiberius? He was higher than a kite. I doubt he'd be dumb enough to drug himself."

Kayn grinned. It was her turn to appear to have a secret.

Lexy smiled and pressed, "Oh, just spit it out."

"It was me. He kissed me, right before I passed out and I'd taken some of Astrid's ability." Lexy knit her brow but said nothing. *Was that a hint of jealousy over Tiberius, she detected?*

Lexy responded to her private thoughts, "Not jealousy but confusion. I kissed him and it had no effect on me."

*Lexy kissed Tiberius?*

"It's because you're already crazy," Grey teased.

Lexy gave Grey a dirty look. Kayn smacked him without her having to ask and she smiled.

Kayn heard the blinkers. Lexy turned off the highway and began to drive down a gravel road.

She explained, "The others will be up soon, everyone is going to need to use the bathroom. Lexy motioned to Grey. He opened the glove compartment and handed Kayn a gold ring with the symbol of Ankh on it. "This one is for you. Wait until she wakes up, give her the speech, brand her and kill her."

With the ring between two fingers, Kayn stared at it. *Was she really the best choice for this?* She slipped it on her finger, nodded and flippantly responded, "Why not?"

Lexy gave her a genuine smile. She winked and replied, "Now, that is how a Dragon responds to a challenge."

They turned off at a sign for a campground and when the motorhome came to a complete stop, Kayn walked back to the bathroom. Mel was standing at the bathroom door when she arrived.

Mel questioned, "Who was driving?"

"Lexy was, and the girl is in the bathroom." Kayn grinned as she read the piece of paper, they'd taped to the door that warned, *Waitress in bathroom.*

The door opened. Grey's voice yelled from outside, "It's hooked up! You're good to go!"

Lexy's voice hollered from the front, "Come have breakfast before you kill her. I'm sure there's plenty of time."

Mel shot her a strange look. Kayn showed her the ring on her finger and a lightbulb visibly glimmered above Mel's head.

"You're going to do it?" Mel questioned as they made their way back to the kitchen. "How did we get her? What happened?"

"Lexy and Grey took her from Triad," Kayn responded.

Mel gave her a peculiar look. *She probably didn't remember anything past leaving the bathroom.* As they ate a bowl of cereal, she relayed the story.

They chatted as the rest gradually awoke from a Triad induced slumber and made their way to the table where they were given the details of what happened as they lay dreaming. Grey had this enormous grin on his face. He kept looking at Zach and then at her. *The others didn't know about what they'd done to try to conceal themselves from Trinity before they understood that Trinity had always known they were there. Keep your mouth shut Greydon.* They'd all been awake for a good hour when she began to wonder if the girl in the bathroom was still asleep. *Was she smart enough to know she shouldn't call out for help?*

Zach stood up and complained, "I really need to go to the bathroom. We need to find another place to store the waitress."

Grey casually took a drink of his coffee and urged, "Well, what are you waiting for? Go back there and see if she's up."

Zach sighed dramatically, wandering back to the tiny, locked bathroom, muttering under his breath about how this wasn't his job.

Kayn took that as a hint to get up and go with him.

He tapped lightly on the door and said, "Are you awake? Don't freak out. I'm opening the door." Zach unlatched the lock on the outside. He was immediately smoked in the face by the toilet plunger and shoved out of the way by the crafty waitress with an escape plan.

Kayn stood in front of her, rather effectively blocking the small hallway. The girl gripped the toilet plunger and swung it back as though she were going to do the same thing to her. Kayn stared the girl down as she threatened, "I wouldn't do that if I were you."

"Why not?" The tougher than she looked tiny built waitress declared.

She moved in one direction and Kayn manoeuvred to block her. She dodged in the other and Kayn aggressively pinned her against a bunk until she stopped struggling without even breaking a sweat.

The girl defiantly lifted her chin and hissed, "Wasn't massacring my whole family enough?"

Kayn tightened her grip and stated, "If I'd done your families Correction, you wouldn't be standing here." The feisty young girl started struggling again. "It wasn't us," Kayn clarified. "You must want to know why they died? I still remember how it felt when my family was killed. How fresh is this for you? When did they die?"

The girl stopped struggling and whispered, "It's only been a couple of months. What is this? Who are you?"

Kayn released her grip on the small-framed teenager and the girl bravely stood to face her. *She didn't seem ready to flee. This girl was prepared to fight. She was so numb from the loss of her loved ones, she had nothing left to lose.* Kayn looked into the girl's eyes as she questioned, "Did you die too, or did you fight and survive?"

Looking at her like she was certifiable, the new girl countered, "If I died that day I wouldn't be standing here right now, would I?"

*She knew nothing about what was coming for her.* Kayn explained, "When the Correction came for my family, I was in a coma for seven months. I started to remember things about the period while I was asleep. I was told three Clans of immortals would be coming for me. I also knew I had to go with the first one that came. We're Clan Ankh and you were granted a second chance at life as a sacrificial lamb for the greater good, just as we all were." The girl's expression changed. Her words had triggered a memory. She saw it in her eyes. She looked at the name tag on her uniform. *Convenient. Her name was Molly.* Kayn began the speech, "Molly, this isn't the end of your life, that's already happened. You made a choice and this is the result of that decision. This is the beginning of your new life. Are you ready for it?"

Molly raised her eyes to meet hers and bravely replied, "Yes, I am."

Kayn rotated the ring to the inside of her hand as she continued, "This symbol prohibits you from entering the hall of souls each time you die. You will be bound to us and we will be spiritually bonded to you. We will be your new family. Give me your hand."

The brave girl extended her hand without hesitation. Kayn branded her flesh with the symbol of Ankh. The girl only had time for a shriek of pain as Kayn snapped her neck and she crumpled to the floor. *It was done. She was Ankh.* She twisted her ring around and walked back down the hall to the others. She met Lexy's eyes and knew she was proud of her.

Mel got up, asking, "Shall we bring her back now?"

Smiling, Lexy remarked, "I'm so happy there's another Healer. Neither of us will have to die to bring her back. She followed Melody down the hall, patting Kayn on the shoulder as she passed. "Good job Brighton."

Kayn suggested something unusual, "If one of you lets me absorb some of your ability, all three of us can do it."

Lexy knit her brow as she enquired, "Are you sure you're ready for that?"

Kayn smiled and responded, "Why not?" She grinned and

motioned for Zach to come along, just in case. *She knew the drill.* The others stayed behind as they dragged Molly's body into the open room at the back and knelt around it.

"I'm the strongest, use mine," Lexy offered, holding out a hand.

Kayn held out both of hers. Lexy took the hint and gave her the other one. She let go of her inhibitions and her hands began to warm and tingle. They heated until the sensation began travelling up both arms. It surged into her torso with shivers of adrenaline that overwhelmed her with a euphoric sense of power. *She didn't want to let go but she was trying to prove she could control her ability.* Kayn winced as she yanked her hands away. Mel took Lexy's hand after, refreshing the healing energy Kayn siphoned.

Zach took Melody's hand and urged, "Use mine, I'm not doing anything."

With the two Healers running at full capacity, Kayn realised she had no idea how to pass the energy out of her body into somebody else's. She questioned, "How do I pass this on?"

Lexy and Melody placed their hands on the newest member of Ankh. Kayn followed suit, a little concerned she'd continue siphoning energy and take them all down.

Seeing the concern in her eyes, Mel assured, "You can do this."

*She was going to try. Maybe the ability would work on autopilot as Frost's had and guide her actions. She thought about what she wanted to do.* The sensation reversed as it warmed her torso, surged in her chest, travelled down her arms instead of up and left her body from the palms of her hands. She felt lightheaded as Molly opened her eyes.

They all smiled as the girl who looked too small to be sixteen declared, "That sucked." Her abrupt declaration was followed by nervous laughter. They helped her up and introduced themselves.

Weeks passed before there was a chance to meet up with the rest of the Clan. *According to the texts Grey and Lexy received, the others had acquired a new boy. She'd been staring at her cheap burner cell for weeks wondering why she even had it. Not one message. She'd been told to keep it on. Why?* Her phone beeped. Kayn smiled as she looked down at the screen. *It was from Zach. He was sending her a message because he knew she wanted one.* She grinned as she sent one back even though he was only a few feet away. This became a thing they did from time to time. She was going through serious Frost crush withdrawals. She'd been spending her nights lost in her twin's memories of him. The dreams of Kevin and what he was doing or who, were now few and far between. Most nights as she drifted off to sleep, she'd think about the night Frost appeared in her bedroom and changed her life. She'd carry on dreaming of the naughty things they'd do if only they were allowed. After a night in his arms lost in a dream that had been nothing less than earth-shattering bliss, she heard his voice. She opened her eyes. He was sitting on the bunk next to her and by the look on his face, he knew exactly what she was dreaming about.

He stretched out next to her on the bunk, teasing, "I was worried you'd forgotten all about me. It's good to know some things never change." He rolled onto his side and whispered, "That Molly girl looks like she's thirteen."

"She does, doesn't she?" Kayn replied as she turned to face him.

"Did you miss me?" He whispered.

She caught herself thinking about the last time they were lying on this bunk together and wished he was under the covers with her instead of on top of them. "You left without saying goodbye," she whispered back. She bit her lip, hoping she didn't have morning breath.

He kissed her cheek and whispered, "I'd never care about that. Now, hurry up and get ready, we're going out for breakfast." He got up and wandered away.

She slipped out from under the covers. With a skip in her step, she made her way to the bathroom in the dark. *Everyone was still asleep. How early was it? Maybe just they were going out for breakfast?* She quickly got ready and tiptoed back down the hallway. *It was just the two of them and it was still dark outside. What was he up to?* Her heart soared. Frost opened the door and she saw Zach, Lexy, Grey and Lily waiting in the truck. Her romantic fantasies deflated like a balloon losing air from a pinprick as she climbed in and asked, "What time is it?"

Grey replied, "It's the crack of frigging dawn. We're going to go somewhere cool to watch the sunrise."

"No breakfast then?" Kayn questioned. *Now that she knew she probably wasn't getting any, she was hungry.*

Frost was sitting in the front with Lily and Zach. She was in the backseat with Lexy and Grey. *Yes, this definitely wasn't the romantic scenario she'd hoped it would be. Maybe she needed to give her head a good shake.* Grey tossed her a granola bar. She grimaced as she took it. *This wasn't exactly what she had in mind.* Frost kept looking in the rearview mirror while he was driving, smiling at her. She stared out the window wishing she could just go back to bed. *It was the dreams. They were messing with her. In reality, she was emotionally unavailable right now. He was too old and wise to walk into that situation. He'd said as much. Well, those weren't the words he'd used. He'd referred to her as being in the train wreck stage.* The others were chatting about stuff that happened while they were apart. *Well, she was awake now, she might as well watch the sunrise and eat her frigging granola bar with a smile.* She bit into the granola bar. *Frost was grinning at her in the rear-view mirror again. What was he up to?*

They kept driving for what felt like hours until the sunrise began and pulled over at a lookout perched above a small town nestled in a valley. They all got out of the truck to watch as the sun peaked over the mountain top in the horizon. The streetlights flickered out in the town below. *It felt like they'd driven a long way to watch a mediocre sunrise.*

Standing beside her, Frost baited, "Guess where we're going next?"

Kayn's face lit up with fake enthusiasm as she replied, "Where?"

Ignoring her sarcasm, he announced, "That town down there has the best breakfast spot. We'll be staying there for a day, possibly two. None of us brought anything with us. I have an Aries Group card. We'll go shopping and get whatever we need. I'm sure we'll find something to do."

She stared at the sedate looking town. *What was so great about this place? The restaurant must be fantastic if it was worth waking up hours before the crack of dawn and driving this far.*

Lexy gave Grey a knowing smile and teased, "Awe, this is so sweet Greydon. You shouldn't have. My birthday isn't until next week."

*She was missing something but suspected it wouldn't be difficult to figure out. She felt queasy.*

Frost motioned to the truck and nudged, "Come on everyone, let's have breakfast."

They were all grinning as they strolled back to the truck like they had a secret. Kayn's stomach cramped and it became clear.

Zach cringed as he whispered in her ear, "This is a job."

She nodded without offering a verbal response. Her stomach cramped again. *It wasn't necessary. It was painfully obvious. She knew it was a job.* Frost kept glancing at her in the rearview mirror. *There was a time when she would have been afraid or nervous, but she was different now and the idea of being in a fight made her almost giddy.* She couldn't stop smiling. She was practically bouncing in her seat as she turned to look at Lexy. Grey was smiling and shaking his head at her. As they drove down what was clearly the main street, she took in the scenery. It was a picturesque little town. *It looked like it belonged on a postcard.* Spotless sidewalks with cobblestone planters full of flowers and perfectly sculpted trees. There was just a hint of fall in the air. *It was quite lovely.* They passed a man walking out to his vehicle with colours surrounding him, like he'd brought his own sunset. *Melody told her about this. All Healers must see auras. She could see them now too. Why was she only seeing this now, though?* Looking directly at Lexy, she announced, "Now, that's trippy."

"You haven't seen anything yet," Lexy chuckled.

Zach twisted around to look at her from the front seat and questioned, "What are you guys talking about?"

Kayn pointed at the man that was now a speck in the distance and replied, "I could see that guy's aura. I guess I haven't lost the healing ability yet. It's been almost a month. I just assumed it would be gone by now."

Zach glanced back as he answered, "You've been on a steady diet of me. Mel and Lexy have been topping me up after every snack. Maybe that's why?"

Lily squirmed in her seat and proclaimed, "There it is. That's the place. Jenna said it was named after a children's poem."

Kayn glanced where Lily was pointing. The sign above the restaurant read, Humpty Dumpty's. *That's original.* Frost parked the truck by the side of the road. They all got out and stretched. *She was hungry and not just for food of the mortal nature.* Her stomach ominously clenched and she grinned.

Zach stopped her and offered, "Take some of mine if you need some."

*Her Handler was becoming more intuitive with each passing day as far as her needs were concerned.* She smiled at him and responded, "I have a feeling you're going to need every ounce of energy you have. I'll be alright."

# 11

# SMELLS LIKE BACON

When the group walked through the doors without the jingling sound of bells, she was a little disappointed. Only a few patrons were dining in the restaurant with visible auras, surrounded by a haze of purples and oranges. *It was quite beautiful. They looked like they'd been on the road for a long time. They were probably the drivers of those rigs parked down the street. A Healer's ability was seriously cool. This whole restaurant was amazing.* It was all burgundy and a class above their usual dining experience. *Why would a nice place like this be open this early in the morning?* A waitress appeared from the kitchen area and froze when she saw them at the table. *Her aura was different. There was a grey and black smoky looking mist around her.* She quickly darted back into the kitchen area. *What was she?*

Lexy kicked her under the table and whispered, "They can't tell that we're anything other than normal people unless they see the symbol of Ankh on the palms of our hands. Just play it cool."

Confused, Zach whispered in her ear, "What are you two talking about?"

"I'd be willing to hazard a guess that our waitress isn't mortal. Her aura is all grey and black. It's a smoky film, not a glow," Kayn quietly responded. She got up to get menus out of the wooden container on the counter. Zach grabbed for her arm. She darted out of the way and chuckled, "I'm just going to go over there to get some menus. They're sitting in plain sight. Our waitress appears to be missing in action." Kayn wandered over to the counter and snagged six menus just as their not so mortal waitress appeared from the back room.

The lady with the smoky aura began to apologize right away and Kayn assured her that it was fine. She was just going to grab the menu's herself.

"I apologize for the wait, we're understaffed. Would you all like some coffee?" The pleasant lady asked.

*She was a wolf in sheep's clothing. If she were a normal girl, she'd be none the wiser.* Kayn smiled sweetly and answered, "Yes, coffee sounds wonderful. How come you guys are open so early?"

The waitress responded, "We get a lot of truck drivers passing through early in the morning. It tends to be our busiest time of the day. This morning is obviously an exception. I'll be there in a second with your coffee." She nodded at Kayn and briskly marched back into the kitchen area.

Kayn strolled back to the table with menus in hand and a knowing smile as she passed the menus out and slid into her seat with a sweet self-satisfied expression on her face.

Frost started to laugh, "You should have seen the look of

sheer terror on Zach's face when that waitress came out of the back room. It was amazing."

Kayn glared at Zach and directed, "Mello yourself out my friend. Have a beer or something."

"It's six o'clock in the morning. Who drinks at six am?" Zach mumbled as he opened his menu, trying to pretend he was interested in ordering and not the least bit terrified at what she might do next.

Grey had the giggles. Lexy scowled at him, asking, "Is something funny?"

"Nope, nothing at all," Grey commented, opening his menu.

Lily slowly shook her head and sighed, "You guys are so whipped."

Looking up from his menu, Zach questioned, "How am I whipped? She's not my girlfriend or anything."

Lily grinned, hid behind her menu and teased, "That's not what I heard."

*Grey must have told her about the kiss, during that first job alone. Wonderful.*

"That was a distraction to get out of a sticky situation with Trinity. It went a little further than it was supposed to because our Kayn has amped pheromones and I'm..." Zach stopped speaking because Frost looked stricken.

*He hadn't been told. Oh, it's not like he doesn't use his ability every chance he gets.*

Frost looked at Zach and questioned, "No headaches or anything when you kissed her?"

Raising an eyebrow, Zach gave him a strange look as he responded, "No, why would I get a headache?"

"Interesting," Frost replied, reading his menu.

*He was jealous. When he attempted to have a more intimate relationship with her, he'd been stopped and Zach hadn't. It was easy to decipher the reasoning behind it. Zach was her Handler. They were supposed to be forming a close bond. It was Frost, she wanted. This wasn't her fault.*

Frost glanced up from behind his menu, and as their eyes met, she knew he'd heard her inner commentary. The door to the kitchen opened with a squeal and a groan.

"They should grease the hinges on that door," Grey noted, studying his menu.

The waitress arrived at their table coffeepot in hand. They passed her mugs. When she finished pouring, she said, "I'll be right back to take your orders."

Lexy mouthed, "I'd avoid ordering anything with meat."

Kayn knit her brow. *Vegetarian omelet it is.*

Lily gave Frost's arm a squeeze when the waitress appeared, saying, "It's your turn."

*The intimate gesture stung a little.* Frost ordered oatmeal. He handed the waitress his menu and started playing with his phone. *Anything, to avoid looking at her*. The door to the restaurant opened. A half a dozen strangers with ominous smoky grey and black auras strolled in. Adrenaline pulsed through her. *She couldn't worry about Frost's wounded ego. It would make her weak. Instinct told her she'd be needing all of the strength she could find today.*

Lexy kicked her under the table, quietly scolding, "Shut it down."

Kayn nodded at her fellow Dragon as her stomach growled so loudly everyone looked at her. Every hair on her body was standing on end. *She was starving.* Seeing the energy in the room was making her come unhinged.

Zach slid his hand over hers as he quietly instructed, "Just breathe."

"I need to get out of here," she whispered, trying to get away. She could hide in the bathroom until she managed to calm her ability.

Frost glared at her and ordered, "You're not going anywhere."

Meeting his eyes, Kayn explained, "I need a minute. I'll get it under control."

"Just think about something else. Someone else," Lexy directed.

Frost's leg touched hers under the table as the waitress appeared with their breakfast. She placed the omelet in front of her. *It looked delicious. The sight of real food stifled her need for the spiritual kind.* Kayn politely thanked the waitress as she dumped a disgusting amount of hot sauce on her omelet. She took a burning mouthful and felt a touch of relief. *This must be the reason she craved hot sauce.* With each bite, the tension within her drained away. She had a sip of piping hot coffee and felt his eyes on her. *He was still stewing about her kissing Zach. It wasn't that she'd made out with her Handler, it was his lack of repercussions. She was intuitive enough to know that everything happened for a reason.* She still recalled the conversation with Winnie in the in-between. *She was supposed to be discovering who she was, and what she was capable of, but with her twin sister's soul fully merged with her own, all roads led back to Frost. There used to be a tug-of-war between Chloe's desire for Frost, and her own for Kevin, but since Testing, the scales had tipped in Frost's favour. Her attraction to him was beyond reason or logic. It was an instinctual pull. She still wanted him even after experiencing his ability and knowing the trouble it could cause. She understood him now.* She peered up from her coffee cup to find him staring at her, smiling. *He'd been eavesdropping on her internal dialogue again. Wanting him back wasn't a secret.*

"I think there's something wrong with my bacon. It smells off. Should I tell the waitress?" Zach complained, scowling at his almost untouched plate.

*Zach was eating meat. Oh no. He hadn't seen Lexy's warning against ordering anything with meat in it. She'd been so off in her own little world that she hadn't noticed what he'd ordered.*

Picking up one of Zach's pieces of bacon, Kayn sniffed it. *She'd smelled that scent before. Where had she smelled that scent before?* Intently observing Zach, Lexy was waiting for his reaction. Kayn's eyes widened as she recalled where she'd smelled that scent. *He'd only taken a small bite but he'd already swallowed. It would come back up if she told him what it was.*

Shaking her head, Lexy mouthed, "Don't tell him."

Kayn whispered in Zach's ear, "It's probably gone bad. Don't eat it."

Zach grimaced and mumbled, "That was a waste of money."

*Please don't notice what it is. Please don't remember.*

The waitress popped back to refill their coffee and Zach said, "I think there might be something wrong with the bacon."

The waitress gave her token response, "I apologize. We serve thin strips of moose meat as bacon, not pig. I keep telling them they should have that written on the menu somewhere."

That seemed to pacify Zach's need for an explanation. He sniffed a piece and took a bite of it, right in front of the waitress.

*No, no! Don't do it, Zach.* He looked at her and she had to look away. *If he heard her thoughts, he couldn't react.* Smiling as he chewed it up and swallowed, their server wandered to the next table to refill coffee. The restaurant was now full and everyone was surrounded by the black and grey smoke. *If she said anything, Zach would cause a scene. It felt so wrong allowing him to eat bacon made from people. Her emotions had led her to make rash decisions in the past but she was different now.* She repeated, *brains before brawn,* in her head until he finished every bite of people meat on his plate.

"Let's go buy some toiletries and clothes. Then we'll find somewhere to stay for the night," Frost announced rather loudly.

As the waitress walked past their table, she suggested, "There are great cabins with a lake view a few blocks away. You'll see the sign for, Eagle Perch. Those are reasonable."

Frost smiled at her and said, "Add an extra ten dollars for the tip." He handed her his card.

She thanked him and replied, "I'll be right back with your receipt. She ran it through the machine and brought it back to the table. They rose from their seats and made their way out of the restaurant.

Kayn caught up to Frost, whispering, "So, what's the plan here? Are we really spending the night in a town full of...?" He lifted a finger and pressed it against his lips, to signal, she shouldn't say what she was about to say.

They got into the truck. As they started driving around to scope out the town, Frost explained, "We're going to rent a cabin. We'll stop by every business in this town and make sure they know where we are, and that we'll only be here for one night. They'll come for us and we'll show them what two Dragons are capable of."

*It's kind of funny how things change. She wasn't the least bit nervous. She was stoked. The idea of letting her inhibitions go and seeing what she was capable of was exciting.*

Concerned, Zach enquired, "What are they? How many are we fighting?"

"This is a demon infestation," Frost replied. "The sign as we arrived said the population was two hundred and seven."

*This was going to be so much fun!* Kayn couldn't stop smiling. *It was like Dragon Christmas. Her Handler's lips were parted like he had more to say but shock slowed his roll.*

Pulling it together, Zach declared, "There's no way we can kill two hundred demons, it's impossible."

Laughing, Frost sparred, "You survived the Testing. Nothing is impossible."

They turned down the dirt road leading to the cabins. Lexy glanced at her and they grinned at each other. *This was going to be awesome.* They parked and everyone got out.

Wandering to the office, Frost hollered, "Wait here. I'll be right back." He winked at her.

*The cheesy horror movie line had been directed at her. He knew she loved that stuff.* Kayn stretched her arms above her head and cracked her neck. *This was going to be epic.*

Jogging back with a key dangling from two fingers, Frost filled them in, "I told them we needed privacy. They put us in a cabin by the water. Everyone get back in, it's a bit of a drive."

They got in, pulled out and continued their journey down a narrow road. There wasn't room for more than one vehicle. If they met someone coming in the opposite direction, they'd be screwed. They drove for a few minutes through lush greenery before, pulling down a numbered driveway. Frost parked in front of a rustic log cabin. *It reminded her of where they stayed before Testing.* Grey got out, climbed into the back of the truck, unlocked the plastic storage box and hauled a case out. He lugged it to the door as Frost unlocked it. He glanced at the welcome mat and lifted it up. There was a key under the mat. Grinning, Frost held it up, commenting, "This is how they planned to get inside." He strolled into the cabin. Grey followed, hauling the heavy case.

Walking in behind Grey, Zach whispered, "Tell me this isn't going to be a bloodbath. Our bloodbath."

Grey grinned at Zach and stated, "We won't even have to leave the cabin. Lexy and Kayn are going to enjoy this. It'll be a cakewalk." The case was full of ten-pound bags of salt. Grey instructed, "Grab one. Start circling the room on the inside.

Lifting a bag, Lily piped in, "This happens. Demonic souls have possessed the entire population. These are just strong shells. There won't be any big scaly ones or sedating mist involved. We're just sending them back to where they came from. The Aries group will clean up after us."

Lexy walked in carrying a plastic case and placed it on the bed. She opened it. Inside were a dozen silver daggers engraved with the symbol of Ankh.

*This was something new.*

Noticing Kayn there, Lexy explained, "We use these on large demon count jobs. These daggers will send them to where they are supposed to go without us having to mark them with our blood and say anything."

*This must be the routine. Somebody comes into the diner and they suggest the cabins. One narrow road in and out. There was no way for a mortal to escape. These demons had quite the sick and twisted little operation going on here.* Kayn wandered around. *Everything reeked of bleach. They probably opened the door with the key from under the mat and killed the travellers in their sleep, then served them in the restaurant. Gross.*

Frost came out of the bathroom, announcing, "Time to get to know the town's residents. We'll drive in together, then split up. We'll cover more ground faster that way. I'd like to come back here and relax. It's a beautiful lake. It's a shame the whole damn town is full of cannibals."

Zach looked at Frost and said, "What did you just say?"

Lexy elbowed him. Frost answered, "Nothing. Don't worry about it. Let's go." He strolled out of the door.

*She felt guilty about not telling Zach what the bacon was made of but knew there was no time for drama.*

As they drove back into the town filled with cannibalistic demons, only some were anxious. Others were excited. The two Dragons in the backseat couldn't wipe the smiles off their faces.

Lexy took off her rose quartz bracelet and passed it to Kayn, saying, "Wear this. Take it off when we get back."

Without bothering to ask why, Kayn slipped it on. She smiled at Frost's reflection in the rearview, he grinned. *He was enjoying her enthusiastic response to the job.* They pulled over a block from the diner where they'd eaten their sketchy breakfast and all got out. The girls started walking in one direction and the boys in the other.

Lily took a card out of her pocket, announcing, "Let's go buy new clothes."

Lexy grimaced at the idea. Lily was stoked. Impartial, Kayn sighed. *She could use shorts, tank tops and yoga pants.* They entered a trendy looking boutique. *She wasn't going to find anything comfortable in here.* Lily was a girl with a mission. She moved around the store with the skill of someone who worked there. She grabbed jeans for them to try on. Kayn took the jeans from her and wandered to the back of the store in search of the changerooms. She found them easily while Lily told the ladies who worked there about the cabin they were staying at by the picturesque lake. Kayn slid the first pair of jeans on. *They fit perfectly. There was a bit of stretch in the material, they were easy to move around in.* She turned in the mirror for a rearview. *Her butt looked amazing.* Some shirts were tossed over the top of her dressing room. Lily told her to try them on. Kayn put on a delicate lace top. *It was much sexier than what she was used to wearing but she like it.* Lily was a rock star at picking out clothes for other people. They each left the store with a bag and it wasn't nearly as painful as she thought it'd be. She even had a dress. They stopped into the local florist and chatted with the people in the store about where they were staying. They asked directions to the pharmacy and went there for toothpaste, toothbrushes, and makeup. Every person they met was a demon with a smoky black and grey cloud trailing behind them. They started talking about food, Kayn glanced at the time. *It was almost three o'clock. Time flies when you're visiting every business in a small town making your whereabouts known, so demons will attempt to murder you in your sleep.* While ordering food, Lily texted the others. They needed to eat something and relax before the fight. When their take-out was ready, the guys showed up. Zach was waiting in the truck with the groceries. They passed off bags to Frost and Grey and followed them out to the vehicle loaded with stuff. Zach was beaming as he waved through the window. *What had they bought? Why was he so happy? He knew what was coming.* When she climbed into the truck, she knew why. *He was drunk. Those idiots.*

Lily sighed, "Really you guys?"

"He's a little drunk," Grey chuckled. "Not wasted, just happy. Nobody is coming until after nightfall. It won't be dark outside for hours."

Lily slid into the front seat beside him and he stared at her until she said, "What do you want Zach?"

He preened, "You're so beautiful. I really want to touch your hair."

She glanced into the back and hissed, "Greydon, I'm going to smack you for this when we get out of the truck."

Grinning, Grey sparred, "Sounds good, gorgeous. I'm willing to take one for the team... again." He glanced at Frost.

He hadn't been openly flirtatious with Lily since the banquet before the older members of Ankh left for the Summit. Kayn knew what he meant by again.

Lily rolled her eyes, turned to look at Zach and called his bluff, "Fine, go ahead."

Zach reached over to touch her glistening silky black hair. As he ran his hand down the length of it, the strands trickled over her shoulders like a midnight waterfall. Zach started laughing, "I can't, it's a joke. I'm not drunk. Do you think I'm a moron?" He winked at Grey and ribbed, "You owe me one if that spanking's amazing."

Lily smoked Zach's arm. He giggled, "Hit me harder. I can take it."

"You think you're pretty funny, don't you?" Lily sparred.

With game far beyond his years, Zach taunted, "I'll be anything you want me to be beautiful."

Lily shook her head, but she was still smiling when they pulled up to the cabin. They carried everything inside and sat down to eat. Grey and Lexy were sitting on the bed together. Lily was observant. She usually tried to guess what everyone wanted to eat. It had nothing to do with abilities. It was just something she enjoyed doing. This late lunch was more difficult. She had to order everything without meat. Kayn took a bite of her vegetarian caesar wrap and searched through the bag for the hot sauce, she'd asked for, pouting when she realised the restaurant forgot it. Frost smiled as he stood up and grabbed a small bottle of hot sauce out of a plastic bag.

*One million brownie points for Frost!* Kayn smiled and said, "Thanks."

Frost winked at her and replied, "We'll be stuck here until we've rid the town of demons and the Aries group shows up. It made sense to grab groceries." He passed her the bottle and their fingers touched. She bit her lip and met his eyes. *He was insanely gorgeous. It wasn't allowed to happen between them... yet. Yet, being the operative word. It was going to happen. It was only a matter of time, and time, was something she had an overabundance of.* She took a bite of the wrap and scowled, wishing it had chicken on it. *She knew they were relatively safe because her stomach had ceased its constant complaints.* Lexy was standing by the table staring at her when she glanced up from her meatless wrap.

"It sucks, doesn't it?" Lexy remarked.

Kayn grinned, for many things sucked at this moment. "Which thing?" She placed a hand over her mouth as she responded, still chewing her thoroughly unsatisfying wrap.

"Wanting something you're not allowed to have," her fellow Dragon replied without missing a beat.

Kayn grinned, for that could still be one of a dozen things. "It does," she answered. *She knew Lexy was talking about Grey. That wasn't a secret. Not anymore. Frost wasn't her Handler though, Zach was. Eventually she'd be in control of her ability then being with Frost would no longer be an issue.* Lexy smiled as she took another less than satisfying bite. Frost was talking to Zach. She tuned in to the conversation as he questioned, "This new girl, Molly. What's she like? She certainly doesn't look sixteen."

Zach replied, "She does look way younger, doesn't she? She's a sweet girl and much tougher than she looks."

Looking at Frost, Kayn interjected, "She's funny and a bit goofy. I can't picture her in the Testing though. I can't wait until we take her to the in-between for the first time."

Lexy grinned at her and teased, "I couldn't picture you in the Testing. I have a feeling you're going to miss out on that. She's there with the rest of our Clan right now. Do yourself a favour, don't get too attached. They rarely come back out of Testing."

*She already was. She'd been the one to mark her Ankh. It felt like she was responsible for her.* Kayn nodded as she ate the last bite of her less than satiating wrap.

Grey wandered up behind Lexy and baited, "Don't be so negative." He wrapped his arms around her waist from behind and playfully kissed her neck. She squirmed out of his arms and swatted him away.

Kayn could see it, Lexy was already trying to shut her emotions down. *Her Handler wasn't being helpful. Zach had been staring at her for a while. He seemed worried. She knew what each of his expressions meant.* Zach asked her to come for a walk. She pushed out her chair and followed him out into the crisp autumn air. They walked away from the cabin onto the rocky beach area where they sat down on a log. He picked up a rock and tossed it into the water without even trying to skip it. *He always tried to skip it along the surface. He wanted to say something.*

Zach looked at his shoes as he spoke, "I haven't been your Handler for long. Bringing you back after what you're about to do, feels like it's way above my skill level. I don't even know how the Handler Dragon thing works. It's just been happening." He picked up another smooth stone and rolled it between his fingers. He gripped it in the palm of his hand as he verbalized his fears, "What if I fail you? What if this job is too dark and I can't bring you back?"

Kayn held out her hand. Zach dropped the small rock into it without her having to ask. She closed her hand around it and urged, "Stand up."

Grinning, he rose to stand beside her. "You really want to skip rocks...now?"

She sparred, "Why not?" Kayn wound up and skipped the stone once across the shimmering surface of the lake. A fish jumped. She exclaimed, "Did you see that fish it was huge!"

Zach found another rock, explaining, "It needs to be a flat one like this." He showed her the stone. It was smooth and flat on either side. Kayn opened her hand. He dropped it into her palm. She wound up as Zach instructed, "A little more to your side."

This time when she pitched the stone it skipped three times. She raised her arms above her head, cheered and did a dance. "Bet you can't beat that one."

Zach grinned and baited, "Oh yeah?" He found another one, reeled his arm back and skipped it four times across the surface of the water. He obnoxiously cheered and danced around.

Her heart twitched as her memory flashed a picture of

Kevin as a child doing the same thing. She closed her eyes and willed the sentimental thought away. *They'd been having a moment and the joy of it had been dampened by a memory of her mortal past.* Tears formed in her eyes and she blinked them away. *Dragons don't cry. Dragons never cry. Especially Dragons that are expected to fight 207 demons at dusk.*

Zach stopped obnoxiously cheering as he noticed her solemn expression and probed, "Are you alright?"

She tried to smile as she responded, "I'm fine. You just reminded me of somebody that I used to know." *And that was who he was to her now. Somebody that she used to know. It was another life. A life that could not be compared to this one. Why was she feeling like this right now? This was an inconvenient time to rediscover her useless emotional connection to someone that was now and would always be, her enemy.*

He grabbed both of her hands and whispered, "Are you afraid you can't do it? You can tell me the truth. I know it seems impossible. It would be for me, but I don't believe for one second it's impossible for you."

"I know I can do it," Kayn disclosed. "The only thing I'm afraid of is losing myself."

Understanding what she needed, he vowed, "I know I wasn't sure I could do this. Hell, even fifteen minutes ago, I wasn't certain. I can promise you this much, I won't ever stop trying to bring you back. I'll never give up on you."

They embraced by the lake with a surface still as glass, mirroring the mountains and sky. Kayn whispered in his ear, "I know you won't." She allowed him to hold her longer than she was comfortable with. *They were both unsure of what they were capable of but her being a Dragon, was a certainty. She feared letting go of the thin thread of humanity she'd regained since their*

*Testing. He was afraid he would fail her. Their concerns were warranted. They weren't in the Testing anymore. This insanity was about to happen in the real world.*

Their touching Dragon Handler bonding moment was cut short by Lexy's booming voice, "This isn't the time for mushy crap. It's almost time to shut your emotions down. We should feed your Conduit ability and top up the healing ability. You need some of my energy. We have a plan and we're running out of daylight."

They turned to face their friends. *There was a concerned expression on Frost's face. They'd been standing there for a while.* Lexy held her hands out. Kayn walked over and took them. *This was one thing she'd never have to be asked twice to do.* Her hands gradually warmed until Lexy's healing energy travelled up her arms. Every hair on her body stood on end as the euphoria of her ability took hold. Lexy abruptly yanked her hands away, breaking the connection.

Strolling over, Grey explained, "We have a plan. We want to see how many you can hold at once. Take some of mine. I'm not sure what will happen. My Pyrokinesis was stifled by the Third-Tier."

*Why not?* Kayn took Grey's hand. *This was different.* Her hands were burning, it felt like her arms were on fire. Her tortured brain exploded. *Her pain tolerance was amped up but not this high.* Her knees buckled. In agony, she managed to keep her grip on him. She didn't break the connection until it felt like there were flames within her lungs. Grey yanked his hands away. She remained on her knees, regaining her bearings. Shivering as adrenaline surged through her, Kayn rose as power she'd never experienced pulsed through her being. Concern was silenced in preparation for the insanity ahead.

She heard each falling pinecone as haunting wind whistled through the trees. Jumping fish splashed and the nervous beating of everyone's hearts. *It was a lot to take in, but it didn't overwhelm her as it once had.* Lily tossed a knife. Sensing it sailing through the air, Kayn caught it.

Lexy grinned as she instructed, "Now cut your hand."

Kayn dragged the blade across the centre of her palm without flinching. The blood didn't even have a chance to pool at the slice before it closed. *It healed instantly. This was new.*

Grey prodded, "Try to use mine."

Kayn waved her hand but nothing happened. "I don't think I can," she admitted.

He explained how, "You're doing it wrong. Envision it on fire. Want the flames to appear, then do what you just did with your hand."

Staring at the log, Kayn imagined it on fire. Without breaking her train of thought, she pointed. It exploded with crackling flames. *This may come in handy.* Adrenaline surged through her as her emotions dimmed. *She wanted more.* She spun to see if Frost was willing. *He was already giving Lexy energy. Everyone appeared to be back to normal, except for her.* Zach doubled over, grabbing his stomach.

With warning cramps of his own, Frost grabbed Zach's arm, directing, "Leave her like this. She's ready to go. They're coming."

*Why was he whispering? She could hear everything. There was no pain in her stomach now, just a pleasurable twinge of something unusual. She was ready.*

# 12

# DEMON FIGHT CLUB

The sun had begun its ill-omened decent behind the mountain's summit. The darkening sky above cast an ominous shadow throughout the forest, as it crept slowly towards the Ankh. This darkness had the appearance of a living breathing being as it methodically extended its menacing grasp until night captured the woods.

Staring at the mountain's peak, Lexy grinned as she began her speech, "First things first. She grabbed an object out of her pocket and dropped it on the ground. "I'm sure you remember what this is. Just in case you've forgotten. This object is for blocking spiritual energy. It will also keep the demons locked within the confines of this town, so we'll have a controlled circumstance in which to send those abominations back where they belong."

Mesmerized by what Lexy dropped on the forest floor, Kayn watched. *The last time she'd seen one of these contraptions was the night the Clans fought at the house she'd grown up in. That was the night she lost her older brother Matt and Jenkins. The night Kevin was taken by Triad. Kevin...His name had to mean nothing now. If she kept saying these things to herself, perhaps one day, it would be the truth.*

Grey chuckled, "The first rule of demon fight club is, you must always clean up the evidence after demon fight club."

*Grey's sense of humour was always an effective tension breaker. It was as though they weren't about to do anything out of the ordinary. Killing two hundred and seven demons wasn't even an issue.*

Frost laughed aloud and disputed, "No, the first rule of demon fight club is you must stay the hell in the cabin while the Dragons fight. Get it right, Greydon." He turned to look at Zach and clarified, "That's your cue. Run back to the cabin, toss our Dragons a few of those Ankh swords and get the hell inside."

Grey made a revision to the list of demon slaying does and don'ts, "Okay, if that's the second rule. The third is, "Do not break that line of salt at the door of the cabin while you're running through it. Jump over it."

Zach leapt over the line of salt and came running back with demon slaying daggers in his hand. He tossed one at Lexy. She caught it in midair. He tossed one to Kayn. Zach asked, "What happens if they drop them?"

Frost looked directly at Kayn and instructed, "Fun fact, demons can't even touch those blades. With the slightest graze, they'll drop to the ground and be expelled from their shells."

*The slightest graze. She planned on doing more damage than that.*

"We're all going to go inside and find our seats for the show. This is where we find out what you two are capable of together. Take out every demon who has the balls to show up here," Frost instructed. Everyone but the two Dragons strolled back into the cabin.

Seconds later, Frost appeared in the doorway. He cast more daggers into the dirt outside. They concealed their spare weapons. *Fully prepared for this, she felt more ready than she'd ever been for anything.* Lexy motioned for her. Flush against the cabin, they noiselessly crept around the side, concealed in the shadows. With a hushed voice, Kayn probed, "What's the plan?"

Lexy whispered back, "We're going to let them walk their cannibalistic ass's right into our trap. They've sent in scouts. We'll take these first ones out easily."

*She heard snapping twigs.* Giddy with anticipation, Kayn tightened her grip on her blade. Music blared from within the cabin, making it impossible to hear anything. *That was how she'd been gaging the distance of her foes. Fricking Greydon. Her demon fight club buddy appeared to appreciate his choice in battle tunes.*

Noticing her scowl, Lexy explained, "He knows I like listening to eighties rock when I'm fighting. It's one of our things. I love a good ass kicking anthem." Lexy gingerly crept around the back of the cabin. She paused, tugged her fingerless glove off and tossed it into the dirt.

Kayn smiled for it felt like her fellow Dragon was shedding the pretence of normalcy. Just as they were about to step out of the shadows, a half dozen shells emerged from the brush. Lexy glanced back at her and remarked, "Allow me to show you how easy this is going to be. I can take all six without breaking a sweat. Watch and learn." Lexy confidently strolled out of the shadows with a dagger in hand, ran at the demons and in one swift movement, she slashed one above his collar. The shell staggered backwards clutching his throat with blood spurting from a severed artery. A cloud of smoke spewed out of his mouth into the ground. She spun around grazing multiple demon's arms and the same thing happened. The fifth assailant ran at her with a knife. She kicked him in the chest. He landed on his back with a thud. Lexy didn't finish him off while he was on the ground struggling to catch his breath. She stood there watching as he scrambled to his feet. A female shell burst out of the bushes and sliced Lexy's back with her weapon. A pool of red expanded on her light-coloured shirt. The Ankh symbol on Lexy's hand lit up and the game changed. The demons froze as Lexy lifted her shirt so they could see she was healed. Kayn's symbol heated up. She tugged her glove off and tossed it on the ground. *It was time to let these abominations know who they were dealing with.* The shell Lexy kicked to the ground fled into the bushes as she finished off the fifth demonic assailant with a swift slash of her blade. *They couldn't let him get away.* Sprinting out of the shadows, Kayn chased after it, manoeuvring uneven terrain with the agility of a mountain lion seconds from subduing its prey. The shell was fast but nowhere near as fast as she was while free to be her supernatural self. She leapt into the air and knocked him down. Raising a blade, she thrust it into his back, watching as a black cloud of smoke funnelled out of its mouth into the forest floor. Someone grabbed her by her throat and yarded her off the creature she'd subdued. Flipping it over her shoulder, she spun around to see how many there were and laughed. *She was surrounded by fifty, maybe sixty demons adorned in human flesh.* Adrenaline surged through her being as she revealed a hidden blade. With one in each hand, she provoked, "Bring it on, demon bitches!" *They had her surrounded. She was having far too much fun to care about silly things like being outnumbered. All it would take was the smallest slice to send them back to purgatory.* The hoard closed in on her. She slashed assailants from every angle until her vision was obscured by an endless mist of red and smoke as it left the parted lips of stolen bodies. She felt it each time the shell's blades penetrated her flesh, but it wasn't painful, there was an adrenaline induced pleasurable response. *How long would she last?* Operating purely on instinct, Kayn kept swinging and spinning in a continuous circular motion, with blades clutched in both hands. When the fine mist cleared and the last body dropped to the forest floor, she was standing there soaked in the blood of her enemies with piles of bodies surrounding her. *Had she accidentally killed the other Dragon in the haze of blood and demon smoke?* She heard the clinking of metal and darted to the other side of the cabin. *Lexy was dealing with a similar hoard.* Kayn sprinted around the outside of the swarm of cannibalistic beings, slicing their backs. They were now dropping from both the inside and outside of the herd. She remained on the outskirts to take each one on as they emerged from the bushes. Lexy had a method to her madness much the same as she did. Another surge of demons burst out of the bushes and Kayn took them out, one by one. The next hour was a haze of blood spray and smoke until the two Dragons were the only beings left standing.

The front door of the cabin opened, Frost announced, "I'm personally impressed. There's got to be close to two hundred out there. Great job ladies. I'll bring you some towels. Consider this immortal combat halftime. We'll check the bodies and make sure none are only playing dead. We'll do a count. After, we'll have to go door to door and make sure none have been left alive."

Incapable of responding, for she no longer had a single thought. A blank emotionless canvas, she remained there unable to move a muscle, until a voice in her mind whispered, *sleep. You need to rest.* She curled up in the fetal position in the dirt. Her eyelids grew heavy as she heard Frost's voice in the distance, "*We'll search the town at first light.*" Kayn closed her eyes and deafening silence became nothing at all.

She awoke to the overpowering scent of bleach. *It was too dark to see.* She was lying on a bed next to someone and sensed it was Zach. She felt clean and knew he'd bathed her but this time she didn't care. She was wide awake, staring into the darkness of the cabin. *Had they completed the job without her?* Having no concept of time while lost in the emotional void, she took a deep breath in and expelled air slowly. She vaguely recalled the mist of blood and smoke in the air. Her last memory was of lying down in the dirt and closing her eyes. *She needed to use the bathroom.* Kayn swung her legs over the side of the bed and manoeuvred her way through the darkness towards the crack of light glimmering from the almost closed bathroom door. She stepped into the washroom and closed the door behind her. After doing what she'd come in to do, she stopped in front of the mirror and stared at her reflection. Her eyes were vibrant green. She lifted her shirt. Her wounds were completely healed. There wasn't a mark on her flesh to show that she'd just been in an epic battle with the undead. Someone opened the door. *It didn't startle her. She knew it was Zach.*

Leaning against the door's rustic wooden frame, Zach whispered, "There's only five missing, but that's going by the population sign. In the morning, we'll go door to door and do a thorough search of each residence. Once we're certain we've killed them all, we'll call in the Aries group to dispose of any evidence."

She nodded at him while staring at her reflection. *She didn't feel like speaking... not yet.*

Zach stepped out of the doorway as he quietly urged, "Come back to bed."

Barefoot in the dark, Kayn followed the faint noise of his footsteps. She climbed under the covers. He slid in beside her, leaving space between them. *She was glad.* She needed him to be close by while maintaining the emotionally void cocoon around her. When she was ready, she would burst free and become a butterfly with a rainbow of emotions but not tonight. On this night, she needed to feel nothing. Kayn closed her eyes, and for a while, she fought the slumber her exhausted body required. Without knowing, she slipped into a dream.

In her dreams, she was standing in the silky sand of the in-between beneath the watercolour splashes of blue in the sky. She knelt in the sand. While on her knees, she picked up handfuls of glorious feeling grains and allowed them to trickle through her fingers. Feeling something amiss in her heavenly hideaway, she glanced up to the multihued majesty of the sky. A swirling black circular object was hovering above, beckoning her closer. It felt like she was being hypnotized.

A baritone voice spoke, "Come to me. I have something to show you."

Fascinated by the whirling ominous vortex, she stood directly below it.

"Do you know what you are?" The deep, disturbing voice prodded.

She confidently baited, "If you want me, I'm right here." The blackhole turned into the funnel of a tornado. She didn't move an inch or cower from the unknown. Growing impatient, Kayn stood her ground and shrieked, "What are you waiting for!" The funnel descended from the heavens, snatched her up in its swirling vortex and sucked her up into oblivion. It dropped her onto the bed where she opened her eyes and tried to scramble out from under someone who was trying to restrain her. She flailed and lashed out with every limb until she was being pinned down by something. *No! Noooo!* She clawed and scratched at what restrained her. She felt heat on her hands and euphoria, followed by a surge of adrenaline so glorious it overwhelmed her. Her back arched in response to the energy surging through her being.

Lexy's voice ordered, "That's enough Kayn! You're taking too much!"

She felt the absence of contact from her energy source. A sense of calm washed over her being and she was able to focus on her surroundings. *She'd obviously been taking Lexy's energy. Her friend looked more than a wee bit pissy.*

Kayn groggily mumbled, "What happened? Did I hurt you?" She tried to sit up, the room wavered around her and came into focus once again. *What was this?*

Lexy sat on the edge of the bed, saying, "You absorbed some dark energy last night, didn't you? It can send you on one hell of a disturbing trip."

*She honestly didn't remember. There was no way she would have had the time to do that in the middle of a fight.*

Grey wandered over to Lexy and offered, "Take some of mine."

Zach was sitting on the bed beside her. He whispered, "That was one hell of a nightmare."

Kayn sat up as she tried to explain, "I was in the in-between and there was this swirling black hole above me in the sky, it dropped down and sucked me up into it."

Lexy let go of Grey's hands. He crumpled to the floor. "Whoops," she chuckled. "My bad? I gave you shit and then took too much myself. I'll deal with him in a second. Can you move him to the other bed Frost?"

Frost grinned and sighed, "I've got him." He dragged his buddy to the other bed. Lily grabbed Grey's legs and they tossed his limp body onto the bed together.

Lexy sat beside Kayn and disclosed, "I've had that dream before. It's just a nightmare. It's no big deal. I thought you might have internal injuries that didn't heal properly. We're kind of flying blind here. We've never dealt with a Conduit's abilities before. We don't even know how long you have between siphoning someone's ability and losing it. Hell, we don't even know if you lose it. Maybe you keep them all."

*She hadn't attempted to use Grey's ability the night before. She hadn't had the time to figure it out. Did she still have it?* The sun was shining. Particles of dust pirouetted in the stream of light through the curtains. *It was such a simple moment. She'd always thought this was beautiful. The magical sight of a million particles of dust shimmering in a ray of light. Kayn allowed it in. She felt joy as her heart soared.* Kayn smiled, knowing she had found her way back on her own and managed to burst free of her emotionless cocoon in record time. *It felt like a miracle. Perhaps it was.* With an animated grin, she embraced her Handler.

Confused, Zach stiffly gave her a sturdy pat on the back. She whispered, “I’m alright. I found my way back. I’m me.”

Squeezing her tighter, Zach whispered in her ear, “Oh, thank God. That was one dark night of demon disposal.”

*She knew this was what she’d been created for. She was a weapon. A sacrificial lamb for the greater good and last night was only the tip of the iceberg.* She peered up at Frost. He was quietly watching their exchange, smiling. When their eyes met, he quickly looked away. *There was something in his eyes that she couldn’t quite place.*

Lexy had finished healing Grey. She cleared her throat and announced, “It’s time to go. We’ll separate into two groups and go door to door. One person at the front and the other at the back of each house. The third person does the internal search. We’ll work our way through the whole town, leaving no stone unturned. We must have every one of those shells accounted for and disposed of.”

*That sounded easy enough. In this line of work things were never as easy as they seemed.* Kayn was the first to step over the line of salt that hadn’t been broken the night before. She paused mid step as she laid eyes on the enormous pile of bodies in front of the cabin. *They were empty, nothing but shells.* She stood before the pile of soulless corpses and wondered who they’d been before the darkness had taken them away.

Grey proclaimed, “There’s another mountain of bodies just as large out back.”

*She didn’t need to see that one. She’d created it.* They got into the truck and headed into town. *It was an eerie drive, with not a soul in sight.* They pulled up at the diner. *Home of the sketchy people bacon.* She glanced at Zach. *He still didn’t know.*

Zach glared at her and questioned, “What?”

She smiled and replied, "Nothing important." Kayn turned away, silencing her thoughts. She climbed out of the vehicle, taking in the picturesque trap. *It was the perfect cover. How long had it taken the demons to takeover this town?*

Lexy started barking orders, "Kayn! Come inside! I'll show you how it's done!" She motioned for her to follow.

Kayn wandered after her. They slowly strolled past each booth.

Lexy grabbed the broom, tapped on the ceiling and pushed up a panel. "These panels can't hold the weight of an adult, but they might hold a child. I'm sure you remember what that demonic toddler did to you. We'll have to find the opening to the attic. It's usually in a closet."

Kayn nodded as she followed Lexy into the kitchen. *It was empty. They would have sensed the presence of any unsavoury beings. No survivors were hiding in this restaurant. She was certain of that.* Kayn opened a metal door. *It was the freezer.* She grimaced at its contents. *If she'd had any residual guilt over slaying two hundred demons the night before, the freezer's contents cured that glitch.* She called Lexy over, "Take a look at this sick shit."

Lexy peered into the room full of icy bodies eerily suspended from the ceiling by meat hooks. She stated, "It's a shame it took so long for us to find out about this place." She stepped into the freezer and wedged the door open with multiple things. "If you watch what I'm doing here. It might save you from getting locked in a freezer in the future. First, you always take the necessary precautions. You're going to want to make sure you've inventively wedged the door open, with more than one object. That way you'll always have enough warning before you get locked inside."

Kayn watched as Lexy wandered through the creepy display of frozen people meatsicles. *This is so messed-up.*

Her fellow Dragon disappeared in the back of the room and reappeared with an announcement, "The entrance to the attic is in the back, it's all clear. Off to the next store."

They searched the whole town this way, store by store and residence by residence. This continued for hours until they were only a few houses and the school away from having thoroughly searched the entire town. *They hadn't found one demon. Perhaps they'd all been killed and their job here was completed?* They decided to split up for the last two houses and search the elementary school as a group. Kayn wandered up the cement walkway of a light blue house with a mailbox that was a miniature version of the home. *It was kind of cool.* Zach stood watch as she broke a small decorative stained-glass window beside the door, reached inside and unlocked it. Smiling pictures of the family that dwelled within the house prior to the demonic takeover adorned the walls of the landing. *A vision of her own family's pictures flashed through her mind. She blinked the images away. No, she wasn't going to think about that.* Opting to search downstairs, Kayn descended into the dimly lit basement. She felt around for a switch and turned it on, revealing a child's bedroom. Whimsical clouds were painted on pastel blue walls. Teddy bears, dolls and books were lined up on the shelves. She sat on the toddler sized bed and picked up the family portrait poised on the miniature nightstand. A little boy with a cherub's face grinned while cradled in his father's arms. His mother proudly beside them. *The child was two years old, possibly three. He looked like the baby pictures of her brother Matt.* She considered taking the picture out of the frame, folding it up and putting it in her pocket. *They weren't allowed to keep pictures*. She put it back where she found it. *Something furry touched her ankle.* Kayn tossed the toddler bed aside. A black kitten sprinted across the room. She sat on the floor and called the emaciated feline over. The scrawny kitten cautiously crept towards her. She sat for a while, stroking the kitten's soft fur, listening to soothing purring. *They'd be waiting for her.* She kept the kitten in her arms as she got up and peered down at the happy feline cradled in her arms. Stroking its soft fur, she whispered, "They're not going to let me keep you." Kayn brought the kitten with her as she searched the rest of the basement. In the next room was a freezer. *She didn't want to open it. Leave no stone unturned. Please let there be no toddler. Please let there be no toddler.* She took a deep breath and opened it. *The freezer only had normal freezer contents.* Kayn scaled the stairs and continued searching the house. She came back outside with the tiny powder puff of a kitten in her arms.

Zach had been patiently waiting outside for her. He chuckled, "What do you have there?" He wandered up and stroked the tiny feline in her arms.

Frost appeared beside the house. His eyes softened as he saw her. He smiled and said, "You know we can't keep that." He opened his hands. Kayn passed him the kitten. "It's time to search the school. I've got fluffy here. Go catch up with the others you two."

Zach and Kayn wandered over to the inconspicuous looking elementary school. *There wasn't anything dangerous in the building but there was something. She could sense it. Maybe it was more kittens?*

Lexy looked back as they approached. She questioned, "You feel it too, don't you?"

Kayn nodded and confirmed, "There's something." They

shoved open the weighted doors at the entrance and methodically made their way down the dimly lit hall, searching each classroom they passed. *There was something here. She sensed life. That was the only way to explain it.* The group searched each room thoroughly. *The walls were adorned with student's creations. She hadn't fought any children last night. Where were they?* Kayn reached up and touched one of the pictures. Directly under the picture was a snapshot of the little girl that created it. *Mary was five years old. She liked the movie, 'Frozen' and her favourite food was spaghetti. Something was drawing her towards the room at the end of the hall.* Kayn left the group, Lexy followed. She hesitated before opening the final door and glanced back. Lexy nodded, she tried the door. *It was locked. That's strange?* Kayn laid her ear against the wood. *She could hear giggling. What in the hell? Instinct told her there was nothing to fear but there was something she needed to protect.* They shoved on the door at the same time. The lock broke and it swung open. Tiny feet scurried in the darkness. Lexy reached over and flicked on the light. Three toddlers were cowering in the corner. There was a yellow aura around the babies.

Lexy's jaw dropped. She whispered, "Do you know what that aura means?"

Kayn recalled hearing about it but she'd never seen it for herself. *These children were possible Second-Tier. They might have abilities.* "I thought a yellow haze was only around the newly claimed?" She whispered.

Lexy responded, "It is. The glow means they've been Corrected and survived. I'll need to check to see if they've been marked. I think someone is trying to break the rules." She knelt on the ground and whispered, "Little ones, we've come to take you home."

The toddlers hesitantly came out of the corner and shyly moved towards where Lexy was kneeling on the floor. Kayn knelt by her so she'd be less of an intimidating presence. She recognized one of the toddlers. *It was the little boy from the picture in the basement where she'd found the kitten.* She whispered, "I have an idea." Kayn slowly stood up so she wouldn't upset the little ones. She stuck her head out of the door and motioned for Frost. They all began making their way down the hall. *Frost still had the kitten in his arms. He hadn't wanted to let it go either. That big softy.* She pointed at Frost, motioning him closer. *She needed the kitten.* He placed it in her arms. She slipped back into the room. Kayn knelt, whispering, "Look who I have." The child's face exploded into an enormous grin and he ran to her. She placed the kitten in his arms and whispered, "Is this your kitty?" The little boy nodded, cuddling it. *There was something in the way he moved. His mannerisms were so familiar. It couldn't be. She knew his name.* "Matty?" Kayn whispered. "Is that you?"

The child nodded. He smiled and squeaked, "Kay."

Her heart skipped a beat as shivers crept across her skin. *How was this possible? Her brother died almost three years ago, in his early twenty's. Matt died trying to protect her.* Her lips parted in disbelief as she opened her arms to receive him. Matty placed the kitten on the floor and dove into her arms, with the blind trust of a child who'd always known and loved her. She embraced him as tears of joy trailed her cheeks. Kayn whispered his name against the nape of his neck, "Matty, it is you. It's really you." With her vision obscured by the flood of tears in her eyes, Kayn looked up at the group gathered at the door and gasped, "How is this possible?"

With her eyes full of tears, Lily came in and knelt beside

Kayn. She whispered, "Hi Matty. Do you remember me?" Embracing Kayn, the cherub-faced toddler met Lily's eyes and nodded. Lily whispered, "I guess you've finally earned your wings." She got up and left in tears.

Kayn heard Lexy say, "They've been marked. Finding and holding them captive until they're of age is against the rules."

"We can't undo it without breaking rules," Frost stated.

Kayn's heart tightened as she embraced her brother's reincarnation. *He wasn't mortal this time around. How was she going to protect him when nobody had been able to protect her?* She insisted, "There must be somewhere to hide them until we find out what's going on. We have to keep them safe."

"There is," Frost declared from the doorway. "I've already called, they're on their way."

Kayn peered up at him. Frost was grinning, watching the momentary happiness she'd found.

He knelt beside Kayn and sweetly said, "Hey, little man. I remember you."

The cherub-faced toddler smiled. *She could tell Matty remembered him. She'd never seen Frost interact with a child before. It did something to her. Even though she knew she could never have a child of her own without serious repercussions, she found herself imagining what it would have been like to have one with him. It was a beautiful, silly, ultimately useless thought.*

Frost stood up, squeezed her shoulder and whispered, "I'll explain everything once we're alone. He's going to be alright. They'll hide him and take care of him until he's old enough to be claimed. The Aries Group has hidden quite a few orphaned Second-Tier for us in the past."

*She didn't want to let Matty go but knew she had to. The life they lived was no life for a child. She needed to hold the reincar-*

*nated version of the brother she adored for a moment longer and will herself to have the strength to let him go. The happiness she felt was tainted by the knowledge that Matthew wouldn't have the carefree existence he'd had the last time around. Her brother's soul had been given a bump up the food chain.* Something flashed and she glanced up. *Zach took a picture. He wasn't allowed to do that.* He took pictures of the other toddlers and slipped his cell back in his pocket.

Frost winked at her and assured, "I didn't see a thing." A loud clank, followed by the humming of voices, alerted the group. Frost stuck his head out of the door and warned, "They're here. Say whatever you need to say. Lexy is over there explaining the situation."

Kayn held Matty tighter. The miniature version of her brother was lapping up her adoration. She whispered in the toddler's ear, "These people are going take good care of you. We'll see each other again, I promise." *He seemed to understand.* She forced herself to let him go and rose to stand by his side, protectively keeping a hand on his head.

Zach caught the little black kitten and placed it back in Matty's arms. The tiny version of her brother snuggled with the kitten and smiled up at her. *She knew they couldn't keep him. He had to be hidden away until he was old enough to fight.* A well-dressed lady strolled into the room, introduced herself and asked the children to come with her.

Matty looked back at her. The miniature version of her brother spoke a full almost decipherable sentence in an adorable squeaky voice, "Goo bye Kay."

"Wait!" Kayn called to the lady. She paused and looked back. "His name is Matt. He likes to be called Matty."

The lady gave her an understanding nod as she ruffled the

toddler's hair and introduced herself, "Well, it's lovely to meet you Matty." He beamed up at her as they wandered out the door.

Kayn stood there, attempting to compose herself. She blinked away the tears each time they formed in her eyes. She took a deep shuddering breath as the others walked away. Zach placed his arm around her, tugged her into a partial hug and guided her out of the room. *He didn't need to say anything. He was wishing one of those children was a member of his family. Happiness allowed things to surface that she'd rather not think about. Emotions were better left buried. Shut it off.* She willed her heart to do what she needed to get through the rest of this day. *Shut it off.*

Sensing what she was trying to do, her Handler cupped her cheeks in his warm hands. Gazing into her eyes, Zach scolded, "Don't you dare. You have to feel the hard stuff sometimes. You can't always take the easy way out."

*Maybe, he was right about that, but it was too late. It was already done.* Staring blankly into his eyes, Kayn responded, "It's already done." *He appeared to be disappointed in her. She didn't care.* They stepped out of the school as the toddlers were being loaded into a vehicle. *She felt nothing about it as they drove away.* A thought entered her mind. *Perhaps it showed more strength to feel the pain and get through it. Maybe next time.*

Grey addressed the group, "Lily went back with the truck to collect our things. The Aries Group is collecting DNA samples. There's no need to go back to the cabin. We can leave as soon as she gets back. Ankh had to leave the state, they had a run in with Triad. We'll be hoteling it until we catch up."

They sat on the curb of the sidewalk to wait. The others were joking around. Kayn was just listening. Aware things were funny yet unable to respond, embracing the peace in her mind. *There was nothing. No anger, no sadness. Nothing at all.* She closed her eyes, waiting for the steady hum of tires. *She was capable of such dark things but the purpose of her darkness was to maintain the light. She'd played a part in preserving the balance between good and evil. This was why Dragons were created.* A feeling stirred within her, even though she wasn't ready for it. *It was pride. She was proud of what she'd accomplished.* She opened her eyes to the whirling hum of approaching tires. *And now, she was ready to turn the page.*

# 13

# WHAT HAPPENS IN VEGAS?

The six Ankh drove for a full day and night, only stopping to trade off drivers. They came to a unanimous decision while cruising through Vegas. They were staying for the night. Kayn was absolutely exhausted from travelling but excited at the same time. *She'd never been to Vegas before.* They chose a hotel off the main strip with a half decent club and restaurant downstairs. *This always made things convenient.* The plan was to leave by the ten thirty check out the next day. *It had been a long, painfully boring ride. Frost had barely spoken to her. Maybe, it was the whole mass murder thing?* Kayn smiled as she lugged her backpack out of the back of the truck. This time she'd be sharing a room with Lexy. Lily had her own room. The boys were plotting a long overdue night of male bonding and debauchery. So, they made plans to pamper themselves in the hotel's luxurious spa. They planned to dress up afterwards and go out for drinks after eating at a nice restaurant. This excursion would be a first for her, she was looking forward to it.

After making themselves comfortable in their rooms, they met at the spa and enjoyed being pampered for the day. Kayn felt like a new woman when she was done. She'd had a massage, a manicure and a pedicure. Her hair was in an updo and she was wearing her new dress from the town they'd slain the demons in. *She felt classy. This was also a new experience. It was difficult to feel elegant while being jostled around in an RV, sleeping in bunk beds and ingesting nothing but food from roadside diners. The closest she'd come to feeling this beautiful was at the celebration after Testing, but that experience had been tainted by the whole virgin sacrifice thing. The fact that Kevin was there added extra anxiety to an already messed-up situation. Today there was no need for stress. This was a magical drama free day.* They sat in a restaurant and ate whatever they wanted without worrying about where the meat came from. They sipped their glasses of wine and tried to find normal things to chat about. It was a quiet dinner. Lily flirted with their sexy waiter and they watched her work her magic. The night was going splendidly until thoughts of Frost crept into her head. *They couldn't be together. She wasn't foolish enough to believe he was sitting around waiting for her. She wasn't that naïve anymore. She'd had a taste of his ability. She understood what he needed.* She'd been staring into her empty glass of wine for a while, trying to steer her mind away from thoughts of Frost with someone else when Lexy cleared her throat. Kayn snapped back to reality as the girls started talking about going to the club to dance. *Maybe she'd meet someone. It could happen.* After a short ride back to the hotel, they arrived to pounding club music. As per usual, they strolled past the lineup into the club. *This was one of the perks of hanging out with Lily. No line ups, ever.* Lily strutted in with glistening jet-black hair and curves for days. Lexy's crimson hair was in an updo with a short dress that left little to the imagination. Kayn wandered in with a messy bun and sensual ringlets framing her face. Sure enough, the guys were chatting up a flock of female admirers. They made their way through the crowd and ordered drinks. Kayn snuck a peek in Frost's direction. *He was pretending he hadn't noticed she'd arrived. This was Frost's signature move whenever he was trying to make a point that was far too silly for her to bother with. Grey couldn't take his eyes off Lexy. He was trying to pay attention to the girl who was speaking to him, but his eyes kept wandering back to her.* Kayn nudged her and whispered, "Grey's staring at you."

Lexy didn't look up from her drink as she replied, "I promised myself I wasn't going to backslide with him."

*She could read between the lines. She'd always suspected there was more to their Dragon, Handler relationship.* She nodded, saying, "Understandable." Kayn took another sip of her drink and enquired, "How did movie night with Orin go? I totally forgot to ask you about that."

"It's Orin. He's trying to move on but he's still in love with Jenna. We hung out. Nothing happened," Lexy said as she took a casual sip of her drink and slyly glanced over at Grey.

*She was having a conversation about guys with Lexy. She'd never thought that would happen.* Fishing a cherry out of the bottom of her drink, Kayn snuck another peek at the boys. *He was coming. Grey was coming over.* She elbowed her fellow Dragon.

Lexy turned to look and whispered, "Shit."

Grey slid up beside Lexy at the bar. He leaned in and seductively whispered in her ear, "Looking good, Lex."

Lily slowly shook her head and chuckled, "Here we go."

"We should dance," Grey flirted. He got up and spun Lexy's barstool to face him. With a roguish grin, he tried to kiss her cheek.

Playfully batting him away, Lexy sparred, "I'm not into dancing tonight. Go dance with someone from the ever-expanding harem of hussies over there. Surely, one has to be interested in you."

He ran one of her sexy ringlets between his fingers and whispered, "Come on Lex. You know you want to."

Crossing her legs tighter, Lexy bit her lip. "I don't want to dance," she sighed.

He kept pouting and giving her puppy dog eyes until she cracked and agreed to dance with him, "Alright."

Grey grinned as he tugged her to her feet and towed her out on to the dance floor.

Lily casually stirred her drink as she commentated, "He has a dark gift that one."

Kayn glanced over to where they were dancing. They were laughing. *Grey was openly hitting on her. He didn't appear to be kidding around. She'd never seen him do this before.*

Watching it play out, Lily whispered, "Apparently, it happens randomly just like it did tonight. Lexy loves him so much, she folds like a cheap deck of cards. Dragons and their Handlers aren't allowed to be intimate. If they sleep together, he's spelled to forget about it. How harsh is that? I didn't even know it was going on until we had a heart to heart a few weeks ago. After she shared it with me, it all made sense. If she'd told me, I would have walked away. I hooked up with Grey for a long time. I'm sure you remember how awkward that was when it was over. I knew Grey thought he loved me. I wasn't into anything serious. I, of course, can separate sex and love quite easily. It's part of who I am. Grey can't do that. That's not who he is."

*Frost and Lily were similar creatures. Someone capable of having an adoring hoard of women surrounding him at a moment's notice was a ridiculous choice for a boyfriend.* Kayn shook her head and responded, "It's a shame they can't be together. They'd probably be happy." She found her eyes gravitating to Frost. *Was he trying to make a point? He was usually a little more discreet with his conquests.* She noticed Lily observing her watching Frost.

Lily took a sip of her drink as she pointed out, "You know you can stop that anytime you want."

*Should she? That was the question. It may end up with a piercing headache for Frost and a night of frustration for her.* Lily cleared her throat. Kayn turned to look at her.

Smiling, Lily asked, "Are you going to be upset if I take off on you? Our waiter from that restaurant is here. I have ability related issues to deal with."

*She had no interest in watching Frost being a man whore.* Kayn shook her head, urging, "Go have fun. I'm going back to my room to watch Netflix." Getting up, she gave Lily a hug and whispered in her friend's ear, "Don't do anything I wouldn't do."

Lily chuckled her breathy response in Kayn's ear, "So, nothing then?"

Pulling out of the embrace, Kayn laughed, swatting Lily. They glanced at the dance floor. Grey and Lexy were making out. Kayn smiled. *At least they were going to have a good night.* She looked for Zach but he was already gone. *It was time to go.* She strolled by Frost only meeting his inquisitive stare for a flash as she manoeuvred through the club. Kayn stepped outside into the warm night air and looked up at the Nevada sky full of thousands of sparkling stars. *It was gorgeous.* The differences in the states never ceased to amaze her. Her mind travelled back to the fireflies Frost captured for her after the Testing. She contemplated the insanity of going back inside. Just as she'd talked herself out of it, Frost called her name. She spun around. He was standing under the light of the pink neon sign. *He'd all but ignored her for days. She didn't blame him. Who would want to be with someone who could slaughter that many demons without even breaking a sweat?* She waited for him to come closer but he didn't.

He stood there and loudly baited, "Are you leaving? It's still early."

*Why was she leaving? She didn't have an answer that wouldn't make her sound like a jealous shrew.* She replied, "I'm grabbing snacks from a vending machine, and going back up to my room to watch Netflix in bed."

Frost took a few steps towards her and asked, "Mind if I join you?"

She sparred, "Are you sure you want to? It's not going to be nearly as exciting as what you had going on with that harem of girls in the club."

He grinned as he walked beside her and teased, "You happen to be the most exciting person I know."

*Sure, if mass murder excites you. I'm your girl.* They strolled to the elevator. When the door opened, it was insanely packed. She hesitated and he playfully nudged her into the herd. They ended up chest to chest on the side furthest from the buttons.

A voice boomed, "What floor are you guys going to?"

Kayn responded, "The second floor." His chest was pressed

against hers, she could feel it rise and fall with each breath he took.

He intimately toyed with delicate material on the front of her dress, whispering, "This is a good look for you." His fingers grazed her skin while skillfully tracing her revealing neckline. "It's soft."

Knowing she was blushing, Kayn silently mouthed his name. They were in a packed elevator. He was thoroughly enjoying having her as a captive participant to his naughty games. He deviously grinned as he unhooked his finger from the dangerously low neckline of her dress and placed it on her waist. The sensual electricity between them was making her think all kinds of sinfully reckless thoughts. *They could let everyone off the elevator, press the alarm and...* The door opened on the second floor. They moved with the herd of hotel patrons as she anxiously searched through her handbag for the key card. *He was so close. His presence was making it difficult to focus on even the simplest of tasks.* Kayn slid the card in the slot. A green light turned on. She smiled, it felt like that's what she'd given him by allowing him to come up to her room with her to watch a movie. *A green light. If she'd spoken that sentence aloud, she would have had to use air quotes with two fingers.* She opened the door and stepped into the empty hotel room with Frost behind her. *This was insane. He'd get a migraine, courtesy of Ankh's Oracle the second he attempted to kiss her.* She kicked off the torturous heels. She wanted to take off her tight dress and put on something more comfortable.

Frost chuckled, "You can change. I promise I won't get the wrong idea." He winked at her.

She dug in her backpack for a tank top and shorts to sleep in and wandered into the bathroom barefoot. She tried to take off her dress but couldn't reach the clasp in the back. *She didn't want to wreck it.* "Can you help me with something?" She questioned, walking across the room. He was already sprawled on the bed with his shirt off and jeans on. She sat on the bed with her back to him and asked, "Can you undo this hook for me? I can't reach it."

Crawling up behind her, he unhooked it and tenderly kissed her exposed shoulder, prompting, "What do you feel like watching? There are new movies we can rent."

She got up, responding, "Something funny. I'm not sure scary movies would do anything to me now." As she closed the bathroom door, she heard him say, "Probably not," from the other room. Kayn slipped out of her dress. Manoeuvring material over voluminous hips, she allowed it to drop to the bathroom floor. The scent of lavender from her massage still lingered on her skin. She took the pins out of her hair, allowing sexy untameable curls to cascade down her back. Her ample bosom was screaming to be set free. She took off her bra and put on a tank top. Slipping on shorts, she wiped off her makeup and came out of the bathroom. Frost stopped methodically clicking through the channels and stared at her. She climbed under the covers beside him, snuggled in and said, "See anything you like?"

"You're such a tease," Frost chuckled as he tossed the remote at her and got off the bed. He slowly unbuttoned his jeans. "If you get to be comfortable then so do I." He grinned at her as he tossed his jeans on a chair.

*What had she gotten herself into?* Laughing on the inside, she flipped through channels and tried to keep looking at the screen without watching his every movement.

Frost tossed her play on words back as he slid under the covers next to her, "See anything you like?"

She cleared her throat nervously and answered, "Yes." She ordered a movie giggling.

"Oh, you think you're pretty funny, don't you?" He teased, tickling her sides. She rolled over attempting to squirm away and buried her face in the pillow to muffle her laughter. Frost was poised on top of her from behind, they were both laughing. She felt the warmth of his breath on the nape of her neck as he hardened against the back of her thighs. Instinctually, she arched her back and reached out to touch him.

He abruptly rolled off her and explained, "I'm sorry. I'm honestly trying to behave myself. What you just did there. It's so much like..."

*He knew better than to say her twin's name aloud.* She didn't move a muscle, with her nerve endings humming from being close to him. *One of her twin's memories popped into her mind but it was more than that, there was no line anymore. It felt like she'd already been with Frost. The sensation of him behind her triggered a memory of what she was supposed to do and how his lips would feel on hers. The taste of his skin and the feeling of him within her as they moved together until...* Her heart was racing as she turned around. Their eyes met and he saw it. *It wasn't a dream that belonged to her sister anymore. It was a memory.* Her lips parted in anticipation as he inched closer, pressing his lips softly against hers. When there were no repercussions, Frost groaned her name and deepened the kiss, darting his tongue against hers. All in, Kayn slid her hands into his hair, shamelessly tugging him on top of her. His hand slid beneath her shorts, caressing her silk panties. Breathless as their lips parted, she whispered, "Don't stop."

Deviously kissing her neck, his lips travelled a naughty torturous trail to her chest. Looking up as his lips reached her abdomen, he whispered, "Tell me what you want me to do."

*Don't stop. Please, don't stop. She wanted this in a crazy way.*

Yanking her shorts to her thighs, he kissed her all the way down to her silky panties as she gasped and squirmed. *The heat from his breath was driving her insane.*

Peering up, he suggested, "We should go back to my room. Lexy might come back here."

Breathless with anticipation, she nodded. He gave her a quick peck on the lips before jumping off the bed and racing for his clothes. *She was going to his room in her tank top and shorts. She didn't care who saw. She was really going to do this. She must be insane.* They were both laughing as they reached the door. He backed her up against the wall and kissed her again, naughtily running his hands over the sparse material covering her chest. He groaned as he pulled away and reached for the doorknob.

Frost opened the door, turned around and whispered, "You look incredibly hot with your hair all messy and that tank top with no..."

Kayn's eyes widened. *Jenna was standing there smiling.*

Frost spun around to see what she was looking at and groaned, "Oh, come the hell on."

Jenna chuckled, "Not tonight, Romeo. Go back to your own room. We need to be out of the city before eight am. I left the instructions on how to find the others with Lily. I'd imagine she's not happy with me for similar reasons."

Looking back at Kayn, Frost vowed, "To be continued. I'll see you bright and early tomorrow Brighton. Sweet dreams."

*He'd used her mortal last name as a nickname instead of Froggy or Princess. She was alright with Brighton.* Sheepishly, Kayn said, "Good night," closing the door. *Guess she'd better add sheep to the list of animals in her inner dialogue's repertoire. There was no way she was going to be able to sleep.* She peered out the peephole, contemplating waiting until she walked away, texting Frost for his room number and sneaking up there. With hilarious timing, her phone buzzed on the nightstand. She raced over and looked at the text.

It read, "You are killing me Brighton."

Gathering her guts, she responded, "Ditto. What room are you in?"

The next text read, "Would you actually come?"

She nervously bit her lip as she texted back, "Yes."

There was a long pause before he responded, "318."

*She needed this.* Kayn opened the door and peered both ways down the long hallway. *Nobody was there. The coast was clear.* She sprinted down the hallway to the stairwell and ran up the flight of stairs to the third floor. When she shoved open the weighted doors, Jenna was waiting on the other side.

Jenna teased, "Do I really have to explain this whole Oracle thing to you?"

*Awkward.* Humiliated, Kayn apologized, "No, you don't. I'm sorry. I just..." *She lost the words to explain what she was doing. I'm insanely turned on. I died a virgin. I'm ready for this and I don't want to be one anymore? I now feel like Chloe's memories are mine. He's irresistible. I can't be held accountable for my actions. All of those things couldn't be said aloud.*

Placing an arm around her, Ankh's Oracle justified her reasoning, "A Dragon's first violent confrontation in the real world can turn them into a bit of an adrenaline junky. I promise it won't be long and the choice will be yours to make."

*That was reasonable.* Embarrassed, Kayn nodded. *She'd heard her, I'm all horned up inner commentary.* Jenna walked her back to her room.

She counselled, "Go ahead, call Frost. Explain why you didn't show up. We'll keep this between us."

Lexy was in bed when she snuck back in. *She'd been gone all of five minutes.* Kayn sat on the bed and texted Frost, "Lol, I got caught."

He answered, "It was worth a try. Jenna has serious Oracle game. Sweet dreams beautiful. I'll see you in the morning."

She threw herself on the bed and screamed into her pillow. Lexy quietly chuckled. *She'd been pretending to sleep.*

Lexy teased, "Jenna caught you guys to, didn't she?"

With her face buried in her pillow, Kayn gave her a muffled reply, "Yes, she did. She also caught me trying to sneak up to his room after she vetoed our hook up."

Lexy started to giggle. Kayn lifted her face from the pillow and tossed it at her. She started to howl.

"Glad you think this is so funny," Kayn complained.

Her fellow Dragon sparred, "Tomorrow morning when you wake up, this whole fiasco will be nothing more than a laughable memory. Jenna expects you three newbies to throw some rebellion into the mix. It's totally normal for someone your age."

*Lexy was right. She was only nineteen years old.* While she had Lexy all to herself, there was a question she'd been dying to ask. *She had no idea how long each of these abilities she'd siphoned would last but there had to be a way to shut down the trippy glow that surrounded everyone. Surely Healers didn't see this all the time.* Kayn blurted out, "Can you turn the viewing everybody's aura part of being a Healer off?"

Rolling over to face her, Lexy responded, "No, it just becomes normal. It's strongest when your body has been freshly healed. You'll notice it beginning to dim over the next couple of days. Well, that's only if you haven't used your healing ability for anything."

*Her healing ability. It would be cool if she could keep this one. Well, minus the trippy aura part. Nothing good came without a price in this new life.*

"We'd better get some sleep. The alarm is set for five am. We need to be back on the road in four hours," Lexy whispered.

Kayn whispered, "Night Lex." She snuggled beneath the sheets. She closed her eyes and tried to think of happy things. As she drifted off her last semi-conscious thoughts were of Frost.

*In her dreams, it was a different story.* She was on a balcony overlooking a red desert, wearing a flowing red dress. The material seemed to have a life of its own as it rippled in the breeze. Millions of luminescent stars lit up the night sky, creating a sensual glow on the surface of the crimson sand. A door closed, followed by the shuffle of feet. She knew someone was behind her but didn't turn to see who it was. *She was waiting for something to happen.* A shadow from the crypt containing the Immortal Testing travelled by the enormous moon. She relaxed against the person standing behind her, watching the shadow of Testing disappear as it left the light of the moon.

A male voice whispered, "My daughters will change everything. The Prophecy has begun."

*She recognized the voice but couldn't place it.* When she turned to see who'd spoken, nobody was there. The buzzer went off.

She groaned and covered her face with her pillow. *No, no, no. She wasn't ready to get up. It felt like she'd just went to sleep.* She opened her eyes. Lexy raced to the bathroom so she could be first. *She recalled every second of her dream. She sensed the voice she'd heard had been her father's. Her soul was fully merged with her sister's. Maybe it had figurative meaning? She'd dreamt of saving the people they'd lost in the Testing before. Survivor's guilt?*

Dressed, Lexy ran over and leapt onto her bed, "Wake up! Wake up! There's no time to waste. I'll explain on the way to the truck."

Launching herself into an upright position, she yawned and stretched. Kayn snatched her backpack off the chair on her way to the bathroom. *She didn't look half dead from lack of sleep.* Quickly brushing her teeth, she applied a touch of makeup. Raking uncoordinated fingers through her wavy mane, she put her hair in a messy ponytail. *There, she was ready for the day. Sort of.*

# 14

# NEVER MESS WITH A DRAGON

Two exhausted Dragons ambled down the long emerald-green carpeted hallway towards the elevator. Lexy pressed the button as she explained what she'd insinuated, "Jenna's premonition says, we have to split up. Jenna, Markus and Orin have the boy. Astrid, Mel and Haley are hiding Molly in a small town in the desert. It's only a few hours' drive on the highway. We'll have to take the backroads to ensure we're not being followed, but it's a scenic drive. Zach has already gone to get the truck.

The door opened revealing Frost, Grey and Lily with bags. As Kayn stepped into the elevator, Frost flirtatiously teased, "Going down?"

With no reaction to his innuendo, Kayn straight-faced responded, "Yes, we're quite obviously both going down." Everyone's cheeks burst into a smile.

Lexy elbowed her and sparred, "Speak for yourself."

Kayn gave in and laughed. *Everything was going to be hilarious until she got her second wind.* Lily took everyone's key cards and left them on the desk. In a minute, they were all standing outside waiting for Zach. *The morning air made her feel a bit better though. She really needed to go for a run.* Kayn saw the truck coming down the street. *There wasn't a parking spot.* Zach pulled over and they all quickly got in. Lexy traded places with Zach saying she wanted to drive first. He nodded and moved to the backseat. They were about to pull out when someone knocked on the window.

Lexy sighed as she it rolled down and said, "Is there a problem sir?"

The shady stranger replied, "Your back tires are almost flat and you have a broken taillight. I thought I'd warn you before you drove too far and bent the rim."

"Oh, thank you for telling me," Lexy responded. "I'll be right out sweetie." She rolled up the window.

Zach leaned over, whispering, "The tires are fine."

Glancing back with an innocent smile, Lexy countered, "Oh, I'm sure they are."

Attempting to be the voice of reason, Frost cautioned, "There are cameras all over the place. You're going to have to handle this tool carefully."

*This asshole sure picked the wrong driver to carjack.*

Stretching, Lexy cracked her neck, instructing, "Lock it as soon as I get out. I'll only be a second." Appearing to be a naive southern belle in the big city, she got out.

Grey grinned and slowly shook his head. He locked the door behind her, chuckling, "That poor dumbass."

Lexy strolled around to the back of the truck, looked at the tires and stated, "The tires are fine. Are you really sure you want to do this?"

Realising she was on to him, the man yanked a gun out of his pocket and threatened, “That’s right bitch. The truck is fine, so fine it’s screaming my name. Tell those shits to get out. I’d hate to wreck your beautiful smile by forcing you to eat a bullet.”

Checking for cameras, Lexy dared, “Oh, would you like my keys? If you can take the keys from me, you can just have the truck.” He pressed the gun into her shoulder with his arm around her neck as he searched her pockets. She laughed as he pushed her towards the driver’s door.

Her assailant threatened, “Do you want me to shoot you? Tell those assholes to get out of the truck! What kind of sadistic friends do you have? They’re all smiling at me. I’m going to effing kill you.”

“No, you’re not. They know I’m allowing you to point your little gun at me and they also know I’m going to kick your ass as soon as I grow tired of playing along,” Ankh’s Dragon countered. He tossed her against the hood of the truck and she laughed harder.

Grey rolled the window down a touch, commenting, “Hey, honey. While you’re playing with this moron, don’t let him shoot the engine. It would be inconvenient. We have places to be. Can you wrap this up?”

Lexy sighed, “Alright, the game is over my friend. I’ll give you one more opportunity to walk away.” As she took a step towards him a shot rang out. Lexy barely flinched as blood seeped through her shirt.

*Holy shit. He shot her in the shoulder.*

Lexy moved aside her shirt to show him the wound as it closed and spit the bullet out. “Now, that wasn’t very nice.”

"What are you?" he stammered as he dropped the gun and ran away.

For a second Kayn thought Lexy was going to get into the truck. *They'd drive away and that would be the end of it.*

Glancing at the bloodstain, Lexy scowled. "He wrecked my new shirt," the Dragon hissed, sprinting after the man who shot her.

Grey yelped, "Oh, shit!" He scrambled out of the truck and chased her.

Frost slid into the driver's seat, chuckling, "Buckle up, we can't park here."

Seeing an opportunity to go for a run, Kayn opened the door, winked at her Handler and sprinted down the street after Grey.

"Well, go get her kid," Frost instructed.

Sidetracked by Zach's presence, Kayn glanced back. *Sure enough, her Handler was chasing her. Catch up if you can buddy.* She regained her focus. *She'd lost Grey. Shit! Time to use those predatory instincts. Lexy wasn't far behind the guy who shot her. She'd want to teach him a lesson. They'd be somewhere without cameras.* Sprinting down the alley, she came across Lexy duct taping her naked assailant to a fire escape. *What was she doing? Where in the hell did she find duct tape?* Grey was shaking his head, letting her do her thing as she taped the gun to his forehead. His shirt was stuffed into his mouth to muffle his screaming.

Smiling proudly at her impressively twisted work of art, Lexy announced, "I'm willing to bet this wasn't the first time you've used that weapon. Don't worry the police will be here soon to get you down. If you haven't used that gun for any other crimes, you'll be free to go." The man started squirming and wriggling in his duct tape suit. Grinning, Lexy provoked, "That's what I thought. Gee, I sure hope it's not excruciatingly painful when they remove the duct tape from your butt crack. You know people pay big bucks for the Brazilian you're about to get for free. No, need to thank me. Have a lovely morning." She wandered away with a little skip in her step.

When Kayn was finally able to pry her eyes away from the evil genius revenge scenario, she couldn't stop smiling. Zach was standing with his mouth agape and as the others pulled up in the truck. They all got out and just stood there in awe of Lexy's duct tape creation.

Staring up at the wriggling scumbag, Frost questioned, "Why does the kid look so mortified."

*He was talking about Zach.* Kayn grinned as she replied, "He's naked under that duct tape. He's also wearing a duct tape G-string. Think about it for a second. Let it sink in." They were silent as the bad karma worthy mortal valiantly attempted to free himself. Lexy was in the truck calling the police with Grey.

Grey opened the door and hollered, "Let's go. This guy has a date with a body cavity search."

The man let out muffled screams as they climbed into the truck and sped away. Grey couldn't stop laughing, "She told the police a drug smuggler who just arrived on a flight, tried to carjack us and we caught him."

For hours, they laughed whenever somebody brought up duct tape guy. Frost turned off the highway. Glancing in the rearview mirror, he explained, "We need to drive the rest of the way on the backroads. We're almost there. I need to see if we're being followed. On the highway, it's difficult to know for sure."

Grey piped in, "Hey, when are we stopping to eat? My stomach has been singing for over an hour."

"We can't stop for longer than a few minutes. You can heat up something at the next convenience store we find. It'll be a good opportunity to grab drinks and snacks to have in our rooms for later," Frost answered.

It took a good hour to find a convenience store on the road less travelled. They raced inside, famished by then. As Kayn strolled down the aisles, she was reminded of the old saying, never shop on an empty stomach. *She was so hungry it all looked amazing.* She grabbed Twinkies, knowing Frost would have a moment when he saw them. She brought her stash of snacks, drink and premade sub to the counter and dropped it in front of Frost because he already had the card out.

He ran her stuff through the till, teasing, "You'd better share those Twinkies with me."

*This was so much fun. He'd be thinking about the Twinkie thing all afternoon.* Kayn innocently wandered over to wait for her turn at the microwave. After everyone finished heating subs, they had a final bathroom break before trudging back out to the truck in the sweltering heat with bags full of junk. She ate lightning fast, chugged down a lemonade, and asked Zach if she had anything in her teeth.

"I'm not sure you had time to chew. You're all good," Zach laughed.

*It felt like the air-conditioning wasn't working. It was devil's sauna hot outside.* She dozed off to the sound of spinning tires.

Zach's voice announced, "We're here!"

*Seriously?* Kayn opened her eyes and knit her brow as she saw the sketchy motel, they were staying in. It looked like one of those places a serial killer would use to find his victims. Half asleep, she was the last one out of the truck.

Grey yelled, “Heads up!” He tossed Kayn her backpack from the locked storage in the back.

She caught it, before it hit her. In her partially awakened state, it would have knocked her over. She made her way to the large outdoor pool where everyone was laughing and embracing.

Mel strolled over. They joyously embraced as she said, “I’ve missed you guys.”

Hugging her, Kayn answered, “Ditto.” They helped bring stuff up to their rooms. *She didn’t have a swimsuit. Her bra was passable. Nobody would care.* In her bra and shorts, she went back down to laze around at the pool in the sunshine. There wasn’t many guests at the hotel, so everyone was able to enjoy an escape from reality. She sprawled in the sunshine watching Frost swim back and forth. With the urge to join him, Kayn stepped into the water and pushed off. *It felt amazing.* She swam the length, almost forgetting why she got into the pool. Frost saw her and waited, holding onto the edge of the pool in the deep end. She surfaced and grabbed on beside him. It took her a moment to catch her breath.

“I was hoping we’d have a chance to spend some time together. After last night,” Frost whispered.

*He’d taken the words right out of her mouth.* She confessed, “I was too.” Their moment was wrecked by an ill-timed cannonball. The wake left them dishevelled, choking and sputtering, clutching the side. They were laughing as Grey surfaced.

Joining them clinging to the cement ledge, Grey spit chlorinated water out of his mouth, chuckling, “It looked like you needed a tension breaker.”

Pushing off, Frost swam back to the other side of the pool, leaving Kayn clinging to the pool's edge with Grey. Frost climbed out of the water and wandered away. *What in the hell? He regained his title as the king of mixed messages.* Grey interrupted, but something about his mannerisms suggested he felt justified in doing so. Kayn called him on it, "It'd save time if you just told me what that was about."

As water splashed the edge, Grey replied, "Frost is one of my best friends. I love the guy to death but you're also my friend. The only thing you should be worrying about right now is learning how to use your ability. My brother from another mother over there, tends to be relationship phobic. With good reason, some might say, but you should give yourself five minutes to regain your balance before getting on that roller-coaster ride."

*Really? Frost was the one with drama? He was the rollercoaster ride? She was sure she could hold her own in that department. She wasn't blind. She'd always been able to see him coming from a mile away. She wanted him despite that.* Grinning, Kayn explained, "Grey, I've already been on this rollercoaster, I remember everything about the ride. So, I happen to have firsthand knowledge that it's going to be worth it, even if the ride only lasts five minutes. This isn't a normal situation. Thank you for your concern, but I can handle Frost. I've already handled Frost, literally." Kayn watched as the lightbulb began to glow above his head.

"Oh, I see. The twin thing. Sometimes, I forget about that. You remember everything? How does that work? I mean, I know you were having the dreams about Chloe's memories before the Testing," Grey questioned, curious.

Kayn suggested, "Let's talk about this in the sun while

we're drying off." She kicked off the ledge and sparred, "I'll race you there." He was right behind her as she swam for the other side. She climbed out, raucously dancing at the top of the steps, cheering.

Shaking his head, Grey didn't utter a word as they strolled over to where the others were lounging in the sunshine. Kayn stretched out on a recliner. The warmth of the rays instantly dried the droplets of water on her skin.

Flipping onto his stomach for a better vantage point to finish their conversation, Grey whispered, "Ultimately, I think you should do whatever makes you happy. It's hard to see you as both. I get the concept, but it's difficult to wrap your mind around. I'll get there."

Kayn attempted to explain the impossible, "In my head and heart, all of her experiences are mine. My experiences are also mine. It doesn't even make sense when I try to rationalize it."

On a lounger next to Grey, the new girl asked, "What are you guys talking about?"

Nonchalantly shifting his tanned, muscular torso to face her, Grey gave young Molly a hilarious rundown of Kayn's backstory, "Freja, an immortal friend of ours got pregnant. She gifted her baby's soul to Kayn's mortal mother, but her egg split creating identical twins, each with half of one soul. Chloe had abilities, Kayn didn't. They were corrected at sixteen. Chloe died and Kayn survived. Always meant to be one, their souls had to rejoin. Before that could happen, Frost had a naughty fling with Chloe's ghost. Kayn was in love with her bestfriend Kevin, who turned out to be the leader of Triad's grandson. Are you still following along?"

On the edge of her lounger listening to the crazy story, Molly asserted, "Keep going."

Grey chuckled and kept telling the tale, "So, the twin's souls rejoined. Frost lost Chloe. Kayn lost Kevin to Triad, and his memory was wiped. Eventually, Frost and Kayn sort of started seeing each other. In a selfless move, Frost let her go before the Testing so she could figure things out with Kevin. In a sick plot twist, I knew nothing about, the Clan arranged to have Kevin kill Kayn so she'd become a Dragon and lead the others out of the Testing."

Molly stared at Kayn, then back at Grey. Shaking her head in disbelief, she declared, "That's a horrible story."

Kayn grinned. *Hearing it back sounded like absolute insanity.* "What you overheard was Grey's reaction to me explaining that my twin's memories and emotions are my own, in my mind and heart." *She liked this kid. It was a little funny to speak to someone only a few years younger as though they were lifetimes apart. Perhaps it was because she'd been to hell and back. For every time she'd died during the Testing, it felt like she'd gained years. Molly was dealing with everything she'd been told with remarkable maturity.* Noticing Molly staring, Kayn probed, "Yes?"

The new Ankh enquired, "Are you and Frost a thing?"

*She wasn't sure how to answer that question. They were a confusing thing. She should go find him.* Kayn stood up and before walking away, she replied, "We're something." *She was becoming attached to Molly. They'd better not lose her to another Clan before her eighteenth birthday.* She looked back at her. *Her eighteenth birthday was years away. Being on this side of the situation felt weird.* Wandering down the seamless cement walkway barefoot until she heard his laughter, Kayn followed the voices into a private area surrounded by a marble wall. There was a secluded hot tub full of scantily clad people. An attractive brunette had her hand on Frost's chest, shamelessly flirting with him. Zach noticed her standing there, contemplating yanking her out of the hot tub by her hair. Zach got out of the water and suggested they go back to their room to get out of the sun for a while. *He was either running interference for Frost or doing his job as her Handler by trying to save the mortal from her unhinged temper.* Frost noticed her just as she was about to walk away. Kayn glared at him, pressed her lips together and nodded. *Yes, I saw that. You jackass.*

He shifted away from the girl and made the mistake of far too casually saying, "Are you coming in?"

*Was he asking her to join them?* Kayn venomously sparred, "No, I'm not feeling it now. That water looks a little too dirty." Frost tossed his head back and laughed.

Taking her arm, Zach led her away, whispering, "Let's go before you go full psycho. You're reading way too much into this my friend."

*Was she really? Did he have to let some chick touch his chest?* She followed Zach up to the room. *He had a key pinned to his shorts. Weird.*

He opened the door and sweetly suggested, "Let's sit at the table and relax for a while." He strolled over to the coffee machine by a red microwave.

Wandering into the room, Kayn noticed the kitchenette had white cupboards covered with graffiti. As she took a closer look, she realised it was whiteboard decorated with washable markers. The table was one of those folding card tables. It was also covered in graffiti and initials. She sat on a flimsy child-size chair, hoping it wouldn't collapse. *The room had the vibe of the interior of a kid's unfinished treehouse. The bed was the only normal piece of furniture. She'd stayed in some strange places. This room would definitely be added to her list of the weirdest hotel rooms in North America.* It felt like only a minute as Zach placed a mug of coffee on the table in front of her. *Would the heat from the mug destroy the washable marker art on the table? She was so going to forget, lean on something and be covered in washable marker. This was who she was as a person.* Zach placed a plastic cup full of packets of sugar and coffee whitener on the table. He sat on the other side and asked her to pass the whitener. Kayn swiped her hand, without touching the cup. It slid across the table to him without flying across the room. She'd done it on a whim because they were alone, but doing it properly with control had been cool.

He tried to do the same thing. It flew off the table and clinked on the floor but didn't break. She picked it up and placed it back on the table. Giggling, Kayn cheered him on, "Try it again." Zach moved his hand slowly this time and it slid right into her hand. He beamed and she grinned. *They were learning new things every day.* Forgetting she had powdered whitener, not milk from a fridge in her coffee, Kayn scalded her tongue, and fired off an impressive list of obscenities.

Zach cleared his throat. As she peered up at him, he confessed, "I'm not sure how I'm supposed to help you with these anger issues. Did I word that properly?"

*What was she supposed to say? This was all new for her too.* She tried to take another sip of steaming coffee without responding. *She didn't necessarily see it as a bad thing. She'd spent so long filtering herself. She wanted what she wanted, and when she felt anger, she showed it. She'd never felt freer.* She met his gaze and replied, "I know you miss who I used to be but this is who I am now."

His eyes softened, Zach backtracked, "I'll reword that. Frost always flirts with everyone. Hell, sometimes I feel like he's hitting on me. Why would some girl flirting with him in a hot tub make you want to yank her out by her hair?"

She chuckled, "I thought it. I didn't do it. We haven't had a chance to talk privately since Vegas. You're missing the back-story. Calm down, I wasn't going to hurt her, she's mortal." Noticing the washable markers on the table, Kayn plucked a cap off and decided to play hangman. He started guessing letters without even talking about it.

They'd been playing for less than five minutes when Zach guessed, "I almost slept with him in Vegas."

Kayn laughed as Zach started his hangman without a word. Once he was finished, she started guessing letters. A few minutes in, she guessed the sentence, "But Frost is a man whore."

Grinning, she started hers. *Fair enough. He was right. He had been. She knew that but she also knew they could be more.* The door opened and Frost walked in. *Oh Shit!* Zach placed his mug over the name Frost. Kayn nonchalantly smeared her seedy info with her arm.

Frost strolled over to the table, commenting, "These are weird frigging rooms. In mine, everything glows in the dark." Looking directly at Kayn, Frost asked if she wanted to come check out his room.

*Lord help her she did, but she was still ticked off at him. She couldn't make it that easy.* She glanced at Zach and invited him along, "Come on, Zach. Let's go check out Frost's room." Frost grinned, knowing he was in the doghouse. When they walked next door, they suspected Frost heard their unfiltered game of hangman. He drew the blinds and it became dark.

*His room was cool.* She excused herself, "I need to use the washroom."

He turned the lights back on and replied, "It's over there."

She strolled across the room, closing the door behind her.

Zach announced, "There's pizza in Grey and Lexy's room. The keys are on the counter. Lock up when you're done."

"Alright, I'll be right there," Kayn replied, washing her hands. Wondering if there was glow in the dark writing on these walls too, she turned off the lights. *There was writing everywhere.* On the back of the door, she saw their initials and a heart. *I'm sorry, I'm trying,* was written underneath it. She recalled the romantic cabin with their initials carved into the door. *The one they'd almost stayed in together. He knew she'd see this. He'd known the initials on the back of the door meant something to her. She wasn't ready for it back then. They had an adjoining door. Would he try to use it?* She walked out, expecting Frost to be waiting. *She was alone.* She went outside and locked up. Down the walkway balcony, she saw a group of strangers approaching. Her heart clenched. *Was that Kevin?* As they came closer, she realised it was just somebody who resembled him. She smiled and waited for them to pass. *Why was she thinking about him now? She'd put him behind her. Had she really put him behind her, or had she stifled all thoughts of Kevin by hyper-focusing on Frost? Suddenly, everything became clear. Jenna might have been right. Her emotions had been either shut off or amped up since the banquet and virgin sacrifice fiasco. She needed to find her normal. Whatever that meant. She didn't plan to slow anything down with Frost. Even if they were short-lived, it'd be worth it.* She heard familiar voices and smiled as she walked in. Saying she was tired, Kayn took a few slices of pizza with her and wandered back to her room. She devoured it, cleaned up and snuggled beneath the comfy covers. *She was exhausted.* Her eyes were drawn to the adjoining door. *Was it locked? This wasn't the night for that life event. Thinking she'd seen Kevin messed with her resolve. The Testing wasn't that long ago.* She aimlessly clicked through the channels until her eyes grew heavy and sleep stole her away.

Music filled her senses. She was standing in front of a mirror in a strapless teal prom dress. She recognized the bathroom. Her curiosity peaked as she followed the music out of the washroom down a long dark hall of lockers. At the end were the gymnasium doors. *She'd gone to this school and had this dream before. This was what could have been. He would be waiting for the domesticated version of her former self, Kayn Brighton the track and field star. She was just a girl, and this was just the dance she'd never gone to.* She shoved on the doors, revealing cheesy space decorations. Silver stars had been painstakingly hung by long strings from the ceiling. Planets adorned the gymnasium walls. *The best part about this dream was that each time she had it, the theme of the prom changed. Last time it was under the sea.* Familiar faces were everywhere but there was only one person she was searching the crowd for. *He didn't appear to be here.* Derek, the boy who'd been taken by Abaddon, under the guise of meeting up with her was eating something that made his cheeks bulge. Derek covered his mouth when he saw her, waving with his free hand. *This was another reality. One where they hadn't been forced to fight to the death.* Somebody slapped her butt. She spun around and had to catch her breath. *It was Chloe.* Her twin flounced away. She stood there in awe watching her sister, making her rounds. The crowd separated and she saw him having an animated conversation with someone. From this vantage point his hand gestures were rather comical. The music slowed, making it easier to manoeuvre through the crowd.

As she reached him, Kevin teased, "I was wondering where you went. One second you were standing beside me and the next you were gone."

Her eyes filled with moisture. Kayn blinked away her tears. *That's what happened. He was standing beside her, and now, he was gone. It was hard to see him as he was and comprehend that he was destined to be her enemy.* Kayn took his hand as she would have before everything changed between them. Kevin pulled her into his embrace. She rested her head on his shoulder as they began to sway to the soothing rhythm of the music. *This was really him and these were the moments they'd lost.*

Kevin whispered against her hair, "I love you. That will never change."

Kayn pulled away so she could look into his eyes. *These were the words they'd never had a chance to say.* Tenderly touching his cheek as a surge of tears swelled, the emotional damn within her broke. "I love you too," she confessed. Their lips met sweetly at first, then deepened with the passion building between them for their entire lives.

Lost in the moment, they heard someone say, "Get a room."

Kayn laughed nervously, searching the crowd for the comic culprit. *She'd heard that barb before. Something Kevin said snapped into her mind. That will never change. Why had he added that to his declaration of love? What was this?*

Sensing the change in her demeanour as she backed away, he pled, "Don't leave. I'm not ready for this dream to end."

*It couldn't be? She needed to know.* She closed the space between them and aggressively unbuttoned his shirt.

Kevin taunted, "Right here. Really?"

She yanked it open revealing the symbol of Triad, branded on his flesh above his heart. *He'd tricked her.* Rage tightened in the pit of her stomach. Shooting daggers of hatred with her eyes, Kayn grilled, "How are you here? Why?"

Amused by her instantaneous change in attitude, he flirtatiously sparred, "What are you doing here?"

They were staring each other down as Chloe came to break up their visual standoff. With a smirk, Chloe probed, "You need me, don't you?" She stepped into her and they became one as they were always meant to be.

Blinding white light exploded, causing her to shut her eyes. When the glare ceased, Kevin had vanished. Her senses were assaulted by the putrid scent of sulphur. She was standing in a dance full of misshapen faced hollow-eyed demons with open mouths twisted in torment. In her hand was a demon blade. There was a time when this would have been a terrifying sight, but her pulse raced with anticipation. A voice in her mind whispered, *'You don't need a knife.'* Kayn dropped the blade, making melodic clinks on the floor. She marched over to a demonic entity, grabbed either side of its contorted face and smirked. Her hands heated up, followed by the addictive sensation of life-force travelling up her arms and gathering in her chest. Her fingertips tingled. *She knew what that meant.* She touched the tips together and pulled them apart, moulding herself a ball of energy. The demons merged into a massive snake-like abomination with the legs of a centipede and slick tar black glistening scales. Operating on instinct, Kayn raised the orb of energy and pitched it at the creature. Blood, meat and tissue splattered everywhere. Demon intestines were hanging from the decorative stars on the ceiling. After redecorating the gymnasium with a macabre display of demonic innards, she stood there alone wondering what came next.

She gasped and woke up. *That was an insane nightmare.* Relief washed over her. *She was in bed.* She glanced at the untouched bed beside hers. *Zach hadn't come back. Maybe, he met someone? Maybe it was still early? The others could be a couple of rooms down, hanging out.* She glanced at the clock on the nightstand flashing midnight. *Well, that's not helpful. She vaguely recalled unplugging something to plug in her phone. It was probably the alarm clock.* Kayn rolled onto her stomach, buried her face in her pillow, closed her eyes and drifted off to sleep.

# 15

# A KIDNAPPING AND A KISS

Kayn awoke sensing something amiss before opening her eyes. *She was in an odd position. Her arms were bound above her head. Shit, seriously?* She opened her eyes. The room was dark. The clock was still flashing midnight. Kayn struggled to free herself. *What in the hell was she bound with? She should be able to snap handcuffs like twigs. What was going on? Someone was in the room with her. It couldn't be?* She hadn't been gagged but she knew the drill. *There was no point in screaming for help. From who? A mortal passing by. What were they going to do? Situations like this were less emotionally taxing when you knew you couldn't die. If it was a serial murderer, it would seriously suck, but it wouldn't wreck her week.* Sensing someone in the shadows, she sighed, "Would you like a chance to explain yourself before I rip these restraints off my wrists and kill you."

A familiar voice chuckled, "You'd be wasting your energy but go ahead, give it your best shot."

Kayn swallowed the lump in her throat. *Why was he here?* She struggled against the chains. *They wouldn't budge.* Kevin stepped out of the shadows into the faint light glowing from her cell by the bed. *She'd wondered when their paths would cross again. Seeing him was less confusing now. He was her enemy. It had been a smart move on his part to restrain her.*

Kevin grinned as he sat beside her and asked, "So, how's life been going for you?"

Rolling her eyes, she sparred, "Just frigging wonderful. How's yours?" She struggled against the restraints again before comprehending resistance was futile. *They were obviously created to restrain immortals. She'd known of their existence but never had the annoyance of being bound by them until now. She'd thought he was grinning at her frustration until she realised what he was really smiling about. She'd flailed until she lost her covers. She was playing this all wrong.* Wearing only underwear and a tank top with no bra, Kayn flirtatiously smiled. *He'd forgotten to tie her legs.* His eyes were darker, colder than they'd been the last time she gazed into them. His expression amused, yet far from emotionless. Choosing to go with the situation she'd found herself in, she baited, "You could have just called me on the phone instead of opting for this kinky medieval bondage game."

His eyes flickered in response to her inappropriately timed flirtation. He chuckled, "Are you flirting with me Brighton? I thought you wanted to kill me? I guess it's true what they say about the thin line between love and hate."

Kayn met his intrigued expression and stated, "Oh, I'm still going to kill you." Kevin burst out laughing as he climbed on top of her, poised above her on all fours. *Was he trying to intimidate or flirt with her? She wasn't sure.*

Straddling her, he tenderly stroked her cheek as he replied, "Not today. Today, I'm going to drag you out of here and chuck you in in the backseat of my car. Then, I'm going to drive you out to the desert and leave you stranded with the rest of your Clan while we steal that sweet little dark-haired friend of yours. Of course, we'll have to make it extremely difficult for you to catch up with us. I'm sure if our situations were reversed, you'd do the same to me."

Kayn struggled as she clicked into what was happening. *Triad was taking Molly. She was supposed to protect her.* She wrapped her free legs around his waist and squeezed with everything she had.

He chuckled, "Hot as this moment is..." He sprayed a mist in her face. She coughed, her vision flickered and everything went black.

Kayn awoke in the backseat of a car, to the sound of tires rumbling down a road. *She was still restrained. Nobody was stupid.* She kept her eyes closed, so she could listen to what they were talking about.

Kevin's voice spoke first, "She won't be out for long. Did we manage to get all of them?"

Stephanie responded, "We're only missing Lexy and Grey."

"Only Lexy and Grey are missing. Well, that's not good," Kevin chuckled. There was a brief pause in their conversation before he threw in, "That spray is great stuff. None of their symbols were triggered. They might not even know their friends are in trouble."

Kayn felt around for something to cut herself with but her options were limited because her hands were bound behind her. *She had to set off her symbol and alert the two that hadn't been captured.* She shoved her fingertips into the cushions of the bench seat she was laying on. *She needed something sharp. There was always random crap shoved between the seats of cars.*

Kevin's voice came from the front, "Kayn, I made damn good and sure there was nothing you could hurt yourself on back there."

She smiled and countered, "Then, why didn't you gag me?"

Stephanie replied, "He's a sentimental guy. He wanted to have a chance to visit with you before we killed you."

Kayn scrolled through the escape options in her head. *She had one clear way to signal her distress to Lexy and Grey. Although, it was a difficult one to wrap her mind around. She'd only get one chance. It had to be now. Self-inflicted cannibalism was never something anyone's mind was prepared to wrap itself around.* She glanced at the front to make sure their eyes were still on the road ahead before biting into her own shoulder. At the point where her mind began screaming at her to stop, she knew, she'd have to be downright brutal to signal the cavalry. She fought against instinct as she tore a chunk of flesh out of the top of her arm by her shoulder and spat it onto the floor of the vehicle. With the taste of blood in her mouth, Kayn said nothing as it flowed from her wound into the cushion. Her hand was warm but tied behind her, so the light from her symbol was concealed. Laying there listening to their casual conversation, she smiled to herself. *They thought they'd covered their bases. They hadn't.*

The car stopped. Stephanie got out of the passenger seat, opened the backdoor, saw the blood and sighed, "We should have gagged her."

Kevin looked through the door, smirked and chuckled, "Creative Brighton, extremely damn creative."

It was stiflingly hot outside as they hauled her out of the

backseat into the sand. The heat beneath her bare feet was a little more than uncomfortable. She saw where they were taking her. *What in the hell?* They walked her up a ramp towards the back of a metal storage container. *She'd roast in there.* Kevin slid open the door, revealing epically pissed off Ankh. They were gagged and chained to the wall, literally roasting. *She was totally in the right mental state to appreciate the genius of this messed-up scenario. Torturous genius. They needed to hold them somewhere long enough for Triad to get away with Molly.* She was grinning as Kevin attached her chains to the wall beside Frost. *He probably thought he was being ironic.* Her shoulder had healed leaving no evidence of her backseat antics, besides the bloodstain on her white tank top.

With a genuine smile, Kevin admitted, "I should have known better than to underestimate you. Unfortunately, your shenanigans in the car leave us no time for a proper goodbye." He slipped the material off her shoulder and kissed her freshly healed skin.

She stiffened in response to the tenderness of his lips. The intimate act brought her heart back to the moment in the Testing when she'd allowed him into the sleep chambers with her, against her better judgement. She recalled the cruel words he'd spoken to work up the nerve to do what he'd been ordered to do, kill her. *He was staring at her like he wanted to say something more but couldn't find the words.* She'd slumped forward, kept upright by the chains burning her wrists.

Kevin lovingly brushed her sweat dampened golden ringlets out of her face, whispering, "Sorry Kayn. This is going to be extremely unpleasant."

She coldly mumbled, "For you, when I get out of these." Kayn struggled against the metal cuffs that bound her once more. Kevin cracked a grin and began to walk away. He paused, turned around, marched back over and passionately kissed her on the lips. Her lips parted as his left hers, partially out of shock, but also because she'd felt the familiar pull of their connection. That telltale tug in her heart, she'd assumed was gone. He smirked as if to say, you still want me. Then turned and strolled away without saying a word. *He sure was ballsy now, she'd give him that.* The sunlight disappeared as he closed the door to the sweltering container. There was a moment of silence as she tried to figure out what she should do. She heard tiny clicking footsteps on the roof. *It was probably buzzards. Those things creeped her out. They were always waiting for someone to die.* Kayn struggled against the chains as sweat began trickling down her brow. *It's like a sauna in here.* A droplet reached her upper lip, she licked off the salty perspiration. *Perhaps, she could pick up someone's thoughts? There was nothing. Shit.* Kayn spoke aloud, "Lexy and Grey know we're in trouble. I'm sure they're already on their way." *The others would be weak. They'd probably been in this sweltering heat for a while without water. The others were gagged, nobody could respond.* The temperature inside the container was rising at an alarming rate with the door closed. *The only thing worse than the heat of the sand was the heat of the damn metal storage container under her bare feet.* Perspiration was trickling down her brow into her eyes. *Her throat was so dry.* She couldn't work up enough moisture to swallow. Dizzy, Kayn struggled against her restraints. She heard a buzzard's uncoordinated tap dancing on the top of the container. *The others wouldn't be conscious for long if she was already in this state. How close was she to Frost? Could she touch him? If she could take his energy and double the tension on the restraints, maybe she could break free.* Kayn hollered to get their attention, "I might be able to get us out of here. I need you to try to touch the person next to you with a part of your body. Frost, lean towards me or stretch out one of your legs. These restraints are meant to bind one of us, but they might not be able to hold back the energy from all of us." *She could hear them rustling. They knew what she had planned and were pissed off enough to withstand the pain.* Kayn stretched her leg out. *It touched Frost's. Her motor skills were already succumbing to the rising temperature. She required energy.* Closing her eyes, she focused on the connection between Frost's skin and her own. She shivered as heat coursed up her leg into her torso. Her chest tightened as energy gathered there. She experienced euphoria, like nothing she'd ever felt as the powers of each Ankh travelled through the connection they created. It coursed through her body until it felt like energy was going to burst from her skin. She yanked her restraints off the wall, easily tore her wrists free and heaved open the storage container door. Sunlight lit up the torture chamber. *Death by sauna, pure genius.* Kayn took in the disturbing visual of slumped bodies dangling from the walls. *If she'd killed them, it was only temporary. There was an insane amount of adrenaline coursing through her, she wanted to punch a hole through the metal wall. It was too much power. She'd taken too much.* Kayn marched over to Frost and tore his chains from the wall. He crumpled to the floor. She heard something sizzling and peered down. *His cheek was cooking on the metal floor. It was hilarious. Why? She had no bloody idea.* She continued down the line to Lily, Zach, and then to Mel. *They were all sizzling on the floor.* She giggled as she made her way to Haley and Astrid. She became side-tracked by an ominous painting on the wall and reached up to touch it.

Mel's voice gasped, "Don't touch that."

*Healers never stay down for long.*

"What is that hissing sound? Do you hear that?" Mel asked as she got up and noticed it was cooking flesh. "They're cooking from the heat of the metal floor! We have to get them out of here!"

Kayn far too casually said, "Does it really matter. I had to use their energy to break the chains. It's just their shells. I planned to refill them once I got them all down."

"Yes, it matters," Mel scolded.

They towed roasted friends down the ramp, depositing each one in the sand at the bottom before going back for the next. Once her fellow Ankh were all off the grill. They stood there gazing out at the healing job ahead.

Mel glanced at her, questioning, "So, right now it's safe to say you're rolling on the energy from all of us?"

Still reeling from the euphoria, Kayn nodded. *It was frigging magical.*

"Can you give the energy back by healing them?" Mel walked down the ramp and began feeling pulse points. She looked up and announced, "They're all still alive!"

*Whoops, perhaps she shouldn't have left them sizzling on the floor. She'd assumed she'd killed them.* Kayn wandered back in and retrieved the chains from the floor. *Where did Triad get these chains? They'd rendered them all helpless. The symbols looked familiar. Had she seen them somewhere before?*

Mel cleared her throat and said, "Earth to Kayn."

Kayn snapped back to reality as she strolled down the ramp towards her slightly perturbed friend.

"You're obviously on another channel still." Mel said, "If I heal them, will you heal me?"

Gloriously gapped out, Kayn pressed her fingertips together. She slowly pulled them apart and a glowing orb appeared. *It was mesmerizing. She'd almost forgotten she could do this. Mel was still talking to her.* She glanced at her friend and asked, "Did you just say something?"

Mel's eyes were wide as she ordered her to stop messing around and put her hands in the sand.

*She was not a child.*

"If you put your hands in the sand, it might stop the buildup of energy. I'm going to need you to heal me once I'm finished healing everyone else."

Once Mel had reworded her prior order as more of a suggestion it became more appealing. *Why not?* Kayn knelt, placed her hands in the sand and the granules began to glow with a creepy yellow hue that expanded in a circle around her until it reached her fallen Ankh. Their burns healed. They all opened their eyes, gasping for air. *Well, that was extremely cool. She'd healed them all in seconds.*

With her lips parted in awe, Mel declared, "Now that was amazing." She reached for Zach's hand and helped him up.

Once Kayn released the excessive amount of energy she'd borrowed, her sanity returned. *Awkward.*

Zach dug around in his pockets. He held his phone up in the air and cheered, "Yes! My phones still here!"

*Why hadn't they taken his phone? It seemed like the obvious thing to do when you kidnap someone.*

Astrid dug the phone out of her pocket and declared, "Mines dead but I have mine too." Astrid opened up the back of her cell and laughed, "I thought we got off to easy. They took the batteries."

Opening his cell, Zach chuckled, "There's no battery in mine either. Look in the sand. Maybe they just chucked them."

They searched for their batteries in the sand but they were nowhere to be found. Kayn was standing in the tiny amount of shade created by the storage container. Zach noticed her bare feet and asked, "Do you want my socks or my shirt?"

Kayn smiled at him, knowing he'd probably give them to her. She replied, "I can heal myself from a sunburn, you can't. I'm sure they'll be here soon. I have clothes back at the motel."

Zach shook his head and teased, "My grandparents were from Mexico, my half naked freckle-faced friend. When have you ever seen me with a sunburn?" He bent down and looked underneath the storage container.

Kayn got on all fours and copied his actions. She questioned, "What exactly are you looking for?"

He accidentally bumped into her with his shoulder and she toppled over on her side in the sand. Zach grabbed her arm, helped her up and apologized, "I didn't mean to do that. I was wondering if this would work for shade, but the metal is too hot." He sat up and enquired, "How are you doing, with the Kevin leaving you to die in the desert thing?"

Kayn sat beside him and drew a picture in the sand with her finger as she answered, "Well, that's how it has to be now. I'm sure someday I'll be the one that leaves him somewhere to die." Zach didn't keep the conversation going, he just sat there watching her playing with the sand. She raked her fingers through the sand full of tiny pebbles, grabbed a handful and strained it through her fingers, leaving nothing but a handful of rocks in her palm. *She'd survived her first official run-in with Kevin. He'd kidnapped her in her underwear and left her chained up in the desert.* She grinned and dropped her handful of pebbles.

*It's a good thing she found damn near everything funny right now. Where were Lexy and Grey?* Kayn stood up and offered a hand to Zach. She tugged him to his feet, noting that she was still quite a bit stronger than usual. They wandered over to the others, just as they all noticed the cloud of sand rising in the distance. Kayn knew who it was even before she could see them clearly. *It was Grey and Lexy.* As they came into view, there was someone in the back. *Holy crap. They have Molly.* They all began to laugh as they sprinted towards the approaching vehicle.

Frost leaned into the window and chuckled, "I have to know how this happened."

Grey grinned as he began to explain, "We were on our way back to the motel when Triad drove by with Molly. We hung back and followed the car, instead of trying to find you guys. We ran them off the road, killed them and stole her back. We saw the dust from a second car and thought, maybe that was the other vehicle Triad was using. It was and here we are."

Raking her fingers through damp hair, Lily opened the door and asked, "Where did you find this beater and how does it still run?"

Grey passed her a bottle of water as he replied, "Let's just say our options were limited. We should get out of here. They'll be back soon and they'll be seriously pissed off."

As Frost got into the backseat of the sketchy vehicle, Lexy glanced back and prodded, "How in the hell did they capture all of you?" She passed him a bottle of water.

He shrugged, twisted off the lid as he replied, "I came to, sweating to death and chained to the wall in the back of that sweltering storage container. I have no bloody idea how it happened." Frost chugged the entire bottle of water and began passing bottles to everyone else.

Mel piped in, "We all woke up in there, except for Kayn." She passed a bottle of water to Kayn.

Kayn twisted off the lid and downed the entire bottle. *She'd needed that*. She peered up from her empty water, wishing she had ten more. *Lexy was staring at her. She was probably wondering how they'd taken her without a fight.* Kayn started to explain, "I went to sleep early and woke up with my hands chained. Kevin was in my room. He used this spray chloroform on me. I came to in the backseat of his car. Stephanie said he left me ungagged because he wanted to talk to me. I overheard Stephanie say they hadn't found Grey or Lexy so I bit a chunk out of my shoulder to signal you. They brought me to that stifling storage container and chained me to the wall with everyone else."

Frost spurned the tale on by saying, "Oh, don't stop now. You're leaving out the best part of the story."

Meeting his penetrating gaze, she glared at him, saying, "What part is that?"

Frost smirked and teased, "Kevin kissed her before he left."

Grey chuckled, "While you were chained to the wall in front of everyone, kinky."

Lexy asked the obvious question, "How'd they chain you to the wall?"

"I'll be right back," Kayn said as she ran back to the storage container and reappeared with the chains.

Lexy took them from her and stated, "I see what they used. These are supposed to be foolproof. How did you get out?"

She wondered how it was going to sound but decided to just spill it all, "I got them to touch each other so I could drain their energy to overpower the spelled chains. I ripped the lock off the storage container, opened the door, then tore the restraints off the walls, and removed their cuffs. *Mel woke up while they were all baking on the metal floor. She'd just leave that part out of the narration.*

Mel covered for her by skipping the unsavoury part of the story, "I woke up and we dragged them outside into the sand."

Zach gave Kayn a hug, saying, "Thanks buddy."

*She'd left them all sizzling on the floor for a good five minutes. Don't be so quick to thank me.*

Lily prodded, "Thank her in the car you guys. Squeeze in everyone. We really have to get out of here."

When everyone was in, the only spot left was on Frost's lap. It was just how the attempt to sandwich way too many people into a tiny backseat had gone down. *She knew he'd be the one to bring up that kiss. It wasn't like she'd asked for it. She'd been chained to the bloody wall.* The windows were rolled all the way down. Her hair kept whipping her in the face but if they slowed, they'd all be eating sand. When they pulled onto a cement road, her hair started blowing behind her. She tried to tuck her crazy locks behind her ears. Frost twisted her hair in a knot, but it didn't work. She leaned against him, so he wouldn't have to spend the drive back to the hotel with a mouth full of her hair.

"I'm sorry I brought that up," he whispered.

Kayn sighed, "I knew you weren't going to let that one slide." She looked at their reflections in the rear-view mirror. *He appeared to be pissed off. This was going to be a fantastic drive.* She turned and questioned, "What?"

Frost scowled as he asserted, "Oh, come on. You can't

possibly be that naïve. You saw the way the kid looked at me after he did it. That kiss was a territorial guy thing."

*They were packed like a can of sardines in the backseat. She didn't have the patience for any jealous hissy fits while in this claustrophobic situation.* She gave him her best fake pageant smile, stating, "It wasn't about you. He was clearly messing with me. Next time I see him I'll make sure he understands you were only interested in a serious relationship with me when you were certain I'd be dead soon." *Why had she said that?*

Amused by her feisty behaviour, he wrapped his arms around her waist, pulled her against him and whispered in her ear, "You're onto me. However will I sleep with you now?"

His warm breath travelled delicate tendrils behind her ear. She shivered and exhaled. *She wasn't fooling anyone. Not even herself. She wanted him so badly, sometimes it was all she could think about. She was trapped on his lap in her underwear, if they weren't sardined in this car full of people... Why was she this ticked off?*

He seductively taunted, "Who peed in your cornflakes this morning?

*Once again, she saw his expression in the rear-view. He was loving this.* She removed his arms from her waist as she sarcastically jousted, "Maybe, I'm just finished with your passive aggressive bullshit. Now, I want you, but wait, I can't sleep with you as quickly as I'd like to so, I'm going to just walk away and ignore you." *Then I'll let strange slutty girls touch my chest in the hot tub.* "I want to be with someone who wants to spend time with me. Someone like Zach, for instance."

Zach looked at her and chuckled, "Oh, don't you dare drag me into this."

*It occurred to her for the first time that they might both be idiots.*

Frost was quiet for a second before he cupped each of her sparsely covered hips with the palms of his hands and whispered in her ear, “I know exactly what you want.”

Her breath caught in her chest. *Don’t look back at him. Don’t look in the rear-view mirror.*

While driving, Grey chuckled and teased, “I’m a little disappointed that you’re not wearing superhero underwear today.”

Grey, Lexy and Molly were in the front. Everyone else was in the back. *There were far too many of them sandwiched into this tiny car.* Kayn ignored Grey’s teasing. She tapped Molly on the shoulder and said, “I’m glad you’re still with us.”

Molly smiled as she glanced back at her and answered, “I’m glad I’m still with you guys too.”

Mel squeezed Molly’s shoulder and declared, “That was a close one.”

“It was too close,” Lily decreed. “She’s only sixteen. We have to keep her with us until she’s eighteen. I talked to my father. Their group might have to stay close to us for a while. They have another teenage boy named Dean. So, we already have three and this never happens. They are going to pass them off to us and shadow us as back up.”

Kayn smiled, finding herself a little excited to meet this new kid. It was going to be tight in the motorhome. She asked, “How old is Dean?”

Turning with her ebony hair whipping in the wind, Lily responded, “He’s almost eighteen, and by almost, I mean his birthday is either today or tomorrow.”

*Even covered in dust with insanely windblown hair, Lily was still the most beautiful girl she’d ever seen. She wished she could hate her but she was a wonderful person. They had to be almost there.*

Zach elbowed her to get her attention. He tapped Grey on the shoulder and provoked, "Are we there yet?" Grey swung his arm in the back and he ducked out of the way.

Grey threatened, "I will pull this car over, maim you and leave you incapacitated by the side of the road as an afternoon snack for the buzzards."

They all started to laugh. Kayn smiled as she stared out the window at the surprisingly scenic desert landscape. She was exhausted and felt herself relaxing against Frost.

Frost whispered, "Don't be mad. I was just jealous, that's all."

"Forget about it. I was shocked to see him. I was frustrated and angry. I'm sorry I took it out on you," Kayn quietly answered.

Grey whispered, "Awe, is everybody friends now?"

There was a loud crash. *Shit!* The car lurched and flew into the barrier. *They were going over the cliff. No seatbelts, over a cliff... Crap.* The second impact tossed the vehicle over the side of the cliff.

Molly cried out, "We're going to die!"

They gave each other a comical knowing look as they plummeted towards what would have been certain death if they'd been mortal. The first impact with the cliff tore the door off. Kayn grabbed Molly's arm and squeezed it for a second. Feeling no fear as she was launched out of the missing door. She felt her bones break, agonizing pain. Her mind whispered, *shut it off*. She heard the crunching of the vehicle as it descended and crashed at the bottom. Her vision flickered in and out, then there was nothing...

# 16
## GONE

*She heard faint voices.* After a short blackout, Kayn awoke unscathed in a precarious position on a ledge halfway down a ravine. *How long had she been out?* She peered over the ledge. *The vehicle was at the bottom. Awesome! That was a long fall. She'd have to jump. She could stop her descent in the in-between, but would she be able to stop it here? If she couldn't, it would be excruciatingly painful but death wasn't a permanent situation anymore.* She looked up. *She'd fallen a long way. There didn't appear to be witnesses. She should jump right now before anyone else showed up. The Healers were awake.* Lexy had climbed out of the wreckage, she was helping Mel. She sensed someone above her and looked. *Good thing she didn't jump. She would have been caught.*

A man called out, "Want me to call for help?"

Thinking on her toes, Kayn yelled, "We're filming a crash for an independent film, everyone's fine!"

Lexy sarcastically hollered up, "It's just dummies in the car, they're fixable!"

"That scared the crap out of me, it sure looked real!" The flustered man shouted.

*It was challenging to look serious while laughing hysterically on the inside. Lexy just referred to everyone in the car as just dummies.* Kayn called out, "Thank you for offering to help, we're all good here!" *He'd better not ask any questions. How in the hell would she explain where she was? She was halfway down a cliff filming the movie with no camera. The story had more than a few holes in it but once you gave someone a reasonable explanation, they usually didn't dig deeper.* He waved and disappeared.

They waited until they heard him driving away before speaking. Lexy bellowed, "Molly's gone!"

Kayn yelled back, "Dead?"

"They took her!" Lexy shouted.

Kayn's heart sunk as she looked around. *No cars were driving away in the distance at the bottom of the ravine. Where did they go?* She jumped off the ledge, slowing herself easily before hitting bottom, she landed on her feet. *That was cool, it totally worked.* Mel and Lexy were healing the others. In minutes, they were all standing in the sweltering sun at the bottom of a ravine in the desert, without transportation or Molly. *They'd been overly cocky.* Her stomach tightened. *Talk about a delayed response. It would have been handy to be warned before being forced off a cliff.* She smiled and asked, "Was that Triad?"

Shaking her head, Lexy replied, "No, it was Trinity. Glory was driving. She's hard to miss."

Something inside of her relaxed at the mention of Trinity. *Molly would be alright with Trinity. They had two years to get her back. She was only sixteen. If it had been Triad, they wouldn't want her back after two years. She'd never be compatible with the others for Testing. They could still get her back.*

Lily held up her cell and laughed, "I was all excited for about five seconds when I still had my phone but then I remembered Triad took our batteries."

Grey snatched it out of her hand, took off the back and laughed aloud, "That's so evil. I guess we should be thankful they left you guys phones. We need to go. Let's get out of here before another 'Good Samaritan' shows up."

Frost was leaning against the hood of the trashed beater, aimlessly picking away at the rust and peeling paint. He chuckled, "Go where? We're at the bottom of a ravine in the stifling heat. There's nowhere to go but up. We'll have to scale the side. I don't know about you but I'm not in any hurry to climb up there in this sweltering heat."

Lily knelt, picked up a pebble and pitched it at the side of the demolished car. It tinged off the metal an inch from Frost's leg. He scowled at her and stood up. She sighed, "You're such a baby sometimes. We just went over a cliff. Markus' group is already looking for us. Now, quit being a whiner and climb. Better to scale the side of that now than when you're dehydrated."

Standing at the base of their inconvenient climb, Lexy touched the stone, stared up at the feat before her and declared, "I can climb it."

Kayn looked up the steep ravine. *There were ridges in the stone that went almost all the way to the top. It wasn't impossible. Nothing was anymore. There was a clear area of difficulty. They'd need to make more steps.* She strolled over to the annihilated vehicle and began searching for sharp solid pieces that could be driven into stone. Lexy saw what she was doing and came over to help because Dragons were problem solvers. *The descent severely compromised the trunk. It was smashed inwards, but the contents may still be inside.* They grabbed raised metal and yarded it open. There was a roadside assistance kit. Lexy opened it, finding a tire iron. *This might be useful.* Kayn opened a toolbox. *Bingo!* Inside were various sized screwdrivers, wrenches, and even, long thick metal nails. *No hammer? A hammer would have come in handy. They could use the tire iron as one.* Lexy tucked various metal objects into her jeans. In the netting on the back of the right passenger side, Zach found a hammer. He squeezed her shoulder where Kevin kissed it and passed it to her. *She wasn't sure why her mind snapped back to it, but she didn't need to be thinking about that crap right now.* Kayn passed the hammer to Lexy. *There was a time when she would have spent hours dwelling on a first encounter. Now that she had the ability to compartmentalize her emotions, it was different. She'd altered her perspective. She allowed herself anger in the moment she felt it and stopped hiding the parts of her personality meant to be wild and free.* Her pulse raced. She looked at her arms. Her veins were raised and visible. *It was a good thing she had energy to burn off. She was going to need it.* Kayn stared up the ravine, seeing where they'd need to add steps. *It could be done. If she fell to her death, it wouldn't be more than a slight inconvenience. Once they'd made it to the top, the others would follow. The stifling heat would create obstacles like sweating brows and sopping hair but everything about the climb was doable.*

Kayn glanced at Lexy and said, "I've got more than enough energy to drive those spikes into the side of that ravine."

Her fellow Dragon smiled at her as she responded, "That's

why I'm going first. If your ability operates like mine, the more you burn off, the more you'll need."

Kayn watched where Lexy placed each hand and foot, mirroring every action as they climbed to where they had to drive steps in for the others. Lexy hammered the first ones into the side of the ravine easily. Scaling after her, Kayn grasped the third makeshift metal stair. *It was slick with perspiration.* Her fingers started to slip off. *Shit, she had no choice.* Pressing her body against the rock, she slid to the spike below it. Adrenaline shivered through her as sweat streamed into her eyes. *It was frigging hot against the stone. By the time the others came up the nails would be too hot to hold onto with bare hands.*

Lexy called out, "Are you alright?"

Kayn answered, "I'm fine. The nails are slick. They'll be too hot to hold onto soon. They'll need to wrap their hands in material to climb it."

Growing short of breath, Lexy gasped, "Good idea. We're almost there. I don't need to drive in more spikes. It'll be easier now."

Relieved to grab the stone underneath Lexy's foot, Kayn glanced up. *They were closer than she thought.* She was dizzy and dehydrated by the time she reached for the ledge. Her sweaty palms were a second from causing her to plummet to the bottom when Lexy's smiling face appeared. She grabbed ahold of her wrist and yanked her up over the ledge. They both sprawled out flat on their backs to catch their breath. Kayn's vision wavered and she started to giggle. *She'd been far too cocky about that climb.* She closed her eyes and exhaled.

Lexy called out to the others, "You'll need to wrap your hands in material. The spikes are hot and slippery."

Kayn opened her eyes to find Lexy standing above her holding out her hand. She assumed it was to help her up.

Lexy whispered, "Quickly, before the others make it to the top. Don't take too much, we might have a full day's hike through the stifling desert ahead of us."

Kayn grinned as she took Lexy's hand, and hers began to heat. Just as she felt a wondrous rush of energy, Lexy snatched her hand away.

Feeling like a new woman, Kayn scrambled to her feet, looked at Lexy and confessed, "Thanks, I needed that." She peered over the ledge. The others were following their lead.

Lexy grinned and replied, "I know what it's like."

One by one, they helped the others in those final moments as they reached the summit of the climb. Once they were all at the top, they stood as a group and stared out at the seemingly endless span of nothing. *There was not a vehicle in sight on the lengthy span of desert road. No water supply in their near future either.* Kayn swallowed to wet her dry scratchy throat. She licked her lips.

Grey grabbed her, cautioning, "Don't lick your lips, it'll only make it worse."

Choosing the direction they were headed when they were forced off the road, the exhausted immortals began their journey down the deserted stretch of desert road. She'd been tuning out the heat of the sand under her bare feet for a while, noting she could opt to walk on the pavement instead of the sand by the side of the road. She stepped on the cement and hopped right back into the sand. A light breeze made her senses spring to life. It felt truly amazing until she inhaled an unwelcome mouthful of sand and choked on it. Zach patted her on the back. She noticed the sand caked on her sweaty braless chest as her bits and pieces dangled in front of her and was suddenly self-conscience. *Everyone else had clothes on and here she was wandering through the bloody desert in her underwear and the tank top she'd worn to sleep the night before. This was bullshit. She'd have to keep this day in mind the next time she chose her bedtime attire.* The breeze tickled her skin again. She got an eye full of sand. Kayn leaned forward and rubbed her eyes as she tried to blink the irritating grains away.

Zach placed his hand on her back as he consoled, "I know it sucks. Don't rub them, just keep blinking until it stops."

Still leaning over, she willed enough moisture to form in her eyes to stop the insanity. *It didn't hurt, it was just irritating. She knew that was one of her triggers.* Her eyes cleared. Zach was standing in front of her when she looked up. He lifted the corner of his t-shirt and used it to wipe the accumulation of sand out from the corners of her eyes. Grateful he had her back in her mini moment of need, Kayn smiled and decided to walk on hot cement versus getting more irritating sand in her eyes. They picked up their pace and caught up with the others in no time. After hours of trekking a deserted stretch of road, barefoot on sizzling pavement with scorching afternoon sun glaring on her, Kayn started to shake. Recalling Lexy's warning, she knew, she'd siphoned too much energy from the others that morning. Lexy had given her a touch of what she needed after the climb, but it wasn't going to cut it anymore. Her chest started burning and her head began to pound. She looked at her fellow Ankh, knowing none of them had extra energy to give her. *They were all barely hanging on in the heat. She had another day before she'd be risking the inconvenience of death by dehydration. That wasn't what concerned her. She was worried about what she'd do to the others if she lost control of the ability that she knew so little about.* After another hour of staggering through the desert, she started shaking uncontrollably. Her healing ability fed her adrenaline just as something shrieked above her. Kayn dove into the sand by the side of the road and started choking on the cloud she'd created. *An enormous red Dragon had attempted to snatch her up in claw-like talons as it swooped past.* The dust settled as she watched it soar off into endless blue sky until it became a tiny speck in the distance. She noticed everyone's legs. *Nobody else reacted.* They were standing around her with concerned expressions. She heard the sound again. When she looked up it was a hawk soaring above her. *This was embarrassing, her mind was starting to play tricks on her.*

Zach knelt beside her in the sand and teased, "Seeing things already? We could be walking for many more hours, even days." He took her hand in his and whispered, "Take some energy from me. I'll be okay for a while. We'll make finding shelter and water our priority."

Afraid she wouldn't be able to control the urge to take more than Zach had to give, she looked at her Handler and whispered, "I can't. I don't want to hurt you. You can't heal as quickly as some of the others."

"It's my duty as your Handler," Zach assured as he held out his hand to help her up.

Fearing what she'd do if she took it, she felt guilty. *She'd been offended when he hadn't wanted the job as her Handler. She'd felt like a burden because she was one.* Kayn refused his offer by standing on her own and faking self-control. *He would have given her his last breath long before it became his duty. That was how close the three of them were when they entered the Testing together.* She glanced over at Mel and she smiled back as their eyes connected. *She could do this. She had to.* She took shallow breaths, walking a few paces behind everyone else with Zach by her side. Frost and Grey were so far ahead, they looked like specks. They were searching for a shady place to wait for the arrival of the others. *Good luck with that. She just had to buy some time. Once nighttime arrived, they'd be granted a reprieve from the sweltering sun scorching their skin and sucking moisture from their pores. What time is it?* She attempted to look at the sun but couldn't focus. *There were six suns in the sky? She was clearly hallucinating.* She staggered again.

Zach grabbed her shoulders to stop her from falling. He held her against him and urged, "Do it. You have to."

Noticing the predicament, Lexy asserted, "Not you, Zach. We'll start rotating between Mel and I."

Appearing to be fine, Mel held out both hands and declared, "Me first. You probably can't stop cold turkey after the amount of energy you siphoned this morning."

*That made sense. She'd broken bones and healed faster than the others after the accident. When she'd fed from everyone to break free of the chains, she'd obviously taken the immortal cork out of the bottle.* Kayn took Mel's hands and hers began to heat up, drawing energy into her body. With each passing second, she felt more alert.

"That's enough Kayn," Mel whispered. "I have to be able to walk."

Kayn abruptly let go of Mel's hands, surprised she'd been coherent enough to follow orders. *That felt amazing.* She took a moment to gather her scattered thoughts before saying, "Thank you. I needed that."

Mel grinned at her and replied, "No problem hun."

Their attention was drawn to the road ahead as Grey let

out a hoot and began sprinting back down the road towards them. He spun around and pointed at the horizon. *There was a building in the distance.* Frost took off ahead to get a closer look. At least there was a possible end to the stroll through this sweltering hell on earth. Everyone's spirits perked up a touch as they began to joke about what the building might be. Her brain ceased to care about the need for energy. *Please let there be running water and a restaurant.* Her stomach turned. *Crap. That was never a good sign.* They walked until it became clear it was a motel. They picked up their pace. As they grew closer, they saw the massive industrial fence surrounding it. *Was it under renovation?* There were a few cars parked out front. They were all older models with a thick layer of dust. *Nobody had taken the time to write rude messages. This place had been deserted for some time. It had been her experience that people always wrote on dirty cars.* The hotel's large stained double doors swung open with a pitchy squeal, startling everyone. Frost was standing there grinning. Her stomach grumbled and twisted into a knot, but she didn't even wince. *Her feet had been on fire since that morning.*

Frost announced, "I have good news and bad news. Which do you want first?"

Zach rolled his eyes and sighed, "Always the good news. Let's just make that the new rule. We all have the same queasy sensation. I'm sure we can all hazard a guess at what the bad news is."

Grinning, Frost started with good news, "Well, there's food in the freezer. The kitchen is stocked up, the water is turned on and nobody lives here but I think I know why this place was closed. Saying it's haunted, would be an understatement. I know you're all exhausted but we're going to have to clean house before we can relax. I also found a couple of creatively deceased workers. They were probably killed by the entities that are stuck in here. I also found police tape from a crime scene. So, I'm running under the assumption the workers were in here cleaning up after something that happened. The main entry is thick with dark matter. Do you three remember the dark entity in that house before your Testing? Well, there's at least a dozen of those demonic entities in there. I know it's been a while since Astrid and Haley have had to deal with these things but you never forget dealing with these assholes. We are going to have to work first so we can play later and by work, I mean take a small scenic stroll through hell."

*They'd been cramped into a car, forced off a cliff, climbed up a ravine and walked for countless miles through the desert. She needed water before endeavouring to do anything else.*

Frost looked directly at her and teased, "There's a case of hot water in the back of that car. Cold water won't be on the menu until we've worked our way inside."

Grey started walking over to the car. Lexy beat him there and smashed the window with a boulder. He sparred, "See, this is why we never have nice things. The bloody door is unlocked." He opened it. Lexy shrugged and climbed into the backseat. She grabbed the water and passed each of them a bottle.

Scrunching up his face, Grey stated, "If bottled water has been in the heat for too long it's like poison."

Lexy wiped the layer of scum off a lid, passed him a water and chuckled, "Suck it up buttercup. It's liquid and if I have to kill myself in five minutes time, I'm going to need to drink this nasty stuff first."

Casually accepting a bottle from Lexy, Frost disclosed,

"One more thing. I found the workers in the freezer. I opened the door with no problem. It was just locked. I bet they hid in there from whatever evil shit came after them and were locked inside. They're dead and frozen solid. So, they don't smell. That's always nice. Especially if we might be stuck here for a few days, while we're waiting for the rest of our Clan to show up. After we're done here, we'll drag them out of the freezer and burn the place. It would probably be fair to assume nobody's come looking for these guys."

Lily shimmied past Frost at the door to sneak a peek inside. She came back out with a solemn expression and didn't say a word.

*That was never a good sign.*

Grey chimed in, "A situation messed-up enough to render Lily speechless. This, I've got to see." He stepped inside and dashed back out a second later. "How in the hell did that happen?" He laid his hand on the side of the building and said, "We'll need a plan. There's no way our usual routine will work for that many."

Kayn tried to slip past Frost to get a look. He blocked her and cautioned, "You've been in a volatile state ever since you siphoned that energy this morning. You should stay out of this one."

*He was right. She was doing a half decent job of controlling her urges, but a room full of demons in this state might be too appetizing for her to handle right now. She'd taken it from her own Clan and accidentally siphoned from mortal demon filled shells. What would happen if she ingested a demon's energy in its true form? Something this dark would be powerful. You are what you eat.* She smiled as she wondered if that quote applied here. *Maybe she could control it? She'd been in darker places. She'd managed to find her way back after the Testing...sort of.*

Frost walked over to the side of the building, grabbed a few bags of salt, tossed one to Grey and announced, "I found these in the kitchen. They didn't attempt to stop me from entering or exiting the building. We can create a circle in the doorway and see if we can disperse them old school demon style. It won't kill this kind of entity but it might scatter them. It'll be easier to take them out one at a time."

*She'd had a dream about demons, she'd taken their energy and made one of those orbs.* Frost walked into the building and poured the circle of salt. He stood in the centre of it while Lily held the door open and called the rest of them into the building. They all walked inside and dove into the spiritual safety of the circle. Ignoring Frost's wishes, Kayn entered the building. *He hadn't noticed her standing there yet. This was incredible. She couldn't wait.* In awe, she whispered, "Shit, how is this even possible?" Irritated by her inability to follow instructions, Frost glared but didn't order her to leave. The entire ceiling was a snaking web of black intertwined spindly spider legs of energy. They writhed, moving through each other, entangled limbs reached out, beckoning her closer, willing her to become a part of the darkly twisted dance of vile entities. The rhythm of the creatures made Kayn's chest heavy. She felt her skin beginning to heat. *She was so hungry. What was happening to her?* She held one of her hands in front of her face. *Every vein was darkened and raised from her skin.* Her brain began to give her instruction based on instinct. *She was hungry. So very hungry.* They joined hands. As Mel reached for hers, Kayn stepped away, pointing out what should have been obvious after this morning, "Look at me. I'll take your energy the second you touch me."

Curious, Lexy probed, "This morning, when you took energy from everyone to break those chains, created to immobilize an immortal, how did you know what to do?"

"It felt like logic," Kayn replied. "I could channel someone else's energy to make myself stronger in the Testing."

Mel's eyes lit up as she explained, "Oh, you should have seen her in the Testing. She created this ball of energy, tossed it at Kevin's girlfriend and blew her into a million pieces."

"Do you think you can do that again?" Frost asked. "Lexy and Mel can save their energy to disperse them after you've scattered them."

*Maybe.* Kayn nodded as she replied, "I'll still need to use energy from you guys. I was feeding from the walls of the Testing. I have no idea how many of you it would take. When we destroyed these things the last time, you had to allow it to feed from one Healer and then send a jolt of energy through the other. What if we tried the same thing with one of the Healers and I sent the jolt of energy? I can send more of it. Maybe, even enough to take them out two or three at a time. Lexy can come in after and heal us. Then, we'll go back in and deal with the rest." She sensed Zach and turned around. *Her Handler was agitated by what she was offering to do. That was a first. Their connection was becoming stronger.*

Livid, Zach met her eyes, firmly asserting, "Absolutely not! You don't know how to control this. Frost was right when he suggested you should sit this one out. Go wait outside. We'll join up and send a jolt of energy to separate the cluster on the ceiling. We can take them out one by one after that if we have to."

*Party pooper.* Kayn scowled at him. *It was Zach's job to rein her in.* It had taken him a while to stop being angry about it. *Inconveniently, he appeared to be all in now. The others saw this.*

She watched as Grey squeezed Zach's shoulder as he stood behind his decision, "He's her Handler. If Zach feels like this might be too much for her, then it probably is. It's not worth the risk. How about we stick with the original plan. We'll bring her in once we've exhausted all other possibilities."

Kayn shook her head. *It was bullshit having someone else tell you what you should or should not do.* She met Lexy's gaze and read between the lines. *Lexy also thought she should go outside and wait. It was going to be difficult to do.* Her mind whispered, *wait till they're dead and do what you want.* Kayn conceded, "Fine, I'll wait outside." She slipped out the door and waited for the show to begin. She knew when they started dispersing them because all she could hear was screaming. *All of this for air-conditioning and a soft bed to sleep in.* She heard a crash and assumed one of her friends had been launched across the room. Kayn wandered around in the shade of the building. She wasn't worried because being immortal meant death wasn't permanent. It always took the sentimentality out of the situation. It was torture most aspired to avoid. She still heard wails of torment coming from within the walls of the motel. *Once it stopped, she'd be able to go inside.* Looking forward to finding out what she could do, Kayn picked up a rock and pitched it but it didn't make it over the fence. *Personally, she didn't care if she avoided the torture part. Pain was also only temporary and she could shut down a lot of it. This was the high point of embracing the abilities of a Dragon. Danger was exciting and pain was quite doable.*

As sunlight hit the car's window, a vision of the first time she saw Kevin after he'd been taken by Triad flashed through her mind. *She'd fallen and he was standing above her with the sun shining behind him. He'd reached out his hand to help her up. She recalled the hope she'd felt in that moment. She'd spent the whole year before the Testing dreaming about it. Hope wasn't a word that applied to her life after the Testing. She didn't hope for things anymore. She made them happen. She'd believed in so many things she didn't have faith in anymore. With every inch of her being, she'd been sure their bond was so strong he would regain his erased memories of her. He'd never be able to hurt her when it came down to it. She'd believed they could overcome the fact that they were in different Clans and find a way to be together, but she wasn't a child anymore, and those had been immature fantasies based on lack of life experience. She now understood why he'd haunted her dreams for so long. You dream the most about the things you can't have. She still dreamt about him sometimes but most of the time it was more like she was watching him move on with his life from afar. Any romantic dreams she'd had of him since she'd come out of the Testing always ended with something messed-up happening.* She found herself smiling, knowing all future interactions would be a gong show.

She'd gapped out. Kayn snapped back to reality. *No sound... total silence. It was time to go inside and see what she was capable of when there was nobody to tame the Dragon.* She entered the building and noticed only half of the creepy ceiling dwelling beings. Lexy and Mel were face down on the stairs. The others appeared to be missing. She had to act quickly if she wanted to test out her abilities before the Healers awoke to scold her. *She was starving*. Kayn climbed the staircase and raised both hands above her head, daring the half dozen black swaying entities above her. They expanded in size as they grew closer. Kayn looked up at the dark masses and spoke to them, "You'd better hurry up." Her pulse raced as the beings attached to her and raised her body into the air. Resembling a sick version of a marionette, Kayn allowed them to take from her, until her chest began to burn. Instinct took over and she felt her body humming as she drank them down, ingesting the dark beings as though they were nothing more than demonic milkshakes. Deliriously giddy, Kayn dropped to the stairs, drunk from the excessive energy swimming through her. *It was amazing. She had to get rid of it now.* She stood up, touched her fingertips together and slowly separated her hands, until a pastel yellow haze formed between them. *What was this? It wasn't blue this time, it was yellow. It was just like her dream.* When the orb reached a certain circumference, she knew it was ready to use.

Lexy sat up. Her eyes widened as she interrupted her moment, "What do you have there?"

Kayn grinned. *She'd heard Lexy's voice and noticed that her fellow Dragon was awake, but it seemed inconsequential and it sounded like it was coming from far away.* She continued to mold the hypnotizing orb between her fingertips. *Where another one of her Clan members would have attempted to subdue her, Lexy did not.*

She heard Lexy speak from the somewhere else again, "Show me what you can do with that light before our wardens wake up."

This time Kayn focused on her. *Lexy understood because she was a Dragon too. She had no intention of stopping her.* Kayn scaled the stairs and paused at the beginning of the hall. The lines of red doors on either side appeared to go on forever. The ceiling from about halfway down was thick with writhing madness. *Throw it.* With fear no longer an issue, Kayn strode towards the writhing mass of demonic entities. Lexy took cover as Kayn tossed the glowing orb into the centre of the wicked things and they disintegrated. All that remained was dust on the burgundy carpet where each entity had been. Everything became normal. Her pulse slowed and her sanity returned.

Lexy stepped out of one of the rooms, chuckling, "That was frigging amazing!"

*Kayn knew what she was supposed to do with her light. She was supposed to rid the world of the dark things.*

Mel was standing on the stairs as they turned to go back down. She asked if they knew where the others were and of course they didn't. They'd been doing things only a Dragon could appreciate. The trio began to search the hotel, ironically finding the others almost drained of life in the freezer. Above them was a whirling mass of dark things. This time, Kayn knew what to do.

Lexy grabbed Mel's arm and towed her out of the room saying, "Trust me. Kayn's got this."

The dark mass swirled above her as Kayn raised her hands up to the twisted abominations and enquired, "Are you guys hungry?" The demonic infestations began to drink from her essence, levitating her body in the air as they devoured her spirit. They dragged Ankh's bodies out of the freezer while Kayn kept the darkness occupied. She allowed them to feed until instinct whispered, *Now.* She pulled energy back into her and dropped to the cement floor with a thud. She touched her fingers together and began to mold a yellow orb.

Seeing what she was doing, Mel stammered, "Crap!" She slammed the freezer door just as Kayn hurled the orb into the mass of demonic entities.

They turned to ash and became nothing but piles of dust. Kayn's grasp on reality instantly returned as she comically knocked on the back of the freezer door.

Lexy opened it and said, "Are we back to normal now?"

"We are," Kayn replied as she strolled out of the freezer to curious eyes.

# 17 FINALLY

With everyone healed, they raided the vending machines and retired early to the rooms they'd chosen for a well-deserved demon free slumber. Just as Kayn was about to close her eyes, the emotionally taxing events of the last couple of days began swimming through her mind. *What she needed was a break. A whole week where she could just sit back and take the time to absorb the crazy events of the last forty-eight hours. Matty was alive. He'd been reborn. He remembered her and this time around, he was Second-Tier. How had that happened? She'd been actively trying to shut that tidbit of information down inside of her head. Any enquiries she made into his whereabouts, could lead Abaddon straight to him. He'd need to be hidden away for at least fourteen years to have a shot at survival. She wanted to see the picture Zach took.* After spending a few minutes scouring the impressively dusty room for Zach's cell, she knew he must have taken it into the bathroom with him. *He'd been in there for a good hour. He was sitting on the toilet playing video games.* She climbed back onto the bed, stretched out on top of the covers and sighed. *She could either stare at this white stucco ceiling until he was finished or go find something else to do. There was no way she was going to be able to shut her mind down.* Far too amped up to sleep, Kayn sat up, slid off the bed and thought about knocking on the bathroom door to ask Zach if he wanted to explore the motel with her. In the end, she opted to go alone. She wandered down the hall. The burgundy flowered wallpaper oddly matched the red doors of each room. Everything blended together giving it a creepy feel. It resembled a scene from an old horror movie. Kayn almost expected to see ghostly twins riding tricycles at the end of the hall. She peered in each direction, hearing nothing but total silence. *Everyone was sound asleep. She should be exhausted, but for some reason, she had energy to burn.* Kayn sauntered barefoot down the hall, descended the stairs and glanced to her right. The swinging doors lead to the kitchen. To her left was a hallway she'd yet to explore. Curious, she strolled past a conference room into what she assumed had been a restaurant because there was a large sign listing the specials of the day. It was a neat little diner with high wooden tables and a bar with stools. *Perhaps it had been more of a pub?* She could picture the hum of people's voices with country music blaring from the jukebox beside the pool table. *It had probably been a cool place before the demon infestation.* Kayn's stomach growled. *This time, she knew the complaints were hunger induced and not a sign of trouble.* She made her way to the vending machine by the washrooms. She needed real food with nutritional value, but this would do. She scoured the contents for something besides the potato chips and Twizzlers. She'd eaten those earlier from the machine upstairs. *There were Snickers bars. Score! At least they contained peanuts.* Instead of smashing the glass, she decided to try a creative approach at obtaining the snack. Focusing on the Snickers bars, Kayn motioned her hand towards her. Packets of Skittles beside the Snickers fell into the metal tray. She tried again and everything dropped into the bottom. *Yes!* She did a victory dance before retrieving the spoils of her small magical victory. She attempted to shove them into her pockets but had none. She'd forgotten she was wearing underwear and a tank top. Kayn placed the candy on the dusty bar, opting to come back for them after she'd done more snooping. As she wandered down the hall to the washrooms, there was an unlabeled door. Inside was stairs descending into darkness. Feeling like nothing could harm her now, she went for it. Once she'd reached the bottom, she felt around and flicked on the lights. It was a rustic wine cellar. She searched the shelves. Most of the bottles were empty but she managed to find a few dusty bottles of bourbon. *Zach liked bourbon.* She'd never tried it so she brought one with her. She scaled the stairs, bottle in hand and wandered over to check out the jukebox. *There was a lot of country music, mostly Rascal Flatts. That group had always meant a lot to her. This wasn't the day to be listening to country songs that reminded her of everything she'd lost along the way.* Sitting on a tall barstool, she peeled open the wrapper of a Snickers bar and devoured it in seconds. She twisted the lid off the bourbon, grimaced as she smelled it but took a swig from the bottle anyway. *It was nasty tasting stuff but Zach would love it. She owed him a present.* Gathering the spoils of her exploration, Kayn made her way back upstairs to her room. She strolled down the hallway of identical red doors, opened her room and wandered in. *Zach was still in the bathroom. Good thing she hadn't waited for him.* Kayn placed the bottle on the dresser.

She was staring at her reflection in the mirror as the bathroom door opened. *She was in the wrong room.*

A half-naked Frost teased, "Were you feeling like our conversation earlier wasn't finished?"

Her pulse raced at the shirtless sight of him. Instead of darting out of the room, she coolly handed him the bottle of bourbon and acted like she'd meant to come to his room. His fingers grazed hers as he took the bottle from her hand. She held onto it instead of letting go. As he moved the bottle to his chest, he brought her along.

With his face dangerously close to hers, Frost baited, "Aren't you going to let go?"

She released her grasp feeling like an idiot.

He grinned as he strolled over to the sink and grabbed a few cups. He poured them each a glass and handed one to her. Frost took a sample taste and remarked, "This stuff is damn strong." He took another sip before adding, "I heard about what you did today. Those skills of yours will come in handy down the road." He raised his glass and saluted her, "To slaying demons like they're nothing."

They clinked plastic glasses and drank. Kayn hadn't really wanted more of the vile tasting liquid but the need to push her limits when it came to him was overwhelming. She grimaced, looked at the liquid in her classy plastic cup and stated, "This stuff is truly horrible."

Frost winked and chuckled, "It's definitely not my favourite deviance." There was an extended moment of silence before he teased, "You accidentally came into my room, didn't you?"

Kayn cracked a giant grin as she replied, "I expected to find Zach wandering around shirtless, not you."

He pretended to be stabbed in the chest. Frost stared into

her eyes as he confessed, "I'm glad you ended up in the wrong room."

She peered into her almost empty plastic glass. Frost snatched it out of her hand and refilled it. Kayn hesitated but took it from him, admitting, "I shouldn't have more."

"Why shouldn't you?" Frost probed as he gazed back at her with unflinching amusement.

She didn't answer. *There was no reason why she shouldn't... not anymore.* Kayn apologized, "I'm sorry about earlier."

He chuckled as he took another drink and provoked, "You mean when you accused me of only wanting you when there was a convenient time limit to our relationship? I'm lost, you've had a busy day. Maybe you're referring to that kiss from Kevin?"

*A part of her wanted to drop kick Frost in the junk and watch him squirm around on the seventies brown shag carpet. Another part of her wanted to keep stretching her boundaries.* Kayn met his eyes and provoked, "Shut up."

Frost locked eyes with her and sparred, "Make me."

*He was daring her to do it. She wanted him to see her as an equal, not a scared little girl.* She took a few calculated steps closer. *He didn't believe she was going to do it. She never could resist a dare.* Kayn leaned in and paused a breath from his with parted lips. Raking her fingers through his hair, she boldly pulled him closer. As his lips touched hers, every nerve ending in her body lit up. *She was done fighting this.* She shivered as he darted his tongue against hers. Her breasts became aching peaks straining against the thin material of her shirt. In a swift movement, he lifted her, clutching her behind in the palms of his hands as he carried her across the room and pinned her against the wall. His tongue darted between her parted lips as he caressed her with only a thin layer of material separating his hands from her until she was shivering uncontrollably. He put her down for an agonizing second as his hands slipped beneath her top. He nibbled the tender flesh of her earlobe as he groaned, "Say you want this."

Every inch of her was aching for him. *Was it not obvious?* Her hands were pressed against his taunt ab muscles. She found the courage to slide one into his pants, letting him know what she wanted without playing his game by having to say the words aloud.

Zach opened the door and said, "Hey Frost. Have you seen?"

*They'd been caught.*

Frost stepped back, grinned and remarked, "She's right here."

Absolutely mortified, Kayn manoeuvred out of Frost's reach, grabbed the bottle, a few snickers bars and slinked out of the open doorway past her grinning Handler.

As Zach closed the door behind her, he teased, "If you were having fun, it wasn't necessary to leave on my account."

She passed the bottle and gave him a curt response, "We're not going to discuss this."

Grinning, Zach ribbed, "Alright, it didn't happen. I saw nothing."

He ushered her into their room. *It was next door. She'd miscounted by one door.* Kayn excused herself and disappeared into the bathroom, stopping to look at her reflection in the mirror. *It was worse than she thought.* Her lips were swollen and there was a mark on her neck. She touched the slight discolouration and smiled. *She'd never had one of these before.* Every part of her was pulsating with need. *She was going to have hot dreams tonight*. Kayn turned on the shower, stripped off her clothes and stepped under the spray. Her skin was all tingly from his touch. She heard the shower next door and touched the wall separating them. *Yes, he drove her crazy, but she wanted to be with him so badly she couldn't think straight. Frost was undeniably hot but that wasn't why she wanted him. It was the way he looked at her when he thought she couldn't see him. It was how he'd cared for her from a distance and allowed her to figure out what she wanted. It was the expression on his face when she did something goofy. It was that ring from the bubblegum machine and the fact that he let her go, so she could have the time to say goodbye to Kevin without feeling guilty. It was because she'd always found solace in the knowledge that he was close by. There were easily a million other little things. Why had she left? She knew it was a Dragon's instinct to run from anything requiring emotions. It was also a Dragon's instinct to run towards danger and he was certainly that. If she could have found a way through the wall without Zach seeing her, she would have*. Kayn touched her lips. *She'd be replaying that kiss in her dreams all night*. She rinsed herself off, turned on the freezing cold water and allowed it to pummel her face. *It helped a bit*. Stepping out, she dried herself off and put her underwear and top back on. Her tank top was disgustingly dirty. Zach was out cold lying on top of the sheets. *Good idea, this place had been deserted for a while*. She was too tired to worry about it. She fell asleep the second her head hit the pillow.

Kayn awoke to the light streaming through the sheer curtains. She rolled over, groaned and buried her face in the pillow. *After that night of steamy dreams, she'd have to get her game face on before she ran into him*. Zach stirred and peeked in his direction.

He stretched and taunted, "Sleep well last night?"

"I slept just fine," she sighed. He glanced at her. They both leapt out of bed and raced for the bathroom. He beat her, giggling as he locked the door. Kayn left and wandered down the hall to figure out which room Lily was in. *If there were toiletries in this hotel, she'd have them.* A door opened. She held her breath, knowing it was him.

A glorious bare-chested Frost teased, "Had you stuck around last night this would have been your walk of shame."

Glad he'd said something funny so she could retaliate without feeling awkward and inexperienced, Kayn rolled her eyes at him and sparred, "Good thing I left." She kept walking, more determined than ever to find Lily's room.

Following her down the hallway, he groggily flirted, "Don't knock it until you try it."

*Don't knock it till you try it, seriously?* She knew she shouldn't turn around but couldn't help it. Kayn stopped walking as she glanced back at Frost and they bumped into each other. He grasped both of her arms to keep her from going anywhere and she bit her bottom lip.

He gazed into her eyes and whispered, "All lame jokes aside, you know I don't want to just hook up with you. I want more than that."

Lost in the intensity of his gaze, she still managed to find the words, "I've made it clear I want more from you but I don't want to keep playing these games with you Frost. We can't keep starting over from scratch."

Moving his hands seductively down the length of her arms, he whispered, "We're almost done playing games." He kissed her sweetly on the forehead and backed away from her.

*What in the hell did he mean by that?* A door opened, down the hall. *It was Lily.*

Holding toothpaste and a bar of soap, Lily remarked, "You'll have to share, that's all there is."

He got there first and baited, "Guess you're going to have to come with me if you want some."

Resisting the urge to grin, she followed his muscular back into his room.

Grinning, he glanced back at her and teased, "Yes, I caught what I accidentally said." Frost turned to face her and flirtatiously instructed, "Hold out your finger if you want some."

Kayn smiled. *She wouldn't have been able to contain that one even if she'd wanted too.* She shook her head as she held out a finger. He squeezed toothpaste onto it and did the same with his own. They both stood in front of the bathroom mirror, rubbing their teeth and tongues with toothpaste. He passed her a plastic glass of water first and she rinsed and spit into the sink. He did the same. *It was kind of adorable.*

He handed her the bar of soap and offered, "You can shower first."

*It felt like a dare. They'd showered the night before but neither one had been able to use soap.* He didn't leave as she slipped out of her flimsy top and underwear without breaking eye contact. Feeling like she'd won their flirtatious game, she stepped into the shower and turned on the water, certain he was going to leave. The curtains opened. *Was he getting in with her?* She exhaled.

He stopped her from turning around, by pressing up against her and whispering in her ear, "Don't worry, I don't want our first time to be in a shower either."

Frost washed her back, and as he rubbed suds on her

front, she bit her lip, breathlessly anticipating his touch. He soaped her down everywhere but the places she wanted him to touch her. *He was doing this on purpose.* She leaned back against him, attempting to give him a dose of his own medicine.

Frost groaned in her ear, "I've been thinking about doing this to you all night." He abruptly got out of the shower and left her standing there, covered in suds, wanting him more than she ever had.

She heard him chuckling as he left the bathroom. She rinsed herself off and got out, but he was already gone. There she was standing in his room just as she'd left him the night before, turned on and confused. She started to giggle. *He was good. She hadn't even seen that one coming.* Kayn put on her dusty panties and slipped on her top. *Fine, two can play at this game.* She grabbed the toothpaste off the counter, wrapped the soap up and went to find the others.

Zach was waiting for her in the hall. He grinned and probed, "What was that about? Frost left with the biggest grin on his face."

She passed him the toothpaste and countered, "I'm assuming it was payback for leaving him last night."

Giggling, he taunted, "Please tell me he got you going and left you standing there."

*She could admit it when she'd been had, or in this case, not had.* Kayn admitted, "He left me standing naked in the shower covered in soap."

Zach howled. Fake pouting, he playfully harassed, "I guess you know how it feels now."

As they strolled down the hall, she sighed, "He made his point but paybacks a bitch."

Her Handler chuckled, "It's possible he was thinking more about making his point than who he was making it too."

They heard Markus' voice. *The others were here.* Kayn felt self-conscious, aware she was only wearing the underwear and tank top, she'd been kidnapped in.

Zach nudged her, assuring, "It looks like your wearing spandex shorts. Don't worry about it."

*Right, don't worry about it.* The duo wandered downstairs into the foyer that had been covered in dark things only the day before.

Jenna's voice loudly announced, "Kayn, I hear you've been a busy girl."

Her eyes widened. *For a second, she thought Frost had told her everything, then realised she was talking about the ball of energy she'd used to destroy the demons.* Kayn disclosed, "I learned a few new things about myself." She made eye contact with Frost and he smiled at her. Jenna looked directly into her eyes, grinning. *She always knew way more than she let on.* Kayn took the bait and asked the question teetering on the tip of her tongue, "If you know everything, why don't you just tell me what I can do and save me some time?"

Their Oracle sparred, "What fun would that be?" Jenna placed her arm around her, teasing, "I'm just waiting for the shit to hit the fan over what you did, and when it does, I'll know for sure."

*Why did she always have to speak in code?* Kayn questioned, "Know what for sure?" Jenna smiled as she walked away, disappearing through the swinging kitchen doors. Kayn called after her, "Know what for sure?"

Markus responded, "Who your father is."

A shiver ran through her. *It was an odd response to talk of who sired her. She felt uneasy. She'd had a father. He'd been a wonderful father. He was dead and she didn't need another one.*

Standing beside her, Zach whispered in her ear, "Who do you think it is?"

Making herself comfortable, Kayn sat on the bottom step as she replied, "I have no idea and I don't care." She saw Mel chatting with Orin. Their relationship had been growing slowly but steadily since they'd returned from the Testing. *Would it really be that bad to have family? Her Uncle Frey had been a disappointment and her mother was just gone. She had her Clan, the promise of something more with Frost and the knowledge that she would see Matty again. That was all she needed to keep a glimmer of hope alive for her future happiness.* Everyone was gathered at the door, having an animated chat about the events of the last three days. Kayn remained seated, assuming they were waiting for a speech about what was going to happen next.

Grey walked over to her and piped up, "I think it'd be cool to know where my father is. He just disappeared and never came back. I barely remember what he looks like and I've never run into him."

Lexy elbowed her Handler teased, "Would you, take ownership of you?"

Grey glared at her and sarcastically sparred, "That was uncharacteristically harsh Lex."

Kayn pressed her lips together to stop herself from giggling. *That was totally characteristically harsh.* Grey winked at Lexy, she socked his arm. Kayn was enjoying watching everyone's interactions. Frost walked out of the swinging kitchen doors. He grabbed her hand, tugged her to her feet and led her away. *Where was he taking her? She'd thought about snatching her hand away, but heaven help her; she still wanted to go with him.*

*Wait a minute. What was she doing?* She wrenched her hand away and provoked, "Why would I go anywhere with you?"

He chuckled, "Oh sweetheart, I'm sure you're aware it's more fun for me if you don't go willingly." Frost flung her over his shoulder.

She was laughing as he kicked the kitchen door open. It swung shut as he carried her over the threshold. He was laughing as he put her down on the island in the centre of the kitchen. He gave her peck on the lips and disappeared. *Had he seriously left her there again? Oh, she was going to have to kill him.*

Frost reappeared moments later, announcing, "Here we go. No more games, starting right now. If you want a relationship, you've got one. Do you want steak for breakfast?" He fired up the stove, turned and winked at her. Then walked over to the fridge and opened it. A nasty scent wafted across the room. He feigned choking and said, "I guess it's just steak."

Kayn slid off the counter and wandered over to try to peek at what he was doing. He chuckled as he obscured her view. She suggested, "Maybe if you broil that steak, it'll be edible."

Frost grinned at her and declared, "I'm a thousand years old. I know how to cook a steak."

It felt like they were a couple cooking together in their kitchen. She walked up behind him, wrapped her arms around his waist, kissed his bare shoulder and taunted, "Don't remind me."

He leaned back, kissed her cheek and sparred, "You're a hitman. I think it all evens itself out, doesn't it? I'm willing to date someone who'd kill me first and ask questions later."

*He had a point.* Kayn kissed his shoulder once more before releasing him from her embrace. She began to roam around, opening cupboards on a search for steak sauce. She found some. It was still sealed. She hollered, "Heads up," as she chucked it at Frost. He caught it a split second before it smoked his head.

Grey burst through the swinging doors, saying, "I hope you're making some for everyone. It smells gamey and freezer burnt, but if I have to eat one more bag of potato chips this week, I might lose my frigging mind."

They were standing there staring at the meat sizzling in the frying pan when Lexy appeared through the swinging doors. She wandered into the kitchen, commenting, "You know that's human meat."

Frost turned off the stove and dumped the steaks into the garbage, admitting, "No, I did not, but if you say it's human. It's human. Well, that cute idea is done. Let's go see if Markus and the others want to try to pile us all into their vehicle and drive to the nearest town for something to eat."

On the counter, Grey sighed, "They've already left."

Frost swung around, questioning, "They left?"

Grey slid off the counter and explained, "Mel and Lily went. They need three Healers and extra muscle for a job."

Kayn grabbed the steak sauce and placed it back where she'd found it.

Searching for something, Frost turned and said, "Wait a minute. They left us with one Healer for two jobs. That doesn't make sense?"

Listen, I'm only the messenger. Don't get your panties in a twist. We have Lexy and Kayn is rechargeable. I've got us a couple of vehicles. We can take the highway back to the RV and truck. The new kid's eighteen."

Putting the frying pan in the sink, Frost questioned, "They left the new kid with us?"

The boy earlier referred to as Dean, wandered into the kitchen and proclaimed, "I have a name."

Frost shook his hand politely as he greeted him, "Nice to meet you, kid."

The teenage boy looked at Frost, saying, "It's Dean. My name's Dean."

Lexy took off and Grey followed her. Pausing in the doorway, Frost teased, "Go with it, kid."

Kayn smiled at the new guy but didn't bother to shake his hand. *She wanted Molly to be standing there, not this kid. He meant nothing to her.* She saw him appreciatively following Frost with his eyes. *Maybe, he isn't into girls?*

Grey hollered from the stairs, "Drag the bodies out of the freezer. I'm lighting this place on fire."

They strolled into the freezer to drag the corpsicles out of cold storage into the kitchen while discussing their favourite kinds of eggs benny. Dean did what he was told, moving stiff icy bodies with a confused expression. *Drag the bodies out of the freezer. I'm lighting this place on fire. The sentence hadn't even registered as abnormal.*

Frost clapped his hands, declaring, "We've moved the bodies. Let's burn this shithole to the ground and go find us some eggs benny."

*If the new guy was Trinity, they were grieving the people they'd lost in the Testing. Nobody would be joking around.* The rest strolled out. Dean was standing there with an eyebrow raised. Kayn touched his shoulder, enquiring, "Which Clan did you come from?"

Dean shoved open the doors with dark muscular arms and

they squinted as sunlight came streaming in. Holding it open for her, he replied, "I came from Trinity."

"How long were you with them?" Kayn questioned.

Looking at her, Dean replied, "Eight months. I had to wait for the next group to go into the Testing. I wasn't eighteen yet."

*It was worse than she thought. He was friends with the kids who hadn't come back out. She remembered Leanne. She'd liked her.* Kayn responded, "I knew a few of your friends. They were good people."

"They were," Dean replied as moisture filled his eyes. "I turned eighteen yesterday. I missed going in with the last group by months. They would have made it back out if I'd been in there."

"You'll get the next group out. I know you will," Kayn assured. Dean smiled as they stepped up their pace to catch up with the others. *She was trying to be optimistic, but she knew it would go one of two ways. Either he'd fight extra hard for Ankh because his friends hadn't made it out, or he'd have difficulty attaching to the new group and trap them all in the Testing.* They piled into the vehicles. Hoping Greydon checked to make sure they ran, Kayn poked his shoulder, taunting, "Exactly how far do we have to drive these beaters?"

Chuckling, Grey said, "I know they're sketchy. They paid for our rooms for another night. They only need to run until we get back to the last hotel we stayed at. The RV is still parked out back with our truck. They couldn't take Dean for some reason. He's eighteen though, he's sealed to Ankh. Markus' group kept the other kid. We have a couple of jobs this week. We're driving up north to fix a little mistake and there's a girl up for Correction. If she survives, we're going to try to grab her before the others get there."

*Just going to grab her before the others get there. It sounded like it wasn't a big deal at all. She knew better. Were they ever going to get a couple of days off?*

Frost stuck his head into the vehicle she'd gotten into, asking, "Want to keep me company? I'm driving the other car."

Smiling, Kayn got out of the car. Before walking away, she peered through the open window and said, "See you later Dean." She made her way over to the vehicle and sat next to Frost. Between them was a bag of munchies from the vending machines. She peeked inside the plastic bag. *It was mostly Twinkies. Hilarious.* As they drove away, the third floor was engulfed in flames. *It occurred to her that demons were like a plague of locusts destroying everything in their path. She could devour them before they devoured everyone else.* As they left the smouldering demonic stronghold, Kayn knew she'd only touched the surface of what she was capable of.

# 18

# ALL THIS TIME

During the drive back to the motel they'd been kidnapped from, they talked about normal things couples would chat about on a long road trip. They inappropriately ate some Twinkies, and on several occasions, she found herself wanting to hold his hand. When they arrived at the motel and it was time to get out of the car, Kayn was disappointed. She got out and grabbed the plastic bag off the seat. They'd have to stop at the office to get new keys, their's were long gone. She turned to talk to Zach, and when she glanced back at Frost, he'd taken off.

Putting his arm around her, Zach gave her a buddy squeeze and declared, "I have it on good authority that we have a couple of hours to shower, change our clothes and order food that doesn't come from a vending machine."

They rushed up the steps. When she entered their room with whiteboards and marker graffiti, Kayn glanced at the adjoining door. *Was he in there yet?*

Her partner in crime, suggested, "Have a shower and change. I bet they're ordering the food to Lexy and Grey's room. Do you know what you want?"

She smiled at him and replied, "I'm starving. Order me a chicken burger and a salad. I need something green after a day of junk. Maybe an order of onion rings? Just in case the portions are small. I'd hate to be starving an hour from now." Kayn brought her bag into the bathroom. After a shower with shampoo and conditioner, along with a few minutes at the mirror with her toiletries and clean clothes, she felt like herself again. Zach showered next as she sprawled on the bed and closed her eyes for a few minutes. Someone knocked on the door. She got up and darted across the room to answer it before realising it was from the door to the adjoining room. *It was Frost.* She grinned as she rushed over and yarded the door open. He grabbed her arm, towed her into his room and kicked the door shut. Kayn giggled as he tossed her onto the bed.

He climbed up after her, scolding, "You were such a naughty girl, eating those Twinkies like that while I was trying to drive." He tenderly kissed her lips and tickled her.

They laughed and wrestled until she ended up poised on top of him. Pinning his arms to the pillow above him, she altered the playful moment, tempting, "I say we lock the door."

Allowing her to keep him restrained, Frost answered, "We're going to have a thousand occasions where we can just lock the door. Not for your first time. You deserve more. Next time we come to this hotel, I promise I'll take you anywhere you want."

"Right up against that door," Kayn teased, nuzzling his neck, she nipped the tender flesh of his earlobe.

Groaning, he stated, "Alright, Brighton. You'd better get off me. Our food will be here soon. If we keep this up, I'm not going to be able to go over there without having a cold shower."

She grinned as she got off the bed and strolled to the door. Glancing back, she flippantly provoked, "Enjoy your shower."

Frost leapt off the bed and chased her out the door. He caught her outside of Lexy and Grey's room. Backing her against the door, he playfully kissed her lips while turning the doorknob behind her. The door opened. He remained standing as she fell backwards onto the carpet with an ungraceful thud. He knit his brow and sighed, "Brighton's been hitting the sauce already. I hope this isn't becoming a thing?" He grinned down at her and casually wandered inside.

*Awkward.* She sat on the floor plotting her revenge before scrambling to her feet and explaining, "He opened the door without warning me. That's hilarious, Frost."

Smiling, Lexy passed Kayn her styrofoam containers and whispered, "Wait a second." Lexy straightened her up and patted down her hair. "I hate it when I accidentally fall down and end up with naughty hair." She winked before sitting next to Grey, who was also grinning from ear to bloody ear. Astrid and Dean were sitting on the floor by the window, laughing.

*They were all freaking hilarious. A room full of comedians.* Wandering over, Kayn sat in the empty chair by Frost and opened her meal. *No hot sauce.* Before she had a chance to pout, Frost jumped up and returned with a bottle of hot sauce. *So many brownie points.*

He placed it in front of her, kissed her neck and teased, "If that sexy behind of yours is still sore later, let me know and I'll kiss it better."

Her cheeks heated as they turned shades darker. *She wasn't ever going to be able to stay mad at him.*

Passing her a wrapped-up straw for her drink, Frost toyed, "Nobody in this room can judge. Especially those two."

Scowling, Grey questioned, "What do you mean by that?"

Lexy rolled her eyes and sighed, "Just eat your damn burger Greydon."

*Where was Zach? She glanced towards the window. Lexy seemed to know exactly what she was thinking.* "Zach was already here. He grabbed Haley's stuff. They must be having something to eat in your room."

Kayn shrugged as she dumped a disgusting amount of hot sauce on her bun and put it back together. She took a bite of her messy chicken burger. It dripped down her chin. Frost handed her a napkin. She gobbled up the whole thing in under a minute. When Kayn took a moment to breathe, she noticed everyone was staring. She'd inhaled a chicken burger, the side salad, and a full container of onion rings before Frost managed to eat his burger.

Lexy got up, walked over to Kayn and suggested, "Take some of my energy. We'll leave Zach and Haley alone. I have a feeling if you take some of Frost's, we'll be stuck here for days."

Frost grinned at Lexy and baited, "Party pooper."

Lexy glared at Frost as she gave him a little speech, "We'll be at the next stop for a week. I'm sure I could be convinced to look the other way for a day, if someone was super nice to me instead of being a pain in my ass."

"Point taken," Frost politely answered.

Reaching for Lexy's hand, Kayn explained, "I thought I was hungry for food this time." *Well, food and something we don't have time for.* She peered over at Frost, certain he'd heard her naughty inner dialogue.

Lexy smiled, disclosing, "I overload too. Sometimes, I need to injure myself so I can heal to feel normal. You occasionally feeding from me might help me out."

Grey chuckled, "True story."

Kayn glanced over at Dean and Astrid, watching from their rather odd choice of seating on the floor. *Who chooses to eat on the floor*? Holding Lexy's hands, she felt hers warm. The energy travelled up both arms and heated her chest.

Lexy yanked her arms away. Grinning, she shook her head as she walked away, thinking, *"That is quite the ability."*

Kayn heard her and smiled. *She'd just keep that to herself.*

Astrid stood up, looked at Frost and asked, "How long do we have before we need to leave?"

Up collecting the garbage, Frost replied, "I'd love to stay for another night but we have a tight schedule. There's somewhere we need to be."

"So, right now," Astrid laughed, helping him clean up. The others finished eating and tossed their garbage away.

Frost directed, "Grab your bags and make your way out to the back parking lot. Dean, you can come with me. We'll drive the cars back and meet up with you guys."

It was time to collect their belongings and ditch the vehicles in lieu of their truck and RV. Kayn offered, "I'll go get Haley and Zach." She snuck into Frost's room and burst through the adjoining door trying to catch them doing something, but they were innocently sitting at the doodle covered table. She walked in, announcing, "We're leaving. Grab your bags. We're supposed to meet at the RV. It's parked out back."

They began to clean up. Haley said, "I need to grab my things, I'll see you guys in a few." She unceremoniously left.

Grabbing her backpack, Kayn looked at Zach and asked, "Are you ready?"

He flung his bag over his shoulder, responding, "Ready as I'll ever be."

They strolled out together and quickly descended the stairs. Kayn was excited to get back into the RV. Grey was already there when they arrived, creatively shoving plastic bags from the vehicles into the cupboards. *They had junk food galore.* She watched him for a while. *He must have been good at Tetris. As he shut the last cupboard, he appeared to be quite pleased with himself.*

Grey glanced back and answered her inner commentary, "I kind of miss Tetris."

Kayn was still grinning about Grey missing Tetris as she slid her backpack in the tight-fitting compartment under the bunks. Zach chose the first shift driving the RV. Grey and Lexy were planning to take turns driving the truck.

Kayn wandered back to the front. She sat beside Zach for a minute and said, "Mind if I go to the washroom?"

"Take your time," Zach chuckled.

*He knew where she was going.* She smiled at him and sang, "I owe you one."

Kayn strolled to the back, finding a sexy once again shirtless Frost sprawled on the bunk she usually slept on. "Changing bunks?" She asked.

Grinning, he teased, "You're supposed to be up there with Zach."

"I happen to be on my way to the bathroom," Kayn toyed.

Frost grabbed her arm before she could go, flirting, "I hope someone brought the bag of Twinkies. I have big plans for those."

Dying to climb under the covers with him, Kayn baited, "Grey put it in the cupboard by the microwave. If you have big plans, you should hide them before they're gone." His hand slid down her arm to her wrist as she stepped away. He revved her engine by seductively moving his thumb in a circular motion on her wrist. She yanked her hand away and gave him a dirty look. He started to laugh.

Zach shouted, "Put coffee on!"

"Sure, I'll just be a minute," she yelled. Kayn sat on the bunk, kissed his lips and whispered, "Have a nap. I'll make sure I'm the one who comes to wake you when it's your turn to drive." She shimmied off the bunk and walked back to the tiny kitchen to brew a pot. She quickly scooted to the bathroom. When she came back, she filled a few travel cups full of coffee, using whitener because the milk was outdated. Carefully carrying them up to the front, Kayn handed one to Zach and scooted into the seat beside him.

"Did you get a chance to tuck Frost in?" He teased.

Smiling, she confessed, "I did."

Curious, Zach questioned, "Were you trying to catch us doing something when you burst into the room?"

Grinning, Kayn admitted, "I thought it would be funny. I'm surprised you didn't burst into Frost's room looking for me when you got out of the shower."

"I've already done that once this week. I think once is enough. I'm your Handler not your stalker," Zach taunted.

Kayn took a sip of her coffee and smiled. *Not so long ago, she'd accused Frost of stalking her.*

Grimacing, Zach bitched, "This is powdered creamer."

*She knew he'd catch that.* "If you prefer sour milk, I can make it happen," she countered, staring at the road ahead.

Laughing, Zach replied, "I'm good."

After a minute of silence, Kayn remarked, "I always pictured immortals living a classier life with big mansions and fancy cars."

Zach took another sip, commenting, "That's probably just Vampires."

"Do you think we'll ever have to deal with Vampires? I wonder if they're like they are in the movies?" They heard the group gathering at the table behind them. Kayn said, "Cards or Monopoly?"

"Scrabble," Zach chuckled, watching the road.

Astrid leaned over Kayn's chair and announced, "Zach wins!"

He fake cheered and enquired, "What do I win?"

Astrid playfully provoked, "Haley, what does Zach win for guessing which game we're playing?"

A chorus of laughter came from the table. Dean's laugh really stood out. Haley yelled her response, "Tell him, I'll stay awake and drive with him next time."

Kayn glanced over at Zach and quietly ribbed, "I don't think you should try to drive while you're doing that. It can't be safe."

Grinning at her, Zach whispered, "I can almost guarantee that's not what she meant."

"Move over a bit," Astrid urged. "I'm going to sit up here with you guys. Your commentary is always far more entertaining than a silly game of Scrabble."

*Yes, their commentary was rather magnificent.* Kayn shimmied her butt over, saying, "Come on up. Our boring four-hour long party is just getting started." They spent hours chain drinking coffee while joking around. Kayn felt like she was living a normal life as they talked about superficial random things. It was almost seven thirty pm when Zach pulled into a roadside diner. She got up as they slowed down.

Astrid suggested, "You should go wake Frost up."

Kayn rather ineptly attempted to manoeuvre her way to the bunks as they cruised into a bumpy gravel parking lot. He was fast asleep, facing away from her. She sat on the mattress, rubbed his shoulder lovingly and whispered, "It's time to get up. We're stopping to eat before the next four-hour stint of driving."

Frost rolled over and smiled at her with sleepy eyes. Stretching, he baited, "Look at you, being true to your word." He yanked her onto him and held her in his arms cuddled against him.

She met his eyes and whispered, "I'll always keep my word."

He cupped her cheeks in his hands, stared deeply into her eyes and replied, "I know."

Her heart leapt. *It felt so good to be with him like this.* With the pretence gone and their burgeoning feelings out in the open, it felt like she was finally moving on. She was looking forward to every step they'd take together. When Kayn stepped out of the RV, she took a deep breath of evening air. Soon they'd be up North. *She couldn't wait to go for a trail run.* They'd been working steady since her Testing. It had been so long since she'd felt the exhilaration of a run with nobody in pursuit of her and no one she was trying to catch. She'd found similar feelings in various acts over the last couple of months but she was far past due for soul recovery time.

Approaching her from behind, Frost wrapped his arms around her and pulled her against him, "Go for that run. I'll order your dinner. You can sit up front and keep me company while you eat it."

She turned to face him. Without speaking, she set the timer on her cell for fifteen minutes. She'd run for fifteen minutes in one direction, turn around and sprint back to the diner. She wouldn't be holding anyone up if she only used half an hour of time. Kayn took an elastic band off her wrist, pulled her hair back in a ponytail and took off through the gravel parking lot towards the highway. As her running shoes hit pavement, she was blessed with the euphoric sensation, she'd been longing for. It felt like only five minutes had passed when her cell phone beeped. She sprinted back to the roadside diner. Her brow was slick with perspiration as she returned to the parking lot. *That was exactly what she'd needed.* Kayn shoved on the door and entered the diner to the sound of dual high-pitched beeps instead of jingling bells. She noticed her group right away. Haley's neon pink hair signalled her to the table like a beacon. *Haley's hair looked cute with just pink tips at the banquet. She missed the makeup job they'd done on her. Perhaps, she should try stepping out of her box, versus attempting to put her friend back in one?* Kayn wandered over to their double-sized booth and everyone on one side shifted over to make room for her. *Clearly, only one of her butt cheeks was going to fit on the seat.* Without saying a word about her humorous predicament, Kayn perched on the edge. Zach handed her a container. She took it and politely explained, "I should wait a few minutes before eating anything after that run. I might puke. I'll eat it once we're back on the road." Smiling at her, Zach used his napkin to wipe her cheek and showed her the streak of mud.

*How did she always manage to get mud on her face?* Feeling tension from somewhere, she looked around the table. *It was wrecking her happy place. Grey was perturbed about something. Lexy and Grey were sitting far away from each other. Was this still about the Summit? It had been months. They'd appeared to be over that drama.* She met Grey's hostile expression with a giant grin and decided to bring it up, "Do you have an issue?" *He was just sitting in the corner boiling rabbits with his eyes.*

"Ask Lexy," he hissed.

Lexy didn't even look up from her food as he said her name. She popped a fry into her mouth, slowly chewed it and took a drink of her pop. She was being far too casual about it, making it more than obvious she was purposely ignoring him.

Furious, Grey cleared his throat and stated, "I need to get out of here. Can you guys please let me out?"

Everyone shimmied off the bench and released him from his corner. He strode away without looking back as Lexy continued to eat without even looking up from her plate. Frost followed Grey away from the table, leaving his food behind. *That was awkward.* Everyone finished eating rather quickly after the drama and left the table. Kayn stayed behind with Lexy.

When the waitress showed up to clean the table, Lexy politely asked, "Can we please have those two meals wrapped up?"

The waitress took them with her and Kayn took that opportunity to ask, "What was that about?"

Lexy glanced at her and began her little speech, "I know I've said this to you before, but don't ever sleep with your Handler. In the morning, he's been spelled to forget about it and your heart gets thumped out repeatedly. If you're super lucky, he'll want to spend four hours talking about a girl he wants to sleep with the next day. Some days I can take it like a champ and on others, I just want to grab his head and smash it into the damn steering wheel a thousand times. I can shut down my emotions for everything and everyone but him. I end up retaliating by telling him little tidbits of information I know will hurt him. Which is what I did today, just so I could shut him up."

Kayn probed, "What did you say?"

Her fellow Dragon smiled and replied, "I told him I agreed to give Tiberius what he's always wanted from me if he helped me with something during the Summit."

*Lexy had made a deal with the devil to save her. That's why Tiberius was there.* The waitress appeared with their takeout containers. They thanked her and left the restaurant. Kayn stopped her before they walked out of the door and asked, "Are you really going to do it?"

Lexy smiled at her as she quietly replied, "Let's just say I saw another side of him during halftime while we were fighting together at the Summit. I don't want to be with him, but I definitely wouldn't kick him out of my bed for eating crackers."

Kayn strolled beside her with an enormous grin on her face. *She knew the feeling. It was funny how their friendship was beginning to evolve.* They walked out of the beeping door together and made their way back to the RV. The engine was already running.

Lexy grabbed Grey's container and climbed the couple steps at the entrance as she said, "Good talk. Hopefully, Frost had enough time to talk him down. He's always had a way with those greater good speeches. He's probably in the backroom pouting. He'll be happy I saved his food."

She followed Lexy up the steps and parted ways inside as she went up front to bring Frost his dinner and eat her own. He was waiting with a grin on his face. She handed him his container. He quickly scarfed the rest of his burger down before they pulled out of the gravel parking lot onto the highway. She ate her cold meal. *At least it was a chicken caesar wrap. It didn't matter if it was cold.* They sat watching the small patch of highway lit up by the headlights until her eyes began to grow heavy.

Slipping his hand over hers, Frost squeezed it, urging, "Go get some sleep. In seven hours, Zach will be needing his copilot. I'm alright. I'll wake you up when it's your turn."

*She needed to brush her teeth. That wrap was potent.* Half asleep, Kayn wandered to the bathroom as the motion of the road jostled her around. She grabbed her backpack so she could wash up. She used a spritz of someone's body spray, put on yoga pants and a t-shirt, then staggered to her bunk and climbed under the covers. *The pillow smelled like him. His scent was heavenly.* That was her final thought as she drifted off into a dream.

Kayn felt his arms around her as she groggily opened her eyes and it felt perfect, until she became nervous that she'd overslept. *He'd just climbed into bed beside her and fallen asleep. He was supposed to wake her up*. She tried to move.

He tightened his embrace and whispered against her hair, "Haley drove and now Astrid is driving. You're fine."

*What time is it? Where were they?*

He chuckled, "I drove for three more hours after you went to sleep. I came to bed around twelve thirty. Astrid was planning on driving for four hours with Haley. After they were done, Dean was going to take over until Zach woke up. Lexy and Grey have a lot to talk about. They're still trading off in the truck."

She relaxed in his arms, closed her eyes and tried to go back to sleep. *It wasn't going to happen. It felt like she'd had more than eight hours.*

Frost slid his hand down to her hip and seductively whispered, "If I were you. I'd get as much sleep as I could right now. As soon as we reach our destination, we get a whole twenty-four hours... alone."

Her pulse raced. *No chance she was going to sleep now.*

Frost started to laugh. He groaned, "Well, now that I've put that out there, I'm wide awake. If you want to get ready first, I'll go and make us some coffee."

*She didn't want to leave his arms.* Kayn slid out of bed, grabbed her backpack, and made her way to the bathroom. After she closed the door behind her and locked it, she stared at her reflection in the mirror. *She wasn't nervous or stressed out about the day alone with him. She'd been ready for this part of her life to begin for a while. It felt right.* She brushed her teeth, washed her face and even put on a bit of makeup. *Oh, shoot!* She soaped down her legs and did the fastest shaving job ever accomplished by a human being without having to go to the emergency room for stitches. She wandered out and balanced her way down the hall as he not so innocently brushed past her. He removed his shirt at the end of the hall. She watched until he vanished into the bathroom. Fighting to keep her thoughts on G-rated things, Kayn stuck her head into the front and asked Dean if he wanted a coffee. He opted out, saying he only had an hour left before it was his turn to sleep. Kayn poured one for herself and before she'd done anything to it, Frost reappeared wearing a black t-shirt with a v neckline and jeans. He hugged her and nuzzled her neck with his freshly shaven face. His aftershave made the intoxicating scent of his skin even more amazing. She draped her arms around his neck and sighed in his ear, "How many hours are left in this drive?"

He chuckled as he nuzzled her neck again and teased, "Only eight or nine more hours and we're on our own."

*That sounded heavenly.*

Frost poured himself a coffee, sat down at the table and announced, "They're splitting us up for the next job. My crew, Grey, Lexy and Lily will be doing one of the jobs. You five will be doing the other."

Kayn slid onto the bench seat next to him, took a sip of her coffee and questioned, "Which group gets Dean?"

He swallowed another gulp of coffee and replied, "We do. This next job will be another first. You and Zach will be enrolling in high school. The Aries Group will take care of the paperwork. The others will remain at the campsite as your back up. You'll be hanging out and going to classes while you wait for someone's Correction. If they survive, you'll take them with you. We'll meet up when both jobs are finished."

*It didn't sound that hard.*

He smiled at her and disclosed, "I never does."

She smiled back. *He'd responded to her thoughts like she'd spoken them aloud.*

He rested a hand on her knee as he leaned over and whispered in her ear, "There's an upside to separating us into two groups. We'll be able to get through the list of jobs faster and have more downtime."

Zach appeared from the hallway and enquired, "Hey lovebirds, is that coffee fresh?"

Once her shift with Zach started, time whizzed by. In the blink of an eye, they'd crossed the border into Canada. By midafternoon they turned off and drove down the winding dirt road to the campground they'd be staying at.

# 19

# TOUCHED

Kayn stepped out of the RV. Her senses were flooded by the fresh scent of the forest as she wandered out into the campsite. *They'd be staying here for a whole week. The idea of planting temporary roots even if it was teeny tiny weeklong ones felt glorious.* She stared up at the familiar feeling lush greenery. *She adored this Province. It felt wonderful to be back where the trees towered majestically above her. It was oddly comforting.* She'd be escaping to go on a trail run at some point. The group was already rushing around, doing their usual part in setting up the campsite. Someone grabbed her shoulder. She spun around. *It was Lexy.*

Her fellow Dragon said, "You two need to be back here, no later than noon tomorrow. Go inside and grab your bag." She released her shoulder.

*What was she supposed to say? Thank you for giving us time off for an uninterrupted booty call?* Kayn grinned at her thoughts as she scaled the steps into the RV and grabbed for the handle.

Lexy called after her, "Have fun!"

*And this situation just became even more awkward. If that was possible.* She turned back, gave her friend a slow nod and disappeared into the RV. *That was embarrassing.* The door dramatically slammed behind her. *She hadn't meant to do that.* The second she was alone, her mind flooded with nervous energy. *She'd evolved in so many ways since she'd become Ankh, but this particular scenario was intensely mortal and long overdue.* She grabbed for her bag and missed. Giggling, she reached for it again. *Oh, she was a nervous wreck.* She strolled back to the door. *She was really about to do this.* As she reached for the handle it occurred to her, *they all knew exactly where she was going and what she was about to do.* Kayn winced as she opened the door and descended the steps to the ground. *She was fairly certain she'd be able to maintain a straight face as long as nobody attempted to give her any pointers. Enter stage left, her Handler.* Zach raised his hand in an epically inept attempt to high five her. She shook her head and winced. Giggling, he dropped his hand to his side. *Where in the hell was Frost? They needed to leave before someone else tried to high five her.*

He appeared from the other side of the RV with his bag in hand and asked, "Ready to go?"

Zach gave her a thumbs up. She pursed her lips to stop herself from laughing, cleared her throat and replied, "So ready. Let's get out of here." As they strolled away from the group, she heard the snickers coming from the peanut gallery. *Yes, she'd walked right into that one with her response. The lack of privacy within their Clan was a double-edged sword. It was good because you were never alone. If something was wrong, you had this amazing extended family that always had your back, but this situation was just mortifyingly awkward.*

Frost unlocked the truck. They quickly got in. He turned the key and she smiled at him as they drove away. As soon as they turned the first bend in the dirt road, they both burst out laughing.

He looked at her, teasing, "Think of the bright side, after tonight, nobody will care about what we do. The novelty will be gone."

*That was true.* She slid her hand onto his and asked, "Do you know where we're going or are we just winging it?"

Paying attention to the road, he responded, "It's not far."

They turned back out onto the highway. The trees and mountains made it feel like they might be close to her hometown but she knew they were on the mainland. They drove for twenty minutes down the highway before pulling into a fancy hotel with a log cabin look and a scenic view of the mountains.

He smiled at her and announced, "This is it."

*It looked like a place you'd book for your honeymoon.* She was nervous as she grabbed her bag and got out of the truck but didn't doubt her choice for a second. *It felt right.*

They strolled towards the entrance together. He held open the door for her and she walked in first. *It was incredible.* A waterfall ran down the side of the wall into a stream that flowed through the centre of the lobby with see-through glass. They walked over it on their way to the desk. The man working behind the counter referred to them as Mr. and Mrs. Brown and congratulated them on their nuptials.

The kind looking man ushered them to the elevator and announced, "You newlyweds will be staying in one of our most luxurious honeymoon suites. You will find your little slice of heaven on the sixth floor. It's clearly marked on the door. There's room service at any hour and the items you've requested are already in the room. Please call me if there's anything else you need."

Frost opened his wallet and handed the man a few bills. The door closed and he backed her into the corner of the elevator. His lips met hers tenderly. He tucked her stray curls behind her ears on either side, gazed deeply into her eyes and whispered, "Are you sure it's me?"

He'd grazed his palm against her cheek, ever so slightly during the intensely loving gesture and her pulse raced in response to his innocent touch. She'd been attracted to him long before she'd fed off his ability. Perhaps, a part of it had come from her twin's love when their souls joined, but if she was honest with herself, he'd awakened something reckless within her the moment she found him shirtless on her bed, the night he'd marked her Ankh. He'd kept his distance when it was the right thing to do and selflessly let her go to have closure with Kevin. He'd been the one to stand with her before she dropped into the Testing. He'd given her little information but the look in his eyes had warned her of the horrors beneath her feet. He'd been there for each defining moment in her afterlife. Nodding, she tenderly cupped his face with her hands and asserted, "You told me a long time ago that all you needed was for me to say these words." She pressed her lips against his, pulled away and whispered, "I want you. I wanted you long before I should have." The elevator opened before he had the chance to respond, revealing a wide luxurious hardwood hallway.

Frost stepped out of the elevator, looked back at her and held out his hand. His eyes overflowed with emotion as he said, "Let's go."

There were only two doors in the hall. One had a gold

plaque on it that read, "Honeymoon suite." Frost swiped the key card and blocked her from entering the room as she attempted to walk past him. *What was he up to?* Frost grinned as he chucked his bag into the room. It slid across the floor. He grabbed hers out of her hand and tossed it inside. She was laughing as he gallantly scooped her up and carried her over the threshold. It was just as she'd always fantasized until he accidentally clipped her head on the door. *That smarted. A romantic gesture followed by a concussion, seemed like a normal expectation in her accident-prone existence.* She giggled as he kicked the door closed and carried her to the king-sized canopy bed. *He hadn't noticed she hit her head.* He tripped over one of their bags and his chivalry faltered as he dropped her like a sack of potatoes on the bed. She bounced around, laughing.

Wincing, he chuckled, "I'm so glad you have a wacky sense of humour. I tried. I really did."

Stretching out on the silky bedding, she smiled up at him. *The way he'd worded it sounded like he was saying he dropped her on purpose.* She started giggling again. *He was trying. That was more than obvious.*

As Frost walked across the room, he spoke, "I know we could both use some champagne but there's something I need to do first."

Kayn winced and rubbed her head while his back was turned. *That would have left a nasty goose egg if she'd been mortal.* She watched him sprinkling salt and placing stones around the room. He uttered a familiar phrase in Greek, and she smiled, knowing what he was doing. *He didn't want anyone to hear them.* He strolled over to the small table with a bottle of champagne and poured two glasses. She glanced around the room. *He'd truly outdone himself.* One of the walls was made of glass, there was an enormous tub and a fireplace. She was sprawled on a gorgeous king-sized canopy bed with silky sheets. *The room was incredible.* He turned around with a glass of champagne in each hand and came over. Excited for so many reasons, she sat up.

Frost smiled as he passed her a long thin wine flute and suggested, "We can order an early dinner if you're hungry?"

*He looked nervous.* She took a sip of the champagne he gave her and placed it on the nightstand. *He'd lost his cocky immortal exterior. In this scenario, he was just a boy nail-bitingly nervous about taking her virginity.* He remained standing by the bed with his glass in hand. Kayn got up, took the glass out of his hand and placed it by hers on the nightstand. She turned around and confessed, "I don't need anything right now but you." She bravely slipped her shirt off and tossed it onto the floor. Staring into his eyes, she undid the button and slowly unzipped her jeans. Frost exhaled deeply as she slid the material over each rounded hip. He continued watching appreciatively as she tried to seductively step out and ended up awkwardly kicking her pants aside because her foot got stuck. *That had almost been sexy.* She was about to walk over when his expression stopped her cold. *He was afraid. What could he possibly have to fear?* Frost snapped out of it and began his striptease. He undid the buttons of his shirt, exposing glorious, chiselled abs. Her lips parted. Her heart fluttered with anticipation as she bit her lip. *This was happening.* Watching her reaction, he regained his sexy cocky demeanour. Frost smirked as he tossed his shirt on the floor. He licked his bottom lip as he mischievously unbuttoned his jeans. She couldn't tear her eyes away as his pants dropped to his ankles. He smoothly kicked them away and smiled at her. He was wearing form-fitting sporty briefs. *They left little to the imagination. He was as excited as she was.* She tried to maintain eye contact but her eyes kept darting to the one part of him she'd never laid eyes on. He came to her, caressed her shoulders and seductively ran his hands down the length of her arms. She shivered as every nerve ending lit up. *What was he doing?* Stopping at her wrists, he sensually massaging her pulse points with his thumbs. *He drove her wild when he did this.* She gasped as the skin beneath his thumbs heated and her heart raced. *He was using his ability.*

Grinning, he disclosed, "Women have so many sensual places to stimulate." He lifted her wrists to his lips. His eyes glinted deviously as he tenderly kissed the delicate flesh of each pulse point. She was aching with need as he lowered her wrists from his lips. Continuing his naughty game, he seduced, "There's another one right here behind your ears." Without breaking contact with her tingling flesh, he mischievously slid his fingertips up the length of her arms to her neck and felt her racing pulse. She thought he was about to kiss her but he left her with parted lips, nuzzled her neck and whispered in her ear, "Do you trust me?"

*Sometimes.* He grinned at her inner commentary as his fingertips travelled her jawline to her ears. He caressed her lobes between two fingers on either side and then slid his talented fingers to where her ears joined with bone. Kayn shivered as goosebumps peaked on her arms. He gently, rhythmically touched her there until her lips parted as an intense wave of pleasure overcame her. She gasped as a single tear of ecstasy trickled down her cheek. Her knees buckled. He caught her, swept her up in his arms and placed her on the bed. She nervously squirmed up the mattress until her head was resting on a pillow anticipating what came next. Frost grinned as he kissed her ankle and joined her on the bed, feathering naughty kisses up her legs until he reached her panties. He hovered above there with the heat of his breath between her legs but kept going, slowly climbing up the length of her until his eyes met hers. She could feel the pressure of his manhood straining against her. Only a thin layer of material stood between her and what she was desperately aching for. She reached for him.

He stopped her and looked into her eyes as he confessed, "It's not time for that sweetheart. If we don't go slowly, I might lose control."

*He was afraid he'd lose control of his ability. She understood that feeling but didn't care. She wanted it to happen.* Frost sensually trailed erotic kisses down to her abdomen. He sat up. *What was he up to?* With a devious smile, he hovered his hands just a hair above the flesh of her abdomen without even grazing her silky skin. The area heated. Her body began to tingle and pleasurably ache. An intense euphoric sensation building within her made her squirm beneath him.

Holding her in place with his muscular thighs and the weight of his body, he seductively teased, "Are you ready?"

She moaned aloud in reaction to the intensity of the carnal pleasure he was creating within her. She arched her back in response as his deviously magical hands contacted her tingling flesh.

"Give in...Let go," he tempted, watching her squirm.

Clutching the sheets, overcome by pleasurable agony, there was a mind-blowing explosion from within. Her back arched as she cried out, each time a soul-altering wave of intense pleasure rippled through her. After the waves of carnal bliss ceased, she laid there with her eyes shut unable to even think. Kayn covered her mouth with her hand, still in awe of what he'd done to her with only a touch. When she opened her eyes, he was watching her. His eyes were a haunting shade of pale green. He'd received gratification by giving it to her with his ability. *She wanted him right now. No more games.* Grinning, he moved down. *No, don't stop. She was going to lose her mind if he took off on her again.* He playfully hovered his hands above her ankles creating warm bliss, travelling up both of her legs. He grasped her ankles, and as his hands touched her flesh, another tsunami of soul-altering ecstasy overcame her. Clutching the sheets, she cried out, sobbing his name, writhing on the mattress. Temporarily blinded by the carnal gratification he'd given her with only his touch, she lay breathless in the aftermath gripping the bedding with adrenaline pulsing through her being. She could hear her blood rushing through her veins as the predatory urges in her brain fired up. *He'd triggered her ability.* She made eye contact, knowing he had more deviously sinful party tricks up his sleeve. *There was an obvious way to force his hand and she needed energy.* Kayn motioned for him to come closer with her finger.

With concern in his eyes, he obeyed and cautioned, "If you use that ability, I won't be able to control myself."

*She didn't want him to have control.* "I know," Kayn baited. She placed her hands flat against his chest and stared into his eyes as her expression darkened. Her palms warmed as his essence coursed up her arms into her chest. He whispered her name as she removed her hands. *There it was, that euphoric scent was in the air again, it was coming from both of them now. She needed him to lose control. She wanted this so badly.* She took off her bra, tossed it aside, slid her panties down the length of her silky legs and bit her lip as another sensual intoxicating burst of pheromones released from her skin. His expression changed as primal need ceased all ration. In an instinctual frenzy, he tore his underwear off. *Now. Right now.* Making her desire clear, she reached for him as their lips met passionately. He seduced her with his tongue and groaned as she aggressively wrapped her legs around him, sliding him into her with a momentary tinge of glorious pain where there was a touch of resistance. It was instantly gone and all she felt was the all-encompassing pleasure of their union. Groaning her name, he began slowly moving. *He was trying to be careful. She didn't want that.* She aggressively grabbed a hand full of his hair and demanded, "Harder." Her words snuffed out his control. He vigorously pounded into her until her limbs began to shake as a tidal wave of pleasure swelled. Overcome by volatile euphoria, she bit into his shoulder and sunk her nails into his back. He bucked as they simultaneously cried out. Her toes curled as ecstasy shook her to her core. Every nerve ending in her body was blissfully humming. Neither one moved as they regained their bearings. *Holy crap.*

Breathless, he rolled off onto the bed beside her and gasped, "Holy crap!"

*He'd taken the words right out of her mind.* They both started to giggle. They looked at each other. *She wanted more. More kisses, more lovemaking, more of everything involving him.* Lured like a moth to a flame, she mounted him and provoked, "You're not done."

He roughly grabbed her hips as she started moving and cockily demanded, "Harder."

His bold assertion triggered the urge to dominate him. She gyrated faster and harder until pleasure was rippling through her. Moaning loudly, she tightened her thighs, arched her spine in abandon and gasped his name. Without a second to recover, he rolled her over. On top, he kissed her and told her he wanted her on her stomach. Her pulse raced. *What was he going to teach her next?*

"You'll like this sweetheart," he naughtily tempted. He lifted her hips and roughly took her from behind.

As he started moaning, his ability skilled hands heated up on her hips and took her over the edge. She muzzled her screams of ecstasy with bedding. In the aftermath they were staring up at the canopy blissfully exhausted. After a brief silence, Kayn cheekily provoked, "I hope you're not done."

He chuckled and sparred, "Don't worry honey, you're not going to be able to walk when we leave this room."

She pulled the covers up over herself and watched his rear view as he sauntered across the room like being naked was no big deal. He rolled a table over with bottled water, champagne and a tray of chocolate dipped strawberries. He climbed onto the bed, casually passed her a water and she downed the entire bottle in seconds.

"Cold or nervous?" He ribbed, playing with the sheet.

In uncharted territory, she countered, "It's probably a little late for modesty, isn't it?" She let the blanket fall around her waist. He mischievously dangled a chocolate covered strawberry in front of her lips. *This was so sweet. He was going to be trouble.* She bit into it. Her taste buds revelled in the combination. He passed her another one. Distracted by strawberries, Kayn gasped as he poured champagne from his flute on her breast and mischievously cleaned it up with his tongue. Enjoying his naughty game, she laid back as she bit into the strawberry and ate it as he poured champagne on her abdomen and drank it out of her navel. He was about to pour it somewhere else when he stood up and left her laying there with a half-eaten strawberry in her hand. *What was he up to?*

After digging around in his backpack, he returned with something hidden behind his back. He grinned and baited, "There's this naughty dream I've been having ever since I watched you eat one for the first time." He presented her with a Twinkie.

*Touché. They'd been playing flirtatious games with these. Where was he going to take this?* She bit off the end, dipped her finger into the creamy filling and seductively licked it off as he watched with a pained expression. As she licked off her next finger full, he disappeared under the sheets with a devious smile. Gasping, she became lost in his naughty talent until her toes curled as she imploded with abandon.

Her unrestrained screaming was muffled by his hands and laughter. When she started giggling, he removed his hands and chuckled, "We don't need anyone busting in here thinking you're being murdered."

*If she could choose this as her next demise, she'd sign up for it.* Humming with pleasure, Kayn snuggled against him. He was lying there with a self-satisfied smirk, finishing her half-eaten Twinkie. *It was dark outside already.* She slipped out of bed and attempted to look sexy as she walked away from him to the bathroom with Jell-O legs. *He'd already accomplished what he'd set out to do.* She gazed at her reflection and smiled at her birdy. *Her lips were easily double their normal size. She'd finally done it. There were no words for how much pleasure he'd given her. He'd outdone every one of her sister's memories. The whole experience had been in a league of its own.*

His voice came from the other side of the door, "Are you okay in there? I didn't hurt you, did I?"

*She felt like there might be steam rising from her nether regions, but she'd never been better.* Kayn pressed her lips together to stifle her giggles and replied, "I'm fine." She strolled over and opened the door. He was standing there concerned about how aggressively he'd taken her.

He tenderly cupped her cheek and disclosed, "I didn't plan on being that rough but when you took some of my ability and used it on me, I lost control. I'm sorry if I hurt you."

She kissed him gently on the lips, gazed into his eyes and whispered, "I wouldn't change a thing. It was perfect." They embraced and she breathed him in. *She'd never get tired of his scent.* Kayn mumbled against him, "I'm starving."

He nuzzled her neck as he replied, "I've already taken care of it. I ordered two of their dinner specials. I thought we could share the Seafood Alfredo and Steak Neptune with croquet potatoes. Both entrees come with soup, salad and a desert. There's a fridge in the room. Anything we can't finish, we'll heat up later. I'm fairly certain we'll manage to work up an appetite a few more times before morning." Frost pulled away from her and teased, "You're cold. I'll go start a fire."

Kayn grinned. *Yes, she was. How had he known that she was cold?* She glanced down at her front. *Her girls had probably been daggering him in the chest.* She smiled as Frost knelt in front of the fireplace and attempted to pull the glass cover off. *He was going to break it.* Kayn walked over to the wall and said, "Hey, hun. I think this is a natural gas fireplace." She flicked on the switch and it lit up.

He chuckled as he stood up, wrapped his arms around her

waist and tenderly kissed her lips. Frost nuzzled her neck and whispered, "Awe, you saved me from breaking the fireplace."

She kissed his neck, inhaling the intoxicating scent of his skin with her head resting comfortably in the crook of his neck. *It would be so easy to allow the words teetering on the tip of her tongue to slip out. She knew she shouldn't, not yet.* As they embraced in front of the dancing flames. Kayn found herself wanting to dance with him. She usually never wanted to dance but, at this moment, it felt like they should be.

Frost whispered in her ear, "One second." He walked over to the hearth grabbed his cell and music quietly added ambiance to the already incredible moment.

He took her in his arms, they began swaying with their nude forms, magically lit by flickering flames of the fire. It was a beautiful moment. He dipped her and held her there as she laughed, then pulled her against him again. *The memory of this night would be filed away in her heart as one of her favourites.* There was a knock on the door. They raced for the robes in the bathroom. She put on a luxurious robe and sat on the edge of the tub, waiting for room service to leave. *How she felt could not be described with only one word. She felt gloriously wild and free. It was more than happiness; it was euphoria. She knew they were drugging each other with their abilities. She'd ceased to care about anything but the intoxicatingly addictive sensation of being with him.* She heard the door close and practically skipped out of the bathroom. She ran across the room and leapt onto the bed, bouncing before coming to a stop.

Frost left their dinner on the tray and crawled towards her on the bed, unwrapping her robe as though she were a present at Christmas. He kissed her breasts, nipping at each aching rosebud with his teeth. He deviously grinned as he continued his naughty exploration. She arched her back in response to the tantalizingly sensual trail of his lips and tongue as he travelled down to her abdomen. Kayn started to giggle as she wished she had a Twinkie.

He peered up from his devilishly sinful exploration and enquired, "Is something funny?"

She roughly clutched a handful of his hair and ordered, "Don't you dare stop."

Grinning at her savage libido, he urged, "Hold that thought, dinners getting cold."

*He was going to leave her in a partially satisfied state. That jerk.*

"I think I've created a monster," he taunted, hovering his hands above her abdomen. She moaned and writhed as the sensation built with the pressure of a volcano about to erupt. He laid his hands on her stomach. She screamed with no ability to filter the ecstasy as she exploded from within and remained there unable to move a muscle as every inch of her hummed with pleasure.

Grinning, he casually enquired, "Do you want to eat at the table over there, or do you want to stay right here in bed?"

Kayn glanced across the room at the table and started giggling. *There was no way her legs were going to hold her.* Still trying to catch her breath, she gasped, "Here, let's just eat right here."

He split the dinners up so they each had a little of everything as she managed to manoeuvre herself into an upright position. Frost passed her a plate, handed her a full glass of champagne and sat down next to her to eat.

*She was starving.* Kayn ate a few mouthfuls of steak and looked at him, grinned and asked, "How do you fight the urge to do that to random strangers while you're walking down the street? I'd be doing that to everyone just for shits and giggles."

He laughed and choked on the mouthful he was trying to swallow. She patted his back. When he managed to stop coughing, he teased, "Of course you would."

"Oh, Come on. You've totally done that to people. I know you have." Kayn playfully accused as she downed her glass of champagne.

His eyes had a devious glint as he gave her the token response, he would have given her before she became a permanent member of their Clan, "We're not supposed to use our abilities in public."

*Bullshit.* She rolled her eyes and exclaimed, "You are so full of shit."

Downing his entire glass of champagne, he answered honestly, "I used to do it all the time but only to strangers who were bitchy and uptight. I'd just hover my hand there for a second as I walked past."

*She was beginning to feel tipsy.* He refilled her glass and she took a drink without really looking at it. *It was water.*

He leaned in, sweetly kissed her cheek and explained, "Champagne hangovers suck."

Kayn finished the last bite of her meal and noticed he was already done. He took her plate from her. She placed her glass on the nightstand as he put their empty plates on the cart and rolled it out into the hall. He closed the door, strolled back over and slipped under the covers beside her. Looking at him, she sparred, "If we ever get into a fight, you're totally going to do that to me, aren't you?"

He grinned back at her and teased, "Wouldn't that be the fastest way to end an argument?"

She laid her head on his chest, slowly tracing the outline of his abs with her finger, listing to the rhythmic beat of his heart in her ear. *She was happy. He made her happy.* He snuggled against her. She felt the warmth of his breath against her hair. She closed her eyes, for only a second...

She awoke in his arms to his rhythmic breathing. Kayn squinted in the harshness of sunshine streaming through the glass wall. She tried to stay completely still so she could bask in the feeling of this moment for a second longer before they'd inevitably have to get out of bed and go back to the others. Kayn smiled as her mind did a quick recap of the events of the night before. She'd woken up from that nap and they'd inventively used every surface of this hotel room. They bathed in the tub, drank everything in the minibar and knocked paintings off the walls. They'd been slightly intoxicated and it turned into a naughty free for all. They'd tried to watch the sunrise together and both passed out just as the sun was beginning to peak over the mountain. *What time was it? She felt well rested.* Kayn reached over and grabbed for her cell. *Holy crap. It was after ten thirty in the morning!* Kayn whispered, "It's after ten thirty, we have to get up."

Squeezing her tighter, he playfully nuzzled her neck and mumbled, "Not a chance. I'm never letting you leave this bed." Then he groggily murmured, "Is it really after ten?"

While wishing never leaving the bed was an option, she turned to face him, which was quite difficult to do under the dead weight of his muscular arm. She gazed into his brightness induced squinty eyes and kissed him lovingly on the lips as she whispered, "If you want to be able to do this again, we shouldn't be late."

He lifted his arm, released her and sat up before she'd had

the opportunity to. Frost chuckled, "Oh, wow. Have you seen this yet?"

"No, I haven't been out of bed," she mumbled. Kayn sat up. They'd trashed the room. Pictures on the floor, couch cushions everywhere. Water was all over from the overfull bathtub. "We need to clean this up," she sighed.

Frost swung his legs over the edge of the bed and suggested, "Get in the shower. I'll clean this up. If we shower separately, we might still be able to grab something to eat on our way back to the campsite."

Glancing back at him, Kayn smiled as she wandered through the mess. When she walked into the washroom, she howled. The shower curtain was on the bathroom floor. They'd pulled the rod off. *It was fixable.*

He appeared in the doorway and asked, "What?" He laughed as they put it back up. Kayn got into the shower. Frost pulled back the curtain and questioned, "Do you remember showering together last night?"

*She didn't recall that round of their alcohol and ability induced sexcapades.* She began to soap herself down, knowing there wasn't enough suds in the world to wash away the naughty things she'd done the night before. *She'd had the time of her life.*

Kayn wandered out into the room ready to go and was surprised to see, he'd clean the room to perfection. After he'd showered, they tossed the sopping wet towels into the tub, grabbed their bags and held hands on their way out. They were both in the truck when they got the giggles.

He turned to look at her as he remarked, "I wish we'd woken up an hour earlier. It's going to be a long week."

*She did too. It was going to be a long week.* Kayn took his hand as they pulled out onto the main road. *This felt so right.*

They quickly went through a Tim Horton's drive through to grab breakfast. By the time they turned down the dirt road to the campsite, they'd finished eating. He let go of her hand to manoeuvre the winding road. She sipped her coffee and smiled. *Sex like that was how people became obsessed.* Kayn squeezed his knee and urged, "Pull over before we get there." Just before they reached the campsite, he parked. Kayn hopped out of the truck and ran to the driver's side. Frost got out before she made it to him. She leapt into his arms and they held each other.

He whispered in her ear, "I'm going to miss you like crazy."

Kayn pulled away from him, looked deep into his eyes and praised, "That was by far the best night of my life."

Caressing her cheek, he teased, "I'll make sure I outdo that next time."

He leaned in and kissed her. As his tongue danced with hers, their impromptu make-out session took a naughty turn. He aggressively pinned her up against the truck, slid his warm hand under her shirt, rested it on her abdomen and set off fireworks within her. She cried out as her knees buckled with her arms draped around his neck. He stopped her from falling. She moaned into his ear as he chuckled. Still breathless, she gasped, "You asshole."

He slid his hand out from under her shirt and quietly taunted," Pull yourself together, we have company."

Still in a euphoric tingly blur, she heard Lexy's voice say, "I thought that was you guys."

# 20
# CORRECTIONS AND ANSWERS

Kayn managed to compose herself as Frost kissed her cheek and stepped away.

Grinning, Lexy didn't say a word about where they'd been or what everyone knew they'd been doing. She stated, "Well, now that you've said your goodbyes, it's time to go. Kayn, make sure you've grabbed your bag out of the truck. I don't want to accidentally drive away with it. It's happened to me before."

*Her bag was on the floor on the passenger side.* She opened the driver's side door and leaned across the seat. She felt him staring at her behind. Kayn glanced back, teasing, "Were you just looking at my butt?"

He grinned and sparred, "Guilty as charged."

Kayn yanked her bag off the floor and got out. She closed the door and said, "I guess it's time to say goodbye."

"For a week," he completed her sentence. He leaned in, gave her a quick peck on the lips and asked, "Can I carry your bag to the RV?"

*He was trying to be sweet.* Kayn gave it to him and replied, "Why not?" *Anything for a few more minutes.* They began their adorable stroll to the next campsite with the sun's rays streaming through the branches on regular intervals creating flashes of light. *His group was ready to go.* They were standing there, holding their bags. She was grateful he was walking beside her as they met the crowd of enquiring eyes. Frost passed Kayn her backpack, kissed her sweetly on the lips and as they embraced, he whispered in her ear, "I'll see you in a week. Be good."

She started to giggle as she quietly replied, "You should see everyone's faces."

Frost whispered, "They're just jealous." He squeezed her so tight, her feet lifted off the ground. As he put her down, he added, "You should erase those pictures."

*What pictures?* He winked at her as he turned around and walked towards a confused looking Grey. *He appeared to be in shock. He'd probably never seen him do the whole public display of affection thing. She honestly hadn't expected him to do it either.*

Lexy sighed as she wandered away and teased, "Frost is in love. Heaven help us all."

*They'd both been avoiding that word.* Kayn waited until she heard the scratching sound of the tires driving away in the gravel before she went inside. She strolled to her bunk and flopped down on it, beaming. *Her cheeks were going to be sore if she kept smiling like this.* Hedonistic flashes of the night they'd shared flickered through her mind.

Mel joined her on the bunk and whispered, "Tell me everything! Where did he take you? Was it romantic?"

Kayn couldn't give any details, mainly because most of the night was a kinky hedonistic blur. She could tell her a few things, "We went to this gorgeous hotel and stayed in the honeymoon suite. It was perfect. He's incredible. We like each other a lot." *He has crazy abilities and he's probably destroyed me for all other men.*

"So, is it love?" Mel probed, listening intently.

*Yes.* Kayn filtered her response, "It's a bit early for that word."

Mel smiled at her and said, "Sometimes you just know it, even before you're ready to say it aloud."

*She had a point there.* Kayn took Mel's hand and pled, "Can we please not make this a big deal." The RV door creaked a complaint as it opened. The remaining Ankh wandered over and sat on the bunk across from her. *Oh, wonderful.*

"Was it awesome? Your skin is glowing," Haley preened.

Astrid seemed concerned as she started in with the questions, "Are you guys together? Are you totally over that Kevin guy? I'm happy for you guys. Don't get me wrong. I just don't want him to be hurt. I heard him ask you to be good. What was that all about?"

*She was seriously contemplating the merits of smothering herself with her own pillow so she could end this conversation. Really? Twenty-four hours ago, she was a virgin.* Kayn looked at Zach and said, "Do you have anything to say? You might as well get it out now while everyone else is."

Zach grinned at her as he chuckled, "Was it worth it?"

*That just totally lightened the mood.* Kayn addressed everyone as she exclaimed, "I'm going to answer these questions and then we are never going to speak of this again. Are you all with me?" They nodded. She smiled at Haley and replied, "It was amazing." She gave Astrid a detailed response,

"I think we are. I'm not sure you're ever one hundred percent over anyone. I seem to have permanent use of my twin's ability, which is like his, but I think that was a joke. Is there anything else before we close the topic of the loss of my virginity forever?" *Everyone's curiosity had been shut down by her witty responses.* She changed the subject, "So, who can tell me more about this job?"

Actively trying not to smile by pressing her lips together, Astrid managed to get her serious expression back as she replied, "You and Zach will be going back to high school tomorrow. Your information will be waiting for you in the office. You'll be using your regular first names to avoid complications. Your backstory is, your parents met on the internet and they just got married. It's the whole blended family thing. You'll be watching this girl and getting to know her daily schedule. Make your faces familiar but avoid conversations. If you do this right, she won't think twice about going with us after her Correction. If she doesn't survive, we just leave and meet up with the rest of the Clan." She stood up and declared, "We have rentals to drive while we're here. You two will have one to go to and from school."

Zach shrugged and responded, "That sounds easy."

Haley gave him a playful smack and sighed, "Don't ever say that. It's like asking for something messed-up to happen."

*They were starting school tomorrow. It was time to hurry up and wait. This meant board games and movies.* They all got up and silently separated into either the backroom or the kitchen area. Kayn followed Zach into the back, knowing she didn't have the brain power for board games right now. *She could watch a movie though.* Kayn heard her cell phone buzz and went back to her bunk to dig it out of her backpack. It was a message from Frost, reminding her to be careful where she left her phone. *She didn't recall taking pictures.* Kayn pressed the photo gallery icon and started to laugh. She thought it was going to be X-rated, but it was a just bunch of goofy G-rated selfies of them making funny faces in bed together. They were naked in most of the selfies, but it didn't show anything. She texted Frost back, "These are cute."

"Keep looking," he replied.

She flipped the touch screen a few more times. *Wow.* Her eyes widened and she quickly erased the evidence of their drunken debauchery.

Zach impatiently hollered from the TV room, "Are you coming?"

*It was a little chilly.* Kayn grabbed one of her hoodies, put it on and slipped her cell into her pocket. She peeked into the kitchen area. They were in the middle of an intense game of cards. After that wild night with Frost, she just wanted to bask in the afterglow. Kayn wandered into the backroom, ready to begin the Dragon and Handler movie marathon. *Tomorrow she'd get to pretend she was normal while waiting for someone to be murdered without warning them. If they survived, she would get to plot their kidnapping.* She stepped over the pillows and blankets on the floor.

Zach patted the pillow next to him. He grinned like an adolescent brother as he baited, "So, what are you in the mood for?"

Kayn scowled at him and rolled her eyes. She grabbed one of the large, overstuffed pillows from the floor and smoked him point blank in the face. *It was on!* They began pummelling each other with the pillows. Eventually she got the upper hand and knocked him over.

He was curled up into the fetal position laughing and repeatedly saying, "I'll stop! I'll stop!"

Their sibling style wrestling match drew the others away from their boring game of cards into the backroom. Of course, they joined in instead of breaking it up. After a good half hour long pillow fight, they were all sprawled out on the floor hysterically laughing. After they regained their faculties, the tension from earlier had been dealt with. All five cuddled up under blankets to watch a horror movie marathon. They ate snacks for dinner because nobody felt like being responsible enough to make a proper meal, and eventually, they fell asleep right where they were on the floor.

Kayn heard an old song playing before she opened her eyes. It was, 'Push it.' She smiled, assuming it was Astrid's phone. They'd been listening to music from the twenty years they'd missed out on while trapped in the Testing. She groggily opened her eyes and noticed a few of them were missing. She grabbed the phone and looked at the time. *It was seven o'clock in the morning. Shit. She had to go to school.* Kayn grinned when she realised it was Zach's cell. *Hilarious. He was still sound asleep.* She poked him a few times and harassed, "Rise and shine, Salt n Pepa fan. We have to get ready for school."

He swatted her away and mumbled, "No school."

*She smelled coffee. Somebody had their back this morning.* Kayn stretched as she looked around the tousled-up room. She grabbed her things and quickly used the bathroom. She put on jeans, a t-shirt and a hoodie. Opting to put her wild mane of hair into a ponytail because she felt comfortable that way, she applied a touch of makeup and smiled at her reflection. On the surface, she appeared to be the same fresh-faced innocent girl she'd always been. *This was now her disguise. That girl was gone.* The scent of something wondrous accosted her nostrils as she opened the washroom door. Kayn wandered out into the kitchen and smiled at Astrid. She was cooking bacon on the little stove. Kayn grinned and sang, "Thanks, mom."

Astrid scooped a couple of eggs along with bacon onto a plate and replied, "It's just much needed brain food for my sweet angelic teenage daughter on her first day at her new high school."

Kayn took the plate from her and continued the game as she dramatically sighed, "Zach won't get out of bed."

Astrid grabbed a glass out of the small cupboard and pleasantly said, "Let me show you how this mommy deals with unruly children." She filled it with water, pranced down the hall, a second later, Zach was cursing up a storm. She reappeared, saying, "Your brother is up."

Kayn snickered as she ate her bacon. She looked up and sighed, "You would have been the best mother ever." She winced. *She hadn't known Astrid long enough to predetermine her areas of sensitivity.*

Unfazed by her comment, Astrid placed a cup of coffee on the table in front of her and passed her utensils.

Zach strolled in, ready to go and retaliated with one word, "Funny." Their makeshift mother figure handed her partner in crime a plate with bacon and eggs on it. He winked at her and said, "Forgiven." He sat beside Kayn and tried to steal her coffee.

She stabbed his hand with her fork, threatening, "Next time. I draw blood."

"Mom! Kayn stabbed me with a fork," he complained.

Astrid plunked a coffee down in front of him. Ignoring his complaint, she curtly instructed, "Your backpacks for school are in the closet. You have lunch money in the front zipper compartment. Zach, I got a text from Jenna saying Kayn might have some repercussions to deal with from her extracurricular activities. You're supposed to keep a close eye on her because you might have to deal with it."

*What was that supposed to mean?* Kayn took a drink of her coffee and exclaimed, "You know, I'm sitting right here." *Deal with it?* She stood up and marched into the back to get the backpacks. One was stuck in the closet. She yanked on it growing angrier every second. *It wouldn't budge an inch. The part of her brain that did the problem solving was not cooperating this morning. She wanted to take the frigging door right off.* She tore the door off the hinges with her bare hands just as Mel came out of the bathroom. *Her friend seemed concerned. Yes, it was possible she was going to be easily amped up for a while.* Standing there casually holding the door she'd ripped off, Kayn explained her predicament, "I couldn't get our bags out of the closet." A little embarrassed, she propped the door up against the wall. Her friend crouched down, easily removed the bags from the closet and passed each one up to her. She said, "Thanks Mel," as she meekly walked back to the kitchen where she admitted, "Yes, it's possible, I may be a wee bit easy to anger."

Grinning, Zach took his bag from her and countered, "Knowing is half the battle."

*She did not have the patience for fortune cookie day.*

Placing his arm around her, he gave her a brotherly

squeeze and chimed in, "You just need to think of your cup as half full."

*Of alcohol.* Kayn smiled at her inner commentary as she stepped out into the invigorating chill of the morning air. Her senses were greeted by the familiar scent of the trees, she instantly felt a little lighter on the inside. Her footsteps crackled on the ground. *It was quite icy. It was going to snow.* She glanced at her running shoes, knowing if it snowed, her feet would be soaking wet and freezing all day.

Astrid hollered after them, "Break a leg!"

With hilarious timing, Zach slipped on the icy ground. She grabbed his arm before he went down. Kayn smiled and teased, "That was fortune cookie karma, my friend."

He grinned as they carefully walked to the rental car. Zach pressed the keypad. They both got in. He turned on the heater, warming up the interior. Kayn was about to pass him the scraper when she changed her mind. Delicate snowflakes were already spiralling down from the heavens. *She knew it.* She got out of the car, tapped on the window and bargained, "I'll do it this morning if you do it after school." There wasn't much to do as the heater had already done a great job of melting the thin layer of ice on the windows.

Zach got out of the car and said, "I'll be right back. They'll have to get this motor home out of here and park it somewhere in town before there's too much snow on the ground."

Kayn slid into the passenger seat. *He was right. This campground would be absolute hell to get out of when it was covered in snow. She loved this province. It was warm outside yesterday. She hadn't even thought of putting on a winter jacket. You never knew what you needed to wear from day to day. Welcome to British*

*Columbia.* Zach reappeared with boots and a winter jacket on. *Her winter gear was in his arms.*

He passed it to her as he got in, fastened his seatbelt, and said, "We'll text them after school and find out where they ended up." He plugged in his cell to play tunes.

*There goes my trail run.* She zipped up her boots and stared out the window, watching the snowflakes as they fluttered from above.

Driving the slick gravel road out of the campground like an old pro, he pulled out onto the highway. Zach glanced her way, teasing, "Maybe, we'll all get to stay at that fancy hotel you and Frost just stayed in?"

*He had his irritating brother role down. There was no point in giving him a reaction.* They passed a sign directing them to the high school and turned down a sideroad. After a few minutes of travelling, they pulled into the high school's empty parking lot. *They must be super early. This was a first. She'd never been early for anything. They were going back to high school.* Kayn grimaced and glanced at Zach. *High school had barely been tolerable the first time around.* Images of Kevin began flashing through her mind. She blinked them away. *He's gone. They both were.*

Sensing something amiss, Zach nudged her and asked, "Are you alright?"

"It's nothing," Kayn answered as she opened the door without missing a beat and got out.

He grabbed his bag out of the back and announced, "I guess we'll have to go to the office and get our schedules before we do anything else."

*Her Handler appeared to be stoked about this new experience. She might as well try to get with the program.* "That's how I understood it," Kayn responded as she stood there in the winter wonderland. The landscape was already covered in white powder. *Only a week ago, she was trudging through the desert barefoot so thirsty she was hallucinating.* As the flakes landed on her face, she stuck out her tongue, allowing them to land on it. *What a strange, wondrous afterlife.* Frost entered her mind and she smiled. *He was something to look forward to.*

Zach chuckled, "Earth to Kayn. We should get inside before we're both soaking wet."

They jogged through the flurry of white spiralling snowflakes to the main door. Zach yanked it open and allowed her to dive inside first. She laughed, "Thank you, kind sir." They shook the snow off, by stamping their feet on the large black mat. The office was conveniently right there. After pretending to be siblings to get their class schedules, they strolled through the school to get the lay of the land. They took a seat on a bench and compared their schedules. They were grateful to be in all the same classes. *The Aries Group was good.* Students began to flood the halls and the slightest touch of colour hovered around each person. *She'd ceased to notice it unless she was looking for it.* Kayn scanned the herd of teens for a hint of yellow, there was nothing. The bell rang and the two Ankh made their way to their first class. The seats were full except for two at the back. The teacher pointed to the empty seats without a big announcement. Relieved, Kayn took her binder out. The teacher turned off the lights before she got a good look at the student's auras. She heard Zach say something to her using only his mind, *"Is she in here?"*

She responded back, thinking, *"The lights went out too fast."*

Zach's voice spoke in her mind again, *"Do you remember what class this is?"*

She recognized the movie the class was watching but she couldn't recall the name of it. There was a lame battle going on. *"It could be Social Studies?"* They spent the whole hour watching the movie before the teacher turned the lights on. The girl was sitting a few aisles over. She had glasses that kept sliding down her nose and her black hair was in a ponytail. The bell rang. She startled, dropped her binder and everything fell out on the floor. She scrambled to stuff papers back inside. Nobody stopped to help her, they just walked around her. *It was mortal Kevin but a girl.* Kayn knew wasn't supposed to do it but couldn't help herself. She helped the girl pick up scattered papers. The girl thanked her. Kayn smiled without speaking because she wasn't supposed to speak to her. Zach was standing above her shaking his head when she looked up.

"That was her, wasn't it?" Zach questioned. He helped her up and passed Kayn the backpack she'd left under her desk. *He'd packed up her stuff while she was busy breaking the rules. He was getting the hang of this Handler thing.* They strolled out of the room and began searching for their next class. The girl they were observing walked out of the bathroom and accidentally bumped into someone. They ignorantly shoved her against the lockers. *This was painful to watch. She wanted to follow the bitch who'd pushed her and give her a shove.*

Zach laughed and whispered, "We're supposed to be inconspicuously watching her. Not going all vigilante on everyone that wrongs her. She'll have to be toughened up to survive what's coming for her."

*He had a point, but she still planned to arrange an inconvenient accident for that bitch if the situation presented itself.* The girl wasn't in their next classes. They found her at lunch, sitting alone reading a book. Her table was the only free one by the time they got through the line. They made their way through gossiping teens and sat by the girl they weren't supposed to speak to. Kayn smiled and apologized, "Sorry if we're bothering you. There wasn't anywhere else to sit."

The girl looked up from her book and remarked, "You guys are new here. It won't be good for you socially if you sit with me.

Zach introduced himself, "I'm Zach, and this is my stepsister Kayn. It's our first day. We don't care about stuff like that."

The girl slid her glasses up her nose and wiped her hand on her shirt as she replied, "I'm Hannah. This book isn't important. I'm just passing time until the end of the day. It's nice to meet you guys." The bell rang. Hannah stood up and said, "I have to run. I hate being the last one in the door. I guess I'll see you in class." She smiled like they'd made her year and walked away.

Kayn looked at Zach and declared, "So, we've blown our cover on the first day. What now?"

Her partner smiled and replied, "I guess we'll just have to go with it."

They finished the school day without bumping into her, but they'd introduced themselves like idiots. It was going to be challenging to stalk her without being noticed. They saw her walking in the snow by herself. They pulled over and offered her a ride. She happily accepted. They drove her a couple of blocks and dropped her off. She lived in an apartment building. After saying their goodbyes, they drove away. They pulled over a couple of blocks from the girl's apartment complex and sat there silently for a minute. Kayn glanced at Zach and stated, "We suck at this."

He chuckled and agreed, "We don't just moderately suck. We epically suck. We're horrible stalkers. She's going to be looking for us now. How do you stealthily watch someone who is actually looking for you?"

"Should we tell the others we screwed up? Maybe, we can trade places?" Kayn asked. She looked out the window and noticed someone approaching in the distance. "Shit. It's her," she whispered. Zach ducked in the driver's seat. Kayn smacked him and hissed, "She knows what we're driving you tool. Just drive away." He pulled away from the curb. As they took off down the street, Kayn looked at her equally inept partner in crime, suggesting, "We might have to trade vehicles each day." She took her phone out of her pocket to find out where they were staying. Mel gave her directions. *It was the same place she'd stayed with Frost. Of course, it was.*

Glancing her way, he enquired, "Is something wrong?"

She met his eyes, responding, "Drive back out to the highway. I know how to get to the hotel."

He stared at the road ahead and made a valiant attempt to keep a straight face for a minute or two. Then with an enormous shit-eating grin, he blurted out, "Please tell me it's the same hotel. It'll make this gong show of a day, so much better."

She mumbled, "Yes, it's the hotel. I guess there's a big hockey tournament. There were no rooms in town."

Zach bounced in his seat like a sugar cranked child. Stopping, he prodded, "Tell me we're in the honeymoon suite. Say this is happening."

*This was going to be so awkward. Once again, she'd like to welcome everyone to the all humiliation Kayn show, otherwise known as her afterlife.* He knew the answer by her lack of response and started to giggle. *This day was only going to get worse*. She pointed out the hotel and he pulled into the parking lot.

Staring out the window at the building, he exclaimed, "Frost is my new hero."

Kayn socked him in the arm like five times, as hard as she could, while he laughed, pleading with her to stop. She looked at him and questioned, "Now, how in the hell am I supposed to get up to the room? I just stayed here with my husband, for my honeymoon."

He rubbed his wounded arm and replied, "Your family is in town for your reception. All the rooms were booked for a hockey tournament. I'm your stepbrother."

She shook her head at him as she grabbed her bag and got out of the car. When they entered the hotel, she was relieved to see that it wasn't the same man at the front desk. As they got into the elevator she thought of Frost. *He was going to piss himself laughing when he found out where they were staying.* The door opened to the floor they'd stayed on and there was the little gold plaque on the door that read, 'Honeymoon suite.' *Let the humiliation begin.*

Zach walked into the room. He parted his lips in awe as he announced, "Wow. This is an unbelievable room. Frost has serious game."

*Well, this was happening.*

Astrid gave her arm an apologetic squeeze, explaining, "We'll only be here for a night, and then, we have a room downtown. I'm sorry. This was just how the search for a room played out. We've made a pact to not say a word about it while we're here."

*While we're here. Now there was the smooth loophole in the pact. She noted that they'd brought up a few cots. She'd sleep in one of those.*

Haley sat on the king-sized bed. She bounced around, sprawled, and sighed, "I wish someone did something like this for me." She peered up and quickly apologized, "That was the last comment, I swear."

*On the bright side, the food was unbelievable.* She looked at the others, suggesting, "Let's order early dinner and have a couple of drinks. The food here is incredible. I can pretend I'm somewhere else if you four let it happen."

Mel smiled, grabbed the menu and said, "Alright, let's eat. What do you all want?"

"I'll have Steak Neptune," Kayn replied. The others ordered as she wandered over to the minibar, grabbed tiny bottles of vodka and climbed into the enormous empty tub. She lined up the tiny bottles on the edge. Astrid, Haley and Zach joined her as Mel called room service. After ordering, Mel climbed in. They hung out in the empty tub, talking about life while drinking expensive booze from the minibar. Nobody uttered a word about the off the table subject as they ate. The impromptu waterless tub party numbed her anxiety over where they were. Relaxed, Kayn wandered to the washroom, closing the door behind her. Sitting, she texted Frost, "It snowed and we had to get a room. There's a hockey tournament going on. There are no rooms in town. Guess where we're all staying tonight?" She stared at her phone for a minute and no response. *He was on a job. He couldn't answer.* She got up and looked in the mirror. Her hand warmed. *Crap.* Knowing what it meant, she took off her leather fingerless glove as her symbol flashed. *That was two flashes. There were five of them. She couldn't fight against the Dragon instinct with logic.* Her pulse raced. *Fight it. She had to fight it. There was nowhere to go. She was in the bathroom on the sixth floor of a hotel. Nobody could see her like this.* Her blood scalded her veins with each pump of her heart. *Zach.* Clutching the sink, Kayn stared at her hands. Her veins were brilliant green and clearly visible. *One ability would surely set off the other. She hadn't even thought about feeding the Conduit ability since Frost left.* The headache began. *She knew how this was going to go down. They had to subdue her.* Someone knocked on the door as her palm lit for the third time. *Three down.* Shaking, Kayn opened the door, looked into her Handler's concerned eyes, and ordered, "Restrain me while you still can."

Blocking the door, Zach whispered, "I can get through to you. Listen, we're not their backup. Markus, Jenna and Orin are there. This isn't our fight."

Her stomach knotted into a ball of excruciating pain. Kayn dropped to her knees and groaned, "I can't control it! Do it now!" Agony was radiating through her body in spasms. "Take me out! Heal me when it's over!"

Grabbing ahold of her, Zach tried to give her a pep talk, "You can fight against this. They don't need us, this feeling will pass. Just breathe with me. Deep breaths." He slowly inhaled air and exhaled.

Glaring at him, her Ankh symbol flashed a fourth time. Another surge of adrenaline rippled through Kayn as her chest tightened. Thin threading sanity with dark ridged veins and laboured breathing, Kayn clutched her Handler's wrist, ordering, "Do it!" Her Conduit ability reared its ravenous head. No longer able to fight against her primal urges, she swatted at Zach and growled, "Get away!"

Mel stood in her path and asserted, “You know we can’t let you leave.”

With nothing but a faint hum of restraint, Kayn met Mel’s eyes and darkly urged, “You know what you have to do.” She felt the energy addicted predatory part of her switch on. *They were no longer things she needed to protect. They contained sustenance and they were blocking the door.* She took one step, felt a sharp pain in her neck and the lights went out.

# 21

# LESSER EVILS

Feeling the sand beneath her fingertips and the wondrous warmth of eternal sunshine, she opened her eyes. *Somebody killed her.* Relieved, Kayn scrambled to her feet, smiling. *It felt like she hadn't been here in a while. It had only been three months since her Testing but it felt like years. So much happened in a short time.* She strolled the desert, revelling in the warmth of the silken sand as it slid between her toes with each step. Kayn couldn't recall the exact number of deceased Clan. Unable to pass through the hall of souls, they'd remain here until they were healed. *She could find them if she wanted to.* The scenery exploded with glorious light. There was a time when she would have felt the urge to cower, but she was far past her fear of the unknown. When the heavenly glare ceased, Kayn was standing in a field of buttercups and orange flowers with fluffy dandelion heads and bumblebees. As she took a step, every orange flower in the meadow took flight. *They were monarch butterflies.* They grouped, hovering twenty feet in the air. *The butterflies in Immortal Testing had been an ominous presence, but not here. Not in this place. This was different.* She raised her hands. A few fluttered down and landed on her, strutting a ticklish path with tiny feet on her skin. As she took a step, they fluttered away like a magnificent cloud into the horizon. She smiled. *The last time she'd come here, she'd been so angry. This time she felt nothing but peace within her soul. There were things to look forward. Most importantly, she felt hopeful.* This time she was careful to avoid bumblebees as she wandered the meadow. Inhaling delightful fragrances, she felt the caress of grass underfoot as she opted to relax in the grass to observe the bees. She watched the furry creatures as they darted from flower to flower with tiny legs coated in sticky yellow pollen. With her chin rested in her hands, she witnessed their magical, timeless dance and became lost in it. She sensed someone there and glanced over. *It was creepy black spandex guy. She'd met him after her Correction, and to be quite honest, he'd been a bit of a dick. He'd frozen her solid and messed with her mind by placing her in various macabre situations for his amusement.* She knit her brow and patiently enquired, "What do you want?"

The wicked being tilted his head, questioning, "Do I have to want something?"

*His presence irritated her. He was wrecking her happy place.*

The obnoxious thing tossed a handful of grass at her face and chuckled, "Now, that's not fair. What if this is my happy place too?"

Recalling his ability to hear her thoughts, she scrambled to her feet. *Fine, if he wasn't going to leave, then she would just relocate her moment to somewhere he wasn't.* He started to follow her. Kayn turned around and asserted, "Listen, I just need a moment of peace. Leave me alone. Bother somebody else. I'm sure there are plenty of lost souls for you to traumatize." She spun around and walked away. She heard his footsteps rustling in the grass behind her. Kayn ignored him for a while, hoping he'd lose interest, but he continued his irritating pursuit. Pausing without looking back, Kayn sighed, "Why are you still here?"

He admitted, "I may have been a little insensitive when we first met. What can I do to get a clean slate?"

*Clean slate? Was this tool serious? She was a Dragon. She didn't have to put up with this shit*. Kayn smiled and thought of a boulder. It appeared in her hands. *Bigger. It needed to be bigger*. She grinned as it tripled in size and turned to face him with an enormous boulder in her hands.

The treacherous being grinned. Intrigued by the hostile turn of events, he questioned, "Will throwing that rock resolve your feelings of hostility towards me?"

Kayn grinned and sparred, "It's a start."

Remaining there, he sighed, "Fine, if you must."

She launched the boulder directly at him and he didn't even attempt to move. His head exploded in a blast of bloody chunks. His body slumped into the grass. *Why didn't he move?* She gave what was left of him a boot with her foot, shrugged and walked away. *Problem solved. That was strange. She knew what she wanted to do.* The scenery exploded with luminescent light and she was barefoot in the forest. *It was time for that trail run she'd been dying for.* Kayn leaned against a tree and got annoyingly sticky tree sap on her. She grimaced but didn't bother trying to wipe it off. *She knew better. She'd have to just tune it out. It wasn't really there anyway.*

A voice behind her sang, "Are we all better now?"

*Seriously. This guy was as irritating as tree sap. You happen to touch it and can't get rid of it until you get home. No matter how hard you try.* She explained, "Listen, I want to go for a trail run before I heal and get dumped back into my body. I haven't had an opportunity to do this in months."

The creepy being responded, "Fine, go for your run, we'll continue this conversation at a later date."

Kayn shook her head and agreed, "Sounds good. Have a lovely afterlife." She sprinted down the path. *She needed this so badly.* Kayn darted through the woods strategically missing each root underfoot. She'd only just begun when she felt something peculiar. *Damn it.* She stopped running and looked at her hands. Her fingertips were tingling. They disintegrated into dust, followed by the rest of her essence as she blew away in a faint breeze travelling through the trees.

In the time it took to exhale, Kayn opened her eyes. She was back in the land of the living with her head resting on Zach's lap.

He stroked her hair and whispered, "Sorry about that. We couldn't exactly have you roaming the hotel all covered in veins, ready for a murder spree."

Kayn smiled, sensing it was the middle of the night and it was necessary to be respectfully quiet. She gave a hushed reply, "I'm fine now. Perhaps, that's the only way around that ability related glitch."

"Did you see any of the others?" Zach questioned as he continued to gently play with her hair.

She grinned, knowing he meant while she was trapped in the in-between. Remaining still, she answered, "I spent my time trying to avoid that creepy jerk in black spandex. Have you ever met that guy?"

Chuckling quietly, Zach whispered, "I've never had the displeasure."

Everyone's shallow breathing prompted her to ask, "What time is it?"

"The last time I checked, it was a quarter to three," he whispered. "We shirked our responsibilities yesterday. We should go to sleep."

*The Correction could have come for the girl last night. They'd do a better job tomorrow.* Zach rested his head on the pillow. She closed her eyes again and drifted off.

She heard someone knock and muffled talking. The door closed. Kayn opened her eyes.

Mel pushed the breakfast cart in, announcing, "Rise and shine. Eat and get ready for school. We'll text you with the directions to the new hotel once we're settled in."

They ate, got ready and rushed out. Relieved nobody mentioned her psychotic episode, Kayn left with Zach. A lady in the elevator had magical aura. Recently healed from death, Kayn suspected it was going to be a visually wild day. Zach drove to school as they discussed the job. They parked and got out. The crowded entrance was full of students with trippy auras. *Oh, wow. She had crazy optical sensory overload going on. Everyone was towing a damn rainbow.* Ready for her first class, Kayn sat at her desk. Hannah hadn't shown up. Just as she was succumbing to concern, Hannah walked in. A wave of relief washed over her. *She shouldn't have associated her with the mortal version of her best friend Kevin. Dragon or not, she cared about what happened to this girl.*

They spent the remainder of the week trying to avoid her without hurting her feelings while getting to know her daily routine. With more snow in the forecast, they stayed in a seedy motel downtown. Each day, they watched the trials of Hannah's life and got to know her quite well, even though they were consciously trying to remain detached. Rooting for her to survive her Correction, they came back to the hotel each evening and told the others what they'd learned about the quirky new girl named Hannah. She lived with her grandmother, mother and picked up her little sister from a babysitter after school. Hannah went to music lessons on Wednesdays at five o'clock and played the violin beautifully. She had a loving family who hugged each other and said, I love you each time they parted. As days passed, it was hard to watch Hannah walking home, holding her cherub-faced sister's hand, knowing their end was near. Out of sheer boredom, Kayn began to guess how the sweet girl's Correction would go down. Her mother was a janitor. She came home from work late at night. All Kayn could think about was how easy it would be to follow her to the apartment while everyone was asleep and off them all. It seemed like the obvious route in.

After seven full days and evenings of poorly executed surveillance, they were in class waiting for Hannah to arrive. When her desk remained empty for the entire hour of first class, they knew her Correction happened. After the bell, they raced out to the parking lot, jumped into the car and drove to her apartment. Neither bothered to speak, until they pulled up at her quiet complex.

Stating the obvious, Zach said, "There's no police tape around this place. That's a positive sign."

With an uneasy feeling, she replied, "Maybe, nobody's found the bodies yet?"

"Aren't you a ray of sunshine this morning," he teased, trying to lighten things up as they strolled to the door.

She walked over and glanced around the side of the building, looking up at the small sundeck of the third-floor apartment. Kayn wasn't sure what she expected to see but there appeared to be nothing out of the ordinary. She wandered over to Zach. He pressed call buttons, saying he'd lost his key until someone buzzed him in. Heavy hearted, they scaled three flights of stairs. Zach pushed open the weighted door, and they stepped into the hallway. Droplets of blood led them to a partially open door like a sick trail of breadcrumbs.

Zach whispered, "She could still be alive."

Kayn didn't respond. She knew they were walking into a slaughter. All Hannah had for backup was a feeble elderly grandmother, a five-year-old child and a mother that never looked behind her once as she entered the building late at night. During her Correction, she'd been warned by her sister's screams and hadn't had time to get away.

"Please...please," Zach whispered, lightly bumping the door with his elbow. It swung open. A metallic odour wafted out.

*She knew that scent. It was scalded into her brain during her Correction.* They found Hannah's mother's crumpled corpse a few feet from the door. She'd been followed inside, just as she'd predicted it would happen. *Her throat had been slit. She'd died quickly. This was a small blessing. At least she'd never know the fate that would befall her family.* She turned to Zach. He'd already begun to tear up. *She wanted to shut her emotions off but couldn't. He needed her to be the one that did the thinking.* Kayn opened the first bedroom. It was the grandmother's room. She could tell by the décor without even getting a good look at the body on the bed. Kayn walked over. If there'd been no blood on the sheets, it would have looked like the elderly woman died peacefully in her sleep. *They were all gone. She could feel it. There was a hollow sensation within this apartment. She sensed the lack of life within the walls. They needed to hurry. They couldn't be seen here.* Zach had his hand against the wall. *It was a good thing fingerprints were no longer an issue. Witnesses would have to be dealt with and there'd been enough carnage in this building.* He hesitated, so Kayn took the lead by shoving open the last door. *She didn't need to get a close look at the tiny body under the covers. Some things were better left unseen. The other bed was empty.* Kayn looked in the closet and under the bed. *Where was she? They must have woken her up and given her the opportunity to fight back.*

Zach frantically searched the apartment, repeating his hopes aloud, "She could be alive. Maybe she got away?"

*She got away during her Correction but hadn't made it far…The drops of blood in the hall. She'd assumed it came from the assailant's clothes.* Kayn darted out, purposely leaving the door open, so the bodies would be discovered quickly. She sprinted down the hall, following the morbid trail. *She hadn't noticed blood on the stairs on the way up. She knew what she was looking for now.* There was a droplet every three or four steps. *She was smart enough to put pressure on a wound.* When the trail ended, it was time for instinct. *There were two directions for her to go. Hannah was an intelligent girl. In a terror-driven panic, dying from an injury, she would have been looking for somewhere to hide.* The laundry room was clearly marked and unlocked. They went in. Hannah was propped up beside the hot water tank. Her soulless eyes stared into nothingness. She was long gone. Kneeling before her, Zach closed her eyes out of respect and remained there. Kayn protectively laid her hand on his shoulder and urged, "We need to leave." He nodded and rose with tears glistening in his eyes. *This was the first prospect they'd lost together, and it wouldn't be the last.* She recalled the warnings about allowing yourself to become attached. Neither spoke as they solemnly drove to the hotel. The job was done. A family of wonderful souls had been snuffed out last night. She knew why they'd been sent in alone to do this job. Traumatic events were meant to grow their bond. She could turn off her emotions to avoid the pain, but for him, she'd chosen the alternative. This was a lesson. She just wanted to get away from this place and move on. Her phone buzzed. She took it out of her pocket and looked.

It was a text from Markus, "We've run into a bit of a situation. When the job is done, send me a message and I'll send the Aries Group in to clean up. Drive the RV up north to Alaska. We'll message you with the details of the next job. We'll be a few days late."

*She'd been secretly counting down the days until she could see Frost again.* Kayn texted back, "Hannah didn't survive her Correction. We'll leave today." She glanced at Zach and relayed the message, "We're supposed to drive the RV up north to Alaska. They'll be a few days late. They'll message us the details of our next job. I'll text the others and tell them to meet us at the RV."

Her phone vibrated again. She looked at the screen. It read, "You will find it easier in the future if you don't use names."

*That was probably true.* When they arrived at the RV the others were already there waiting. There was a solemn undertone as they travelled. *Grey's goofy behaviour would have been a pleasant distraction on this trip.* They rotated driving shifts, played board games and watched movies. *Frost still hadn't texted her back.* Kayn stretched out on her bunk to rest her eyes. When she awoke, she wandered up to the front and found out they'd already crossed the border. *They were in Alaska. She'd never been to Alaska.*

Astrid hollered from the driver's seat, "I'm pulling over! You guys have to see this! Get your jackets on, it's going to be frigging cold!"

The RV slowed and parked as she bundled up in her winter gear. Haley tossed her a toque and gloves. Haley was the first to step outside. Icy air wafted in. Her breath was visible. Kayn contemplated opting out but sounds of awe made her curious. She winced as she stepped outside. *Cold was an understatement. Shit, it was bloody freezing.* Her eyeballs felt like the moisture had been sucked right out of them. Every area of exposed skin was in agony. It ceased to mean anything as she looked up at the swirling glorious glowing hues in the sky. The northern lights. *She'd seen them before, but never like this. It was otherworldly.* Mel was standing beside Zach. His arm was around her waist. *Interesting.* He'd been flitting between Mel and Haley. *Each time it looked like something was happening, the poor guy got shoved back into the friend zone. The Handler situation didn't make him an attractive prospect.* Her mind darted back to Frost and his lack of response to her texts. *Perhaps, he had time to think about what he was getting himself into. She needed to concentrate on something else.* Kayn interrupted the moment by bringing up work, "We should text Markus, tell him we're here and find out about this job."

With quivering lips, Astrid pointed towards the RV, suggesting, "Let's go back inside to discuss this."

They all laughed as they darted back in, closed the door, and left themselves suited up in winter gear. The engine had only been off for a few minutes but the temperature inside the RV had dropped. They took a seat at the table.

Mel responded to Kayn's question, "We found out the details of the job while you were asleep. A girl just survived her Correction. She's in the hospital, but there's a glitch, Triad's already here. According to our Oracle, there's a small window of time if we make one. I'll heal the girl then Astrid and Haley will take off with her, while you guys run interference with Triad. If they don't know she's missing until morning, it will give us a good head start."

"Can't we just get them alone, snap their necks and be done with it?" Kayn asked with her arms wrapped around herself, shivering. *Someone needs to start the engine and get some heat going.*

Astrid grinned and replied, "That's not what we were ordered to do."

*Why wouldn't they just kill us the second they saw us?* The lightbulb above her head flickered. *Kevin was here, wasn't he?*

Zach replied to her thought aloud, "Yes, he's here. It's only Kevin, Stephanie and Patrick. We know where they're staying."

Trembling, Haley explained, "Your rental car is at the hospital. You two need to keep them busy long enough for us to get away. We might be on the run with her for a while."

*This was a goodbye*. Kayn leaned over and embraced Haley.

Haley gave her a few pats on the back and said, "We'll miss you too."

Zach shimmied off the bench, announcing, "We need the heat going. I'll drive to the hospital. I don't know how long we're going to be able to give you without any of those funky restraints. We won't even have anything to drug them with, but we'll do our best."

Kayn sat up front with Zach and inched over so Astrid could share the seat. They heard the others go back to the bunks to gather their belongings.

Astrid whispered, "In this temperature, they won't be able to leave the hotel unless they're fully clothed. Jenna says, the two of you have intimate relationships with the three and this should prove helpful."

*Intimate relationships with the three? She'd only had an intimate relationship with one.*

Astrid leaned over and whispered in Zach's ear, "I'm impressed, you have many layers I knew nothing about."

"We were drunk," Zach whispered. "It was a one-time thing."

*Was she hearing this right?*

Astrid quietly assured, "You don't ever have to explain anything to me. I'm just passing this on. Jenna seems to think that's the key. Mel should stay in the room, so she can act as your Healer if shit goes south." She looked at Kayn, saying, "Due to recent events, this situation might be difficult. You don't have to worry about Frost. If anyone understands the honey pot scenario, it's him. It's practically in his job description."

*It was, wasn't it?* They pulled up in front of the hospital and said their goodbyes once more. Mel went in with the others, and they sat in awkward silence, waiting for her to return. Zach flicked through the radio stations and opted to play music from his cell. He plugged it in and a song with hilariously timed inappropriate lyrics came on. They both giggled as he skipped the song. He opted to turn the volume down and address what she'd overheard, "Promise me you won't tell anyone. Not even Frost."

"You could have told me. It's not a big deal. I'd never judge you for being naughty," Kayn assured.

Grinning, Zach said, "You don't have to do anything. You just have to make him think you might. That's all Astrid meant by that honeypot comment. String him along until visiting hours are over."

Mel returned faster than expected. Their exhausted friend was armed with instructions on how to get to the hotel. She sat with Zach while Kayn fixed herself up in the bathroom. *This time she wasn't a virgin sacrifice, but she was being asked to forfeit a fragile trust for the greater good. It wasn't what she was being asked to do. Frost would understand the premise behind the job. It was who she was being asked to do it with. Frost had a sore spot regarding Kevin, and understandably so.* Going through the motions, Kayn applied lipstick and eyeliner. *It was bloody cold. The heater couldn't keep up to the temperature outside.* She sat on the closed toilet, trying to mentally prepare as they drove down the highway. *Why was she so worried about what Frost thought? It takes two bloody seconds to text someone back.* She felt Zach turn off the main road, and when they came to a stop, Kayn got up and stared at her reflection in the mirror. *She was being ordered to do this. It was a job. Dragons don't feel guilty. Dragons follow orders and kick ass.* She stepped out of the bathroom, strolled over and grabbed her bag. *So be it.* The trio stepped out into the freezing night. Zach attempted to hide their RV from view by parking it around the side of the hotel. *It was a long walk to the doors. Make that run.* They sprinted through the snow to the door. They were greeted by a toasty warm lobby and blaring country music from the attached pub.

Mel dealt with the details. They got into the elevator and rode up to their room in awkward silence.

Unlocking her room, Mel explained, "Triad won't be expecting her to be released from the hospital for at least a week. I've healed her. The nurse came in and gave her a sedative. We're going to smuggle her out. They have a half-baked scheme involving nurse's uniforms and gurneys. I'm going to have a nap so I can heal Zach if shit goes south. Kayn, you heal quickly. Triad is staying in this hotel. The pub is the only place to eat without getting bundled up. They'll be there. If you guys are drunk when you show up, they'll be more intrigued than threatened. Have dinner and keep them occupied for as long as you can. Keep them away from their phones. If they don't know she's missing until tomorrow, we might pull this off."

*Drinking was an excellent idea.* Kayn wandered over to the minibar, grabbed a tiny bottle of wine and tossed one to Zach without warning. It exploded against the wall. She scoffed, "What in the hell Zach? You're an immortal. Get it together." She grabbed him another.

Mel chucked their keys and suggested, "Go trash your own room."

They took the key, bid her goodnight and left her to enjoy her debauchery free evening. They walked to their room in awkward silence drinking tiny bottles of wine. They barely even looked inside as they tossed their bags, dropped their coats on the floor and left. *It would be smarter to only act like they were drunk.* Kayn looked at Zach and asked, "Which one of us gets the key to this room?"

He tossed it at her and replied, "If I need to get in, I'll get another one from the front desk." As they walked to the elevator, he asked, "Are you alright with this job?"

"I'm not alright with it but I plan to do it anyway. If that's what you're asking?" She sparred as they stepped into the elevator. Kayn pressed the button to go down, looked at him and questioned, "Are you alright with it?"

"I'm not sure," he admitted. "I was blind drunk last time, and it was fun, but confusing fun. Does that make sense?"

The door opened as she responded, "More than you know." As they strolled towards the pub, they both started laughing. She exclaimed, "Why wouldn't they just kill us?"

Zach put his arm around her, gave her a brotherly kiss on the head and chuckled, "Jenna usually knows how things will play out. If she says this will work, it will."

# 22

# THE HONEY POT CLOSURE

She walked into the bar and scanned the room. They were sitting in the corner on high stools at a dark brown marble pub style table. *They had a couple of choices. They could order dinner and wait for them to notice them sitting there or stroll right up to their table, pull up a chair and sit down.* She followed Zach's lead by taking a seat at an empty table. They ordered a bottle of wine with appetizers and decided to act like they were oblivious to their enemy's presence. Kayn raised her wine glass and toasted, "To Hannah."

Her partner in crime repeated her words, "To Hannah."

They both downed their glass of wine in the name of the possible Clan member they'd lost. They refilled their drinks and asked the waitress as she passed for another bottle. Kayn rubbed her thumb in a circular motion on her wrist. *She wasn't going to trigger her ability by doing this to herself.*

Raising his full glass of wine, Zach saluted, "To messed-up situations."

She lifted hers and repeated Zach's toast. Before it touched her lips, she felt their presence. *There it was. The irritating sound of chairs being pulled up to their table.* Kayn glanced towards the noise and smiled. *Dragon. You are a sexy frigging Dragon.* She met Stephanie's eyes as she took a casual sip of her wine and coolly stated, "This is our first night off in over a week. If you're looking for drama, go elsewhere."

Her gorgeous dark-haired vixen of a nemesis glared at Kevin and sarcastically complained, "How come we don't get nights off?"

"You're in the middle of one," Kevin countered.

*His presence settled in the pit of her stomach.*

With his glass raised, Patrick winked at Zach and asked, "Who are we drinking to?"

Zach grinned and with a hint of flirtation in his voice, he replied, "I'm sure it's nothing anyone in Triad would be too concerned about."

The one sweet Triad verbally jousted, "Try me."

Zach was solemn for a moment before replying, "Her name was Hannah. We watched her before her Correction for a week. She didn't survive, she was kind of great."

*Patrick understood how they were feeling, so did Stephanie. Their expressions said it all. She couldn't look at Kevin. She knew she had to. She couldn't avoid it.* She was doing a terrific job until he cleared his throat and spoke her name. *Dragon. You are a Dragon.* She locked eyes with her past. *There was something in his eyes, she couldn't quite place. A look she'd never seen in the mortal version of him.*

Kevin curtly enquired, "Why didn't you just go to the hospital, heal the girl and take her? Why announce your presence? What's your game move here?"

She took another sip of her wine as she pondered a witty comeback and went with blunt honesty, "What's the point in rushing? You can't take her unless she's healed. We can heal her anytime we want. Why not relax for a day or two? As I mentioned earlier, we haven't had a day off in a while. Our last job just happened, we're a little upset."

The waitress passed by. Stephanie announced, "We'll have a couple of bottles of whatever they're having." The waitress returned before they had a chance to speak with two more bottles of wine. She uncorked them and walked away.

"What's to stop us from killing you the second you're alone," Kevin questioned as he poured a glass of wine for each one of his friends and topped up theirs.

Zach looked directly at Stephanie. His eyes dropped to her cleavage and lingered there as he flirted, "Why don't we just keep pouring the wine and see where the night takes us?"

After a seductive sip, Stephanie sparred, "That sounds doable."

Kayn quickly drank her whole glass of wine and then grabbed the bottle off the table and refilled it to the rim. A song by Rascal Flatts was playing. *A song they used to listen to. It turned her impermeable Dragon scales to flesh.*

His eyes softened as they met hers. Kevin's demeanour became uncomfortably close to the old version she adored as he whispered, "Brighton, you should slow down. This isn't a race, you've always been a lightweight."

*He was talking like he knew her. Even if he remembered everything, he didn't know her anymore.* "You don't know me anymore," she baited. Kayn picked up her refilled glass and took a rebellious drink from it. As he looked into her eyes again, something flickered in his. *Was that pain. Was it anger or a little of both?*

His eyes darkened as he spitefully agreed, "No, I don't know you at all anymore. Do I?"

*There was some serious animosity in that statement.*

Zach addressed the other two, "Let's play pool. This conversation just became way too intense for my mental state."

The three highly intoxicated frenemies wandered away from the table, leaving them alone. The waitress showed up with pork bites, jalapeno poppers and a mountainous plate of nachos. She was hungry and Kevin looked like he wanted her to choke on a pork bite. She ignored the scowl on his face as she dipped a jalapeno popper in sour cream and ate it. *It was smoking hot! Ouch, damn it!* She was forced to spit it into a napkin. Her goofy moment involving a scalded tongue made his eyes soften. After downing her wine to put the fire on her tongue out, Kayn looked at him and said, "So, how awkward are we going to make this on a scale of one to ten? Everyone else is having a good time. It's horrifically cold outside so I'm not leaving. You're free to go sit at another table if you can't stand the sight of me."

Kevin finished his wine and poured himself another in silence. Staring at his glass, he admitted, "How awkward is this for me? I'd say it's a ten, and if I couldn't stand the sight of you, that dream would have been a hell of a lot easier to swallow."

*He knew about Frost. He'd talked about dreaming about her while he was trying to get into her pants during the week before the Testing. A part of her thought it was part of the game he was playing. The look she'd been trying to place was contempt. She read it now, loud and clear.*

He leaned in, stared into her eyes and whispered, "I had to watch it happen. Do you know what that was like?"

Kayn whispered back, "As a matter of fact, I do. I've spent two years witnessing your sexual exploits in dreams."

Staring into his glass, he whispered, "That wasn't what it was supposed to be like."

*She couldn't look at him. It wasn't what it was supposed to be like for the girl she used to be, but she was different now, and she'd enjoyed every dark, twisted second of it.*

He reached over, grabbed a jalapeno popper, dipped it into the sour cream and ate it. He smiled at her and assured, "They're alright now. You won't burn your tongue."

The pub kept playing a list of songs that reminded her of her mortal life. *A simpler existence. A time when they'd been each other's worlds and the highlight of her day was being with him in a field, watching the clouds drift by. An alternate reality where her soul would have never believed being his enemy was possible.* She forced herself to keep going as she ate a popper that didn't melt her tongue. She met his eyes, knowing a part of her would always miss who they were in that beautiful time before they disappeared.

He slipped his hand over hers and whispered, "What I had to do to you in the Testing, destroyed me too. I think you understand why I had to do it, but I just needed to say the words, at least once. I'm sorry."

*That agonizing moment echoed through her memory more often than she cared to admit.* Kayn whispered back, "I remember the feeling of your blade as it slid across my throat. The all-encompassing devastation. I thought I was safe with you. I used to think that you destroyed me. You were the one person who had that ability. I've been seeing things differently lately.

That blade made me more. Good or bad, you made me the Dragon that I am today... Thank you."

He squeezed her hand, then let it go, releasing her from the carefree mortal memories that would always bind them. Kevin cleared his throat. His voice was thick with emotion as he whispered, "I need to go."

*There were tears in his eyes. Old emotions surfaced, causing confusion. It felt like it was really him.* She struggled to remain on task. "Stay," she persuaded, as sentiment moistened her eyes.

His expression darkened. Kevin wiped her tears away and coldly reprimanded, "Dragons don't cry. Dragons never cry." He walked away and left her there.

Kayn turned down the sound on the cell she'd stolen from his pocket and tucked it into hers. She waved at Zach to signal she was leaving. As she walked back to the room, her mind scrutinized their conversation. *He'd almost had her sucked into believing that their friendship could still exist and then he'd given her what she needed to shut her emotions for him down.* That night she dreamt of who they used to be. She awoke with the beauty of her mortality still fresh in her mind. *Dreams are torture. Bullies that visit you during the night, taunting you with moments lost and things you can no longer have.*

They left as soon as Zach returned from his exploits. They were still drunk, so Mel had to drive until well into the next day. *Her conversation with Kevin had been strangely therapeutic. He had his memories back. They'd had a moment, but it didn't change how she felt about Frost. Time had strategically moved the chess pieces of her life. It had altered her wants and given her the closure she hadn't known she needed.* It felt peculiar having only their original Testing trio driving through the endless Alaskan darkness into the unknown. Kayn was in the passenger seat next to Mel with snow coming at the window like a swirling vortex leading them into another world. Her phone buzzed. Kayn took it out of her pocket and looked. *There was a text from Frost. It was only a week and a half late.* It read, 'Are you still mine?' She stared at her cell for a moment, and then, replied, "Are you still mine?" A second later her phone vibrated. The message on the screen read, 'Always.' Her heart soared and she became instantly annoyed with herself. *Why hadn't he tried to contact her? It had been more than a week. She wasn't mortal anymore. Perhaps, the fact that they hadn't spoken in a week didn't matter in the grand scheme of things? What was a week in forever?*

Mel glanced at her and said, "It was him, wasn't it?"

Kayn smiled as she stared at his words on the screen and replied, "Yes."

Her friend ribbed, "I don't suppose he had a brilliant excuse as to why he hasn't been messaging you back?"

Kayn looked at her, puzzled. *She hadn't said a word about it.*

Mel grinned as she explained, "You didn't need to tell me anything. You've been checking your cell for messages and scowling all week."

She smiled, staring at warp speed snow coming at the windshield. It was a rather hypnotizing sight to behold. Kayn responded to Mel's earlier statement by saying, "I have a feeling Frost doesn't give excuses."

Mel grinned again and replied, "No, I'm pretty sure he doesn't. How do you feel about that?"

"You can always count on people to be exactly who they are," Kayn responded as she smiled, knowing she'd chosen a difficult road.

Zach passed them both a travel mug full of coffee. He was

balancing between the two seats by hanging on to the back as he surfed the snowy highway. He sighed, "Skootch your butt over, Kayn. I'm going to grab one of those for myself, and then, I'm coming up here to sit with you ladies. It's painfully boring back there by myself."

As he released his grip on the back of their seats, Mel purposely swerved. Zach toppled over, falling to the floor with a thud. Mel apologized, "Sorry, sweetie. There must have been a little black ice back there."

"Sure, black ice," he sarcastically quipped.

Kayn heard him fumbling around in the kitchen. Zach reappeared with a spill-proof mug in hand and slid into the seat next to her.

"Thanks for not hitting more black ice while I walked up here," he sparred.

With an icy expression, Mel countered, "You never know when that pesky black ice will reappear. It's such a random thing."

*Mel was pissed. Zach had once again bedded Satan. Had she slept with Kevin it would have made his, 'I had to do it' explanation more feasible. He didn't have to do anything. He wanted too.*

Her phone vibrated. She took it out of her pocket and looked at it. Frost's message read, 'See you in Mexico beautiful.' *This was going to be a long drive.*

Zach read the text over her shoulder. He raucously yelled in the enclosed space of the front seat, "Yes! We're going to Mexico!"

Mel glanced at Zach and said, "With only two of us trading off the driving, it's going to be an exhausting drive. Go get some sleep. We're driving straight through."

As Zach stood up to leave, he added, "Brighton, you're learning how to drive as soon as I get the chance to teach you."

Kayn smiled at him and said, "It's been months since the Testing and we haven't had the opportunity to breathe yet, but I'm all for it."

The days were painfully monotonous as they powered through the rest of British Columbia and the states. Kayn made the meals and got them coffee while they drove for seemingly endless hours. As they travelled south, they began to shed layers of clothing. Once in Mexico, they were given the name of a small town on the coast where they'd be meeting up with the others. They arrived at their destination at dusk the next day. It was an inconspicuous little fishing village. Zach texted Markus for directions and in a few minutes the exhausted trio of travellers pulled up the driveway of a ritzy looking resort. They grabbed their bags full of summer gear, locked up the RV and made their way down the cobblestone walkway towards the sound of voices. Kayn was barefoot, wearing a spaghetti strapped summer dress overtop of her bikini. She couldn't find her flip flops but didn't want to wait one more second to see him. They wandered into a courtyard lit by torches. The vivid colours of the flowers weren't masked by the loss of natural sunlight. The fragrances in the air were glorious but not nearly as wondrous as the sight of Frost sitting with his back to her at the bar. He turned around like he'd sensed her presence. He grinned as he got up and strode towards her. She sprinted into his arms and they embraced. He spun her around in a circle. They joyously laughed as the others began to greet each other and embrace. She ended her moment with Frost to have one with everyone else.

Markus interrupted the group as he announced, "We have

a couple of days here before we travel a little further inland to visit an Ankh crypt with a special purpose, I'm certain the newbies will enjoy."

Standing beside Orin. Mel glanced at her father and questioned, "What special purpose?"

Orin placed his arm around her and teased, "It'll be way more fun to watch you guys if you have no idea where we're going."

Frost approached with two enormous fishbowl sized Pina Coladas and passed her one. He raised his glass and cheered, "To a couple of days off in paradise."

They clinked their hilariously gigantic glasses. Kayn took a sip of her tasty treat as she followed him back to the outdoor bar. She placed the heavy glass down on the counter and took a sip from the straw. *That was better.*

Frost glanced at her and flirtatiously questioned, "Did you miss me?"

Her eyes travelled from his seductively devious eyes to his sculpted chest and then down to his sexy chiselled abs. She sparred, "Did you miss me?"

He took a long drink from his straw, leaned over and whispered, "Oh, I plan to show you exactly how much I've missed you." Kayn laughed and accidentally inhaled her sip of Pina Colada. He gently patted her on the back as he whispered in her ear, "We should eat. Once I get you into my room you won't be leaving it for days."

She felt the heat of his hand hovering above the small of her back. Kayn warned, "Don't you dare."

Frost chuckled as he passed her a menu. Zach asked him a question and they started talking. Frost excused himself and left the bar. Kayn opened her menu. It was all in Spanish. She was Canadian so she'd taken French in school. The Spanish language was enough like French to decipher a tiny bit of the menu. Zach noticed her having a difficult time. He pointed at something, suggesting it to her. Curious, she asked, "Can you speak Spanish?"

He gave her a funny look as he replied, "Of course I can. My grandparents lived with us and they didn't speak English."

"How did I not know this about you?" She remarked, and asked Zach to order dinner for her just so she could hear him speak. When the waiter came over, he ordered her something that sounded super sexy. Stupefied, she exclaimed, "How are you not using this to pick up women? It's seriously hot."

He gave her a funny look as he answered, "I honestly didn't even think about it. You tend to just speak what everyone else is speaking."

"Try it out on Mel," Kayn prodded.

Zach grinned at her. She watched as he strolled down the bar to Mel, leaned in and said something that sounded extremely naughty. Mel looked up from her menu, smiled at him and invited him to sit down beside her. *How had he not been picking up girls with this*? Kayn took a sip from the curly straw. *Well, she'd done her good deed for the day. If that didn't work, nothing would.* She was rather unsuccessfully attempting to fish the maraschino cherry out of her slushy drink when Frost snuck up behind her.

He kissed her neck, handed her a flower, and teased, "Want me to get that cherry for you?"

*All hail to the reigning king of innuendo.* She kissed him on the cheek and sparred, "I think I can get this one." She smelled the flower he'd just given her. *Its scent was heavenly.* Kayn looked at him and teased, "How are you ever going to keep this level of amazing boyfriend up?"

He slid into the empty seat beside her and replied, "We haven't really given this a name yet, but boyfriend works for me. Does that mean I get to call you my girlfriend?"

*Had she just jumped the gun there?* She questioned, "Do you want to call me your girlfriend?"

He intertwined his fingers with hers, kissed the back of her hand and confessed, "I'd be honoured, but just so you know, the whole relationship thing scares the shit out of me. I'm really trying to get past it. I hope you can see that."

She could see the raw emotion in his eyes. Kayn leaned in, tenderly kissed his lips, and assured, "I can." Her meal was placed in front of her. It was an enchilada covered in green sauce. *Intriguing.*

Frost grinned and announced, "That is definitely going to be the spiciest dish you've ever eaten."

*She loved spicy food. It was more than that, she now seemed to require it.* Kayn cut up a tiny bite and ate a mouthful. *It was amazing. It was so hot, she was sweating.* She took a big sip of the slushy drink before having another bite. Frost silently watched her devour the entire contents of her plate, while smiling. When they were finished eating, they wandered over to sit in the hot tub with the rest of their Clan. Kayn slipped out of her sundress and stepped into the luxurious heated tub. Frost and Grey started up a hilarious animated conversation. She closed her eyes and tried to relax but all she could think about was how much she wanted to be alone with him. Frost and Grey randomly got up, raced to the pool, and leapt in.

Lexy nudged her and teased, "It's good to be back with you guys, even Zach."

Zach was sitting in the tub between Mel and Dean. He grinned at her while replying, "Funny, Lex."

"Let's just say, you've grown on me," Lexy provoked as she splashed Zach.

Kayn felt a glow of happiness. *She'd always thought of home as a place. It occurred to her now that a home was created by the people that surrounded you. The RV could be home and the in-between. This hot tub in Mexico was also home because they were all here. Well, almost everyone. They were missing a few.* She stood up, announcing, "I'm going to love and leave you. That was a long drive and bathing at random public swimming pools for a whole week doesn't leave you feeling very fresh. I need a shower."

Lexy smiled at her and said, "You're in bungalow five. The door is probably open. We'll tell him where you went."

She wandered down the path to the secluded bungalow and went in. *Privacy stones were everywhere. Funny.* Grinning, she brought her bag so she could brush her teeth before getting in the shower. She'd already conditioned her hair when the bathroom door closed. Just knowing he was in the room made her pulse race. The curtains shifted as he got into the shower with her.

Pressing his body against her back, he flirted, "Pass the soap."

*Feeling Dirty?* She passed the bar of soap over her shoulder and laughed as his sudsy hands slipped across her midriff slowly massaging her body.

He whispered against her neck, "Is something funny?"

She giggled, "You usually catch those thoughts. That one was far too cheesy to ever be spoken aloud."

Frost chuckled as he purposely missed each of her aching

peaks with his soapy palms and taunted, "Let me guess what you were going to say. I've become quite fluent in your inner dialogue. Was it...feeling dirty?"

She grinned. *He'd guessed her dorky inner dialogue correctly.* He ran his soapy hand down both sides of her inner thigh without touching the part of her that was aching for him. He was playing the same torturously tantalizing game he'd played with her once before but the rules had changed. *She knew how to make him lose control.* She moved his hands to where she wanted them and shivered as the pheromones released from her skin. It was easy to trigger this ability when she was with him. Once her use of his ability had been triggered, what they felt for each other became a violent primal urge. Kayn turned to face him, grabbed a handful of his dripping wet hair and aggressively pulled his lips to hers starting their lustful titillating dance of tongues. His eyes flashed with dark urgency as he lifted her up and took her forcefully against the side of the shower stall. They both lost their filters and cried out as the rhythm of their ecstasy built to a glorious mind-blowing crescendo. They remained in each other's arms as their breathing calmed. She slipped on the soapy tub and towed him down with her, laughing. They both grabbed for the shower curtains trying to stop themselves and ended up on the bathroom floor. She landed on top of him, he cushioned her fall. Recalling the mystery curtains on the floor of the honeymoon suite, they both laughed. She looked into his eyes as she kissed him, nipping his lip with her teeth. He clutched her ample backside with both hands and started up another round of tumultuously rough lovemaking on the tile floor. After hours of christening every possible surface of the bungalow, they filled the tub and had a relaxing bath together. Afterwards, they dried each other off and snuggled under the covers in bed. *He could make her feel more with one touch than anyone could with a thousand beautiful words.*

Tracing her hip with his finger, Frost whispered, "If you only knew what it was like for me when you were in the Testing. I don't let myself care for a reason. The thought of losing you..."

Kayn rolled over, met his eyes, and teased, "And now that I've survived, you're nothing but a scared little boy. Afraid of loving me. Terrified of what I'll be able to do to you."

He smiled as he ran his hand through her damp wavy hair and replied, "I wasn't always this way. I used to believe in the fairytale. Now, the only thing I fear is that sense of loss. The hollow feeling in my chest that whispers...it's gone."

Tenderly caressing his face, she whispered, "Everybody fears loss."

Smiling lovingly, he admitted, "I've lived long enough to know how difficult this is going to be. Relationships are tough. People have unrealistic visions of valentines and flowers, but most of the time, it's gritty down in the trenches work, and a shitload of forgiveness. We're going to have to fight to stay together. Between my ability, job description and the fact that you're a Dragon, the cards will be stacked against us right from the start but, if you can try to forgive me for the mistakes, I'm sure to make. I promise to try to forgive you, for yours. I'll fight for you if you'll fight for me."

*She understood what he was getting at. The reality of being Ankh was much harsher than that of humanity. At some point in the future, they'd be asked to do things that would violate the sanctity of their relationship and wreak havoc on their trust for each other. They would have to make the conscious choice to see past it.*

She met his eyes as she answered, "I want to try." He pulled her to him, kissed her lips tenderly and pulled away with a devious look in his eyes. He leaned over the side of the bed and reached for something. *What was he up to?* He came up with a gift-wrapped box in his hands. He passed it to her. Kayn smiled as she pulled on one end of the bow, loosening the ribbon and it slipped off the package. He was grinning. *This was going to be a joke gift, not something sentimental.* She stopped trying to carefully unwrap it and tore the paper off. Kayn started to laugh as soon as she saw what the present was. *It was a box of Twinkies.* She shook her head at him and provoked, "You know there's more to life than just eating Twinkies in bed?"

Taking her hint to heart, he slid out from under the covers and declared, "Let's go make some memories with our clothes on."

She got out of bed and slipped into her bikini. Frost was already standing with the door wide open, waiting for her. She wandered towards him, wrapped her arms around his neck and attempted to kiss him.

Manoeuvring out of her way, Frost taunted, "Brighton, this is PG memory time." He blocked her exit and patted down her wild mane of curls. "There you go. That looked obvious."

He extended his hand and she laced her fingers through his. *It was the middle of the night. Nobody would even be awake to witness her scary hair.* They strolled into the pitch-black cobblestone courtyard. She couldn't see the flowers but knew where they were by the unforgettable fragrance of their blooms. *Where was he taking her?* It was so dark without the torches lit. All she could see was the outline of the pool area and the little outdoor bar as they made their way through it.

"You're not going to tell me where you're taking me, are you?" She probed.

He quietly laughed, "Not a chance. Be careful, there are steps right here."

The rushing of waves became louder as he led her down cobblestone steps. The stairs ended rather abruptly, she tripped. He caught her in his arms. Standing in the sand, under the sparse light of a slivered moon, they moved together. *It felt like they were dancing to the crashing of waves. She couldn't see a thing but didn't care.* Wildly swept away in the experience relying solely on touch and sound, they swayed to music only they could hear. He dipped her. She had no idea it was coming and laughed. Frost pulled her body against his and whispered something in her ear. A wave roared right as he spoke.

She yelled, "I didn't hear any of that!"

He shouted right into her ear, "Let's make sandcastles!"

Waiting until after the next waves thunderous roar, she answered loudly, "But we can't see the sand?" *She truly couldn't see a damn thing.*

Frost laughed and bellowed back, "That's the point."

She smiled at the premise of just feeling her way around in the dark for no apparent reason. *Why not?* She could see his outline below her. He was already sitting in the sand. She sat next to him. As she raked her fingers through the grains, she recalled a time when one of her fears had been rogue waves. *In this light, she wouldn't even see one coming.* As an immortal, a rogue wave would do little more than wreck her middle of the night sandcastle making experience. She got on her knees and dug her way down to the damp sand. *She was going to make a moat.* For some reason, as a child, she'd always been the one that wanted to make the moat. Matt and Chloe would be scrapping over the big bucket and she'd be there happily digging the hole around their creation. With no ability to see what she was doing, Kayn began to enjoy the tactile experience for what it was. There was gritty sand beneath her nails and it was clinging to her arms. She didn't know what Frost was up to but she was having fun, childish fun. *The kind people didn't have time for as adults. Grey would be the exception. This would be right up his alley*. Once she'd completed her moat, Kayn started to write their initials in the sand but realised she didn't even know his last name. She sat there pondering before reality clicked. *She didn't have a last name either, not really. Kayn Brighton was dead. They may still use her last name as a nickname from time to time, but it was just a nickname now. The Aries Group probably rigged it up to look like she'd died in that house fire with Jenkins and Matt. Did she have a tombstone?* She felt a handful of sand hit her. *He was listening to her thoughts.* He started tickling her and they wrestled until he had her arms pinned above her in the sand as the waves washed behind them.

He playfully reprimanded, "Why are you even thinking about that stuff? Keep moving forward. Anything you see in that rear-view mirror is back there because you've passed it."

She smiled up at him, knowing he was right. A glimmer of light flickered on the water's surface in the horizon. *Had they really stayed up all night?*

He released her from his seductive hold, sat up and urged, "Quick. Sit up. You don't want to miss this."

Kayn scrambled upright and shuffled back until she was leaning against him. Frost wrapped his arms around her waist and held her as the light slowly reached its way across the surface of seemingly endless sea towards their spot on the beach. As the stunning golden orb of light rose into the sky, he nuzzled her neck, kissed her on the cheek, and spoke as waves crashed against the shore. *She wasn't certain, but it sounded like he'd told her he loved her.* Kayn waited until the next crash of waves to whisper, "I love you too." He hugged her tightly, kissing her neck, and she sensed he'd heard her confession over the roaring waves. Frost scrambled to his feet, looked at their sandy creations and started laughing. She got up and stood beside him to gaze at the wonder of their tactile artistry. Secretly impressed, Kayn sighed, "We should get to bed before everyone else gets up."

Facing her, just beaming, he brushed the streak of wet sand off her cheek and teased, "You always get ten times dirtier than anyone else. It's one of your most endearing traits. Just wait until you get a look in the mirror."

Kayn peered down at her arms. *They were caked with sand. She'd known about that. She was digging a moat. It was more than just her arms though, it was funny.* They began the trek back to the bungalow. This time she was able to see the scenery. *They'd have to come back here later and go for a swim when they weren't so sleep deprived. If they tried to go for one now, they'd surely inconvenience the others by drowning.*

Frost grinned as he flung his arm around her, taunting, "I'm not even sure a shower would help. I think we're going to need to chisel it off." The two climbed the uneven cobblestone steps, wandered back through the pool area and ran into Greydon.

Grey gave her a funny look and sparred, "I'm not even going to ask." He winked at her and strolled away.

*He was far too perky for five am. Grey always seemed to be coming back from somewhere early in the morning. What had Frost called that again? Oh, yes. He'd called it the walk of shame.* When they got back to the picturesque bungalow, they showered separately and went back to bed.

She stirred to the clamouring of activity outside. Kayn peered over at the time. *It was already noon.* She snuck out of bed and made her way to the bathroom to get ready for the day. Her bikini was hanging on the shower rod, dry. She put it on and wandered back in to wake up Frost. Out cold, he looked far too peaceful to disturb. She crawled onto the bed. *He didn't even stir.* She hovered her lips above his to see if he'd notice her there. His face burst into a grin. She started laughing as he began tickling her.

He rolled her over, pinned her to the bed beneath him and jokingly accused, "You called me creepy last time you caught me watching you sleep."

*She had, hadn't she?* He began trailing playful kisses from her neck all the way down to her abdomen. It tickled. She laughed so freely, she accidentally snorted and then her stomach growled like a bear. *Sexy moment over.*

He snickered. Pausing his naughty exploration, Frost prompted, "Come on, let's have lunch, you're obviously starving."

Her stomach complained like a ferocious beast once again. He got up and she remained put watching him walk away from the bed. She felt giddy. *Her heart felt open and so full it was ready to burst. She'd fallen for him hard.*

After a few minutes, he reappeared and said, "Let's go have something to eat, grab a few drinks and find a spot on the beach in the sun."

*That sounded heavenly.* She practically bounced out of bed. *Maybe, the girl she used to be wasn't completely lost?* As the urge hit her, she paused and assured, "I'll be right there. I need to go to the washroom. Order me one of those slushy drinks, pretty please."

He grinned at her as he answered, "Sure thing beautiful. See you in a few."

Kayn strolled into the bathroom. She sat on the throne of porcelain and her stomach complained again. *Either it was a warning or she was starving. It was probably the latter.* Only a few minutes of time had lapsed as Kayn wandered out into the courtyard to eerie silence. Everyone appeared to be fine but frozen in place. It was as though someone had hit pause on the remote control of their lives. *Instinct told her this wasn't dangerous.* Someone was able to move behind the bar. She heard a humming blender. Kayn cautiously made her way over. *What in the hell was this?* Curious, she slipped into the empty seat. The bartender from the night before placed an impressive colourful slushy drink in front of her.

The friendly bartender said, "Drink that bad boy."

*It wasn't the bartender's voice, but she recognized it. His voice matched that black spandex wearing jokester from the in-between. What was this creepy tool doing here?* Humouring the being who'd highjacked the bartender's body, she took a sip of his concoction.

He casually leaned over the counter and queried, "It's the best drink you've ever had, isn't it?"

She met his eyes as she replied, "Yes, it is. Why don't you just get to the point of this visit and unfreeze my friends."

The being shapeshifted into a blonde adonis, extended a hand in greeting, and said, "My name's Seth. I'm one of the three Guardians, but you can call me dad."

*What did he just say?*

"It's shocking, I know. We always suspected you were mine, but we didn't know for sure until you sent twenty demons back through the hall of souls with an orb of light. You caused one hell of a shitshow. For future reference, demons have to be pre-approved as redeemable before you're allowed to do that."

Trying to wrap her mind around the surprise paternity announcement, she probed, "You're my father? What does that mean?"

He grinned at her and sighed, "I was hoping someone would have had this conversation with you already but when a boy and girl really like each other..."

Kayn interrupted the immortal's sarcastic shenanigans by raising one hand and saying, "I think I've got that part of it. I'm talking about in the future."

Seth grinned at her as he exclaimed, "Your sister just woke up."

*Sister? What sister?*

Lexy was on the warpath, marching towards them.

*Lexy was her sister? What?*

The fiery crimson-haired Dragon hissed, "Who in the hell is this asshole and why isn't anyone moving?"

Seth grinned as he motioned like he wanted to shake Lexy's hand. She scowled at him and didn't move a muscle.

He began to explain, "Let's catch you up. I'm your father and Kayn here is your sister. Everyone will start moving again as soon as we get back. I'll make sure to return you both to the second you left. Your friends won't even know you were gone."

Her surprise sibling was visibly confused. Lexy glanced at Kayn and then back to Seth as she questioned, "Why would we go anywhere with you?"

With an enormous shit-eating grin plastered on his face,

he responded, "Did I forget to tell you who I am? My name's Seth. I'm one of the three Guardians. Coming with me isn't exactly a choice."

The Dragon sisters glanced at each other as the scenery flashed and they disappeared. They reappeared in the jungle outside of what appeared to be an Ankh crypt. The Guardian Seth walked right through the wall. They stood there. *Were they supposed to walk through it too?* Lexy strolled over and tapped the surface of the crypt. *It was solid rock.* Kayn heard his voice in her head, *"What are you two girls waiting for? An invitation?"* Lexy stepped through the wall and vanished into stone. Kayn took a deep breath and followed her, appearing on the other side unscathed. *She'd walked through stone before but it had always been on the inside of a crypt.* The Dragons of Ankh followed Seth down a flight of stairs, descending into darkness. He reached the bottom before them and spoke in a language Kayn recognized. She even knew what the words meant. *Let there be light.* The stone chamber lit up. The walls were covered with the kind of carvings you'd see in an Ankh crypt. There were three handprints on the wall. *What was this about?*

The Guardian smiled, pointed at the handprints on the wall and ordered, "Kneel and place your hands on those prints."

*He was a Guardian. This wasn't a choice.* Kayn and Lexy obediently knelt before the carvings on the wall, glanced at each other and simultaneously placed their hands on the ancient handprints. For a second nothing happened. Kayn tried to pull her hands away but they wouldn't budge. She looked to the other side of her. Seth was kneeling there with his hands placed in the third pair of prints. Kayn felt her palms heating up and then, they began to burn. *She wasn't concerned. She'd fed from the walls in the Testing.* A burst of pure energy travelled up her arms and her skin glowed with shimmering golden light. *This was new.* Seth removed his hands from the wall. They let go. Kayn looked at her hands. Her flesh was no longer glowing but she knew she was different. *He'd done something to her. She felt stronger.*

Seth placed his hands on the top of both of their heads and announced, "You have both just been granted your birthright. As the daughters of a Guardian, you will bow for no one but the leader of your Clan and the Guardians. Your abilities have been unlocked. They should be easier to control and you will be much stronger now." He removed his hands, stepped back and said, "Get off your knees."

Kayn rose to stand beside her fellow Dragon and as fate would have it, immortal sibling. The two girls looked at each other. In a blink of an eye, they were back in front of the bar he'd taken them from. Everyone was joking around. *It was as though nothing had happened.* The Dragons embraced. She whispered in Lexy's ear, "I definitely didn't see that one coming."

Utterly astonished, Lexy pulled away and whispered, "We're sisters. Should we tell everyone?"

Kayn replied in her normal tone, "You start. I'll be right there. I just need a second."

Frost called out, "Hey beautiful! Hurry up, your drink's melting over here! It's a hot one today!"

Kayn smiled, knowing her Pina Colada had been on the counter in blazing afternoon sun for a while. She heard the thunderous swooshing of the ocean and her eyes travelled there. *She was part Guardian. She had a sister and a father.* Kayn winced. *The immortal that drove her insane was her father. This meant she was Azariah's niece.*

Jenna's voice boomed, "I knew it!"

All eyes were on her as she turned to face the group. Kayn strolled towards the bar in true Dragon form, took the drink from her stupefied boyfriend and affirmed what Lexy had told them, "We're sisters and the Guardian Seth is our father. Let's order lunch." *The strange plot twists in her life never ceased to amaze her.* Frost gazed into her eyes and smiled. *She had a feeling the next chapter in the story of her life was going to be an exciting one. Bring it on.*

***The Beginning***

*Fantasy adventure, magical realism, non-stop action with laughter, tears and a coming of age paranormal romance that will capture every reader's heart. A story of a teenage girl who overcomes tragedy and evolves into something she never knew possible as her immortal destiny comes to light. This series will leave you breathless as it takes you through the darkness and leads you back out into the secret world of immortality triggered by choices in the afterlife.*

*The end of her life was only the beginning of her story.*

# THE CHILDREN OF ANKH SERIES UNIVERSE

There are many books in this universe to keep you occupied while you await the next one. Read on Dragon lovers.

### Kayn's Series

Sweet Sleep
Enlightenment
Let There Be Dragons
Handlers Of Dragons
Tragic Fools

### Lexy's Series

Wild Thing
Wicked Thing
Deplorable Me
Sacrificial Lamb Club

### Owen's Middle Grade Series

Bring Out Your Dead (A short novella)

## *Handlers Of Dragons Teaser*

The musical symphony of exotic birds had Kayn mesmerized. Each step she took through the overgrown brush brought her closer to the next chapter of her story. She ducked, maneuvering under a low hanging branch. The colourful toucan perched there didn't flutter a wing; it remained in place as a steadfast reminder of a love that had dissolved into nothing but memories. Thoughts of the jungle in the Testing instantly brought her back to purple flowers, heartbreaking goodbyes and the devastating events thereafter. Even a momentary thought of her mortal ties still made her want to succumb to the hollow numbness of her Dragon ability. She felt the pressure of Zach's hand squeezing hers. *He'd been listening to her thoughts.* Kayn returned her Handler's gesture and swallowed her emotions down as she always did. *He didn't want her to make his day more difficult.* She closed her eyes, allowing her Handler to lead her blindly into the unknown. Zach yanked on her hand. Kayn was instantly brought back to the here and now. Markus was brushing away the foliage on what appeared to be a small animal's burrow.

The ground opened, revealing stairs descending into darkness, much like the Ankh Crypt in British Columbia. As they followed their leader into the shadows, it felt like a symbolic representation of her life. Zach took her hand again as they reached the bottom of the stairs and she felt the strength of their spiritual tether. *It had taken a while but it was now a certainty.*

*Markus was fumbling around, cursing. He was probably regretting leaving their fire starter Grey behind.* Markus swore again, searching for something to light the torches. *She'd absorbed Grey's gift back in that town full of demons but hadn't attempted to use it since and didn't know if she could.* Just when she was about to offer it up as an option, the light began flickering from a torch, and the five newest Ankh got their first look at the Crypt. It was identical to the last one she'd been in, with ornate tapestries on the walls representing the story of their Clan.

Zach paused by the one with the Brother's of Prophecy and the girl they all knew was Lily. He nudged her and teased, "Your boyfriend is super old… absolutely ancient."

While fighting the urge to touch it, Kayn remarked, "He is, isn't he?" Markus marched down the corridor ahead of the group, lighting each torch with the flames of the first. They stepped away from the tapestry, leaving inconsequential things behind and caught up with the rest just as Markus placed his hands against the stone. He stepped through the solid wall at the end of the hall without saying a word. *They'd done this before.* They followed their leader into the unknown and stepped out into a minimalistic white room. *This was different.* They followed Markus' lead as he strolled right through another wall into a lab, startling the people working there. An attractive statuesque Asian lady, wearing a lab coat embraced Markus like they were old friends. She animatedly chatted, as she led the Ankh down a dimly lit corridor, up an unusually steep flight of stairs and into another sparsely decorated room.

*Where were they? A large plaque on the stairs had read, 'The Aries Group.' It made sense, but she still had questions.* There was the faint hustle and bustle of a busy street and easily identifiable music outside of the walls. *Were they in the Middle East?* The five survivors of the Testing were ushered through the kitchen of a busy restaurant. The employees barely gave six strangers a second look as they were led out a door into the sweltering heat to black jeeps with tinted windows.

Markus paused his conversation with the lady who hadn't acknowledged their presence, long enough to say, "What are you waiting for? Get in. Three per vehicle."

Kayn and Zach climbed into one with Astrid. Mel and Haley got into the other. Zach leaned in and whispered, "We're not in Kansas anymore."

*No, they definitely weren't.* The front door of their vehicle slammed. She couldn't see the driver through the barrier. The engine started and they took off like they were in the Indie 500. Their surroundings whirled by in a blur as they weaved through traffic. *Obviously, road safety was not a thing here.*

They'd been driving in awkward silence for a while when the barrier rolled down and a driver with no accent, announced, "Do what you are told."

*Alrighty then.* They slowed as they pulled into a luxurious walled desert compound with flourishing vegetation. Stifling nervous energy with humour, Kayn glanced at Zach and remarked, "I've already been the virgin sacrifice once this year, it's your turn."

Her Handler sparred, "I'm quite confident there are no virgins left in this group."

# BIOGRAPHY

Kim Cormack is the always comedic author of the darkly twisted epic paranormal romance series, "The Children of Ankh." She worked as an Early Childhood educator and as an aid. She has M.S and has lived most of her life on Vancouver Island in beautiful British Columbia, Canada. She currently lives in the gorgeous town of Port Alberni. She's a single mom with two awesome kids. If you see her back away slowly and toss packages of hot sauce at her until you escape.

Subscribe to The Children of Ankh Universe website and be the first to get updates, contests, and series release info. Hope to hear from you.

Handlers Of Dragons is next. Read it now.

www.ingramcontent.com/pod-product-compliance
Lightning Source LLC
Chambersburg PA
CBHW070805030726
47504CB00003B/702